Lindsey,

"Let l

We hope you enjoy
the read!

♡ Talia Johnson

Misconstrued

Amber Duran and Talia Johnson

ACKNOWLEDGMENTS

We would like to thank Brandon Schulz for being our wonderful cover model. He was instrumental in helping us bring our vision to life. We would also like to thank our families and friends for the support, encouragement, and love given to us throughout the writing process. We are also thankful to our brilliant characters, who now are real and dear friends to us both. Lastly, we are thankful for the God-given gifts of words, writing, creativity, and perseverance.

Misconstrued was conceived on the way home from a movie Thanksgiving weekend in 2010. In true Amber and Talia fashion, the pair were discussing literature, "Greensleeves" in particular. It was late at night, and it had been on the radio. The radio commentator said the song had been rumored to be written by King Henry VIII. A discussion about the atrocities of King Henry Tudor VIII and Anne Boleyn led us, in our pursuit of seeing the best in people, to theorize about a different story for this king, one that explained his heartless pursuit of wives. Maybe there was one girl who got away, one who started it all. Thus, the idea for the novel was born. Although the actual book took about seven years to finish, much of the original storyline, title, and characters stayed true to that night. It was as if the story had been waiting to be written, something already hidden within us.

To us, the book is more than just a great novel, a collection of words depicting a consuming story with characters that are impossibly real. *Misconstrued* is the foundation of our friendship, a summation of countless hours writing and conversing through Google Drive, and the accomplishment of achieving a dream we both have had since we were very young.

We hope you enjoy our dream come true.

1

NEW YORK CITY, NEW YORK
November 2, 1991

"Where there is great love, there are always miracles."
- Willa Cather

White surrounded him, blinding and choking, surrendering him to the captivity of the words he forced out of his hesitant mouth. Just why he was reluctant on what should have been the "happiest day of his life," he did not know.

Her shining, emerald eyes met his, sensing reluctance and smiling encouragingly in response.

He tightened his hands around hers and tried desperately to curve his lips into a returning smile. He could feel his palms perspiring, and he cleared his throat before he repeated his vows back to Anne.

"Good, Henry." The officiant said, before turning to Anne. "And, Anne, repeat after me: I, Anne …"

Her eyes locked with his as she softened the tone of her voice before repeating the officiant's words. "I, Anne."

"Promise to have and to hold, from this day forward …"

"Promise to have and to hold, from this day forward …" Her voice was cool and calm, without a shadow of doubt in her tone.

"For better or for worse, for richer, for poorer …"

"For better or for worse, for richer, for poorer …"

"In sickness and in health, to love and to cherish;"

"In sickness and in health, to love and to cherish;"

Henry's heart pounded faster and faster, and he was filled with the urge to stop the officiant, stop Anne, stop the entire ceremony. He latched onto the words, "from this day forward." Forever. Not for now, for many years. *Forever*. The sudden realization of the promise they were making to each other sent a shudder through his entire body.

"From this day forward until death do us part."

"From this day forward until death do us part." Anne finished her vows confidently and smiled slightly at the officiant.

Henry felt as though the entire crowd, filled with many important acquaintances and just a few family members and close friends from each side, held their breath as they watched the two become joined as one.

"Excellent." The officiant smiled and shut his book. "By the power vested in me by the state of New York, I now pronounce you … husband … and wife. You may kiss your bride, Henry."

Anne curled her lips into a beaming smile of joy and looked out into the crowd before pulling herself closer to her new husband.

Henry bent down to lightly place a kiss on her lips, and the guests clapped, a few even cheered with excitement.

An icy wind blew in from an open window as the recessional music played. Hand in hand, they walked down the aisle toward doors that exposed the frigid, outside world.

Thomas Cromwell, Henry's childhood friend who was like the brother he never had, proudly followed close behind as his best man.

The Boleyn family rose to follow their new son-in-law and daughter with the Tudor's following close behind.

Outside in the fading sunlight, Henry removed his jacket to place over Anne's shoulders as they walked toward the decorated black limousine. She didn't thank him but moved smoothly into the car as the driver opened her door. Henry followed her quickly before he had to accept congratulations and talk with the many guests spilling out of the church. He needed time to collect his thoughts.

"Would you like to get a drink before the reception, Anne? Or just enjoy the limo ride around New York?"

"I would like a drink."

Relieved, Henry pressed the intercom and requested the driver to take them to a bar quite a ways away from the reception.

"Of course, Mr. Tudor." The driver turned the car away from the church and onto the bustling streets of New York.

Henry and Anne sat quiet, staring out their own windows. It was silent until Henry heard Anne start to giggle. He turned his head toward her, perplexed. Her laugh grew until she was sort of rocking back and forth.

"Anne," Henry paused, slightly concerned that this was some sort of delayed shock, and she was now realizing it was all a mistake. The same nervous feeling churned inside him again. "Is everything...are you all right?"

Laughing all the while, Anne replied between fits of giggles."Your face, Henry...you had to have been...the most adorable groom...to ever get wedding jitters," She rested her hand on his leg and suddenly looked at him with feigned seriousness. "I held your sweaty hands, Henry. Never forget that. That takes a very deep love for me to do that."

Henry relaxed at her candor, glad she wasn't concerned by his earlier hesitance.

After enjoying a fine scotch and talking about more of the ceremony with Anne, Henry decided to chalk up his earlier fear to wedding nerves. He was fine. They were perfect for each other.

****

"And now, ladies and gentlemen, I am pleased to announce for the first time, Mr. and Mrs. Henry Tudor!"

Anne and Henry Tudor entered the reception hall to the sounds of cheers. The extensive room was decorated to perfection with no expense spared to make this the most beautiful wedding the city of New York had ever seen. Tiny, white lights glistened out of white gossamer, which gracefully clung to the ceiling and walls. Strings of white flowers dropped daintily from the ceiling. Candles shimmered everywhere, casting soft light around the room. Enormous plates of food filled long, lace-draped tables along one wall for guests to freely fill their plates. The scent of fresh roses and freesias filled the air around the dance floor as couples charmingly waltzed to the sweet, melodic music.

"Please turn your attention to the dance floor for their first dance as a married couple!" The DJ announced.

Henry took Anne's hand and guided her to the center of the floor. An Etta James tune began, and they settled into a graceful waltz of which they rehearsed weeks before. Anne always had been an excellent dancer.

Henry caught her gaze, almost surprised at how stunning she looked. It was as if he never knew or was simply oblivious to it before: the way she half-smiled when she was trying to think of something witty to say, and the way she nervously bit at her bottom lip when she was uncomfortable. These endearing traits were all unbeknownst to Henry until just that moment. Time slowed as he reveled in the fact that this woman was his wife.

Anne coolly complimented his dancing skills, as she had many times before during college dances, snapping him back to the present moment.

Henry thanked her with a nod and tightened his arms around her with a small smile.

As they left the floor to applause and cheers, Henry was pulled away from his wife by a throng of bridesmaids pulling on his arm.

Somewhere in the shuffle, he lost Anne, and he settled in for what was sure to be an exhausting few minutes. He chatted with a few politely while he tried to find Anne in the crowd. Blurs of "Quite the ceremony!" and "So, so lucky" drifted in one ear and out the other. He just as easily could have been somewhere else and that's exactly where he would have wanted to be.

From across the room, Henry noticed Cromwell standing in the corner of the room, casually chatting up a few mutual golf friends who were dressed in expensive, dark suits with silk pocket socks embellishing the sides of their lapels. They were sipping cognac and chewing on stubby cigars, business as usual. Henry could barely distinguish the faces from the plumes of cigar smoking filling the corner they stood in, but he could hear hearty laughs coming from their general direction.

As if she were floating, Anne swept her way into his vision, her white dress causing her skin to glow radiantly. More than one head turned as she walked by, making her way to Cromwell's corner village of smoke.

Henry watched her with a faint smile as she leaned in to receive a casual peck on her cheek in greeting from Thomas. He placed his hand gently on the small of her back. Henry imagined their small talk, "Lovely ceremony, Anne." "Why, yes it was Thomas, the loveliest I believe. I have snagged him, haven't I? Yes, yes the perfect catch."

The two laughed quietly, and Anne placed her hand on his elbow. Cromwell turned and said something quietly to the other men, who silently walked away, leaving them alone.

For a fleeting moment, jealousy tugged at his heart, but the moment passed, and Henry pulled himself free of the crowd and casually strolled over to them.

He nodded at Cromwell and wrapped his arm around Anne's waist. He leaned down and kissed her cheek, pausing to say quietly in her ear, "Are you enjoying the party?"

Her skin fidgeted with goosebumps when his warm breath breezed along her neck. The faint smell of scotch lingered in the air as his words rolled smoothly off his tongue.

Her cheeks flushed with pink, a rare blush forming on them. She smiled up at him. "Of course."

He tried to capture that smile and memorize it. She was his. Her smile flashed for him. "Good. I wouldn't want my bride to feel unhappy," Henry stated with a returning smile. "My parents need us to meet a few people."

Anne nodded. "Very well. Good-bye, Thomas."

Cromwell nodded to them both, watching them as they sauntered off into the crowd. He took a sip of his drink before Henry turned and set his attention on the other guests.

Both Henry's and Anne's parents were chatting over candles and half-empty glasses of wine. The genuine smiles from both sides of the table made it seem like both families felt true happiness for their children. As Henry and Anne approached, the parents stood, welcoming them and commenting on how well everything was going.

"Yes, it was a lovely ceremony." Anne graciously said, holding tight to Henry's hand. It was probably the twentieth time she had repeated the same sentiment. Henry had realized early in the wedding planning process that weddings are as much for the couple as they were for everyone else. People live for occasions such as this. He squeezed her hand back, grateful that he could be the one to comfort her now after his moment of hesitation at the altar. She was always nervous around his parents for a reason she never could fully explain.

Mrs. Tudor lifted the corners of her lips. "You're welcome, my dear." Her hands were squeezed together just as tightly while they talked despite the strong arm of Henry's father firmly wrapped around her waist. They appeared to be a much closer couple than the Boleyn's across from them, who sat apart from each other. Anne's parents answered questions as two separate people, rather than as one entity. They seemed to move about as if each one were unaware of the other's presence, rather than being a complementing silhouette at each other's sides as Henry had observed throughout his life by watching his parents. Theirs didn't seem to be a marriage of passion but rather formality, the image of matrimony that Anne had grown up with.

After many exchanges between friends, family and people Henry barely knew, the newlyweds finally saw the moment they could sneak away to their bridal suite. No one knew they were staying one more night in New York before traipsing off to their honeymoon. Henry wanted tonight to be theirs and only theirs. So much of his life was plastered in the papers. Sometimes other people knew where he was going to be before he did. Not tonight.

****

Soft, red petals daintily covered the expansive floor, sprinkling over the luxurious bed and the marble counter tops. Beautiful artwork decorated the walls, depicting angelic-like people who seemed to peek down at the white dress that lay in the foyer with innocent curiosity. Anne, draped across wide, tan shoulders smiled in her sleep as Henry squeezed her tightly, brushing a strand of dark, silky hair off her face before drifting off to sleep.

He never wanted to forget that moment and the image of his bride looking so sweetly vulnerable. As she dreamed of their future, so bright and unknown, he laid awake, lost in thought. The two expectant lovers had this moment to cherish for years to come. The moment that would become a memory, a memory so powerful it would keep the hope of marriage and love alive, even when such hope sometimes seemed impossible for the two of them to imagine. This memory of love that would last while standing the test of time and trials of life. A love that would endure forever..."till death do the lovers part."

2

THE JOURNEY BEGINS: LEAVING NEW YORK
August 19, 1992

"There is a sacredness in tears. They are not the mark of weakness, but of power. They speak more eloquently than ten thousand tongues. They are messengers of overwhelming grief. . . and unspeakable love."
-Washington Irving

Henry drove as fast and as far as he could from his home in New York, leaving his life behind him. There was no destination, just the goal of putting as much distance between him and his current reality as possible. He headed west, stopping only to fill gas and rest his eyes every now and then. West felt full of freedom and chances to make his life more of a life. He wasn't sure when or where along the way he lost himself, but he was going to get far away from anything familiar in hopes of finding some semblance of who he was before. His mind was filled with questions; they flew through his mind so fast his head spun and as the pavement of the open road buzzed pass, he slowly began to feel a clearing in his mind, as if a cloud had been lifted from his thoughts. What was he doing with his life? What did everyone expect from him? All these questions and thoughts that he had pushed away for so long, he finally faced them head on. Henry felt that everyone was pulling him in all directions. His parents had always demanded extraordinary achievements from him throughout his entire life. He had grown up knowing that he would take over his father's extremely successful business, working with colleagues of his father to expand and grow it. Henry had complied with his father's wishes since high school, working his himself to the bone for years.

College was more or less a six-year long encore of his father's college experience. And after that, it was marriage to a college sweetheart, the perfect image that would fit the role he was to play, and then business, business, business. If he kept at this pace, he would end up like his rich father had been — a tired, grouchy businessman. Only, Henry would be in a loveless marriage.

Henry had been working on a major business prospect with the Weilder & Hauckney firm downtown before he took off. They were looking to go public in the market soon, and Henry had been very interested in their activity. He was engineering the latest revolutionary trends in stock trading, among other things. His company owned many companies. They were mostly in America, but he had just acquired a firm in Spain. And he just left everything. What would his father say? He dreaded the thought of returning home. This had been his father's dream for Henry, but Henry now wondered what his own dreams were for himself. Was Tudor Industries all there was going to be in his life?

Fully enraptured with every thought that flickered to the front of his mind, Henry drove himself slightly mad. His mind spun so fast that the rest of the world seemed enveloped in a thick fog as he flew through Cleveland and the windy city of Chicago. The vast farmlands of Iowa and the dinky ghost towns crowded in between the slightly larger towns were all just a constant blur. They were all, in fact, ghost towns to him, and it didn't matter if they were overflowing with towering skyscrapers or buzzing with the energy of busy bodies. His view on the world outside his car had become quite distorted.

While waiting at a stoplight and gazing at the people outside his dusty window, he would only see himself in the lives of others. In the two children playing hopscotch, he was that one small child who failed at her first attempt. He could feel bitter defeat within himself just from the image of a small failure. It was only in these short, incremental pauses in his trip did he even notice the things outside. His periodic stops for gas allowed him a breath of fresh air from his thoughts, but once back on the road, he was lost again. He barely noticed the majestic mountains, the crystal blue lakes, or the rapidly flowing rivers. He did not even notice the pouring rain and thunderstorm dispersing bright blue spider webs of lightning across the sky.

A giant boom of thunder awoke him from thought, and he saw a sign welcoming him to Nebraska. He let out a sigh and kept driving; his heart leading him into unfamiliar territory, while his mind pulled him back to New York.

3
NEW YORK, NEW YORK
August 19, 1992

He carelessly threw clothes and other belongings into his Louis Vuitton suitcase. He could hear Anne quietly breathing in her sleep, a sound which meant she would be awakening soon. He knew what every twitch and flutter of Anne's meant. He wondered if she had ever noticed his individual quirks and habits.

As he hastily packed, Henry still could not breathe. He had woken up with his wife of about eight months pulled to the very edge of her side of the bed, her arms in an X across her chest and one long thigh caught in the morning light outside the sheet. He had looked down at her beautiful face, and panic had suddenly sunk in.

He needed to get away. He was way too young to be married, especially like this. He did not even know what the word marriage meant. How could no one tell him that marriage was this lonely? His wife was never around, and, when she was, they fell asleep at different times without even a comment or kiss for one another. He was as unhappy as their marriage was weak. Surely she felt it too?

There was just something wrong between the two of them. Marriage was supposed to be more than this. He expected a more intimate commitment, something that defied history books and shouted love at rooftops, something that never lacked passion, and with every ounce and with every breath, the two, entwined with vows, lived for each other. He could not help but wonder if he wanted too much, maybe his secret love for great literature and classic romance was seeping into his reality. Surely, true romance exists outside of a page?

His expectations had been dashed into these torpid hopes, leaving him longing for something greater, with some sense of depth, not this shallow excuse for a marriage.

He couldn't quite pinpoint the root to his emotions, but he knew something was missing. He could only blame himself, he thought.

"I don't know what I'm doing!" He had screamed one day when he got home to an empty house with his wife at her aerobics class. He could have called her, but, instead, he sat on the cold leather couch, lost in loneliness, where he fell asleep to the buzz of Larry King's voice grilling his latest guest.

He needed a break from this monotonous life. Loneliness was exhausting and was driving him to desperate measures. When he was frustrated, he threw himself into work and even that was becoming too much for him.

Henry zipped up his suitcase and grabbed his coat. As he did so, his keys fell from atop the coat and clanged loudly to the floor.

Crap! Henry thought to himself as he saw Anne's eyes flutter awake.

She sat up, looking at his suitcase and then to Henry's face. Tiredness abruptly dissolved, she stared at Henry with scared, pleading eyes.

Henry's hand scratched the back of his head, taken aback by the surprise in her face. Before she could try and change his mind, Henry turned and headed for the door, suitcase in hand.

Anne jumped out of bed, running after him. She desperately called his name, but he kept walking to his shiny, black Rolls-Royce. She stumbled on the foyer rug and clumsily climbed to her feet, chasing after her husband.

"Henry! Please, let me … let me just talk to you about this!"

He put his suitcase in the trunk and walked around to the driver's side, opening the door with a steady hand.

"Henry, please! Please, just, stay with me."

The quiver in her voice caused him to hesitate and look at his wife. Her tiny, silk nightgown moved gently in the cool breeze along with her dark, tousled hair. Anne's panic-stricken face tore at his heart as those wild green eyes, mighty in all their fierceness, shed flowing tears of desperation.

"I need to get away for a while." He said with an obscurity of hesitation as he got in his car, started the engine, and drove away without looking back.

4

HENRY'S JOURNEY
August 20, 1992

Henry's brain began to feel numb from contemplating his life. The haze of the outside world lifted slightly as he put his deep thinking on hold, wishing never to think again. Realizing he hadn't eaten in hours, he stopped in Ogallala, a dusty town, flat and empty.

He had to find some food. His hands were shaking from hunger. When had he last eaten? He couldn't remember. He turned on the radio and tapped the steering wheel to the beat, trying not to think about it.

It was a warm morning with the sun hovering over the town, illuminating small homes and buildings, the type of morning that usually would have him antsy to go for a long run in the park.

Henry thought that this place seemed small, almost cozy, compared to his city back home. From the tinted windows of his car, he observed a mother pushing a stroller down the sidewalk with two small children trailing behind her. The mother did not seem at all concerned that the two would stop and examine something on the sidewalk every once and awhile, even though they were far out of her reach if a strange person appeared. He could see trust in this town and peace, too. To the right, he saw an old man being helped across the street by a young girl.

Henry slowly drove down the street, passing a bank and post office, and, inevitably, the smoky and worn bar that every small town heartily accepts. He noted a small gas station and a bed and breakfast. A few doors down, he spotted a small cafe. It didn't even have a name. A rusty sign jutting from the edge of the roof simply read, "Cafe."

Henry parked his car along the curb of the cafe, ignoring the people passing by who stared wide-eyed at his luxurious vehicle and unfamiliar face. He walked inside the little restaurant, sitting down at the first open booth he found.

The little cafe had a warm, homey feel to it. The locals sipped coffee at a bunch of tables that had been pushed together, gossiping about the latest late-night trouble made by the rowdy teenagers in the town. In the booth next to Henry, a family enjoyed breakfast together. The father sipped coffee while reading his paper. The mother cut her children's food into small pieces while smiling and laughing at their questions and comments. All seemed right in this world.

A waitress came over to take his order. She was a short, grey-haired little thing who smiled as she asked what he would like to order.

"I will just take a cup of coffee for now, please." He wanted to unwind and look over the menu for a few minutes.

"Sure thing, hon." The waitress bustled off, picking up dirty plates and cups from empty tables as she walked.

He looked over the breakfast menu and found just what he was hungry for. Setting aside the menu until the waitress returned, he lifted the newspaper that rested at the end of the table. and scanned the local news uninterestedly.

The waitress returned with a steaming cup of coffee, but quickly walked over to take another table's order. "Be right back, hon." She puffed out to him as she went.

Henry nodded and sipped the strong brew, inhaling the wonderful scent and feeling the warmth fill his empty stomach as he read aimlessly. At the bottom of the fourth page, an ad caught his eye for cabin rentals in Jackson Hole, Wyoming. It claimed to feature quiet, secluded cabins tucked away in the Teton mountains. A cabin in the mountains seemed very appealing to Henry, almost like he was being lured there. He could go fishing, cook outdoors, and just relax, forgetting about the stresses of life. He also needed time to think, time to sort out his thoughts and try to become the man he ought to be or wanted to be. He wasn't quite sure which one was necessary yet, or if a mix of both was the fix he needed.

"Okay, sorry about that!" The waitress whipped out her pad and smiled down at him, still breathing hard.

Henry was pulled from his thoughts. "That is fine." He said patiently. "I will just take some wheat toast and a few eggs scrambled, please." His stomach rumbled. "Oh, and some hash browns!"

"Sure thing, hon." She scurried away, picking up more dirty plates and silverware as she sped toward the kitchen.

Henry looked at the advertisement again and thought of the kind of peace he could find in a cabin hidden away in the mountains. He found a map of Wyoming behind the newspaper and planned his route to Jackson

Hole while he waited on his breakfast, which arrived in a few, short minutes.

"Here ya are." The waitress set down his plate and quickly walked away to the next customer, a permanent smile on her face. She didn't talk much, but Henry could tell she had been a waitress a long time. She was good at it. He made a mental note to leave her a good tip.

The breakfast hit the spot as Henry quickly chowed down. He threw a fifty on the table and walked quickly outside, eager to get on his way again.

He climbed into his car and left the little town behind as quickly as he had arrived. He drove speedily, his mind racing with the rapidity of his pulse. He was thinking of the mountains and the solitude. Impatience urging him on, he pressed the accelerator down a little farther. "Wyoming, here I come." Henry whispered, no longer a wanderer on this journey.

He felt much better now. Henry had a strong feeling that this was what his mind and soul had been yearning for: a purpose, a destination. He needed direction and now he was on a decided path. He paid more attention to the scenery around him that was rapidly changing from flat plains to green hills and mountains.

After two hours of driving, Henry realized he was still hungry. After all, he had polished off that toast so quickly, he had barely felt it!

He pulled through a McDonald's drive-through to get a burger as he thought of his destination. He had not eaten at a McDonald's in years. He didn't remember McDonald's being particularly amazing, but as he swallowed his way through a Big Mac he was overwhelmed by its greasy goodness, and he vowed to try things he had put off for his own "rich guy" reasons. Anne probably had a lot to do with that part of him. But, he was done with keeping up appearances, and he was in the business of breaking down barriers, after all. He was on his way to being a new man. A fresh start was beginning to make its way onto the stage of Henry's life, and who knew that a greasy Big Mac from a Micky D's in a virtually non-existent town could provide such a bright perspective on his new life?

Feeling better about his trip, he continued down the long stretch of Interstate 80. Moving onward, he wanted to do something, anything. He was looking for some exciting, new experience! A little danger wouldn't hurt, either. But what does a guy do for fun in Wyoming? He remembered vaguely that it was the home of the world's largest mineral hot-spring. From what he could gather from Interstate billboards and random signs strewn about the side of the road, rusted and paint chipped, that hot-spring was the biggest tourist attraction Wyoming had to offer.

He then started wondering about how long he would actually be away. It had already been two days since he had left Anne in New York.

Henry stopped himself. He was not going to think of her. He had just cleared his head enough to feel some of the weight of his life lift off of his shoulders. Now was certainly not the time to pile the weight back on again. After all, this was his break from all that. He was going to use it to its fullest potential.

So, he diverted that train wreck and focused on what he could do in dust-filled Wyoming. He had already passed the exit for those glorious hot- springs, but they were out of his way anyway. He wanted to have fun, but he also wanted to stay on track with Jackson Hole as his ultimate finish line.

Just then, he spotted a sign for a rodeo in Cheyenne. Henry decided he was going to get his cowboy on.

"What is the first thing every cowboy needs?" He thought as he pulled into Cheyenne and observed the many people wearing cowboy hats. He was currently wearing an Armani suit with the jacket removed and hanging neatly on a hanger in his backseat. His shirt was silk, from his trip to France last year.

He glanced at his favorite Italian cufflinks that he had gotten when he joined the firm. The smooth Egyptian onyx reflected his face. He laughed. He was a dead giveaway, a fully bonafide city-boy. The clothes in his bag would not do him any better. This soon-to-be cowboy was going to do some shopping.

He took a look around him at the men on the sidewalk. Blue jeans. He was in desperate need of some denim.

While driving the main drag, he saw a few shops to his left and decided to park and check out the stores.

Instead of heading for the obviously appealing mall across the way, sure to have a Gap or something close to his style, he went into a local shop called, "Boot Barn."

With one whiff of the distinct leather smell, he smiled lightly with excitement and shopped the racks. This was as country as it could get, and it was the exact opposite of anything Henry had ever owned.

A woman at the front counter saw him enter. "Can I help ya find anything there, cowboy?" she asked. A sly look of success sprawled across her tan, freckled face, as her lips curled into a smile as if pleased with her not-so-subtle humor. Her head was tilted downward, focusing on a book she was reading, a western no doubt.

But when she glanced up, he saw her golden hazel eyes shimmering with the intensity of a bull, yet somehow calming, looking back at him. A tiny laugh crept out, but she covered it up by clearing her throat.

Henry might have underestimated how out of place he just might look, especially in a store like this one. His gaze shifted around the room for just a second. Trophy bucks and bear skins lined the walls. "Uh, yeah, you see, I'm in a bit of a bind. One of my solid gold buttons is just not as snug as I would like it. I feel like I'm living on the edge here." Henry put his hands out as if unsteady and swayed slightly back and forth trying to play some dramatic rich guy. It was funny because Henry knew men like that. He knew the part so well.

She giggled and set her book down, giving him her undivided attention now.

Henry was surprised at how easy it was for him to casually joke around with a perfect stranger, a very beautiful stranger at that. The truth was he always got nervous around beautiful women. He had always just been skilled at hiding any nervous demeanor that might surface. His nerves gave him this fierce adrenaline that always seemed to make him irresistible to women, or at least, according to Thomas. Honestly, he never quite understood the reasoning.

He carried on a short chit-chatty conversation for a few minutes more. Another customer came in needing help, so she pointed Henry in the right direction and moved to help the next cowboy in need. Everyone was either a cowboy or cowgirl in this town to Henry.

He decided to reinvent his image, starting from head and then to toe. Seeing the need for a fancy cowboy hat, he put a black, sleek one with a metal buckle in the front and black and silver string dangling off the back. He tried it on and looked at himself in the mirror and couldn't suppress laughing; he was never going to pull off a cowboy hat. He looked more absurd with it on than he did with his city clothes.

Just to be sure, Henry tried on a brown one, which was equally amusing. So, putting down the hat, he wandered over to the shirts. Stacks and stacks of plaid, flannel shirts lined the back wall. He knew he couldn't go wrong with the shirts. He had dressed up as a "hot" farm boy one year for a Halloween party back during his freshmen year of college. He knew that chicks dug strong, ruddy, tan-skinned men who knew how to handle a tractor or a gun, especially since the movie "Young Guns" came out that year. Emilio Estevez and Martin Sheen did not make for very convincing cowboys but, then again, neither did Henry. It worked, too; he got three numbers that night.

He pulled out three different shirts in his size and headed over to the blue jeans. He knew his size, but they were looking pretty small on the rack. He pulled a couple pairs off the shelf and headed for the dressing room. He grabbed a random belt as he passed. He would leave boots for last. They would be the hardest, yet most necessary thing for him to get used to if he wanted to fit in around here. He almost dreaded the thought of losing his black suede Armani loafers. But he wanted to look the part more.

Henry walked into the dressing room, closed the door, and proceeded to get undressed. He shed his shirt, and his exposed skin was pale but displayed impeccable definition. Henry worked out regularly; it often helped clear his head or sometimes just allowed him time to fill his life with something other than work. It also served as a much-needed distraction from the dysfunction that was his marriage. He liked to run on the treadmills that faced the windows looking outside and watch the people walk by. He imagined their lives, sometimes even to the finest detail of the color of their front door, and the name of the shaggy dog that barked outside. It was exhilarating to create interesting, comfortable, easy, perfect lives when it was someone else's. It felt great to be in control because he sure didn't have control over his own reality.

He stared at himself in the mirror and imagined an alternative life. His brown hair was slightly shaggy and wild. He usually got a haircut every two weeks, but it must have slipped his mind in the past month of predicaments. Now, his hair fell over his eyes, shading them from view. His look was mysterious, almost dangerous. He liked it. It was a change he was going to embrace. It was a much younger look, like the college version of Henry, only older in and around the eyes, which gave him away. They were the reflection of his heart, a mirror of entwined depths of pain.

Henry sighed and pulled the shirt over his back, zipped his figure accentuating jeans, and flipped his hair out of his eyes and got a good look. *It's now or never*, he thought, walking out of the dressing room with a quiet intensity.

The beautiful saleslady blinked her hazel eyes as she looked him up and down. Speechless, with a slight blush, she told him, "Well, there, you are goin' to be needin' some cowboy boots next." She walked over to the shoe section and showed him a selection of leather boots.

"I will be purchasing this black plaid I have on, along with the green shirt and this brown one here." He told her, his eyes pleading for her help with the right boots.

She bit her lower lip in thought. "Well, you can never go wrong with neutral dark brown. They go with everything." She handed him a nice, leather pair of brown boots and pulled off some shiny black ones for him to see next. "I think these are too flashy … let's see … how about these?" She handed him a set of non-shiny black ones with black stitching.

"Those will be perfect. I need a size 11." He tried on the boots and enjoyed the comfortable, smooth insides. "Mmm, that actually feels pretty nice." He told the sales lady with a smile.

She smiled back. "Well, let's ring ya up and get ya on your merry way."

Just then he noticed an assortment of leather riding gloves on the counter. On a whim, he grabbed a pair and handed them to the saleslady to ring up as well.

Henry handed her his credit card and thanked her for all her help. He took a breath and opened the door. A fully decorated cowboy, he stepped outside. Well, almost fully decorated. He couldn't bring himself to put on the hat.

Looking around the street, Henry realized that the only things he was missing were some spurs that jingled as he stepped and some chewing tobacco. Adding anything else to his getup might be bordering on a little weird. However, he felt pretty great in his new clothes, so he decided to stay as he was for the moment. Dressing like a cowboy just made him feel stronger than his regular, old self, like he could actually be a different person for once.

He turned toward the rodeo grounds. He had never been to a rodeo before and had only a vague idea about what to expect. Henry's thoughts were racing with excitement. He noticed that it seemed like the whole town was going to this thing, too.

Henry walked by little cafes and shops shutting down early and small boys racing with glee toward the rodeo grounds. Every sense seemed vividly multiplied in intensity. The air was wafting with distinct smells, all individualistic in tendency and fighting to overwhelm the other smells, as if to portray a tale. The aroma of warm popcorn lingered with a cryptic presence, as if proud of its smell, teasing the tortured noses whose resistance would soon wear down, the rouged temptress of all smells. The scent of cotton-candy-soaked fingertips and a cold Coke just being popped open were in mid-brawl in the air, one overwhelming the other for just a second, and then the other overtook the short-lived champion.

Another overwhelming scent was, of course, the distinct smell of manure. Henry breathed in deeper, trying to hold back the distasteful, wrinkle of the nose that all city-people form any time that certain smell is around. He tried to mimic the look of the hard-faced cowboys around him. They breathed in deeply, allowing the familiar scent to fill their nose and lungs. Henry breathed in deeply, trying to look content to have the uncomfortable scent far inside his nose. He breathed a little too much, because he coughed and sputtered, causing the tough cowboys to give him strange looks as they passed.

Once recovered, Henry noticed another smell. It was the grandfather of all scents, aged and wise from years of life. It lined every man's boots, every child had it smeared across their face and hands, clinging to the particles of sweat perspired while running around. The boys chased innocent girls with a huge grasshopper in their dust-blackened hand, while the little girls screamed in fright and ducked into the girl's bathroom for safety. Dirt was interwoven in the web of every individual's life. Henry's brand-new clothes were already dusted lightly from this ever-present particle. It smelled of the moments in every single person's life in that town. They were all shared and then swept away by a gust of wind or a casual dragging of the feet.

Not just the smells were imprinted on Henry's mind, but every color was enhanced and almost glowing with energy as he strode to the bleachers and listened to the crowd roar with excitement. The setting sun reflected a soft blue, an almost amethyst haze, off the silver bleachers. Pinks and reds emblazoned the sky and matched the flushed cheeks of children out of breath, who were now taking their seats, anxious for the show to begin.

The interconnectedness of all things was so earth-shatteringly evident that it took his breath away. There was no one there that knew him, nothing that could distract him or pull his attention away from this moment, these unfamiliar people. All these people together, some acquaintances, some friends, some purely strangers, were unified by a single passion. The passion of community, of family, of the Western ideal. He had never been to a rodeo before, but he had been to his share of business parties, gala events, some even in his honor. None of them compared to this event in the middle of nowhere. This looked … fun.

With about fifteen minutes to showtime, Henry got up from his seat and walked over to the concession stand to get the full experience of this place. He requested a Coke, the classic American beverage of choice. The cold glass swiftly chilled his hand, hot from the summer heat. He took a long swig, feeling the freezing, refreshing liquid all the way down to his stomach. "Ahhhh." Henry nodded his head, realizing he had not felt more refreshed and alive in a long time.

Henry noticed two cowboys about five yards away silently observing him. One was tall, even taller than Henry by a few inches, and lean with jet black hair and dark skin. He held his dark brown cowboy hat in one hand, lightly hitting it against his leg in an attempt to knock some of the dust off, but remaining carefree that his efforts were futile. His coal black eyes drilled into Henry as he met the cowboy's gaze. The other man with this cowboy was closer to Henry's height, about 6'3. He was talking in low tones to the dark cowboy. His black, dusty cowboy hat hid most of his face from Henry as he talked, with only his moving mouth and brown mustache showing. His arms were toned, muscles rippling with intensity from years of work.

Henry watched as the dark, taller cowboy curled his lips in amusement at something the muscled cowboy had said.

They both turned toward Henry, walking until they stood right in front of him. The tough, broader man had tilted his hat back slightly, and Henry was frozen under his ice blue gaze. "You ridin' in the rodeo, cowboy?" The cold blue eyes grew colder with mock amusement.

"No, just watchin' today." Henry did his best to add the cowboy accent to his tone, tilting his drink for another swig.

The two men saw right through his simulated nonchalance. With his blue eyes flashing, the man said to Henry, "Well, we heard they have room for one more. Ol' Red needs a rider. You wanna give him a try?"

The taller cowboy chuckled and grabbed Icey Blue's arm. "Joe, you know no one has stayed on that bull for more than a few seconds in years, let alone walked away without serious injuries. C'mon, we need to get back to the chutes. Won' be long now." He headed off with Joe.

Joe turned his icy eyes toward Henry as he walked away. "Enjoy the show, cowboy." He said in a menacing, mocking tone.

Henry was infuriated. Those men had no idea what he was capable of or who he was. He successfully ran a multi-billion-dollar corporation! His newfound zest for life was giving him back the sense of fearlessness with which he used to run his life. He never backed down from a dare.

Henry's eyes were wild with adrenaline. The cowboys were walking away, some distance between them now when Henry shouted out, "Hey, hold up!"

The two cowboys half-turned in surprise to look back at Henry. With strong strides, Henry quickly closed the distance between them. "I want to ride." He said forcefully.

The tall, dark one stared at him, his lips curling into a smile. "All right."

Joe laughed, his blue eyes flashing excitedly. "Follow us." He said, a distinct coolness lining his voice. "You got a pair of riding gloves?"

Henry nodded, grateful for the leather pair he had picked up at the cowboy shop. He could hear the rodeo starting as he followed the two men around the back of the grandstand, through a maze of horse trailers and campers, to the registration side of the rodeo. The national anthem was being played over a crackling sound system as a piece of paper, some sort of liability release, was shoved at him. He signed it quickly before being dragged to one of the small gates in between worn, wooden walls.

A side gate opened, and Henry watched as ten or so beautiful cowgirls came riding out, carrying flags and smiling excitedly.

All too quickly, Henry felt himself being lifted and thrown over the gate. Someone tapped a Stetson on his head. He didn't see who, he just saw red – red, breathing flesh irritated by the weight now added to his back.

"Hold on tight, cowboy."

Henry heard the chill radiating from Joe's voice, but he was focused on more important things now, like the gigantic, dark red bull he found himself straddling.

He grabbed onto the thick rope tied around the enormous animal as a harness. *I sure am grateful for those leather riding gloves,* he thought as the animal reared and snorted, almost tearing Henry's hand off. To his amazement, his hand stayed tightly gripped to the rope. The only thing he could think as the gate was thrown open was *What the heck did I get myself into?* Fear trickled its way up through his spine, but it was gone in a flash as the gate opened.

The bull threw his giant body forward, like the first drop of a roller coaster. Henry leaned with him as well, gripping with both hands to keep his balance during the initial thrust out of the gate.

He threw one hand up as the angry bull twisted, bending opposite the twist. His hand on the rope was iron fused on steel, welded as one unit. His strong legs tightly gripped the bull as the red giant threw himself to the left this time. Henry was completely and utterly focused on the bull and his movements. No one else in the entire world existed.

His hat flew off as the bull turned and twisted at the same time. Henry moved with the bull, throwing his hand the opposite way for balance. To the cheering crowd, Henry looked as if he had been riding bulls since he could walk, as if he was born for this life.

Distantly, Henry heard the buzzer sound, signaling he had made the eight-second round. His focus still did not break. He kept moving and bending with the bull until he felt a hand grabbing his arm from one of the rodeo cowboys.

Henry reached over, gripping the man's shoulder before releasing his iron grip on the bull. The man lifted Henry off and carried him to safety.

As he climbed over the gate, he looked over his shoulder to see four cowboys attempting to guide the bull to the open gate. The bull angrily twisted his body, kicking the wall so violently that the wood cracked.

Finally, he ran into the opening between two gates, snorting viciously as a gate was swung shut behind him.

Henry jumped down from the fence and turned as he felt a hand on his shoulder.

Are you all right?" An excited but concerned cowboy asked him.

Henry nodded, a little overwhelmed at what had just happened. He looked around and saw that a small crowd had gathered around him. Most of the cowboys surrounding him looked exhilarated and breathless as they watched him, like they had just ridden with him and were in that moment.

Henry noticed Joe and his tall friend toward the back of the crowd. Joe was scowling, shaking his head as he talked to the tall cowboy. There were many eyes looking at him like he was some sort of amazing cowboy.

Henry began to feel a little shaky and thirsty, very thirsty. The cowboy who had just spoken to him saw Henry's reaction to his sudden fame.

The cowboy grabbed his arm and pulled him away from the noise. "Here, I got a cold drink in my truck for ya'." He said as they walked away from the arena.

Henry felt very relieved. "I would appreciate it, thanks." He looked at the man beside him. The cowboy was tall, about Henry's height with dark blond hair peeking out from underneath his worn-in, black Stetson.

"Here we are." The man stopped at a dusty '87 Chevy pickup, opening up the passenger door and pulling out a red cooler. Opening the top, he grabbed a couple of cold Gatorades out, popped the tops, and handed one to Henry.

Henry drank in the refreshing coolness. He kept drinking until he had drained the bottle completely.

The cowboy next to him laughed. "Take it easy there. You got another ride left, ya' know." He held his hand out to Henry. "My name's Mitch, by the way. Mitch Taylor."

Henry shook his hand. "Henry. Henry ... Michael." He remembered to give Mitch the name he had registered under for the rodeo. If anyone knew his last name, people from New York would be in Wyoming in two seconds. Once people knew who he was, they would treat him differently and this whole new path he was on would be sodden with the same old stuff he always dealt with – not knowing who his real friends were, never really getting to know anyone. Henry did not want that right now. He was enjoying being a nobody in a town where no one knew him. It was a first for him, and he was going to savor it as long as it lasted.

Mitch leaned against the truck, resting his boot on the back tire. "That was some fine ridin' out there, Henry. Even if it was your first." Mitch's eyes twinkled with laughter and a hint of kindness.

"Was it that obvious?"

Mitch shook his head. "No way. You look like a complete natural. But I've been on the ol' rodeo circuit since I was abou' twelve. I woulda recognized that technique. It is very rare to see."

Henry did not understand what Mitch meant. He still did not understand how he had managed to stay on that maniac for more than eight seconds. The confusion must have shown in his face because Mitch answered his unasked question.

"You rode like you were one with the bull. Like you completely trusted your abilities to stay on him. Not many men can do that. They are too focused on just making the buzzer."

Henry reflected on his ride. He had just gone with his instincts. His gut instincts had always served him well in the past, especially dealing with business and clients. "I just rode him. I don't know." He shook his head. "I guess you might be right, Mitch. So, I have another ride to finish?"

"Ya, with the way you rode, no one else stands a chance, including me. You just gotta make the buzzer again, and you will be golden." Mitch shook his head with laughing eyes.

They turned and headed back to the arena. "So where you headed next, Henry?"

Henry saw no reason to hide the truth. "Jackson Hole."

"No kiddin'? I am headed there next myself. Figured I should at least hit home while I am in the area." Mitch looked at the cowboy attempting to stay on a large black bull in the arena. "Well, looks like I am up next. I'll be seein' you then, Henry."

Henry nodded, looking at the scoreboard to the side of him. He stared in disbelief at his name at the very top. *It had been a crazy day*, he thought. *What New York would think if she saw him now*. He laughed out loud and walked over to see Mitch ride.

5
NEW YORK, NEW YORK
December 20, 1991

"Henry," Anne said coolly as they walked down the frosty New York sidewalk.

"Hmm?" He asked distractedly as he tried to scan the paper for stock sales and navigate the sidewalk at the same time.

"Henry." Her voice had taken on an impatient edge. "Put down your paper, please."

He looked up at her, trying to give his new wife his full attention. "Yes?"

"Henry, we have been married over a month now." She looked pointedly into the window of a jewelry store nearby.

"My beautiful wife needs something pretty?" He asked with a crooked smile, still trying to keep his attention on Anne and not work. Checking his watch quickly, he motioned across the street.

"We have a few minutes before dinner with Cromwell. Let's go."

Anne nodded and walked to the store without a second glance at her husband.

6
HENRY'S JOURNEY
Jackson Hole, Wyoming
August 21, 1992

Wyoming was an entirely different sort of country than he was used to seeing. As he drove, Henry could not get enough of the land. Beautiful, snow-capped mountains stretched endlessly toward the sky with green trees, heavily sprinkling the large, rolling hills at the base of the mountains as the huge sun began to sink behind them. Henry had crashed at a motel in Cheyenne after the rodeo and, exhausted, slept until the early afternoon. He had been driving to Jackson since about 3:30 that afternoon.

It has been a long day, Henry thought as he drove slowly into the town, looking around at the various restaurants, businesses, and houses. The town square had a unique display of deer antlers that seemed to be welcoming all visitors to the West. It was late, but Henry could see a group of teenagers romping around the square, taking pictures and making silly poses. One of the guys paired off with a girl and grabbed her hand. Henry smiled to himself as he drove by.

The town was rustic, yet refined by a rich presence. Henry could see it in the infrastructure. The buildings around him looked as if they were designed to look old, but actually, were quite modern. Rock climbing shops and organic markets showed the area to be prevalent with people of natural hearts and free spirits. He liked that class of people, the ones who could live off the ground and, if they could not, at least there was an organic market in town. They were the type to do anything for a thrill, and they lived each day for the day that it was, at least that's how he saw them in his own imaginary story of their lives. It was a story he wanted for himself, so maybe that's why he saw it that way.

Surrounding the town were the mountains, daring and luring all adventurous climbers to come try their skills. *I'm gonna have to try some mountain climbing while I'm here.* Henry was ready for any and every adventure. He couldn't wait. But first things first. He needed to find housing.

He stopped in at the first bar he saw, asking around for information regarding an available cabin to rent up in the mountains. Two men that were sitting at the bar wearing black, dusty cowboy hats turned around, and eyed his new jeans and shirt before answering.

The tallest one told Henry, "Go talk to Bill. He'll fix ya up." He turned back to his drink at the bar.

Henry nodded his thanks and walked down a ways, pulling a chair out from the bar and, clearly exhausted, sank into it. The weariness of driving all this distance was catching up to him, and the bull riding had really made his muscles ache. He needed a massage.

A tall, thin redhead wearing tight Wranglers with long hair falling past her waist smiled from behind the bar at Henry. "You look like you could use a drink, hon."

"Yes," Henry answered. "I will have a....," He looked around at the cowboys surrounding him. "Whiskey. Any whiskey you have, please."

The bartender, recognizing him as a stranger, poured him a shot. "What brings ya to Jackson, friend?" She said with a teasing smile.

"I am looking for a cabin. Needed to get away for a while."

"How long is a while?" She pried, picking up a cloth and winking at him as she wiped the bar.

Henry looked up and half-smiled, "Long enough."

She nodded and smiled engagingly. Her green eyes reminded him of Anne, causing his stomach to drop sharply. "You should find Bill. He has the best cabins to rent 'round here."

He was sure he looked apprehensive now as he nodded his thanks to her. The image of Anne was a disease in his mind. Even faint memories in the farthest corners of his mind captured any untouched areas of his consciousness and heart.

"Where can I find him?" Henry was starting to picture Anne, tangled in the sheets of the bed, his bed. Her eyes pleading with him, begging him to come back. He shook his head, trying to lose the unwanted image of his wife. She was a dark storm cloud that hung over Henry, looming day and night. It menaced him. He waited for the storm to pass. He knew it would, although not always without repercussions.

Henry forced himself to focus on the redheaded woman in front of him and her friendly yet flirtatious smirk as she watched him.

"He's right over there, playin' cards. He's the one with a sinister smile, which means he's bluffing." She rolled her eyes and pointed at a man a few tables over, playing poker with some cowboys. "I'm Shannah by the way ... if you need someone to show you around later, you know where to find me." She smiled at him before turning to a new customer.

Henry smiled his thanks shortly before rising from the bar. He walked purposefully toward the poker table. The man Shannah had pointed out to him sat facing him, but Henry was unnoticed. The game was obviously absorbing all of this old man's attention. His aged brown face was set heavily in concentration with grizzly whiskers and long gray hair pulled into a tight ponytail under his dusty brown hat. His tight lips curved into a smile as he laid down a full house.

All the cowboys groaned and rose from the table as Bill pulled the chips and money toward himself. He had a toothy, childish grin that made his dimples sink in deep to his face like a draining pool of quicksand.

Henry pulled out a newly vacant chair next to Bill. "Looks like you weren't bluffin' after all, huh?"

"What are you talkin' about, son?"

"Oh, never mind. Bill, is it?" Henry swiftly got down to business. "Name's Henry Michael."

"I have a feelin' you ain' here to try your luck, Henry," Bill said as he counted his winnings.

"That's right, sir. I would like to rent a cabin. I was told you could help me with that?"

"Sure can. How long you in town?

Henry tightly folded his hands on the table. "I have no idea ... just needed to get away," he said quietly while looking down at his hands. The faint tan line from his wedding ring shone up at him.

Quickly unfolding his hands, Henry moved his left hand out of sight under the table and looked back up at Bill.

Bill observed Henry's defeated exterior. "I can fix ya up, sure 'nough. Let's go now. It's gettin' late." He dumped his winnings into a dusty saddlebag and stood up.

Bill nodded to Shannah and said a few words to a few cowboys before leading Henry out into the much quieter street.

Shannah held Henry's gaze as he passed until he was out the door. He gave her a nod and breathed in the fresh air.

The cool night breeze swept over Henry's face, leaving him with the sweet smell of pine, dust, and warm grass. He watched as Bill walked over to a dusty, gold, GMC pickup. He opened the door and hopped in, shouting for Henry to follow him.

Henry quickly walked to his car and followed the old man.

They drove out of town and into the winding trails of the woods. Henry followed Bill higher and higher into the mountains. The mountain air streamed through his window, chilling him ever so slightly, but he kept the window down to allow the heavenly fresh air in. Every once in a while, the stars would peek through the thick cover of the pine trees. Henry just wanted to stick his head out the window and gaze at the stars as he drove.

Bill was getting some distance on him now. He pulled his mind back to driving and caught up to him. After a while, Bill pulled off the road onto a rough trail that led to a cabin tucked into a tight grouping of large pine trees.

Bill opened his door, got out, and slammed it shut.

Henry followed suit, looking around at his surroundings.

"That path over there leads down to a mountain stream." Bill pointed to a faint trail just to the left of the cabin. Henry could hear the softened sound of a stream rushing just down the hill. Bill put a key in the lock and motioned for Henry to come inside as he pushed open the door.

Henry was still gazing around, taking in his breathtaking surroundings.

Bill was talking to himself as Henry came jogging in from outside. "Nothing too fancy. Got a full kitchen, bedroom and bathroom in the back, and a small livin' room." He pointed to a small phone on a wooden end table in the corner. "Phone is hooked up, number is taped to the side, and the machine is set up for messages." He motioned toward the stove in the kitchen. "It can get cold up here at night, real cold. The wood burning stove will do ya good. I'll get that started for ya, 'fore leavin'. Wood piles out back, along with an axe if you should run out. But only split the wood we already got downed."

Henry looked around as Bill spoke. The aged wood floors and walls gave the cabin a quiet, comfortable feel. The scent of cedars and pine hung in the air as the night breeze strode its way inside with them. Henry took a deep breath and let it all out in one relieving sigh. It was small, but exactly what he needed.

There was a mount of a large elk hung above the couch. A date and name was engraved on a gold plaque below the elk, proclaiming the skilled hunter responsible for the kill. A shelf perched just below the mount was lined with old books of history, art, poetry and a few works of Mark Twain. Two colorful pieces of heavy pottery served as bookends.

A coffee table made from driftwood, stained a dark mahogany, sat atop a plain shaggy rug. Two end tables separated a plush couch, of a vintage maroon color, and a colorful love seat that sat itself against the wall with a large window behind it.

Henry looked out the window for a moment, seeing no movement or sign of life besides the trees gently swaying by the slight breeze. "How close is the next cabin?"

"'Bout half a mile. Closest neighbor shouldn' bother you none. She keeps to herself, and owns her own cabin, so it ain't mine." Bill lifted his hat, smoothed back his hair before putting it back down again. "You can have it for as long as you like, say, two hundred dollars a week? That work for you?"

Henry smiled gratefully but shook his head in humble resistance. "How about two-fifty since it is such short notice?"

"Works for me. I thank ya right kindly." He tipped his hat in thanks to Henry and walked toward the door. "I hate to have the cabin empty, seems right wasteful. But I gotta stay on the ranch to see after the horses and such, so a tenant is just what it needs. Now this cabin takes a bit of work. This ain't a city dwellin' by any means. It's got runnin' water and all that, but gettin' hot water is like pulling teeth. So, I would just as well go to the creek for a shower, wakes ya up anyway. It's a snow melt creek, so it'll wake you up better than any coffee could, I'll tell ya that." Bill tossed him the key and smiled.

The pair sat in silence for a moment before Henry broke it.

"Oh, by the way, nice win tonight. Shannah thought you were bluffing."

"Ah I see now, that's what you were goin' on about at the bar. That red-headed beauty don't know a bettin' hand from a foldin' hand. She couldn't call a bluff if I was sweatin' bullets." Bill bellowed a deep laugh from his gut, causing his whole body to shake. He got a kick out of his own wisecracks.

Henry couldn't help but smile and laugh a bit, too. As their laughter came to a close, silence filled the cabin. But it wasn't uncomfortable. Henry liked Bill. He was one of those guys who could be anyone's grandpa. Everyone was comfortable with him and he came off as an honest and trustworthy man. Henry hoped he would use him at the ranch, if only to get to know him better. He could use a friend here.

"Let's get that stove a burnin' eh?" Henry followed Bill out back to gather logs for the stove. The night air had dropped in temperature since they first entered the cabin. He could see his breath in the night and frost lined some of the logs left uncovered by the black tarp.

They each took an armful and strode back inside. The only sounds were the steps they took and the gravel beneath their shoes being kicked around. Bill's boots clicked together with each step, and he had a slight hitch in his step.

They walked back in the back door of the cabin and piled the wood on a rack next to the back door.

Bill lifted a couple logs and instructed Henry to grab some kindling from the bottom cabinet at the end of the counter in the kitchen.

Henry did as he was told, grabbing some old newspaper along with stray twigs and branches.

Bill moved aside to allow Henry to throw it all in. He pulled a box of matches off the sill of the back window, pulled one out, struck it and threw it in. A flame slowly grew and enveloped the kindling and the log caught fire. The fire crackled inside the iron stove.

Henry felt the heat rising from it and rubbed his hands together next to the open door.

"Well, son, I best be going. The wife's probably worried 'bout me. She won't be anxious when I bring home my winnin's from tonight, though." Bill chuckled under his breath. "If you need anything, my number's on the phone next to the bed." He turned for the door, removing his hat again and smoothing his hair in one fluid motion, and replacing it back to his head as he opened the front door.

"Thanks again and let me know about any help I can be for you."

Henry watched as Bill drove away from the front door. Soon, his headlights and the sound of his rattling engine faded away, and silence surrounded Henry. He had driven just over two thousand miles, and this moment made it all worth it. A satisfied smile sprawled across his face.

Henry walked out to his car, unloaded his heavy luggage and strolled back to the house. He heard the comforting sounds of the stream a little ways below and the soft whispers of birds moving about, settling in for the night. He inhaled the fresh air as deep as his lungs would allow. It was delicious as the pure air spread through his nose and chest. The stars shone brilliantly through the minute patches of sky that peeked through the thick clusters of pine trees. Anne was pushed further and further back in his mind again by the wonder of nature. He felt much better.

Henry hauled his luggage inside the small cabin. Exhausted, Henry locked the door and headed toward the bedroom. *The unpacking would have to wait till tomorrow*, he thought. He laid down on the bed, the side of his face found his pillow, and he could just taste the sweetness of sound sleep as his eyes began to flutter shut.

But his eyes flashed open suddenly, and a smile sprawled across his face as he crawled back out of bed. He strode to the front door and looked up and down at the old, wooden, creaky door, wrought with the wisdom of age, and unlocked it. Henry sighed happily, "So, this is what it's like to feel free..." He dove back into bed, alone and happy.

7

NEW YORK, NEW YORK
January 6, 1992

"Henry, watch out." Anne said irritably. She reached over and yanked his hand.

Almost dropping his coffee, Henry looked over at her. "What?"

"You almost stepped on that...man." She said distastefully.

Henry looked back and saw a man dressed in dirty layers of old clothes, leaning against the wall. His beard was long, tangled, and grey with dust. His hands rubbed together furiously in an attempt to stay warm in the cold January air.

The man met Henry's eyes; the eyes were filled with pain and despair and spoke of a journey that no man should ever have to endure.

Henry started reaching for his wallet, but Anne's firm grip on his hand tightened.

"Henry, why are you looking over there? Don't look at him. He'll expect something or try and take it," Anne demanded in a hushed tone, her eyes callous to his pain. "Come on. We are going to be late." She grabbed his arm and pulled him down the sidewalk, but Henry couldn't pull his mind from the pain behind the stranger's eyes and the emptiness in Anne's.

8
HENRY'S JOURNEY
Jackson Hole, Wyoming
August 22, 1992

The sharp light of the sun woke Henry from his deep sleep. Forgetting where exactly he was, he stared at the unfamiliar wooden beams running along the ceiling. As Henry slowly remembered where he was and why, he remained in bed listening to the musical sounds of the birds chirping, about their morning business. A little farther away, the mountain stream noisily pushed the water down the mountain.

He rolled out of bed, anxious to explore his new surroundings. The bedroom was small but clean. The bed was large and comfortable with a patchwork quilt serving as the comforter. A small, wooden dresser stood in one corner with a lamp occupying the other. There were several large windows to see out into the forest along with wooden floors, walls, and ceilings to complete the room.

Henry unpacked some of his things into the dresser before heading into the living room and kitchen. He had looked it over last night but noticed new details with the light of day. Several large windows also filled the living room and the kitchen. There was a small wooden table, wooden countertops, and a yellow fridge and stove.

Henry walked to the fridge and, upon opening it, realized it was empty. His stomach growled, and he decided to clean up and run into town before exploring the woods. *There will be plenty of time for that later.* He thought to himself. He had nothing but time … for now. It was a completely new feeling to him. In New York, he had his entire day planned for him, right out to when he would dine and with whom he would be eating.

He turned on the shower and frigid water poured forth. He waited for it to warm but shut it off remembering what Bill had said the night before. He grabbed a towel and some soap and threw on his boots he had bought back in Cheyenne and headed out the door for the creek. The trail twisted through the trees and the sound of rushing water grew louder and louder, causing Henry's heart to race with adrenaline.

He broke out into a run down the trail and emerged through the trees to the sight of a crystal blue stream racing down the mountain. His eyes widened as he explored the nature of the area. He could see the bottom of the creek, wrought with smooth stones, and larger boulders here and there. A large boulder in the middle of the stream protruded from the persistent water, causing an eddy with white water powerfully swirling around the rock.

Up the stream aways, he noticed a section of the creek with a sudden drop, causing a small waterfall. Just above the waterfall, he noticed a section of flat land. The creek would flow slower there.

He hiked uphill until he reached the flat of the stream. Kicking off his boots, he stuck a toe in the water. A chill shot up his leg and through his spine. Henry let out a shout, and he hopped around shaking his foot. He felt like a child, but, surprisingly, it felt good.

"Cold, cold, cold!" He yelled out and each word echoed through the trees. Bill was certainly right about waking up with the stream.

He got up the courage to get back into the water, this time both feet went in fully submerged. Water came up to his knees, and a cool numbness came over his submerged body parts. At least he couldn't feel the cold anymore. His teeth chattered through a muffled chuckle.

He smiled as he committed in his mind to the task at hand. He pulled off his white undershirt and threw it to shore. He stood in the cold water just in his briefs. He palmed some of the water in his hands and tossed it over his shoulder. His back muscles twitched as the biting water cascaded down his back, soaking his briefs as it flowed back down to the creek. He gasped in air and continued tossing water all over his body.

The sun shone through the trees in gaps, and rays beat against his chest, warming him ever so slightly. He turned his face into the warmth and reveled in the sunshine.

He splashed his face a couple times before bending over and soaking his hair in the water. His scalp was overcome with tingling and the rest of his body swarmed with goosebumps. He flung his head back out of the water. A stream of water came with it, arching around his head and spraying the creek behind him. He arched his back and let his head shoulders relax. Arms wide open, he yelled out, without inhibition, "Woooohoooo!"

Invigorated with energy, Henry washed his hair and skin with the soap he had brought and jumped out of the creek. Putting on his boots, he headed back up the trail to his cabin.

He entered through the front door and headed to the bedroom. He toweled his hair quickly and shook the rest of the wet out. He finished unpacking his clothes and things and picked out what he was going to wear for the day. A denim jean and a plain t-shirt suited him nicely.

He changed out of his wet clothes and replaced it with the comforting dry clothes. A clean, pure feeling washed over him for a few seconds, but soon, hunger set in again. A food run was the first agenda on his list of things to do, and coffee. One thing Bill was not correct on was the need for coffee after creek bathing.

Henry drove down the winding trails and back into the town. There were not as many people about as he had expected. Looking at his watch, Henry was surprised to see it was only eight in the morning.

As he drove up, the town cafe was bustling with ranchers and other men grabbing a cup of coffee and a bite to eat before work. He parked and went inside.

Once again thankful for his cowboy gear, Henry looked around the cafe at a sea of dusty, black Stetsons and sweat-stained, just as dusty, baseball caps. A family of tourists sat at a booth looking over the menu. The parents were discussing the day's activities that were planned, while two little boys were shooting spitballs through their straws. He grabbed a newspaper and a menu, found an open booth, and slid in.

"Hi ya, sir! What can I grab ya this fine mornin'?"

Removing his hat, Henry looked up to see a pretty, voluptuous blond smiling down at him with her pad open and pen ready.

Henry smiled at the waitress. "I would love some strong, hot coffee, a couple eggs over medium, bacon, and a few hot cakes. Can you do that for me, ma'am?" He sounded so country when he said it, he couldn't help but smile up at the waitress as the words came out, pleased with his ability to blend in.

"Sure can, handsome. Be right up." She sauntered away.

His coffee arrived shortly with another cheery smile from the waitress. He sipped the strong brew, feeling the warmth spread from his throat to a comfortable spot in his belly. He made a mental note to get coffee for the cabin. If he was going to bathe in the creek every morning, he would need a hot brew when he got back.

Henry opened up the newspaper and skimmed it, reveling in the fact that he did not have to patrol for stock prices and other competition. It was very relaxing for him to read through trivial news about a new road going up south of town, livestock prices, and a recipe for chicken wild rice soup. Henry flipped over to the back page and read the amusing sheriff's report. He sipped his coffee and chuckled at a few of the stories.

"Here ya are!" The waitress cheerfully announced as she set down his plate, heaped with eggs, bacon, and pancakes.

He smiled, threw his newspaper to the side, and thanked her before digging in. Henry gulped down the delicious meal, barely pausing to sip his coffee.

Pushing his now empty plate away from him, he noticed the advertisements on the front page of the abandoned newspaper sitting to his left. There was a small one near the bottom right about renting rock climbing equipment. Henry suddenly knew exactly what the rest of the morning would hold for him; he was going rock climbing.

Excited, Henry threw down a twenty-dollar bill to cover the breakfast and a tip before heading out the door with the newspaper in hand. He started walking. Shops lined most of the main streets, but he doubted that he could find the right one just by simply walking around.

There was a shop that had a giant bear tucked in the corner, he stepped inside and asked to be directed to the nearest rock climbing rental store. The store clerk, a burly fellow, showed him the way. It was close, just across the street and down about a block. He thanked the man and crossed the street, on his way to a place called, "Jack Dennis Outdoor Shop."

He walked inside the store and was surrounded by all sorts of gear; camping, rock climbing, canoeing, kayaking. Just name it, and Henry guessed they would have it. He walked up to the cash register where a younger guy was sitting, browsing through an issue of "Climbing" magazine. He had his feet propped up on the counter. A hemp anklet with a dangling charm had rolled up his ankle and was sitting taught around his calf. Henry couldn't quite make out what the charm was. It looked like just a plain old rock with a hole drilled in it to run the hemp, though. The attendant dropped his propped-up legs to the floor as he noticed Henry standing in front of him.

"What can I do for you, sir?"

He glanced at his nametag and proceeded. "Well, Charlie, I'm looking to rent some climbing equipment. Is that something you can help me with?" He flaunted his most charismatic smile.

"What's your experience level?"

"I'm a quick learner." Henry smiled coyly. Just because he had never done it before didn't mean he wasn't skilled. Look at how bull riding turned out.

"Sir, we don't recommend or promote unsupervised first attempts at rock climbing. That's how people get hurt. Would you be interested in some lessons?"

"If I buy all of my own gear, could you show me how to use it, or would I have to try my luck on the cliffs as an uneducated rookie?" Henry didn't want to waste time with instructions. It seemed too forced. His journey here had taught him to live, to throw caution to the wind. Taking any sort of class was out of the question.

The attention of the cashier was now focused on the business version of Henry. Ladies found this Henry extremely sexy, a man who knows what he wants. They absolutely swooned. However, other men found him arrogant and vain. In a sense, it was a type of arrogance, but he only ever used it with good intentions. He was always surprised that he could ever keep guy friends, really. His only true friend was Thomas, and that was because he was just as cut-throat in the business world as he was. They understood each other in that way, and they both had that same air of confidence about them. Thomas liked to call it his, "Cromwell Swag," but never in front of a beautiful woman, of course. Henry wasn't sure why he felt the need to be this pushy now, but he knew how to get what he wanted and rock climbing was just what he wanted most at that moment.

The attendant set his magazine to the side and looked at Henry with a feigning look of fear. He wasn't intimidated by him. His mocking expression caught Henry by surprise a bit, and now he was the one feeling shirked by another man's wit. What a new feeling this was.

"Look, you are obviously desperate here, man." He smiled sympathetically. "But I don't like seeing people get hurt rock climbing. So, my deal is this: I just had to cover the first couple hours of someone's shift today, so I get off in an hour. I was gonna hit the cliffs with some friends, and you are free to join us. Deal?"

The long drive from New York to Wyoming let Henry sort of desperate for human interaction. Henry let himself appear deep in thought and then let a quirky half-smile portray his answer. "Let's do it."

They arranged to meet at the shop in about an hour. Charlie said he had all the supplies they would need, and he said he would set him up with a pair of climbing shoes to use, free of charge. His one job was to get some snacks and water for the afternoon. Charlie had three other friends, besides Henry, coming along.

Henry was filled with adrenaline, with a looming hour hanging over his head like a black cloud raining on his rush of energy. He walked around downtown looking for a store that carried some trail mix, a personal request from Charlie. He remembered seeing that health food store when he first rode into town.

He headed over the direction of the store at a brisk pace. Perusing the aisles, he found the needed trail mix and grabbed a few bags. The coolers at the back of the store had some all-natural energy drinks and two different types of water. He loaded his basket with a mix of both. He grabbed some protein bars, enough for two a piece, some fresh fruit, a few apples, oranges and a bunch of bananas. He wasn't exactly sure how long they were going to be out rock climbing. In fact, he hadn't really asked a lot of questions. He had no idea where they were going or how they were all getting there. He shrugged the thought off and felt content with his snack selections. The cashier was pleasant and had an all-natural sort of scent around her, like she just got done rolling around in a grass field or something for her lunch break. He thanked her and she smiled. He picked up his one hundred percent recycled bags and headed out the door.

"Well, that killed about fifteen minutes," Henry said under his breath. He looked around, his gaze hunting out his next way to kill time. His eyes fell on the town square. A fountain was in the center of it and patches of grass sat shaded by the reaching limbs of large oak trees.

Crossing the street with his groceries, Henry found a nice patch of grass, laid his bags in the shade of a tree, and sat down in the warm sun. It had been years since he had a good, natural tan. The heat felt invigorating on his face. A slight breeze every now and then sent the right amount of relief from the heat that he needed.

Henry looked around him, watching people shuffle about whatever daily business they were on. A lot of tourists seemed to be getting out and shopping now. Kids were chasing each other with glee as their mother hastily followed them, certainly not gleefully, back to within her reach. The sun shone brightly with intermittent puffy clouds casting playful shadows on the earth below.

Henry sighed heavily and took off his t-shirt, tucked it behind his head, and laid down in the grass. His eyelids blinked slower and slower until finally he fell into a soft sleep in the middle of town square, shirtless and happy.

9

NEW YORK, NEW YORK
November 3, 1991

The morning after their wedding, Henry had a slight headache from the night before, and Anne still lie sleeping on the bed when the phone rang.

Henry hesitated to answer it. Who calls newlyweds the night after their wedding? Who even knew they were here? They were supposed to be on their way to Aruba.

He picked it up with a sigh of annoyance and was surprised to hear Thomas on the other line, babbling about some business proposal.

"Thomas, Thomas is this really necessary the morning after my wedding?"

"I suppose it could wait ... but you of all people know, Henry, the business world doesn't take days off for any occasion. By the way, was your evening ..." He coughed. "Successful?" The demeanor in his tone of voice was like a crude joke. If he were standing right next to Henry with that statement, he would surely be bumping Henry's elbow with a distasteful grin.

"What? You think I can't close the deal on my wedding night? You must think very little of my charm." Henry didn't feel like he had to explain anything.

"You know what I mean? I meant how was it?" Thomas could be crude, but Henry was well aware of of his best friend's demeanor.

"Well, if you must know, it left me speechless. So speechless that I still can't speak of it." Humor seemed the only way to avoid such an invasive inquiry. Henry wasn't the type of guy to "kiss and tell" as they say. Thomas, on the other hand, was always much more casual and forthcoming, even without being inquired of, about whom he dated.

Marriage was an archaic tradition to him, only still around to appease, in his words, old people. It was no surprise that he would be the one intruding on their morning.

"All right, well, obviously you're busy but gimme a call Monday. We need to work on that back swing of yours."

"Honeymoon, Thomas, I'm on my honeymoon until Wednesday." Thomas knew he would be gone, so Henry came back at him. "But you should take that extra time to work on *your* back swing. I seem to recall kicking your butt last week. Just saying."

"Your recollection must be flawed then."

"Thomas...I'm hanging up now."

"Arrivederci, comrade."

Henry hung up the phone with a chuckle. Thomas was terrible at golf.

He leaned over and softly kissed Anne's shoulder as she sighed with contentment and tangled herself further into the sheets. He felt a little strange after the call, something did not quite sit right, but he was not sure what it was. Rubbing his temples, he lay back down next to Anne and tried to drift off to sleep.

10
HENRY'S JOURNEY
Jackson Hole, Wyoming
August 22, 1992

Henry was stuck on the side of a hundred-foot cliff, alone and the sun beat down on him unforgivably. He screamed out once, "Help ... Is anyone out there?" His voice cracked with dryness, barely audible. He could taste salt as he licked the corners of his dry lips. The edges of his face were caked with dried sweat, his skin cracked, red and blistered.

How long had he been stuck on this rock? Death flashed before his eyes, and he swallowed down the thought of it. It stuck in his throat, no moisture to ease it away. He had an aching thirst, but nothing was around to quench it. He blinked hard as if this whole scene was a mirage but it all remained, the pain, the heat... the fervent heat tormenting every ounce of his being.

His eyes darted around looking for an escape when suddenly a hand reached down from up above. The sun blinded him from seeing fully. A woman, no doubt, with long wavy hair and faceless. Despite his utter agony, her beauty prevailed, and he loved her in just that moment.

He surged upward with all his might, barely hanging on to the rock anymore, and grabbed her small hand. He looked down and saw the evident fate below, as if beckoning for him. He cried out in fear and closed his eyes tight, refusing to see it.

The faceless woman brought him back to her attention and whispered, "I have you." He looked up as the sun was just starting to go behind a cloud. He could see her eyes, wildly blue and fierce. He tried to see more but something was pulling him away. The faceless woman began shaking him and in a flash, Henry woke up.

A man stood over him, shaking his shoulders and calling out his name.

Henry shot awake and rubbed his eyes, the sun blinding him for a moment.

"You're gonna get skin cancer, ya know." The man who stood above him turned out to be Charlie, and he was smiling something fierce.

Henry sat speechless for a moment and then quietly responded. "Charlie ... Hey man, what time is it?"

Charlie laughed, shaking his head. "It's time to go rock climbing. I was walking through the square to get to my car and saw you here. Do you sleep shirtless often?" He was chuckling out loud now, he couldn't hold it back. "Dude, you have one MASSIVE sunburn and a very interesting tanline." He smirked and raised his eyebrows at Henry's chest.

Henry looked down at his chest dazed, but the sleep was finally leaving him. A white hand print was emblazoned on his belly button, bright red skin outlining its shape. He had fallen asleep with his hand on his stomach. He pushed himself up and he could feel the burn on his skin. He sort of half-smiled at Charlie and said, "Well, this should be interesting."

"C'mon," Charlie said, "You can rehydrate on the drive to the cliffs." He patted Henry on his white back. "And would you please put your shirt on ... show off."

They both laughed and walked off to Charlie's "car."

Charlie's car turned out to be an old van. "A 1957 International Metro Van," he informed Henry with a proud, beaming smile as they walked up to it. The back bumper was covered in stickers boasting of all the places she had been: from coast to coast, as far north as Canada and as far south as Mexico. Henry wondered if Charlie had driven it all these places but didn't ask. She held the title of Lucy after the Beatles song "Lucy in the Sky with Diamonds," and her license plates stated so. Apparently, Henry wasn't the only one who named inanimate objects.

They hopped in and went to go pick up Charlie's other friends coming along for the climb: two guys, Roy and Linus. They picked them up at a loft apartment along with a girl named Rena who worked at the National Museum of Wildlife Art. She was just getting off work, so they picked her up on their way out of town.

Charlie introduced everyone to Henry and told them how he came to be on this trip of theirs.

Rena smiled and reached up from the back seat to shake his hand, welcoming him to the group.

Roy and Linus, who were brothers, shouted their greetings from the way back, "What's up man? Glad you could join us."

Charlie quieted the car and announced that it was Henry's maiden voyage in Lucy, so, to celebrate the occasion, he played her tune with the windows down. They all sang out at the top of their lungs, an apparent tradition whenever that song played and headed down the long stretch of highway.

The wind felt good on Henry's sun-singed face. Even though smiling meant his skin was moving and thus causing him the feeling that his skin was burning, Henry and the rest of the group laughed and sang along to Beatles songs for about half an hour until the group quieted.

Rena sat gazing out the window, her long auburn hair tangling with the wind. Roy was reading something, and Henry couldn't quite make out the cover. Linus was reading *On Walden Pond*.

"I learned this, at least, by my experiment; that if one advances confidently in the direction of his dreams, and endeavors to live the life which he has imagined, he will meet with a success unexpected in common hours." Henry smiled thinking about Thoreau and his experiment. It was, in essence, what Henry was doing. In a quest for personal independence, he sought a greater purpose, a longing to be better. His muse was somewhere out in this wilderness of freedom. Now, he just needed to find it.

"Hey, Mr. Lost-In-Thought over there, how's the burn feel?" Charlie broke his thought, and Henry turned his face towards Charlie.

"It's all right ... I hadn't really thought about it until you brought it up. Thanks for that." Henry chuckled.

"Ha ha, very funny." There was a slight hesitation before he continued. "So, what's your story, Burns?"

"Is that my new name now?" Henry shook his head, but Charlie just looked at him, waiting for a response. "It's ... complicated." Still Charlie waited, staring at him. "I'm sort of here to find myself, I guess" Henry said with hesitation in his voice. He felt so vulnerable every time someone asked him about himself. He just wanted to let go.

Suddenly, Henry felt like freeing himself of his little secret, the twisted knot of tension always at his side. He barely knew Charlie and maybe that was just the person he could trust. "The truth is ..." he let out a deep breath and shared his story, as much of his story as he felt that he could in that single breath. It just poured out of him, rushed, but he touched every point, his seemingly meaningless life, his leaving in the morning that day, the undying feeling that nothing ever was nor ever would be right with his wife and his journey that had led him here. He yearned for a feeling aside from torpid loneliness. And although he now ached, it was more rich and deep than he had felt in a long time.

Charlie listened patiently, nodding at the right moments and giving a "mmhmm" when the words prompted him so. He didn't need to talk. Henry just needed him to listen, and he was thankful Charlie silently understood that.

"And so I'm here. This is my Walden Pond of sorts, my fortress of solitude." He leaned forward, resting his hands on the aged dash of Lucy and then rested his chin on his hands, staring out at the mountains.

Charlie turned onto a bumpy dirt road.

"Dude ... you have one heck of a lonely story." Linus piped up from right behind Henry.

Henry sat up and turned around to see all three back seat passengers staring at him, intense with wonder. The guys had moved up next to Rena, and all three were squished onto the middle seat of Lucy, listening to Henry tell his tale.

Henry sat there with his mouth gaping but could say nothing.

"So, let me get this straight ... you are comparing yourself to Superman, now? Shirtless in the park and now this. You are one arrogant guy, Burns!" Charlie smiled wide and toothy.

A gratuitous smile sprawled across Henry's face. They all started laughing, and Charlie smacked Henry on the back as if to say, "It's all right bro," and continued driving. All was at peace as they pulled into the parking lot for Black Tail Butte, ready for some fun.

Charlie pulled the e-brake as he put Lucy in park. Everyone piled out of the van in one immense heap of energy, excited for the day's climb. Charlie had a pack for Henry, and he threw it to Henry as he grabbed his own.

Henry began fitting it to his waist. The others packed their already full bags with some of the snacks that Henry had picked up at the organic grocer.

Charlie finished putting his own pack on and checked the fit of Henry's. Charlie nodded his head and pulled a few strings tighter and then handed him a pair of climbing shoes. "Now they should be quite snug on your feet. You don't want any space in there, or it could mess up your climb." He handed them over to him, and Henry started taking off his boots, but Charlie stopped him.

"Whoa, son, we still gotta hike up to the cliffs." Charlie smiled. He nodded over at the rest of the group as if to say, "Let's do this!" He sure knew how to make someone feel comfortable even when he was correcting them. Henry was glad he had not gone about this alone. "You wear the climbing shoes only when you're climbing. Oh and no socks either, I forgot to tell you that part."

"Gotcha, gotcha. So, how far do we have to hike then?" Henry was excited to climb.

Roy piped up. "A little under a mile probably, then we will have to get the ropes set before you can climb." He snapped his pack on and got right up in Henry's face, clasping both hands on his shoulders. "Don't worry, Burns. We'll let you take your shirt off to even out that skin." Roy continued clasping his shoulders until Henry shrugged them off and laughed mockingly.

"All right, all right, I get it. I'm sunburned. You're probably just jealous you don't look like the red velvet cupcake that I look like. Red in the front, sweet cream cheese frosting in the back. I'm sure I look irresistible." Henry pretended to stretch his arms but flexed his muscles instead.

Everyone laughed, but Rena scoffed and just said, "Boys," before heading up the trail.

They headed up the path behind her. The hike went surprisingly fast because everyone was pumped with adrenaline. Henry could just make out the cliffs as the trail twisted into switchbacks up the side of a steep hillside. The trail was gravelly, and every step moved under their feet.

They made it to the top, and the four started unloading gear while Henry walked around to get a lay of the land. He looked up, and the faces of the rock gazed back at him with curious eyes. His dream from earlier in the day crept up in his mind.

He breathed in deep and kept walking around the site. Small, man-made paths led to different faces of rock. He walked to the very edge, just to the left of the trail they walked up on. Henry looked down to see another face, steep and looming, and then he looked out.

Beyond the branches extended a flat prairie land, mingled with twisting rivers and creeks. The slope of the land increased suddenly in the distance, announcing the mighty peaks of Grand Teton National Park. The Grand Teton sat perfectly displayed as the center of the majestic mountain range, gloriously breathtaking. Henry could gaze out all day long and never get bored of the sight he beheld.

"Hey, Burns!" Linus yelled over to him. "You wanted to learn, right? Get your butt over here!" Henry pulled himself away and jogged over to the group. Charlie and Rena weren't in sight.

"Where is everybody?" Henry inquired. Linus and Roy just pointed up without even looking. Rena and Charlie were scaling up the side of the rock face with no ropes and they were high-tailing it.

"It's called free climbing, and only experienced climbers should do it. So don't get any wild ideas, Burns. Even then … safer just not to do it at all. But Charlie and Rena have been climbing here for years. They'll get up top and get the ropes set up for ya."

Henry realized he was in a group of wildly friendly people. He had just met Charlie this morning and his friends this afternoon, and he already felt like part of their group. Group wouldn't even be accurate, family was more the word. It was pretty obvious they had been together for a long time.

Linus and Roy interrupted his thought to start teaching him the basics about rock climbing, safety harnesses and all. Basically, they told him technical terms: on belay, off belay, take, and various things he would have to say while climbing to keep him safe up on the ropes. In the end, they told him that they could teach him technique, but the best way to climb was your own way, and you just have to discover that for yourself.

Then, they showed him how to harness up and, before he knew it, Rena and Charlie were back. Everything happened so quickly.

They let Henry go first because, as Charlie put it, "Let the rookie go first."

Henry got connected to the rope and walked up to the cliff face. He felt small standing next to it. His shoes were tight, and his harness was an unfamiliar addition to his wardrobe. Totally out of his comfort zone with no clue where to begin, Henry put his hand to the cold, blue rock and felt for a hand hold. "On belay." He was told he had to say this before he could begin climbing. This let Charlie know he was ready to climb. Henry let out a deep breath, rolled his shoulders up and down and stretched his neck from side to side.

"Belay is on, Burns." Charlie hollered to him.

"Climbing."

"Climb away." Henry could hear the smile in Charlie's voice. Charlie seemed to get just as much thrill watching someone else climb as he did climbing himself. Chills ran up and down Henry's back.

"Give ol' Muster Buster Hell, brother." Charlie's idea of a pep talk. Muster Buster was what they had named the face. Linus and Roy had explained earlier in their little lesson that they named all the climbs that they cleaned. Whoever cleaned it first was the one who got to pick the name. To clean a climb you have to touch the top carabiner without letting your weight fall onto the rope, where the person belaying you had to hold you. Charlie was the one who named this climb.

Henry found his first hand hold, but the start of the rock face was eroded away, three or four feet into the rock, so that the whole climb began with a gaping overhang. Henry had upper body strength, he knew that, and so he maneuvered his hands in such a manner that he could brace his body just enough with his arms to get his legs up over the overhang.

He had looked for some points in the climb where he could rest safely before he started climbing. His first goal was to get to an obvious spot in the rock where a gouged hole appeared to be, right below a long reaching crack that went fifty feet up the face. The whole climb was only sixty feet total.

His first goal was to get to that crack. He managed to get his legs hoisted up to the rock, but he was now sideways grasping the wall. He felt like Spiderman and probably looked like him too. He needed a foothold fast. He could feel his muscles already starting to twitch from full exertion. By chance, his foot slipped into a sturdy hold, and he locked his foot into place. His other foot was stretched off in the other direction, so he straddling the rock. He pivoted his hips and found new hand holds. Henry now looked like he was hugging the face of this rock, like a baby hugging his mama.

"Woo! That's it, man."

"Way to stick it."

"Hard parts over, right, buddy!"

He could hear the cheers from behind him. He was only five feet off the ground, tops.

"Is that really the hardest part?" Henry shouted out breathlessly.

"Naw, man, it's just an expression to keep you going." Charlie chuckled but reassured him, "Don't worry about cleaning the climb. Focus on what's in front of you right now, and before you know it, you'll be at the top."

Henry listened and focused all his attention on his next move. He was maybe three feet from the crack, his first goal. *Two or three moves to get to the crack*, he thought. His right hand shuffled along the rock looking for a sturdy hold, nothing definite. He did the same with his other hand but found nothing substantial.

Rena spoke, like a concerned mother almost, "Henry, sometimes you have to trust a hold, even if it doesn't feel perfect. You would be surprised what you can cling to. Just go for it, we got you on the ropes."

He grasped for a hold, only a few fingers holding on, about a foot above his head. His other hand frantically raced to find another hold until he landed on something and allowed the foot with a sketchy hold to find another home for the time being. His thoughts were racing. His adrenaline was making him shaky. He had no idea what to expect or how to face it. So, he just let it all go, he quit worrying about moves and strategy and just took a few deep breaths before continuing.

He shimmied his weight across a slight protrusion on the wall that acted as a shelf for his feet. He let himself rest before going on. He was thankful for those tight shoes that clung to the rock better than anything else. It was like the shoes were hands of themselves. Regardless, he made it to the crack and realized he had barely begun to scale this massive sixty-foot face, and his muscles were already fatigued. He had to keep going. The crack looked like it would be easy to get up, filled with crevices and holes which were sure to be great holds for him. But, to use the holds, one had to have both hands and both feet awkwardly bracing oneself.

Once Henry started up the crack, he looked like he was twisted into some fancy, yoga-balance pose, and he was unsure how he was going to pull himself all the way up this crack. All the while, everyone below was cheering him on. He was so tempted to ask them where a good hold was, but he refrained, wanting to figure it out on his own by using his mental wits against the rock. They probably knew every move he should make.

Meanwhile, as he flirted with different ideas trying to rest his legs, a cramp starting swelling up in his left calf. He couldn't reach down and rub it. He was helplessly contorted against this rock.

Henry had made his way half up the crack, about halfway to the top when he felt his hands slipping. He pinched his fingers as hard as he could, only holding on with four fingers, two on the left, two on the right and a gimp leg about to give way.

He lost all his grasps, slipping off the rock and swung like a pendulum clock from side to side, until he stopped himself with his legs. Charlie caught his fall without a problem. He dangled for a bit before repelling back to the ground. Frustrated, he started unhooking the carabiners.

"Whoa, whoa you are still on belay, sir," Charlie piped up. He took the rules pretty seriously.

"Off belay?" Henry stammered, still short of breath from his climb.

"Belay is off … nice work, man. You got pretty far up. And it looked like you were starting to find your own technique up there," Charlie coiled up his rope into a neat pile while talking.

"What do you mean, what technique?" Henry felt like he kind of just clutzed his way up the rock face.

"You had some yoga thing going on there for a while. You took a different way up than most people do. You took the road less traveled, my Frosty friend."

Henry laughed at that, still trying to catch his breath. He reached down and rubbed his calf, the cramp already easing. His whole body was just sweating with his t-shirt clinging to his skin. The heat of the sun, and the total body exertion wore him out. He took a seat next to Rena, who was belaying Linus next.

Everyone took turns climbing, and Henry watched for a while, trying to get some tips for his next try. They were all extremely experienced climbers, a lot better than they let on to be. All four of them cleaned the climb, but Henry still couldn't quite figure out how he was going to do it.

Charlie took him over to a shorter, much easier wall to practice a bit to get used to climbing.

Henry mastered a climb called, "Mucho Guano," entitled so by Linus because of the bat guano that caked part of the wall at a small opening where bats used to reside. He cleaned that climb without ropes and was gaining some confidence before mustering up the courage to give another go at Muster Buster.

"That's it. Now, you just gotta use that same technique when giving Muster Buster another go." Charlie patted Henry on his back as he got off the climb.

"I really appreciate you letting me come out here with you guys. You've been nothing short of amazing." Henry smiled in thankfulness.

"Hey, it's no problem, man. Climbing's what I live for. I like to show that life to others."

"Well, anyway, thanks. Climbing is amazing, almost as amazing as Lucy." Henry chuckled.

"Yeah, she's great, isn't she?" Charlie looked down at his feet.

"So, did you travel her around the country to get all those stickers, or did she come with them on?"

"Well, some of them are me. Most of them were my Dad's. I just finished it up for him." The expression on Charlie's face changed from all smiles to distant.

Sensing something in the story wasn't exactly happy, Henry quietly retorted, "Did something happen to him?"

Charlie looked up at him with a scarred stare, nodding his head slightly. "He drove her around the country with my mom for years before I was born: California, Arizona, Oregon, all along the west coast. When I was born, they put Lucy in the garage and settled down just outside of Jackson Hole on a nice piece of land. He never got to finish his cross-country trip in Lucy." He hesitated and went on. "My Dad died when I was thirteen." He cleared his throat. "Climbing accident. He's the one who taught me everything about climbing, about life, about everything

52

really. He was such a clear-sighted, intuitive man, noticing every little change in mine and my mother's moods." Charlie smiled to himself thinking about it. "He started the store downtown that you and I met at actually. He had such a drive for life and was just a deeply passionate man. I think I got that part of him in me. After he died I was ... confused but lost more than anything. I didn't know what to do with my life, and I didn't want to try and figure it out. After I graduated from high school, I took all the money I had, packed my bags and drove Lucy out of her eighteen-year confinement. I think it broke my mother's heart, leaving her alone like that. Thinking back, I should have brought her with. It was her trip too, ya know?" Charlie looked at Henry with evident pain in his eyes.

Henry nodded with encouragement and Charlie went on. "I drove everywhere, though. I wanted to do it for my Dad, to do what he no longer could, but mostly I needed to do it to feel closer to him. I looked up to him more than anyone else, still do." He paused for a second and continued. "I was gone about a year, best year of my life. It was like my Dad had specially prepared it for me, leaving me life lessons along the way. I met people, I loved, I certainly lost, and in the end, I still felt lost, but I knew I had just lost a part of myself and learned to deal." He shook his head and barked out a short laugh, a mix of sadness and hope.

"I came home and took up running the store where my father left off. It had been run by my Uncle Ray up until I got home. I helped him out, while taking night classes online at the University of Wyoming. Got my bachelor's in business and here I am, running the family business talking to you, Burns." He looked over at Henry smiling, and Henry smiled back reassuringly, "Sounds like I'm not the only one with one heck of a story, huh?" Charlie shrugged his shoulders and looked at the rocks in front of them. "That's why climbing is so important to me, and I keep doing it. Climbing was when my father was most like himself, free and spirited, and I sort of connect with his memory when I'm doing it."

"Climbing is your muse, then." Henry piped up.

"What do you mean?"

"Well, everyone has someone or something that inspires or, as you say connects us, to things we would otherwise be without. Climbing is your muse."

Charlie thought about it, "I guess that's true...I'm still looking for more though. My dad's number two passion was climbing. Number one was my mother." He smiled and paused for a moment. "So, what's your muse, Burns?"

He looked down at his shoes, kicked the dirt and looked back up, "That's why I'm here. I gotta find my muse."

Linus interrupted them, "Hey, you guys wanna climb or what? We can't be out here all day. Some of us gotta work nights!"

Charlie took Henry by the shoulders, "Such is life, bro. Let's get in some climbing, huh?"

Henry nodded in agreement, and they headed back over with group. He attempted Muster Buster a couple more times. The second attempt ended at about the same point as the first, and, on the third one, he made it three quarters of the way up before falling, completely and utterly exhausted.

Always the winner in every sport, including bull riding now, Henry marveled at this unfamiliar feeling of failure. He climbed a few other faces, cleaning all of them, but he could not finish Muster Buster. Henry curiously wondered why they started him out on what appeared to be the hardest climb there.

When he confronted them with the question, they all laughed and in unison said, "Gotta get big, man," another inside joke to identify this incredibly likable group.

The sun was just beginning to slope downward, signaling it to be about three or four in the afternoon as they gathered their gear. They had eaten all of the snacks Henry packed and only half a bottle of water remained. The group looked exhausted and a tad bit disheveled. They got to the van and piled in slowly, methodically, lacking the energy they had when they had arrived earlier in the day.

Henry sat in the very back of the van, his feet propped up on the seat, his back leaning against the side of the van. Rena sat shotgun with Charlie, and the two brothers were passed out one each other on the seat in front of Henry.

Charlie and Rena were talking quietly up in front, exchanging flickering glances of attention. Henry watched them unknowingly and smiled. He could see the shimmery shades of fondness in their glances, two lovers yet to discover each other's true feelings. It was so obvious once he stopped to see. Eventually, they would stop and see it too.

"Hey," Henry interrupted. "I just wanted to thank you guys for having me along today. Hope I didn't slow you down."

Two hands shot up, sporting the thumbs up sign, from the supposedly sleeping boys, and Rena nodded at him with a smile. Charlie caught his gaze in the rear-view mirror and gave him a nod. "Anytime, brother ... Hey, let me know when you find that muse of yours." They both smiled.

"Will do."

They dropped Henry off at his car after exchanging phone numbers for future climbing excursions, and the van took off minutes later. Henry rubbed his eyes and yawned.

He drove through McDonald's drive-through for a burger and inhaled it on his way back up to the cabin.

He parked and walked immediately into the bedroom. He kicked off his boots and pulled off his t-shirt and collapsed on the bed, succumbing to the fatigues of the day and fell fast asleep.

11
NEW YORK, NEW YORK
February 14, 1992

"Happy Valentine's Day, Sweetheart." With an uncertain hand, Henry slid Anne a white box with a velvet red ribbon tied around it.

She clapped her hands rapidly together and pecked him rapidly on the cheek. A formality, he presumed. "Henry!"

"I hope you like it." Henry said, sincerely hoping he had found the right piece of jewelry this time. He was finding it more difficult to please his wife every day. She always had to have something bigger, better than anyone else. It was exhausting. She was never happy.

"I better..." Anne flashed a smile at him as she pulled the ribbon. Her face twisted a bit.

Henry's heart sank. "Not the right one?"

She set the box down calmly and stood up. "No, Henry. I don't understand how it can be so hard to find a present your wife would actually like. It's like you don't know me at all."

"I will take you to the store tomorrow to find something," Henry promised.

She turned as she walked away, smoothing her perfect hair as she met his eyes. "Yes, I suppose you better."

Henry sat there empty-handed and heavy hearted.

12
HENRY'S JOURNEY
Jackson Hole, Wyoming
August 23, 1992

The sunlight of early evening broke through the blinds and into Henry's eyes as he opened them. Henry was surprised he had slept so hard after rock climbing. He was not usually a person who took naps, but that climb had obviously took a lot out of him.

Stretching his long arms above his head, Henry looked at the wooden beams that formed the ceiling. He felt very calm and relaxed for the first time in months. A deep, savory wood smell filled his nostrils, and he exhaled slowly. The window was letting in a light breeze, gently blowing the warm, calming scent of pine into the room. It was such a deep scent that he could practically taste the trees in his lungs, the earth and all that nature offered.

Henry thought back over the last few days. He had really found himself again, but yet, something was missing … his muse. There was supposed to be a moment, that one moment when everything was right in his world. A hole was still sinking within him, and all he could do was wonder what his whole purpose for this trip was. Flickering thoughts of fate and destiny, like moving frames in a movie, were cruising his mind's consciousness.

Have I really ended up in the middle of nowhere for no reason? He thought to himself. Shaking off any further inquiries of fate, something Henry had never believed in, Henry sat up, stretching out his legs and hips. "Man, am I sore!" Henry had not been this sore in a long time. The pain pulsed through every one of his muscles. The muscles in his back twitched as he arched his back a bit to crack it. It was the same twinge he felt when he was on the rocks. There were moments when he was stuck on the rock face and only one leg was keeping him up. Eventually the muscle began to spasm and cramp and the only thing that kept him going was the hope that he would find a finger hold in the next few seconds, before his leg gave out all the way. He was glad he could feel the soreness. He did love a hard workout, after all.

He walked to the sink, filling his glass with cool water and downing every last drop. He looked out the window at the peaceful forest and decided to take a walk to stretch his sore legs.

He pulled on his Wranglers, his hiking boots, dusty from the rock climbing, and a dark, plain t-shirt before opening the creaky screen door and stepping outside. He breathed in the mountain air, which was even stronger and more invigorating than in the cabin.

The sun was slowly sinking lower in the sky, casting shades of pink, gold, and the beginning shades of a violet twilight. He thought he had better get going as it would be dark soon enough.

Henry followed the road a bit before noticing a faint dirt path that broke through the thick line of trees. He turned and followed the trail. The path was smooth for a few paces before Henry found it wound up quite steeply. The trail turned into a small scree field of larger rocks, making the trek thoroughly rugged. His sore legs protested as he pushed himself to keep going. Small beads of sweat formed on his brow, and his forehead glistened in the colorful light of the sunset.

Henry drew the front part of his t-shirt up and dabbed the sweat, trying to catch his breath. He took another step and then another. His strong will pushed his tired body forward. Henry's breathing intensified before the path finally evened out into a smooth, flat surface.

He walked a few more paces before he came upon a clearing.

Smooth mountain rock formed a tall, jagged backdrop, stretching down to form a crescent shape in the rock. Pine trees encircled the clearing, along with brush and small, white wild flowers. There were yellow-green blades of newborn grass amidst darker older blades that covered the clearing. An icy blue mountain stream rushed over the top of the tallest rock, creating a continuous waterfall down the center, cascading into a small, pristine lake. The water rippled where the falling stream met the still lake and small crests of white surged toward the shore, before evening out into a calm glassy lake. The sun had dropped below the horizon, illuminating the sky in shades of dark blue, amethyst, dark gold, and crimson. The towering rocks cast shadows upon the lightly rippling water. The sound of the splashing waterfall was soothing, almost hypnotic.

Henry walked to the water's edge and dropped to his knees. The ground was moist underneath his body, and the knees of his jeans were darkened with the stains of water as he sunk ever so slightly into the earth. He bent forward and reached toward the clear water, cupping his hands together to catch the cool liquid.

As he lifted the water to his parched lips, he suddenly saw a reflection cast on the crystal water. He drew his gaze upward, and his eyes slowly wandered across the lake to the rocks.

Atop a large rock that rose slightly above the water stood the embodiment of a flawless woman. She stood, her clothes strewn to the side of her, as she unwound the braid in her blonde hair and let it fall to cover her unsheathed shoulders. Her sun-kissed, golden body was like a sunrise, perfect and constant, almost flowing in movement.

With ease she stepped, with blissful grace, off the edge of the rock. Her long, endless legs snapped together as she bent at the knees and gracefully dove into the lake, breaking its crystal surface.

His jaw was dropped in awe. Who was she?

Emerging from the water, she shook her soaking mane of blonde, wavy hair and extended her long, thin arms above her head for another dive into the lake.

She came up seconds later and brushed the water away from her face and ran her fingers through her hair. She twisted in the water playfully, obviously enjoying the peace of this magical place. She flipped onto her back and just floated, placidly allowing her arms to flutter above her head.

The night was slowly making its presence known with a heavy chill in the air, and the sun now fully down. The moon softly lit the night.

He could see her breath in the moonlight. In and out, her chest raised just slightly above the water with every breath. With every breath she took, Henry lost his own, but his pulse raced on.

Henry stood frozen in the growing darkness, mesmerized by the sheer beauty in front of him. A glint of moonlight shone through the trees of the clearing and cast its glowing light upon her face, radiating her eyes of dazzling blue.

The woman dipped under the water and rose shortly after, running her fingers through her hair and sighing softly. The silence of the night accentuated every sound and the buzzing sound of a hum rose in the air.

She hummed as she made her way back to the rock she jumped from. He strained to hear but couldn't quite make out the tune.

Henry felt as though his presence might be felt by her and knew this was supposed to be a private moment for her. He sank back into the shadows of the trees to head back down the path he came, the whole time wanting to turn around and see her again. He allowed himself one last glance as he dragged himself down the trail.

Feeling the chill of the night air, she had reached down quickly and slipped on her clothes before turning on a flashlight and headed down the same path he was on but in the opposite direction.

He released his breath slowly, knowing that this could not be the last time her saw her. He felt drawn to her. Yes, she was beautiful, but something about the freedom she exuded just now in the water, made him want to be free, too. Perhaps, she could bring the liberation Henry was seeking on this journey or, at least, be the vessel by which he finds it. There was something special about her, and he was determined to find out more. Lost in thought, he staggered down the trail, drunk with the wine of her beauty.

13
NEW YORK, NEW YORK
April 2, 1991

"Yes, I am so excited for the gala!" Anne exclaimed, the phone cradled to her ear.

"Anne." Henry looked up from his stack of papers as he tried to concentrate on his work. "Anne?"

"What, Henry? I am on the phone. Can't you see?" Anne rolled her eyes and looked up at the ceiling, as if one word from him could derail all her happiness in the world, as if he had anything to do with her excitement.

"I have an important issue that just came up, so I won't be able to make it." He stuffed his papers into his briefcase as he talked.

"I have to go." Anne said into the phone. "My *husband* just told me he can't make it to the biggest event of the season."

Henry tried to sneak out the door as she finished up her conversation.

"Just where do you think you are going?" She shrieked as he walked quickly to the front door. "Henry Michael Tudor, get back here this minute."

"Anne. I need to take care of this." He tried to be patient and kept the frustration out of his voice. "It is very important." He opened the door to leave. "I will try to make it, okay?"

She glared at him with her hands on her hips. "I will never forgive you for this!"

As she continued to hurl insults at him, he shut the door and walked briskly to his car, shaking his head and trying to prepare his mind for work.

The further he drove from the house, from her, the more the weight lifted from his chest, and he could breathe.

14
HENRY'S JOURNEY
Jackson Hole, Wyoming
August 24, 1992

The soft light of the morning sun streamed into the cabin. Henry opened his eyes and looked at the strange, wooden ceiling staring down at him. Blinded by the fog of deep sleep, Henry momentarily forgot where he was.

It all came back to him in a minute, suddenly remembering what he witnessed last night. Witnessed seemed creepy, like he saw a crime being committed or something. No, he had beheld perfection.

Who was that beautiful woman? Was she a figment of his imagination? Had he actually seen her? He wondered.

He prayed it wasn't just a dream. Letting his relaxed body sink comfortably back into bed, he let his mind focus on this mysterious angel. It didn't feel real, which worried him. How was he going to find her, if she actually existed outside of his dreams? It seemed silly to think a dream could be so real, but then she was almost too good to be true. He thought back to Bill telling him how his closest neighbor was a half mile or so away. Maybe a visit to his new neighbor was in the cards for today.

His stomach growled, reminding him just how long it had been since he last ate. Hunger was always his biggest constraint. *It is time for some more of that cafe food*, he thought. Henry liked the little cafe downtown; it suited him well. In the back of his mind a thrill of anticipation gave him nervous butterflies. He might come across … he shook his head, trying to reign in his hopes and expectations of finding the woman.

Henry rolled out of bed and hurriedly grabbed some clean clothes as he dashed out the door on his way to the freezing creek. He had come up with a name for the creek in his head, "Maestro." It played the tune of morning so well. *No one could play it better*, he thought.

"Good Morning, Maestro," he spoke out loud as he approached the shoreline of the creek. The creek greeted him with her melodious flow and flirtatiously splashed his ankle as he walked in the cool water. Today, as the icy water stung his body, his mind was not at all on the winter lake he had jumped into. He could think of only one thing: her. He was totally unaware of himself, his chattering teeth or where he was in this world, while he thought of her.

Weightless and lost in rumination, the freezing water finally broke into his thoughts. Henry realized he could barely feel his hands or feet.

He jumped out of the water and threw on his clothes, pleading with the sun to warm him faster. He finished toweling off after racing back to the cabin. He grabbed his wallet and sped to town.

He felt a crazy rush of adrenaline as he thought of this woman and how to find her; it was like he had just rode that winning bull ride or climbed that crazy rock, only she was much greater than both of those combined, and he hadn't even met her yet. Dark thoughts were furthest from his mind as he drove into town. He was beaming, and he was sure everyone else could see it too.

Although the darkness of his life back home had been lifting and brightening since he came to Wyoming, true light had finally broken all the way through the shadows. He had a purpose again and was drawn toward the mystery lady for answers. He just knew there was a reason he had found her.

Parking near the cafe, Henry saw the streets were bustling with workers like the previous day, but he also noticed people dressed a little fancier. He looked at his watch and saw that it was, indeed, Saturday. He shrugged and went inside.

Looking around the busy restaurant, Henry saw it was quite a bit fuller than yesterday. He grabbed a paper from the stand and spotted a seat at the high-counter top facing the waitress' station.

Sliding into it, Henry nodded to his waitress from yesterday. Almost knocking her co-workers over in the process, the curvy blond sashayed quickly over to Henry.

"How ya' doin' this mornin', handsome?"

"Just fine, thank you, ma'am." Henry tried to keep the amusement out of his tone.

"Same as yesterday?" She asked with a flip of her hair and a flirty smile.

"Yes, please." He looked down at his paper as she poured him a cup of coffee and sashayed away.

"Well, if it isn't the rodeo star of Cheyenne!" A dry, slightly sarcastic, and yet, familiar voice said from the seat to the right of Henry.

Surprised, he turned, taking in the cowboy next to him wearing a worn-in, black Stetson and a familiar smile. "Mitch Taylor." Henry said with a smile.

"How ya been, partner?" Mitch reached out to shake his hand.

Henry laughed. "Well, I was great 'till I saw you! Sorry I smoked you in that rodeo, Mitch."

The cowboy shook his head with a smirk. "Ah, I can't win 'em all. Then, there would be no competition an'more. Heck, now you got the chance to show me you actually got talent, and it's not all just beginner's luck."

Henry remembered their last conversation. "Oh, is there a rodeo in town?"

"Sure is. Why else you think I would come all the way home to ol' Jackson Hole?"

"You grew up here, then." Henry suddenly knew the best person to help him find the woman from last night … hopefully.

A high, flirtatious voice broke into the conversation. "Here ya are there, handsome!" She set a heaping plate of breakfast in front of Henry. "Anythin' else I can get you boys?" She looked back and forth between them with a wide smile.

"No thanks, Mandy. Get back to work and leave us cowboys in peace." Mitch said with a teasing smile.

She punched him in the arm. "Oh, Mitch. Alright." She giggled and walked away.

Mitch shoved in a few bites of eggs and bacon before he turned back to Henry. "So, you ready to lose to a great rider today, Henry?"

Henry shook his head and moved his fork around his plate. "I was not planning on entering..."

"Why the heck not?"

Shoving in a few, delicious bites, he thought about the idea as he chewed. Last time had turned out to be fun, and if Mitch did not know where this woman he was searching for was, maybe some other cowboys would.

Looking up, he saw Mitch was watching him with a smile.

"I knew you would change your mind." Mitch laughed.

"Well, only 'cuz I gotta prove to you I am a better bull rider than you."

"Whatever helps you sleep at night, partner. So, where you stayin'?"

Henry finished the last few bits of eggs on his plate before answering. "A cabin of Bill's."

"Oh ya, Bill's great. How is stayin' in the mountains for ya?"

They finished eating and both threw money on the counter and stood up, still in conversation as they headed out the door onto the busy street.

"It has been good so far, real nice." Henry tried to remain nonchalant as the beauty from last night swam to the forefront of his mind again.

He stopped by his car, digging the keys from his pocket.

"Whew!"

Henry turned to see Mitch with his hands in his pockets, shaking his head with an impressed look on his face.

"A Rolls-Royce? Really?" He let out a low whistle.

Henry laughed. "Thanks, man. Would you like to drive it? I gotta go up to the cabin quick to get my rodeo gear anyway."

"Are you being serious?" Mitch asked with excitement replacing the tone of disbelief in his voice.

Henry tossed him the keys. "Let's go, cowboy."

He laughed as Mitch yelled happily, "YEEEEHAWW!"

They quickly made their way up the mountain to the cabin. Mitch leaned back in the driver's seat. "Man, I grew up and live in trucks, but this is ... luxury. You must be somethin' back home."

Henry smiled and looked out the window, carefully avoiding the question by saying, "This is the turn here."

Mitch steered the smooth car onto the rough path leading to Henry's cabin. Slowing the car to a halt, he put it in park and turned off the ignition.

They got out and walked inside. "Nice place." Mitch said as he looked around.

"Have you been in here ever?"

"Nope, just to a couple others. I got an ol' buddy in one quite a ways over. But one of my wife's friends lives just about a half mile away."

Henry looked over at him sharply and realized he did not want to give himself away, yet. He looked away. "So, does a family live there then?" He asked casually as he walked into the bedroom to change.

Mitch observed his casual tone, not missing the sharp look. He leaned against the kitchen counter and asked mischievously, "Why do ya ask? You meet anybody interesting?"

Henry pulled on his clothes, hearing the slyness of Mitch's tone. His heart jumped a beat, wondering if he knew of the lady from the lake.

"Well, a man ought to know his neighbors, right?"

Mitch laughed. "I am just goin' to make a guess here. Have you met your closest neighbor?"

Smiling, Henry walked out of the bedroom and shook his head at the amused look on Mitch's face. "I guess I don't know if I have or not."

"Well, if that's how you want to play it, Henry. I guess I won't help you." Mitch shrugged his shoulders. "I will tell you one thing, though, if you had met her, you would know."

Henry's lungs tightened as his heart beat faster. *She had to be the one he was talking about. She just had to be.*

He grabbed his hat and opened the door. "Come on, Mitch. You don't want to miss getting beat again do you?"

Mitch laughed, punched him in the shoulder, and strode quickly to the car. He opened the driver's side door, pausing to see what Henry would say.

But Henry just laughed and got in the passenger side.

Mitch shut the door gleefully and started up the smooth engine. As they drove back down the path, Mitch said "Just so ya know, this neighbor I was talkin' about is goin' to be at the ol' rodeo with my wife." He looked sideways at Henry. "So, if you haven't met her, tonight might be your lucky night!"

Henry just shook his head at Mitch and turned to look out the window. He could picture her so perfectly from last night. Wondering what her voice sounded like, he was sure it would be just as beautiful as the rest of her and wanted to hear it more than anything except her name.

Mitch, sensing that Henry was deep in thought, smiled and turned on the radio to a country station. He kept them fluidly moving down the path right through town to the rodeo grounds. Parking the car next to his trailer, Mitch turned off the engine and hopped outside. "I gotta get my gear on quick," he said. He tossed the keys to Henry and opened the side door of his trailer.

Henry got out and adjusted his hat as he looked around at his surroundings. It looked very familiar, much like the grounds of Cheyenne. He could see the crowd around the bottom of the grandstand buying concessions and some betting on the riders. There were many cowboy hats in the crowd, mixed with a few tourists that stuck out from about a mile away.

Dressed in his black cowboy gear, Mitch came around the side of the truck and handed Henry a Gatorade. He took a swig of his own. "Well, let's get you signed up. Hopefully, you will have an actual mean bull this time, not one so easy to ride." He said teasingly with sarcasm dripping on the edges of his words.

Henry laughed. "Whatever you say, Mitch." He cracked open his drink and let the ice cold liquid flow down his throat. They walked toward the packed grandstand and got him all signed up to ride a bull called Ol' Blue. Henry wasn't sure what to think of that one.

He just followed Mitch to the side gate, taking off his hat to fan himself on account of the heat as he walked. He watched as the cowgirls holding flags rode around in the arena, announcing the start of the rodeo. The national anthem played with a beautiful soprano singing the words over the microphone, a slight echo in the speakers. He looked around but couldn't see where the lady was singing from.

The song was soon over, and the first rider was in the chute.

"Bang!" The rider flew out of the gate on his bull, slid to the side and was lying on his back in the first split second. The crowd moaned with disappointment.

Henry watched as the rodeo clown flew over to distract the bull as the rodeo cowboys helped the man out of the arena. Henry saw Mitch shaking his head with a smile.

The next few cowboys had about the same luck as the first, then it was Mitch's turn.

"Well, I guess it's 'bout time you see a real cowboy ride." He tipped his hat to him to Henry as he headed to the chute.

Henry was interested in Mitch's skills. He knew he had to be somewhat good to make a life out of this sort of thing. He watched intently as Mitch flew out of the chute on a huge bull's back. The bull looked fierce and had a look of immense anger in his solid black eyes. The bull twisted and turned trying to throw his rider off, but Mitch was ready for each move.

Instead of riding with the bull's movements, he anticipated each twist and bend, gracefully balancing himself until the eight-second timer went off and the crowd went wild.

Mitch jumped off the bull and ran to the gate. Henry was impressed. Mitch really was good.

Henry saw with a start that he was up next. He climbed up the bull and reached down to grab the rope around his back. Looking down, he saw the bull was white with a bluish-black tint to his skin. He patted the bull's neck and the chute flew open.

Henry had forgotten how exhilarating it was to ride. He used the same technique as the last ride, gracefully riding opposite the bull's movements to keep his balance. His right hand burned from the tight grip on the rope, but he held on for dear life until he heard the buzzer and the crowd.

He jumped down and ran to the gate as Mitch had, except, he realized with terror, that the bull was still behind him, chasing after him!

Henry saw his life flashing before his eyes as the bull rammed into the back of his thigh as he climbed up the gate.

Using all his strength, Henry hauled himself over the top and dropped onto the ground. His leg hurt, but it seemed okay in general with just some nasty bruising starting to form.

He felt someone pulling him off the ground. It was Mitch.

"Henry? You all right, man?" Mitch looked slightly concerned.

"Oh, I will be fine. It's just a little bump."

"Well, you are about the toughest city-boy I've ever met," he said with a laugh. "Come on, then, let's get another swig of electrolytes before the next round."

They walked toward the busy crowd under the back of the grandstand. People recognized Mitch, saying hello or congratulating him. Some also recognized Henry from Cheyenne.

They rested in the shade, leaning against an old oak tree, and he cracked open his Gatorade.

Mitch suddenly set down his drink and told Henry he would be right back. Henry watched the cowboy disappear into the crowd as he sipped his cool beverage. His leg throbbed slightly, but he tried not to pay any attention to it.

He was looking in no particular direction when he felt his gaze being drawn somewhere to the side of the crowd. His eyes went past the crowded grandstand area over to the right side of a thinner part of the crowd. He did not see anyone or anything that stood out right away. Nothing seemed out of the ordinary. He saw a little girl chasing after a boy who had stolen her ice cream, a woman rocking her baby, and an older man telling jokes to a group of cowboys.

Henry was about to look away when he saw her. The woman was smiling, talking to a couple as she brushed a stray strand of wavy gold blond hair out of her face. From thirty feet away, he could see the dazzling blue of her eyes, shining like the moonlight he first saw her in, and was certain it was her.

He stood motionless, time stilled, staring at her as if he was back at the lake, watching her free spirit unwind in the water. He wanted to just curl up in this feeling, elation, ecstasy, passion, be covered in it, with her. It was so new. He had never felt that way about another person before.

He watched as she lifted a slim hand to shade the blinding sun out of her eyes as she listened intently to the couple. Henry felt as if he should do the same as he stood there, taking in the light that radiated from her. The woman fiddled with the hem of her lavender sundress with just her left hand, her other hand resting casually on her waist, as she talked and listened. Henry thought it was the cutest nervous habit he had ever seen.

Without knowing it, he took a few steps toward her, simply drawn to her.

The woman waved, and Henry could make out the movement of her pink lips saying, "goodbye," to the couple.

As she turned away, she looked up and immediately caught the gaze of Henry, as if she had felt him watching her the whole time. Their eyes met in a clash of what could only be described as destiny, an ocean crashing upon wet sand as the tide comes in, inevitable. He knew in his mind it sounded cheesy, like the stupidest story he could never tell anyone because it was so ridiculous, but it was true.

Henry knew he had been living in a hollow shell of reality, erroneously existing there until this moment. He had stopped breathing, and his heart pounded so loudly the noise around him faded into nothing.

She blushed lightly as they continued to hold each other's gazes for several moments in time. The corners of her lips curved slightly, and she tilted her head softly to one side, letting her hair fall away from her face.

Suddenly, she was out of his sight, two men stepped in front of her, blocking her from Henry. He watched, disappointed but still breathless, as the men talked to her.

She seemed less than pleased to see them but politely flashed that beautiful smile and tried to remain detached. Henry felt a ripple of familiarity as he looked the men up and down. One was taller than Henry, which was quite tall, and the other about Henry's height.

Even though he could only see their backs and cowboy gear, it hit him. They were the men from Cheyenne, the men who had gotten him to ride the bull. A spark of jealous anger and intense dislike filled him as he watched these two men talk to her, his destiny, his hope. He couldn't help but think of her as his already.

The blue-eyed one, Joe, Henry remembered, must have said something she particularly did not like because she shoved him and tried to walk around them. Joe grabbed her wrist and spun her around to face him again, knocking her purse to the ground. Henry was emblazoned with rage.

Before he knew what he was doing, he had stalked over and put a hand firmly on Joe's shoulder. "You leave this lady alone." Henry said with a danger in his voice he himself had only heard once or twice in his own lifetime.

Joe, obviously annoyed by the intrusion, yet very aware of the tone of the man grabbing his shoulder so tightly, turned saying "What's it to...," he trailed off as he saw Henry. His icy blue eyes narrowed, then he laughed. "Oh it's you. The rodeo king of Cheyenne. And, apparently, tryin' to be of ol' Jackson 'Ole too!"

Henry stared him down with intense dislike. "I didn't see you out there today, cowboy." He tried to make small talk if just to keep from hitting him.

The tall man laughed, and Joe glared at him. "I just got in from the ranch. No time to play today."

"Just time to harass a beautiful lady, then? I think you should get back to the ranch."

Joe angrily sized Henry up, who appeared ready and willing to fight, then reevaluated his decision and walked away.

The tall cowboy followed. "Watch your back, city-boy." Joe threw the taunt over his shoulder and disappeared into the crowd, his piercing stare the last words on the matter.

Henry bent down to pick up the woman's purse before turning to face her.

He looked into her eyes, which were boldly smiling up at him, holding onto her gaze for a moment longer. He forced his lips to curve into a smile, and he held out her purse.

She reached out a golden arm and curled her long, dainty fingers around it. "Thank you." It looked like she slightly curtsied as she said it, but Henry couldn't be sure because he was still drawn to her face. She held his gaze for a split-second longer before looking down shyly.

Her voice was music, the melodic tunes of the Sirens of Capreae singing for Persephone but with a country twang to it. "Joe has a nasty habit of botherin' me when he's 'round." She shook her head as if to brush the whole thing off.

Henry shook his head with her, still captivated and unable to speak. She held out her right hand. "I'm Arabella." The words fell from her lips like soft rain.

He reached out, shook her hand, and managed to huskily say, "Henry." He continued holding her small hand in his until a voice interrupted them, and Arabella pulled her hand away.

"Hey! So, I see you have met your next-door neighbor. I knew you were holding out on me, Henry!" Mitch had an excited look on his face, like he had just won the rodeo or something. A petite woman, with chestnut-colored, shoulder length hair and warm amber eyes was holding his hand, smiling and shaking her head at her husband.

"Hey, Mitch." Henry said dryly but smiled at his wife.

"Hi, I am Nicole." She said, shaking Henry's hand as he introduced himself.

"Oh, where are my manners?" Mitch exclaimed. "Henry, this is my beautiful wife, Nicole, and this is her friend, Ara, although I see you two have met." He wriggled his eyebrows suggestively.

Henry and Nicole laughed at Mitch's antics. Arabella shook her head, remaining reserved and quiet but gave Mitch a light punch on the arm.

Mitch laughed loudly and grabbed Henry's arm.

Her hand fell and began playing with the hem of her dress again. Henry melted just a bit inside at the cute habit.

"Well, we gotta get back to winnin' this show, but we will see you beautiful ladies afterwards because Henry is buying drinks!" He put his arm around Henry's shoulder and pulled him away toward the arena.

Henry looked back over his shoulder to see Arabella's eyes on him. As their gazes met, she smiled and turned away. He turned around and followed Mitch who was talking quickly about the next round. Henry tuned out his voice as his thoughts filled only with her, Arabella. Her name melted in his mind as he thought it over and over again.

The rest of the rodeo was a blur for Henry. He blindly watched the few competitors as he replayed his and Arabella's first meeting over and over in his mind, like he was rowing through his memories only he was happily stuck in a pond of Arabella. Everything he saw had a rose-colored haze over it. Nothing could blacken his mood today. Especially, with the prospects of getting together with her after the rodeo. He was determined to speak with her with suavity and poise the next time they met. He felt like an idiot, being barely able to talk or function in front of her. "What she must think of him!" He really did not want to know but at another thought he wished he knew her every thought. Was she as wildly curious about him as he was her? He had never been so intensely attracted to one person before in his life.

More than anything else, he longed just to touch her hand and hear her voice. He wondered if she felt the same connectedness as him. Henry had no idea, when it was his turn to ride, how he ever climbed on the bull and rode straight through to the next round.

****

The spotlight shone through the dusty, night air, straight into Henry's eyes. The crowd roared with applause as he took the shiny, first place medal from the official, shook his hand, and stepped back next to Mitch.

Mitch shook his head at Henry with a good-natured smile as they walked out of the arena. "Beginner's luck." He said, giving Henry a punch in the shoulder.

Henry laughed, but his mind was preoccupied with seeing Arabella again. He was already scanning the area in search of her face. "So, are we getting that drink?" He asked Mitch casually as they entered the outer grandstand area.

"Well, I am feelin' just so tired...that rodeo jus' wore me out..." Mitch glanced sideways at Henry with devious eyes to see his reaction.

"Mitch, you are so convincing, I almost believed you." Henry said sarcastically and shook his head at Mitch. He laughed and gave Mitch a light shove. "So, what bar are we headed to..."

Just then, his eyes found Arabella, walking gracefully out of the crowd toward them with Mitch's wife, Nicole. His breath caught in his throat, and he couldn't finish his words.

Mitch followed his gaze and smiled at the ladies as they approached. "Ya, I thought that was about where your mind was! I cannot believe you managed to stay on that ol' bull with her on your mind." Mitch let off as the two women came within earshot. "Hey, you beautiful ladies!" He said as he put his arm around his wife. "Come to congratulate the toughest men in the show?" Mitch flexed his arm and scrunched his face up in mocking effort.

The two girls giggled, grabbing one another's arm. Henry could not help smiling, with his eyes twinkling in bliss as the two girls sauntered up next to them.

Arabella seemed to notice Henry's attentions and smiled at him before bashfully dropping her head and kicking some dirt under her boot.

"You both did great," Nicole said. "But one of you did a little bit greater, though." She added with a devious smile that matched her husband's. However, she reached down and tightly grasped Mitch's hand to show she was joking.

Mitch pretended to be hurt and made a show of ignoring her. "Well, let's head to the bar to get those drinks Henry owes us." He grabbed his wife's hand and pulled her toward his truck, looking over his shoulder as he walked. "Come on, you two, let's drive together."

Ara and Henry, alone and standing in silence, followed close behind.

They all piled into Mitch's pickup with Henry helping Arabella into the high truck. He extended his hand to help her in, and she took it gladly. His hands still tingled from touching hers as he realized how snug they were, tucked into the backseat.

Mitch started up the loud engine and took off quickly out of the arena. The windows were down and the cool breeze flowed through the cab of the truck. Arabella's bare arms were covered with countless goosebumps.

A fleece blanket was tucked at Henry's side of the truck, and he offered it to her. She graciously accepted, and Henry draped the blanket over her shoulders.

Nicole laughed at something Mitch said and smiled back at Henry and Arabella. Henry thought he saw a glint of concern in her eyes as she smiled.

He turned and looked out the window. People and buildings flew by, but all of Henry's awareness hovered around the woman beside him. She was inches away from him, curled in a blanket and was the most precious sight.

She was sitting quietly, looking out the window with her elbow propped comfortably on the window ledge. Ara must have felt his gaze because she turned her head, startled, and gazed directly into Henry's eyes. In the darkness, her eyes were dark blue, like midnight.

Their stare continued, now a game to see who would look away first. A stubborn smile sported across Arabella's face, and Henry playfully smiled back.

The truck stopped suddenly, jerking both of their gazes away from each other, and Henry realized they were already at the bar.

Mitch was helping Nicole out as he said impatiently, "You two hangin' in there all night or what?"

"No, we're coming." Henry said as he jumped out and reached up to help Arabella out. He noticed she had a faint flush to her cheeks. He thought maybe it was the heat, but maybe ... it was him.

They walked into the noisy bar and ordered their drinks, with Henry paying as promised, before finding a table. He looked around, seeing some familiar faces from the rodeo mixed in with some others he did not recognize. A live band played over in the corner, singing out old country tunes. Country was not his usual taste, but he found, in this environment, he loved it.

Sipping his beer, Henry watched the couples spinning around on the dance floor to the music. Mitch talked about the rodeo, the surprising bulls or falls, and their winnings. It was not long before a cowboy walked over and asked Arabella to dance. Henry watched as she looked to Mitch and Nicole first, almost as if for permission.

When Mitch nodded his head, Henry's suspicion was confirmed. Arabella allowed herself to be led onto the dance floor and then gracefully around it, spinning and twirling in time with the twang of the music.

Henry flirted with idea of just letting it go but shook his head and asked anyway, saying, "Why did she look at you two for permission before accepting that dance?"

Mitch shrugged. "We are pretty protective of her and only want what's best for her." He said simply.

"So watch it." Nicole said with slight daggers in her voice. She poked a finger against his chest.

"Honey, don't you think I have checked him out by now? He is a good guy. Trust me."

His wife looked into his eyes, then at Henry before deciding to trust him. "I will still be watching you, though, Henry." She clinked her glass against his and smiled, slightly reassuring him, before pulling Mitch out onto the dance floor.

Henry watched as Arabella was caught up by another cowboy for the next dance. *With Mitch's approval,* he thought. *I might as well go for it. I will ask her to dance!* He could hardly believe what was happening. This morning he had only wanted to find her, now he was going to ask the woman of his dreams to dance. As if reading his thoughts, the band suddenly switched to a slow number.

It was now or never, Henry thought and stepped out onto the floor. He caught her just as she was headed back to their table and asked her to dance.

She hesitated, just slightly, before accepting. He took her hand in his and led her to the center of the dance floor.

Henry gently but firmly grasped her waist and began to gracefully sweep her around the floor. Together, they swayed in perfect time to the music. The people around them faded; it was just the two of them, close together and deeply gazing into each other's eyes. Henry looked down into the perfection of her face, wondering if beauty had ever been so perfectly portrayed in another being.

He lowered his face to hers, cheek to cheek. He closed his eyes tightly and whispered softly, "Such wilt thou be to me, who must like the other foot, obliquely run; thy firmness makes my circle just, and makes me end, where I begun." [1]

Arabella's eyes widened in shocked recognition. "You know Donne." She said quietly with a mixture of curiosity and disbelief in her voice.

Henry continued to smile down into her eyes. "Yes." He pulled her in a little closer to him and quoted Emily Dickinson. "To see the Summer Sky Is Poetry, though never in a Book it lie — True Poems flee —" [2]

Arabella smiled and blushed lightly, eyes twinkling in wonderment. Henry continued to smoothly glide her around the floor.

Just as the final notes of the song hummed through the room, Ara looked up and met Henry's eyes. They stood frozen, looking into the depths of each other's eyes as the other couples moved around them.

A new song started. The loud, upbeat twang broke the moment. Startled, Arabella looked around nervously, twirling a strand of hair in her hand.

Henry grabbed her hand and gently led her off the floor to their table, calming her nerves. Mitch and Nicole were sitting there, engrossed in each other's presence. They looked up as Henry and Ara arrived.

"Good music." Mitch commented nonchalantly, but the look in his eyes was devious. His eyebrow raised conspicuously.

"Ya ... good music." Henry managed to stumble out. He took a swig of his drink, trying to calm himself down. He snuck a glance at Arabella. Her cheeks were still flushed as she fiddled with the straw in her drink. Henry looked away before she could see him looking at her.

"Well, Nicole wants to head home. She wants to hit the hay early." Mitch announced with a wiggle of suggestion with his eyebrows.

"Mitch!" Nicole cried with embarrassment, not totally opposed to his implications, though. "I really do need to get to bed, though. I have an early day tomorrow."

Henry nodded and threw some dollar bills on the table. They all headed out the door with Mitch and Nicole in the lead.

As they got to the door, a familiar face was entering the bar with a group of other similarly familiar faces. Charlie, Roy, Linus, and Rena came carousing through the door, laughing all together. Charlie and Rena were holding hands which made Henry smile.

Seeing Henry's face, Charlie did not hesitate to flash his big toothy smile right back and give Henry a huge hug. The whole group kind of swarmed around him in a group hug. It was like he had joined their family, their rock climbing, find-who-you-are type of family.

Arabella, Mitch, and Nicole looked at him a little surprised but smiled nonetheless.

"Where ya been, Burns? We went climbing without you today. Charlie left you two messages man, two!" Linus rang out at the top of his lungs.

People turned to stare at the ruckus. He looked like he had already had a drink or two before arriving at the bar. His unfettered smile genuinely displayed his pleasure in seeing Henry, and Henry smiled just as genuinely back, delighted to see old friends.

He glanced at Rena and Charlie holding hands and cast a devious smile at Charlie.

"Sorry, man! I got caught up in a rodeo today." He grinned, "Also, well, I've made a couple new friends. Guys, this is Mitch, Nicole, and ... Arabella." Henry said. As he introduced Arabella he could feel his cheeks flush with heat again.

Charlie caught his attention and his sparkling green eyes smiled a devious smile right back.

Their short exchange was broken by Charlie's words. "It is great to meet you all," Charlie said, he turned and shook hands with everyone, or the closest thing he knew for a handshake. It was more like a clasp and pull because he pulled himself in for a friendly hug for each person.

"Henry makes friends fast, obviously," Charlie interjected. He patted Henry on the back like old pals. Charlie looked around at the new group. "Looks like you are finding your muse all right." He grinned at Henry.

Henry held Charlie's gaze as he nodded and smiled. "Yeah ... yeah man. I think I am." Henry said quietly.

"So how do you guys know each other?" Arabella interjected.

"Well, Charlie here took me out on my first rock climbing experience when I first got to town, which was yesterday," Henry laughed. "It was quite an experience. This is really a great bunch of people right here, and we got along like we were family or something." The whole group beamed like they lived to be someone's friend. They were so good at it too.

Linus got up real close to Henry's face and he could smell the liquor. Linus's eyes were dead serious. "Charlie man ... we climbed a rock together. A rock! That makes us family bro ... for life." He had clasped Henry's hand with his as if their embrace was sealing their family bond.

Charlie came up and pulled Linus off of him. "He ... is really drunk," he laughed, "Don't mind him."

Everyone laughed heartily.

"Well, we gotta get goin'," Mitch chimed in. "The wife needs her beauty sleep and all." Mitch shrugged his shoulders carelessly and snapped his hand around Nicole's waste. "Farewell, boys and lady. Very nice meeting you. Henry, we will be in the truck when you're ready." The two of them traipsed out the front door, Mitch tickling Nicole and the both of them giggling all the while. They were obviously in no rush for anyone to join to them.

"Hey, I have to use the restroom anyway," Arabella chimed in. "Excuse me for a minute?" Henry nodded and she slipped passed to group towards the restroom.

"Well, she seems genuinely amazing, Henry." Charlie spoke up. "Your whole being just seems lit up right now."

Henry dug his hands in his pockets and casually glanced towards the restroom where he last saw her. "Yeah. She's ... she, uh, she lights up a room. So, it's sort of a residual effect that my face lights up when I am around her." Henry smiled. "Don't be surprised if you start glowing too, Charlie. In fact … it looks like you are, but I have a funny feeling that is because of a different girl."

Charlie's eyes glowed with happiness, and he squeezed Rena's hand. "Yeah, well, sometimes something can be right in front of you for so long that it takes an eternity to discover what *really* is in front of you." He looked into Rena's eyes with loving appreciation and Henry was moved by their tenderness toward one another.

"I knew way before him," Rena chimed in.

"Well, I was wondering when you two were going to get together. It was so obvious. I saw it almost instantly and I have only known you guys, what, a day?" They all laughed under their breath but Henry continued, so moved by their love. "But, you both just kind of move around each other like you are meant to be close, ya know. You guys being together is like the confluence of two rivers. It is fluid and an uninhibited, it is almost like, how could you ever have ever been on your own to begin with?" Henry saw their love and was inspired. Seeing their discovery of each other felt like his discovery of Ara: magical. He had just met her but somehow he knew.

"Well, Henry, that was the most poetic thing I have heard all night. And Linus here has been spouting off drunken words of love since we got here." That got everyone laughing.

They were in the midst of their chuckles when Ara returned from the restroom, smiling as she joined their group again. "What's so funny, what did I miss?" she pleaded, laughing still despite her absence.

"Oh, Henry here is a regular, everyday poet, inspiring the daily lives of everyone he comes by is all," Charlie cheered. "Three cheers for Henry."

With that, the whole group cheered at the same time, "Hip, hip … HOORAY!" at the top of their lungs, three times. But after the first cheer the rest of the bar joined in on their carousing and soon Henry was surrounded by the cheers of a bunch of strangers. Charlie and the gang knew how to have fun and were not shy in obtaining it. They couldn't care less what perfect strangers thought of them.

Henry couldn't help but laugh in embarrassment, his cheeks bright red. Ara cheered with them, and her cheers seemed to ring out louder than everyone else's. Henry's heart was so warmed with their love. How had he made such great friends in just a day?

"All right, all right. That's enough," Henry clamored. "I think that's my cue to get this pretty lady home."

"Oh, right! I forgot Mitch and Nicole are waiting for us," Arabella pulled the strap of her purse over her shoulder, readying herself to go.

"Yeah, well it is great seeing you again, Burns!" Everyone took their turn hugging Henry and Ara goodbye.

"If you're not too busy … which I understand if you are," Charlie suggestively wiggled his eyebrows at Ara, and she blushed, "Hit us up for some more climbing. You got my number."

"Right on, will do," Henry shook his head in agreement. He thanked them for embarrassing him to no end and then guided Ara out the door with his hand on her back.

They walked in silence for a bit to Mitch's truck, and Ara was the first to break the silence.

"I love your friends, Henry." She smiled radiantly. "They are so energetic and fun. It was great meeting them."

"Yeah, they are one crazy bunch but just so darn likeable." They both laughed as they arrived at the truck.

Ara tapped on Nicole's window and waved hello.

They were like two teenage best friends, Henry thought as Nicole flashed Ara a devious smile.

Henry held the door for Arabella and helped her into the high truck before getting in himself. His hand tingled from her touch, so he placed his other hand on top to try to steady himself for the short ride back to the rodeo grounds. He looked over and saw Arabella was looking dreamily out the window again. He leaned back and replayed the events of the day in his mind.

In front, Nicole rested her head on Mitch's shoulder and laughed at whatever story he was telling. She leaned up and whispered something in his ear just as they were about to Henry's car.

Mitch looked at her and smiled before saying, "Hey, Henry, would you mind giving Ara a ride home? Nicole and I really do need to get home."

Henry's heart jumped high in his chest. "I can do that." He said, trying to keep his voice steady, forcing nonchalance into his tone. "Is that all right with you?" He asked Arabella.

She looked at him and nodded silently with a little smile. The truck had stopped at Henry's car.

Henry opened the door and carefully helped Ara out.

"Henry?" Nicole said through her open window. "We trust you will get her home safe and sound." She said with a hint of warning in her voice. "Good night." She rolled up her window, and Mitch sped off, kicking up a mountain of dust once again.

Henry thought he heard Mitch's "Yeehaw" before the window closed. Smiling, he unlocked the car from the passenger side and held the door for Ara.

"Thank you, Henry." She said softly as she slid into the car.

He walked around to the driver's side, forcing himself to remain calm. Henry had gone out with dozens of women before he was married, but he had never felt like this before. Usually, he was calm and collected around women. He was the definition of smooth. He opened his door and slid behind the wheel. With a twist of the key, the engine purred to life. He confidently pulled the car onto the road.

"Whew." Ara said. "This is quite a car."

Henry smiled. "You sound like Mitch. It actually is a reliable vehicle, as well as comfortable and fast. The car has never let me down yet. And the best part is … good gas mileage, every man's dream machine." He reached out and patted the dashboard.

Arabella nodded and looked out the window. They rode in silence. The road steepened as Henry steered them toward home. He suddenly realized he did not know where the turn-off to her cabin was. He inquired about it, and she told him, pointing him in the direction. It turned out, she lived quite close to his cabin; it was just about a half mile away.

Henry swung the car into the short gravelly drive to her cabin. The sound of dirt ground under his tires. The cabin looked almost identical to his own, except a wooden porch wrapped around the entire building. A porch swing swayed gently back and forth with the breeze of the night.

He turned off the car and opened his door. The buzz of a cricket's song pierced the silence of the night. He breathed in the fresh air as he swiftly walked around to open her door.

She smiled up at him as he helped her out. "Thank you," she said. "You're a real gentleman, aren't you?"

Henry gazed down into her eyes. "Every lady deserves a gentleman's manners, especially a beautiful one."

In the soft moonlight, Henry saw Arabella shake her head lightly and turned, walking toward the cabin. "You know I am perfectly capable of opening my door, right?" Arabella spoke with a playful, yet guarded tone.

"Of course. But rules are rules. I just abide by them." Henry nudged her arm as they walked toward the porch. They walked side by side, their arms brushing against each other. Henry was caught up in looking at her perfect hand at her side.

"What are you looking at?!" Arabella poked at Henry's arm, and he flinched just to make it a good show.

"Nothing," he pleaded with both his hands up in retreat. "Nothing." He dropped his arms behind his back, walking as if contemplative and returning his gaze to her hand. He released his hands and nudged her again.

She nudged him back softly without averting her gaze from the path to the porch. Henry extended his pinkie and grazed her hand. He could see her smile as she slightly extended hers.

Henry walked with her to the door, pinkie in pinkie, feeling like a boy out on his first date.

They climbed the steps in silence, save for the gentle sound of the creek off in the woods. The two stopped as they reached the front door.

Arabella turned to face him, fiddling with her keys. "A gentleman also walks every lady to her door?" She asked him teasingly, but there was a slight, nervous shake to her voice. The moonlight cast a dark shadow across her forehead, causing her eyes to take on a deeper blue.

Henry nodded as he felt himself getting lost in the beauty of her eyes. He did not know how it happened, but he suddenly reached down and gently cupped the side of her face in one of his strong hands.

She froze and watched him silently as he tilted her face up toward him. With his other hand, Henry lightly brushed back a strand of blond hair.

She continued to be unmoving as she looked up at him shakily, trembling from nerves or the cold. She put up a hand to say goodbye before things went any further.

Henry looked down at her beautiful hand and caught it with one of his.

She watched, breathless, as he slowly pulled it up to his lips and softly kissed the top.

"Good night, Arabella," He whispered before lightly dropping her hand, turned, and walked down the steps to his car. He heard her unlock her door and slip inside.

Henry waited until he was driving back toward his cabin before stealing an exclamation from Mitch that fit the moment, "Yeehaw!"

15
PRINCETON UNIVERSITY
October 17, 1988

"Man, that test was a killer!" Thomas exclaimed, slapping Henry on the shoulder. "Judging by your silence, you must have aced it as usual?"

Henry laughed, running a hand through his hair and looking around the campus. Princeton looked so peaceful at this time of year. Not peaceful in the sense that it was empty, but the crowds of people made him feel at ease. This was his element. He breathed in the woodsy smell of fallen leaves. "I did study last night while you were off with … Miranda?"

"Melinda, I think" Thomas corrected him. "Who knows? The one I find tonight will be a different name anyway." He smiled slyly.

Henry rolled his eyes and changed the subject, "Ya, I could use a drink after that test. Where to tonight? The Barrister?"

"Oh, but of course." Thomas shrugged his shoulders as if it were idiotic to suggest something other than their favorite spot.

They walked the short distance to the Barrister and saw it was busy as usual as they stepped in the door. Henry looked around at the familiar setting, his favorite bar. The place was dimly lit, with dark blue lights and deep wood.

Two women caught sight of Henry and Thomas and made their way toward them with coy smiles.

Henry ordered a round of drinks for the women, himself, and Thomas. While he listened to the two women tell him a story about this crazy party they were at last night, a woman on the dance floor caught his attention. She wore a short, tight black dress that clung to her body as she confidently moved to the rhythm of a rock and roll song. She was dancing with some guy who could not move well with her. She outshined every attempt he could make at keeping up with her, but he never left her side, and she looked as if she just wanted to dance. Henry was used to beautiful women, but she really caught his eye the way her hands would slightly follow the sway of her hips, and the way she seemed free in the music.

Henry tried to distract himself and decided a round of pool would suit his needs. He suggested the idea to Thomas and, after untangling himself from the ladies on his arms, walked over to the tables and grabbed some cues with Thomas. As they played, Henry found himself looking over to the dance floor to watch the dark, haired beauty.

She met his eye once and half-smiled before moving back into the crowd. Henry focused on the game. He lined the cue with the ball at the end of the table and pulled back before strongly slamming the ball into the socket, the cue spun back, lining up his next shot.

"I need another drink," he told Thomas and walked toward the bar. As he opened the top and took a deep drink, he suddenly felt a light hand on his arm. Henry looked down into her green eyes for a second before recognizing her as the woman from the dance floor.

"Excuse me." She said, reaching for her newly filled martini glass. She took a sip with her hand still resting on his arm before taking a step to walk away.

Henry grabbed her hand as she began to move away.

The woman turned, looking down at his hand holding hers before meeting his gaze. "Yes?" she asked.

Just as Henry was about to ask her to dance, a man arguing angrily with another woman crashed into her, spilling her beverage all over Henry.

The woman gasped and reached for napkins, pressing them against Henry's chest to blot up some of the liquid.

"Thanks," he said with a smile.

"Well, it's the least I could do after spilling my drink on you."

"It wasn't your fault, but you do owe me a dance for that." Henry said with a charming smile.

She laughed lightly. "Oh, I do?" She threw the pile of wet napkins away and took his hand. As they walked to the dance floor, she looked up at him and said, "I am Anne, by the way. Anne Boleyn."

16
HENRY'S JOURNEY
Jackson Hole, Wyoming
August 25, 1992

Henry opened his eyes to the bright sunlight rising slowly in the sky, light streaming in through his windows. It seemed every day began with bright sunshine and a sporadic fluffy cloud. There was no smog and, even better, there was silence.

A delicious feeling spread throughout his body as he stretched and yawned his sleep away. *Another beautiful day*, he thought before remembering just why he felt so great. Great couldn't begin to describe his wide-eyed, toothy smile or him jumping out of bed to skip room to room, whistling a familiar tune. The events of the day before replayed in his mind: the rodeo, the bar, the dance, and Arabella.

"Arabella," he whispered to himself. He replayed Arabella over and over again in his mind, every detail better than he remembered the last time he replayed her memory. He was determined to see her again.

Henry bounced around the cabin with childlike glee, threw on the first clothes he found, and was about to run out the door to Ara's cabin when he stopped himself. He could not just storm into her house. Last night was amazing to him, surely she was on the same page as him? Was just popping in going to be okay with her? Henry needed to figure out a game plan.

He caught a glimpse of himself in the mirror. "Whew!" He said aloud. "I need to jump in the creek first. He grabbed some clean clothes out of the dresser and walked out the door for the short walk to the creek, practically skipping his way down the trail.

The water was freezing as usual, but Henry did not feel the frigid ice against his skin as he cleaned up. His thoughts were consumed with Arabella. *How soon should I try to see her? What should I talk to her about? Should I ask her out to a nice, fancy dinner?*

Somehow, Henry doubted Ara would want to go for a fancy dinner. She seemed the simplistic type. He imagined their next meeting in his head as he pulled himself out of the water and put on his jeans and slung his t-shirt over his shoulder.

Still deep in thought, Henry climbed over the rocks leading down to the stream and stepped out onto the road, almost plowing smack into Arabella as he landed.

"Whoa!" She cried, surprised, and tripped over a protruding stone. She stumbled and almost fell.

Startled, Henry reached out and helped steady her. She regained her balance by placing one hand on his bare chest. She was in a soft, white, running jacket with khaki workout shorts that showed off her tanned, endless legs. Her running shoes were dirty and worn from regular running. Her long, wavy hair was pulled back into a ponytail, loosened from her run, small strands blowing with the breeze of the wind.

"Sorry about that." Henry told her, sheepishly smiling, as he dropped his arms from hers and backed away slightly.

She reached up and wiped the sweat off her forehead with the back of her hand. "That's all right, Henry. You just scared the livin' daylights out of me, that's all!" She smiled and shook her head, trying to catch her breath, and placed one hand over her heart as if to feel her racing pulse.

"Ya, I was just washing up in the stream and, when I stepped out on the path, I was just sort of lost in thought, I guess." Henry tousled his wet hair with his fingers and smiled his infamous crooked smile.

Arabella leaned against a rock for support, starting to finally catch her breath. "Ya, I could tell." She breathed in and out before continuing. "What were you thinking so hard about?" She asked.

Henry looked over and watched the stream rushing over the rocks. *So much for a game plan*, he thought. "Um, just, you know, about … the water. It's really cold." He finished lamely. "I'm thinking deeply about the water." He made a mental note to slap himself later for saying something so stupid.

Ara's eyebrows shot up in surprise, and she laughed. "Yes, mountain streams do tend to be that way."

He smiled in embarrassment and shoved a hand through his wet hair to try and tame it down and to buy himself a few more seconds to try and think of something better to say than, "I'm thinking deeply about water."

"So out for a run?" *As if that wasn't obvious,* he could have kicked himself.

She looked at him incredulously and nodded. "I go just about every day. I absolutely love running in the mountains." She gazed around appreciatively.

He decided it might be better to cut the conversation short since he apparently could not trust himself to converse like a normal human being, or at least an interesting one. "Well, I will let you get back to it." He smiled at her in what he hoped appeared to be a casual smile, hoping to successfully manage one thing in this encounter with her. "Sorry again for almost knocking you over."

Ara waved her hand dismissively. "No worries, Henry. Have a great day!" She turned and jogged away, her ponytail bouncing against her back.

Henry headed back to the cabin, replaying every second of their conversation back in his mind. He had never had such a hard time talking to a woman in his life! It was baffling! Who was this woman, and what was this incredible hold she had over him?

Shaking his head in puzzlement, he opened the door to his cabin and heard the phone ringing. He reached over to answer it, wondering who on Earth would be on the other end. "Hello?" He asked tentatively.

"Henry?" A somewhat familiar voice sounded on the other end. "This is Bill, the owner of that cabin you are stayin' in presently."

Henry smiled. "Hey, Bill. What's up?"

"Well, I just wanted to see what your plans for the day were. I was thinkin' of taking you up on that offer to help out at my ranch? But if you're busy, I understand." He sounded a little hesitant to be asking him.

"Nothing would make me happier," Henry chimed. "This cabin is a steal. I should be working on your ranch every day just to make me a fair man!"

"Well, I'm a little behind with two of my ranch hands out sick and another on vacation. I would only need you for half a day, a day at the most. It'll get me caught up."

"Sure thing. Just give me directions, and I'll head out. Is it okay if I grab a quick bite to eat on the way?"

"Oh, no." Bill said firmly. "The wife has made everybody breakfast, and she will be all mad as a hen if you come and don't eat her fine cookin'." Bill gave him simple directions and disconnected the call. The man was abrupt and to the point but didn't come off the least bit harsh. It takes a special kind of person to do that. Bill wasn't the mysterious Arabella, but he was excited to see what this day had in store for him, even if it was sans Ara.

Henry changed into a pair of his Wrangler jeans and a dark t-shirt before grabbing his keys and heading out the door. He followed the directions Bill had given him without difficulty.

Before long, Henry came upon a tight turn and a clearing opened up, revealing Bill's ranch. The entrance had a gate, which was opened for him. He passed through and a hanging sign welcomed him to "Annie Hill." It was a modest place, with a red barn and a matching, lone, red farm house at the top of the hill. The paint was faded and aged, giving the ranch a homey, comfortable feel. He parked, walked up the worn wooden steps, and knocked on the door. A cheery "Welcome Home" sign decorated with flowers was hung on the door, and Henry felt at ease as the door opened.

A smiling woman with softly curling grey hair and kind, blue eyes greeted him. "You must be Henry. Bill told me you were joinin' us today in our time of need. Thank you so much for helpin' us out." She waved him inside and motioned toward a wooden table in a sunny kitchen nook.

"You must be the Annie of 'Annie Hill,'" Henry smiled.

"Oh dear, yes. Bill insisted on it, though, heavens to Betsy, I don't know why." Her cheeks reddened in humility, waving the conversation away in an instant.

He sat down, and she poured him a cup of coffee. "Now, I'll be right back." She disappeared around the corner, and Henry looked around at the many wall hangings depicting various aspects of ranch life. There were several paintings on one wall that took his breath away – one so real, he felt like he was near the top of the Grand Teton in the middle of a winter storm. The blue peaks shot toward the sky like shards of glass, cutting at the thing that dare shed snow on its hallowed ground. The mere thought of being stranded on a mountain top such as this, the cold, the danger, sent a shudder through his whole body.

"Hey there, Henry." Bill smiled his toothy grin at Henry as he joined him at the table, pulling his attention away from the art. He exhaled, and he could have sworn he saw chilled breath escape his lips. He took a long pull on his hot coffee and rested his feet on the chair next to him.

"How is it going?" Henry asked, glad to see Bill.

"Oh, just peachy." Bill sipped a bit of his coffee and smiled a little sardonically. "Just have a downed fence to deal with in the middle of the late August rush." He shook his head and moved his hat up and down, smoothing his grey hair back a bit. "The cows haven't found it yet, though, so I'm thankin' my lucky stars you are able to help me out."

"So fixing fence is my task?" Henry asked, feeling excited. He was pretty sure a cowboy would definitely need to know how to fix a fence!

"Yes, sir. If you are up to the task, that is."

Annie came in with plates heaped full of eggs, toast, hash browns, and fruit. She had hamburger steak as well, covered in brown gravy. "Eat up, boys." She said cheerfully. "You are going to need your energy today!"

Henry and Bill dug in. As they ate, Bill explained the task, how to dig holes with certain shovels, how to string the wire so it was strong and tight, and how to secure everything so it would hold through winter. Henry asked a few clarifying questions, and Bill was patient and clear as he answered.

Once their delicious breakfast was devoured, they stood up from the table. "Thank you for the wonderful meal," Henry told Annie as she moved to clear their plates.

She put a hand on his shoulder. "Least I could do! Now, I'll see you boys back here around the usual dinner time? 1:00?"

"That's right." Bill kissed her cheek.

"I'm makin' somethin' real special." She clasped her hands in delight with a twinkle in her eye. "Now don't work too hard." She winked and headed over to start the dishes.

Bill took Henry over to an old worn truck piled full of fence posts, barbed wire spools, several types of shovels, and other tools. They hopped in and drove out of the yard and toward a pasture Bill pointed to a little ways in the distance. They rode in companionable silence and soon pulled up to a faded approach which Bill turned onto.

At Bill's instruction, Henry hopped out and opened the gate to let the truck in. He climbed back in, and they followed the fence line until they came to a section that was completely open, the fence being torn down by a fallen tree.

"I moved the tree out of the way early this morning when I was checking the fence line," Bill explained. "Let's move this old wire out of the way and unload the posts."

Henry wondered how this old man had moved an entire tree away but noticed a chain saw covered in dust in the bed of his truck. He wanted to ask where all the wood went to and how he had done all of this before the crack of dawn, but the look in Bill's eyes made it clear it was time to get down to business. Henry didn't want to disappoint him. Oddly enough, he felt an unexplained desire to make this man proud of anything he put his hand to, and he set out to do just that.

They picked up the old wire so the cows and horses wouldn't get tangled up in it and threw that into the back of the truck. Next, they unloaded the heavy, steel posts. Henry's muscles strained under the weight, and he enjoyed the way it felt to do actual labor to work his body, rather than work in a gym.

Bill handed him a shovel, and they began to dig the old, broken posts out of the ground. It was rough work, and soon Henry was sheathed in a fine layer of sweat. He wiped his forehead with the back of his hand and peeled off his shirt. Though he was wearing work gloves, his hands simply weren't used to repeated abrasion of the shovel pushing up against the space between his thumb and fore-finger, and the heat building up under his glove was ominous. He pulled off the gloves, and a blister had already formed and broke. Clear puss stung at the fresh wound. He shoved the gloves back on, not wanting to let Bill know he didn't have the hands of a working man.

"Okay," Bill said breathlessly, wiping his forehead as well. "Now we will just dig new holes right next to the old ones so the new posts will hold as we pound 'em in. I will fill those old holes if you want to start diggin'?" He looked at Henry for confirmation.

Henry nodded and set to work without another word. It was satisfying to push the shovel into the hard ground, and he found a rhythm to the work as he dug in and pulled earth out. He stopped periodically to drink water and wipe more sweat from his forehead, never allowing himself a second thought toward his throbbing hand.

Bill checked his work and nodded in approval. "Let's pound these posts in."

They stood up a heavy post, and Bill held it in place as Henry grabbed the tool to pound the fence into the ground. He moved the device up and down, using his arms and his legs to add strength and momentum. With one in place, Henry looked at the ten more laying on the ground in disbelief.

Bill grinned at him. "Only ten more to go!"

They continued the exhausting work for another hour. The throbbing in his hand had ceased and their work was looking like it was nearing completion. Henry was pounding in the last post when he heard the sound of a truck rumbling up the path toward them. He paused and wiped his fore head, shading his eyes to see who was approaching them.

"Ah, I see our ride is here!" Bill stood up straight and smiled mischievously at Henry. "Looks like Annie was too busy cookin' and had to send someone else."

The truck rolled to a stop next to them, and the driver cut the engine. Opening the door, Henry could see that a young woman had been behind the wheel. And not just any woman, it was Arabella!

The butterflies in his stomach roared to life, and his heart beat so loudly that he wasn't quite sure he would be able to hear. He wasn't sure what to do with his hands, so he kept holding the fence pounding tool and prayed she wouldn't notice.

She hopped out of the truck gracefully. Her boots hit the ground and sent a small cloud of dirt into the air, lining her light blue denim in a soft shade of brown. She cast a big smile toward Bill before her gaze fell on Henry's face. Recognizing his face, her left hand immediately fell to the hem of her flannel button-up, and she began fiddling with the fabric.

Remembering the night they first met at the rodeo, Henry smiled sheepishly at the thought that he made her just as nervous as she made him.

"Henry? What are you doing here?" She asked, a nervous smile replacing the familiar one she gave Bill before.

"Fancy running into *you* again," Henry smiled. "Glad that I can say that this time around, and it not be so literal."

That got a laugh, and he relaxed. Henry felt like Henry again, and he was thankful that the "deep-thinker" version of himself from earlier had decided to take a back seat to this particular conversation.

"I see you two have already met?" Bill interrupted the moment.

"Oh, yes." Ara's attention was pulled back to both the men. "We actually met the other night at the rodeo. He knew Mitch from a rodeo they did together in Cheyenne."

Bill grunted in recognition of her comment, but he showed no interest in continuing the conversation about how they knew each other any longer.

"Henry, would ya throw those tools in the back of the truck 'fore we head back for lunch? Ara, sweetheart, I sure hope you're plannin' on stayin' for lunch."

Bill already had his gloves off and was throwing things into the bed of his truck.

"Actually, I was thinkin' of stoppin' by the church this afternoon to check in on a few things," she said, her eyes dancing back and forth between Henry and Bill. "But if you can promise you won't keep me 'til dark, I don't see why I can't stay for a bit."

Her eyes glittered with delight as she met Henry's gaze, and he returned her gaze with similar sentiments.

"Alrighty then, Henry, let's get a move on now. I'm sure whatever Annie's cookin' is hot, and I don't plan on lettin' all that fine food get cold just because you two can't stop making googly eyes at each other."

Henry felt his already warm face grow warmer. He shook his head and laughed, climbing into the truck without a word. Henry thought Ara also looked mildly embarrassed as they drove wordlessly back to the house.

They pulled in, and Annie met them at the door.

"Ah, I see Arabella found you. Henry, did Bill introduce you to our other guest here?"

"No, Annie, I did not. It appears Ara and Henry have already met," Bill said with a smile. He clasped both their shoulders and pushed them into a walk toward the kitchen. "Listen, guys, let's eat, huh?"

Henry couldn't agree more. The day's workload was hitting his body hard. His hands were trembling from hunger and, perhaps, another reason he didn't want to admit to himself at the moment. "I'm famished, Bill. That sounds like an excellent idea."

Henry pulled out Ara's chair for her, and she took it gladly, murmuring her thanks.

The table spread was something out of *Home and Garden*. It was like a pre-Thanksgiving, Thanksgiving-style meal. Slices of turkey were placed in the center of the table, with stuffing, green beans, carrots, mashed potatoes, and dinner rolls splayed around that. Two pies were set on the table, one that had a beautiful fall leaf crust decorating the top and another that looked like it could be the best pecan pie in the world.

Henry took his seat, before realizing he needed to wash hands. He stepped to the kitchen sink as Annie joined them. She pulled out some drinks.

"Henry, what would you like? We've got juice, lemonade, tea, water."

"I'll take some lemonade." Henry motioned to help carry some drinks to the table. "Bill, Ara, can we get you anything to drink?"

Annie graciously passed him the pitcher of lemonade, and she carried another pitcher of water to the table and began filling everyone's glasses.

"So, Ara, tell us, how did you meet Henry?" Annie posed the question. It was clear her intentions were not innocent curiosity.

"Oh well, we he's a friend of Mitch's actually. They did a rodeo together in Cheyenne," Ara volunteered.

"A rodeo. Really? Henry, I didn't know you were on the circuit," Annie pushed.

"Oh, I'm not. It was my first rodeo, literally. Basically, I was challenged by this guy, Joe. You might know him. He's from around here apparently. Well, anyway, I'm not one to turn down a challenge in the first place, and I left New York City in search of something … different and fun. So when the opportunity presented itself, I jumped on it. Seriously, I jumped on a bull!"

Henry could hardly believe he had done it himself when he had to seriously explain it to someone else.

"Were you any good?" Bill inquired.

"I mean, I won, but I don't know that I would call myself good," Henry said.

"No, no, that's good. Isn't it, honey?" Annie bumped her elbow against Bill's shoulder.

"What about you guys? How do you know Arabella? Does she rent one of your cabins, too?" The conversation was casual and warm. This kind of small talk felt good.

"Oh, sweetie we've known Ara since she was a little girl," Annie recollected. "Goodness, she used to come here with her grandparents. Oh, she had the cutest little bib overalls and a little tool belt because she wanted to help fix things around the ranch."

"Yep, you know I believe I still have that tool belt stored away somewhere." Ara looked at home. Apparently, she found home wherever she went – first with Mitch and Nicole and now this lovely couple. Henry was starting to feel like he was coming home, too.

"You know I think I have some old pictures of you, Arabella. Let me just …" Annie was offer before she could complete her sentence.

"She's always on board for taking trips down memory lane," Bill said. "Best finish up eating there, Henry, you're going to want to try both those pies before getting back to work. Annie and Ara make the best pies in the county!"

"I wouldn't dream of missing that opportunity," Henry said. "Is that what brought you by today, Ara?" Henry finally brought the conversation back to her. He surmised he could never get bored hearing her talk.

"Yeah, I like to make it by here at least every other week or so. Bill and Annie are like second grandparents to me. Plus, I mean, Bill always makes me feel so special about my pies." Ara smiled his way.

"It's not just her pies, Henry. You've got to try her cookin' too. She's not my Annie, but she's up there," Bill said proudly.

"I would love to try her cooking," Henry volunteered.

"Well best be makin' a plan to see her again here soon because we gotta finish up our work."

"Um, well …" Henry looked at Ara, who seemed slightly nervous. As much as he wanted to pounce at the opportunity to spend some more time with her, he didn't want to seem overly zealous about getting to know her better. He didn't press it. "We've made a habit of bumping into each other already, I'm sure it'll happen again."

Everyone dug into the pies at Bill's pressing. Ara's was a blueberry pie, and every bite was heaven. Henry scarfed it down just as Bill was finishing his. He picked up his dishes and brought them to the sink. Henry and Ara followed suit. Annie came running into the kitchen waving a handful of pictures.

"Henry, Henry! Look, I've found it. Here she is in her overalls with her momma and daddy. And these two right here are her grandparents, George and Bea. We all grew up together and played our fair share of cards together on a Saturday night." Annie was in storytelling mode. Henry wished he could stay and listen to stories all night, but Bill was getting antsy, checking his watch and patting his back pocket where his work gloves were tucked.

"Annie, thank you so much for lunch and showing me this picture. It sounds like you guys were great friends. I look forward to getting to know you even more in the future," he said genuinely.

"Well, we well just hold you to that then," Annie smiled. "Now you guys get back to work and send my Bill home at a decent hour."

"Will do, ma'am," Henry replied.

She started shoving them out the door. They drove back to the pasture to finish stringing the wire to the new fence posts. Bill said this part would only take about an hour or so. They climbed out of the truck and picked up the large spool of barbed wire. "Ara, did you want to stay for a bit or did you have to rush off?" Bill asked.

Ara hesitated, "Well, I suppose checkin' things at the church could wait a little bit." She walked over to stand next to them.

Bill grinned and had her stand next to Henry to "help" him roll the wire spool.

Together, they moved the spool down the line as Bill held the wire in place next to the first pole. Ara's hair tickled as it brushed his arm, and she smelled fresh and sweet like wild flowers.

Once they reached the end, they set down the spool and walked back to Bill to help clip the wire to the post. He demonstrated how to use the little metal clips and how to twist the clip around the wire with plyers. Henry applied a clip on the next post with Bill supervising his work.

"Looks good, Henry." Bill patted his shoulder and stood up. "Eight more to go on this string." He took off his gloves and headed to the truck. "I'm just goin' to go along the fence line to finish checkin' the rest. Hope no more trees fell down in that last storm." He headed off without another word, leaving Ara and Henry alone.

Nervously, Henry stood up and moved to the next post with Ara at his side. She handed him a clip, and he bent to place it in position, twisting it around the wire with his plyers. "There we go." He said to fill the silence and stood up again.

"Kind of slow work, these clips." Ara commented with a small smile. "Do you prefer this or the fence poundin'?"

He moved to the next post and twisted the clip around the wire again. Looking up into her eyes, he lost his train of thought for a moment. "Um, well, I don't mind the physical work. I enjoyed it, really." He stood up and rolled his sore shoulders. "But after a morning of that work, I am really liking this slower pace." He smiled at her and took the next clip from her hand.

She nodded and smiled to herself as if picturing the hard work he had done that morning. They put on the next few clips in comfortable silence, and, before long, the wire was up.

"Only two more wires to go," Henry said cheerfully, and Ara laughed.

"Well, unfortunately, I do need to get goin', Henry." She smiled regretfully at him, clearly not wanting to leave.

He nodded and put his hands into his pockets. "Thanks for your help. It was nice."

"Okay, well, maybe I will see you around?" She opened up the door to the pick-up and turned back to him with a hand on the handle. "Unless, do you have any plans after you finish … here." She motioned at the fence.

His heart leapt in his chest. "No, I was just going to rest at home maybe …" He finished, knowing how completely boring he must sound.

She smiled and stepped up into the pick-up. "Would you, maybe, like to go for a walk then? Just when you are finished and feel up to it?"

"That sounds great. I'll stop over after I shower and stuff..."

"See you then, Henry." She slammed the door and drove off.

Henry grinned and started to roll out the next wire.

****

After showering off the dust and sweat he had accumulated from his day's work, Henry decided to go into town to pack a picnic for the walk with Arabella. If this was the only chance he was going to get to make a good impression, he was going to do it right.

He revved up the engine of his car and sped down the path and into town. He reached the store and swiftly pulled into a parking lot. He got out of his car, walked into the store, and grabbed a basket.

Henry perused the aisles, trying to think of what Ara would like to eat. An idea popped into his head. He walked up to a store attendant and asked, "Do you sell picnic baskets?" The attendant, a punk kid with dyed black hair and a lip ring, looked at him with intense annoyance. He led him unwillingly to the clearance aisle, filled with Fourth of July decorations. He pointed to some baskets on the bottom shelf.

Henry thanked him and continued shopping. He looked at his watch. He had to hurry. He threw napkins, plastic silverware, and paper plates into the basket and returned to the food section. He grabbed some different blocks of cheese, a box of mixed crackers, a small container of potato salad, some beef jerky, and, on impulse, a pizza lunchable.

He felt frenzied and had no idea what he was buying, but he was going to see her again and nothing else mattered. He also spun through the liquor section and picked up a bottle of Barefoot Moscato, a type of wine that was always a hit with the ladies and one of his personal favorites, much to the dismay of his wine "connoisseur" friends.

Henry checked his watch and flew over to the cashier. The lady rang up his items, and he quickly scribbled out a check. He grabbed his bags, packed the car, and drove back to his cabin.

When he reached home, Henry parked, grabbed the bags, and put them on the kitchen counter. He pulled out his newly purchased picnic basket and began carefully filling it with his purchases. He changed into clean, dark canvas shorts and a soft blue t-shirt with tennis shoes for hiking. He checked his watch again as he walked out the door, basket in hand, and saw that he was going to be right on time.

Henry carefully placed the basket next to him in the car and drove off to Ara's cabin. He saw that she was just stepping onto the porch when he pulled in her driveway. Henry parked the car and put the basket behind his back as he approached her.

She eyed him curiously. "And what is behind your back?" She asked with an amused smile. She wore a lavender t-shirt, a pair of torn-off jean shorts, and tennis shoes. Her long hair was loose, hanging in a wavy curtain down her back. She also had slipped a small backpack over her right shoulder. It bunched by her hip.

"Nothing." Henry said with a teasing grin. He pulled the basket out from behind his back. "Oh, you mean this? Oh, this is for me. Wait … were you hungry? I didn't even think about you." He tilted his head to one side and looked at her with mock carelessness.

Her eyes lit up. "A picnic, for me? You shouldn't have?" She shook her head and grinned.

He loved that she was being playful with him, already at ease around him.

"You are full of surprises, thank you." She turned and walked toward a light path behind her cabin. "Now, the lake is a little walk from here. So, I hope your appetite can handle it. The path is pretty steep, so be careful. I will lead the way." She turned to walk away but stopped abruptly, turned around and grasped Henry's shoulders firmly. She caught his gaze and looked at him with a serious "the world is about to end" look. "Now, stay close." Her lips curved slowly into a smile, and Henry returned the smile to her and laughed.

Henry was pretty sure he knew where they were going, but he did not let on, of course. He followed her through the woods and up the same path he had walked the night he saw her swimming. The walk was shorter than from his cabin. She lived quite a bit closer, so it was only about fifteen minutes on foot. He watched every step she made and followed each footstep with his own. She moved at a swift pace, but he obeyed her request and gladly stayed close.

They walked into the magical realm of the lake, and Henry realized the view was just as beautiful in the daytime. He stood still in his place, taking in the beauty and wonder surrounding him. The night he first saw Arabella flashed in his memory.

"It is quite somethin', isn't it?" Arabella asked him as she took off her pack, letting it slide onto an emerald patch of grass. She sat down next to the pack, taking a bottle of water out for herself and handed one to Henry.

"Thanks. Ya, I have never seen anything quite like it." He told her as he sat down in the grass next to her, taking a sip of his water.

Ara opened her bottle and took a long drink before answering, "I found it when I was in junior high. Nicole and I were playin' in the woods. I got lost and ended up here. I've come here, like, hundreds of time since then." She fiddled with her water bottle. "I have never run into anyone here before or told anyone about it." She had a faraway look in her dazzling blue eyes when she met Henry's gaze. "So, you are pretty lucky," she told him, her eyes smiling. "It's my favorite place in the world."

"I consider myself very lucky ... honored really." He assured her. Henry opened the basket, pulling out the items inside. He watched Ara's excitement at the wine and other food items.

She laughed out loud when he showed her the pizza lunchable. Henry could listen to her laugh forever.

He placed the wine in between some rocks in a shallow spot in the lake to chill. They opened packages, laughing and talking as they did so, and piled food onto their plates. Henry squeezed some pizza sauce onto Ara's little crust, spreading it with a plastic knife.

She smiled, sprinkled some cheese on top, and zealously took a big bite, smearing sauce on her chin.

Henry laughed, handing her a napkin before taking a large bite of his own mini-pizza.

He walked over to grab the chilled wine bottle. "Would you like some wine?" He asked, gesturing to the bottle as he cracked it open.

"MMM! Yes, please."

Henry looked into the basket and realized he forgot glasses. "Oh, man," Henry groaned.

Arabella smiled and rested her hand on his shoulder. She grabbed the bottle and took a pull from it before handing it back to Henry, who sat very impressed by her confidence. He shook his head at her as he took a drink.

They settled back into the grass to finish their plates. "So, have you lived in Jackson Hole your whole life?" Henry placed a piece of cheese on a cracker and popped it in his mouth.

"Yeah, my parents owned this beautiful ranch not too far from the rodeo grounds. I grew up there. I have never even left Wyoming before." She seemed sort of lost in thought for a moment.

Her final statement surprised Henry, but he did not want to dwell on the statement about her family's ranch. Something about it made her very sad. Her eyes had darkened as she talked with her voice taking a hard edge to it. Henry decided to wait until she told him what that was about. He nodded and said, "So, you have known Nicole and Mitch for quite a while, then?"

Arabella nodded, picking up their lunch garbage and placing it into the basket. "They really are great people." He wanted to ask why they are so protective of her and he wanted to prod further about her family. Henry wanted to know everything about her, but he let it go for the time being.

Henry helped her finish picking up their picnic and stretched onto the warm grass. "So, what did you bring to read?" He asked her with his eyes shut tight against the bright sun.

He heard her sit down next to him in the grass. "Just a new book of poetry I found in the bookstore. Would you like me to read a few to you?"

Henry let out a sigh of contentment. "Yes, I would like that very much."

She cleared her voice and read aloud: "A Bird Came Down the Walk" by Emily Dickinson.

Arabella paused in silent reverence to the poem then turned the page and continued aloud: "A Dream Within a Dream" by Edgar Allan Poe.

She finished the last lines in a softer voice as the words spoke to her:

"O God! can I not save
One from the pitiless wave?
In a night, or in a day,
In a vision, or in none,

Is it therefore the less gone?
All that we see or seem
Is but a dream within a dream."

They both sat in silence pondering the poem and their lives. Henry had always had a special fondness for poetry. He always thought that the beauty of a poem is that no matter the reader, there was always some applicable line that revealed a little bit more about oneself than one had known moments before. As the last two lines rolled off Arabella's tongue, sweet and refined, Henry couldn't help but wonder if this was a dream. And if it was, when was it going to end?

A panicked ache swelled in his belly. The feeling felt familiar, and he was reminded of another time when he had felt a surge of panic, minutes before his wedding.

17
NEW YORK, NEW YORK
November 2, 1991

Henry straightened his tie in the mirror and looked around his surroundings to calm himself. The walls of his room were lined thickly with pastel poppies, lightly arrayed in fine gold flakes of paint portraying dainty leaves. A plate of spirits was set on the countertop, and two crystal glasses sweated their prolonged solitude, beckoning for Henry to taste their soothing elixir.

He scanned the luxurious room before turning his attention back to the full-length mirror mounted on the church's wall. He saw the doubt rising in the dark brown iris of his eyes as he thought about the important step he was about to take: joining his life to another.

"Can I come in?" Henry's dad entered through the side door from the church. He smiled the smile of a proud father as he shut the door behind him.

Henry fought down the rising panic in his heart and smiled at his father. "Of course, Father."

"Henry, I have told you many times how proud you have made me. But today, you will take one of the most important steps of your life, and I could not be prouder."

Henry viewed their reflections in the mirror, seeing how alike he looked to this man. They both shared the same charming dimples when they smiled and the same dark hair and dark eyes. Henry saw the wise and elegant confidence in his father that he hoped to one day reflect as well. "Thank you." He said simply.

"I just hope you are sure about Anne, son." His father's brow furrowed with worry as he brought his gaze level with Henry's slightly visible panicked look. "Is she the absolute one?"

Henry felt a surge of sheer pain overwhelm him in a wave. *If my own father has doubts, shouldn't my own thoughts be seriously considered? Am I making the wrong choice here?* He thought wildly.

Then, Henry felt only anger toward his father and wondered why he had waited for this moment to bring this up. He was minutes away from walking down the aisle to commit himself forever to a woman … forever. "Forever" rang like church bells in his head, resounding with possible merriment or sad doom.

He pulled his mind away only to hear the bells outside ringing out, proclaiming this day of holy matrimony. "Why are you asking this now? Henry asked his father, trying to control the anger in his voice.

"I only want you to be happy, Henry. The love I feel for your mother is so strong, so undeniably true. I never second-guessed it. She completes me, son. I want the same for you." His father put a hand on his shoulder. "I just hope you are not doing this out of obligation to me, so you can live up to some imaginary great expectation you think I have for you? The only great expectation I have for you … is your happiness. And that is all I want for you."

His words lingered in the air, hollowing Henry's heart as his father's words collided with his own doubts. His mind was vividly streaming with questions and concerns, and he was overwhelmed with swirling emotions. Henry looked into his father's smiling, yet concerned brown eyes. He thought of Anne, and the last few months they had shared together. Everything just fell together so perfectly; she was gorgeous, and he felt like a different man with her, like he could be anyone he wanted to be. He had thought she was the one, but his heart suddenly tightened with doubt. Had he misconstrued his real feelings for Anne? Their time together seemed to have gone by in a few instances, and he struggled to remember the reasons he had proposed in the first place. He was about to tell his father all his doubts when Thomas walked in, dressed in a perfectly tailored suit.

He smiled at Henry, and his father handed them both a shot glass, filling them with whiskey before filling himself one. "It's time, Henry. You ready for this?" He slung back his drink. "I sure hope so. I just saw Anne, and man, she is going to knock you over with her beauty."

Henry nodded, taking his own shot and shaking hands with his father. He fought down as much doubt and panic as he could as they walked toward the front of the church. Fear still clung tightly to his heart as he climbed the steps and stood next to the preacher.

The organ switched tunes and began to play a different song. Henry took a deep breath and forced a smile as he saw a dark-haired woman in white begin to walk toward him.

18
HENRY'S JOURNEY
Jackson Hole, Wyoming
August 25, 1992

The sound of the water splashing lightly against the rocks brought him back to the present. Henry rolled onto his side and just looked at Arabella. She dreamily returned his gaze and then averted her eyes, saying nothing, ready to read another.

Henry propped his head on his hand, his elbow holding his weight. She began reading again, but the words reached Henry as slurred and fuzzy. His eyes were the intensity of fire, fierce and fighting tears.

Arabella met his eyes over the top of the book. She stopped reading and looked at him. "Henry." She reached out to touch his hand. "Are you okay?"

He swallowed hard, forcing the knot of fear and inevitable tears down his throat. His voice caught in his throat, his words came out crackled, "I'm fine." He cleared his throat. "It's just..." He hesitated thinking of what to say and coming up short. He said the first diversion that spread itself before his mind. "It's a beautiful poem." He shrugged his shoulders pathetically.

They were both silent.

"It is." She said softly as she looked over the lake to the waterfall.

They shared a glance, and Henry shook away his thoughts. But he wanted to get to know her, so Henry took a leap. "So, are your parents still living at the ranch where you grew up?"

Ara played with the cover of the book, turning it over once or twice, and answered, "No, they moved down South for retirement. My mother developed a condition that causes her to need year-round warmth. The cold is the enemy, and the mountains, well, the mountains are not the place for them anymore."

Henry felt sorry that her parents were so far away and told her so. "Do they like life in the sun at least?"

Ara nodded. "Yes." She replied simply. "So, where did you grow up, mystery man?" she teased.

Henry laughed, knowing the question would come up sooner or later. He thought that if she was going to be straight with him, he could at least tell her most of the truth about himself. She probably has never heard of him. "I actually grew up in New York, and I lived there my whole life as well. My family did lots of traveling, though. I saw the whole world before I ever hit my teens."

Ara seemed intrigued. "Where was your favorite place?" She leaned forward, causing her hair to swing forward around her shoulders.

Henry thought a moment. "Well, I would have to say Ireland. I loved France at first, when I was younger. I was a hopeless romantic, if you can believe that."

They both laughed lightly. Ara's eyes flashed with delight as she smiled at him and waited for him to continue.

"But after so many business trips to Paris ... It kinda caused me to see the real city. It's actually really dirty and just not romantic at all." Henry gazed off into the field as he thought of it.

She smiled, slowly twirling a piece of hair with her fingertips. "Ireland. What is it like?"

He laid back down on the grass, raising his face into the warm sun. "It is breathtakingly beautiful, so green and lush. The mountains and scenery here are pretty amazing as well. I would rank it pretty close to Ireland." He turned his head to look straight into her eyes.

"Just pretty close?" Arabella said, looking down at him with a teasing smile.

"Very close." He said and thought that Ara put Wyoming ahead of Ireland, but he kept that thought to himself, for now at least.

They listened to the lake rippling against the shore for a moment. "So, I have to ask. Why do you live in the middle of nowhere in a cabin? Is it just for some peace and quiet?" He waited for an answer, but he could only hear the lake. "Ara?" He turned, placing his head on his elbow and looked at her.

She was looking down at the grass, gently twisting it with her fingers. "Partly." Her voice was strained. "I do love the mountains."

"What about your family's ranch?"

She said simply with a hardened voice, "I lost it." Ara stood up quickly. "Let's swim. I'm feelin' warm." She began skipping to the water's edge, pulling off her outer clothing in the process.

Henry decided not to press the subject and upset her. And Ara in the lake ... he couldn't turn that down.

He jumped up and ran to the lakes edge, tearing off his shirt and jeans in the process. He yelled out with excitement as he gracefully dived into the water, "YAHOO!" The water felt icy and cool against his sun-warmed skin. It felt like the first time he bathed in the creek, only he wasn't taken by surprise. He swam up for a breath and felt a second splash.

Henry saw Ara surface and watched as she brushed her wet hair from her face. He swam over to her, and she turned and faced him, smiling.

"Oh, it feels so good! I just LOVE this lake!" She said with glee, smiling from ear to ear.

Henry nodded. "It feels good to swim circles around you ... slowpoke!" He laughed and swam quickly around her with powerful strokes.

She giggled and pushed him as he swam. "Ooh really?!?" Ara said, acting as if she was impressed. "But did you know I am part fish?!" She flew through the water to the other side of the lake with surprising speed.

Henry laughed and shook his head at her. With strong arms, he sliced through the water until he was right in front of her, so close that she moved back to touch the rock wall behind her. He smiled dangerously. "Maybe I am part shark?" he teased as he moved in closer to her.

"I sure hope not." Ara said shakily, whether from cold or from being nervous, Henry did not know.

"And why is that?"

"Because ...," she whispered.

Henry began to lean toward her, his eyes on her mouth. "Ya?" he asked, moving even closer.

She gazed deeply into his eyes and slowly put her arms around his neck.

Henry's heart beat so fast that he could hear it in his ears. He closed his eyes, but not before he caught a devious glimmer in hers. Dazed, Henry did not figure out what it meant until his nose was being flooded with water as she jumped on his shoulders, thoroughly dunking him.

He kicked hard until he broke the surface, blowing water from his nose and shaking out his ears. He looked across the lake and saw Ara climbing out.

She pulled her shirt over her head and caught him watching her, giving him a victorious smile. "Sure you're the shark?" she asked laughing.

He looked at her with stifled amusement, shook his head, and laughed with her. "Wait 'till I get you, then we will know!" He swam through the water toward her, using his arms to pull him effortlessly out of the lake.

He picked up his clothes and walked toward her soaking wet. He thought he saw her attraction to him reflected in her face as she watched him walking, dripping with water and shaking his hair out of his eyes.

But she tried to look away as he neared her. Henry reached out and lightly caught her arms, gently forcing her to look at him. He just smiled down at her and shook his head, dripping water on her.

She wrinkled her nose and tried to pull free of him with a laugh. Henry let go with an answering chuckle and pulled on his clothes. He turned, noticing the sun dipping lower into the sky. "Should we start heading down the hill?" He asked.

Ara nodded, and they started packing everything back up. Henry put Ara's pack on his shoulders before she could grab it and picked up the picnic basket. Ara just shook her head and led Henry back down the path.

As she walked, she started to sing:
"Won't you come see about me?
I'll be alone, dancing you know it baby
Tell me your troubles and doubts
Giving me everything inside and out and
Love's strange so real in the dark
Think of the tender things that we were working on
Slow change may pull us apart
When the light gets into your heart, baby
Don't You Forget About Me
Don't Don't Don't Don't
Don't You Forget About Me
Will you stand above me?
Look my way, never love me
Rain keeps falling, rain keeps falling
Down, down, down
Will you recognize me?
Call my name or walk on by
Rain keeps falling, rain keeps falling
Down, down, down, down … hmmm, hm, hmm." [3]

Henry could tell that music moved her just as poetry did. She danced circles around him as she sang as if she were singing it just for him, a private show. He thought her voice was perfection. The silky and smooth notes gracefully emanated out of her mouth.

The walk down the path went much too fast in Henry's eyes. He could not get enough of her voice. It was like that of an angel's, pure, fresh, and innocent.

They neared her cabin just as the sun sank below the horizon. Rays of color shot off her amber roof. Ara's singing lulled into a low hum as they walked up the porch steps.

Henry put down the basket and placed her pack on a little table. Ara fished her key out of her pocket and unlocked the door. She turned to Henry and smiled. "I had a great time today." Her eyes sparkled as she leaned against the door frame.

Henry nodded. "Me too."

"Well … have a good evening, then." Ara started to go through her door.

"Ara?" Henry asked, hesitating, not sure how to express just how much he had enjoyed the day.

She turned back toward him. "Yes, Henry?"

"Thank you. For everything." Her eyes lit up a little. "Good night, Arabella." He turned and walked down the stairs toward his car.

"Good night, Henry."

He looked toward her as he opened his car door.

Leaning against her porch, she blew a small kiss his way. She smiled laughingly and walked into her home.

.

19
NEW YORK, NEW YORK
May 19, 1991

Henry snapped the small, black box, which contained the five-karat princess-cut diamond set in perfect, white gold, shut. He had looked at the ring a hundred times since buying it yesterday. Over and over he watched as it sparkled in the sunlight before being shut out in darkness. He hoped Anne would like it and was worried she wouldn't. He imagined the scenario in his mind of Anne turning him down and the devastation that would result. Thomas had agreed with him on the ring choice at the jewelry store, saying it was perfect for her, so he tried to reassure himself with that fact.

Henry tucked the box into the inside pocket of his black suit jacket and checked his watch. "Time to go. Wish me luck." He said grimly to his reflection.

Henry walked out into the chilling night air and climbed into the back of one of the family limousines. "To Anne's house, please," he politely prompted the driver before rolling up the partition between them.

On the short drive to Anne's, Henry rehearsed his plan, along with the perfect words he hoped he would be able to relay to her. His palms were sweaty.

The car pulled to a slow stop in front of Anne's front step, and Henry jumped out and walked to let her doorman know he was there. He walked back nervously to the limo and straightened his tie in the dark window.

Less than a minute later, she came down the steps gracefully, in a tight fitting black dress that flowed out lightly at her hips. She graced a pair of black leather stilettos, her smooth legs shining in the moonlight.

Her hair was loose, smoothly curled to flow around her face and down her back. Her lips were crimson, and her eyes were piercing.

She smiled at Henry, taking his hand and allowing him to help her into the car. Henry saw the approval in her eyes at the limo. He preferred to drive his own sports car, but Anne liked the limousine.

Henry kissed her on the cheek before telling the driver over the intercom to take them to the restaurant. Anne asked which one they were going to, but Henry shook his head, smiling as he told her it was a surprise. Anne looked amused as she grabbed onto Henry's hand and kissed him softly. Within a few minutes, they pulled up to the Chaterelle, Anne's favorite French restaurant.

Anne gasped with excitement as Henry helped her out of the car and up the marble steps. They stepped onto the plush, deep purple carpet and to the hostess stand, passing a crowd of waiting guests who all turned to stare at Anne as she walked. She always stole the stares of every room she walked into.

The hostess greeted Henry, "Good evening, Mr. Tudor." A staff member took their coats as another showed them right to their table. Their table was beside a tall bay window, set up specially for them. The moonlight was playing the shadows on the street outside, and a man walking a dog passed by as they began to take their seats.

Henry pulled Anne's chair out for her, kissing her cheek lightly as she settled into the rich comfort. He moved around the table, seating himself, and looking at her beautiful face in the soft candlelight.

Henry spoke to the waiter in French, telling him their orders. "As you wish, sir." The waiter responded. Another waiter filled their glasses with Anne's favorite red wine.

Anne smiled, "You are spoiling me tonight, Henry." She looked around the room in cool happiness.

"Believe me, Anne, there is plenty more spoiling to come." Henry reached across the table for her hand. He curled his lips into a timid smile and looked into her green eyes.

Their salads arrived. Henry moved most of the lettuce around on his plate, eating some but not tasting a single bite on account of his nerves. He kept feeling his pocket to make sure the ring was still there, making him appear fidgety and nervous. Every time he felt the corners of the little box, he sighed a sigh of relief.

"Are you all right, Henry?" Anne asked, looking at him in a mix of amusement and worry.

"Just fine, mademoiselle." Henry squeezed her hand and smiled.

Anne began to gossip softly about others in the room. Henry listened to her voice, taking in none of her words.

The main course arrived. Henry bit into his delicious food, as Anne gushed about hers. He agreed with her, and they shared light conversation as they ate and drank wine until right before they were stuffed.

Henry reminded Anne to save room, and a few seconds later, Anne's favorite French chocolate silk trifle arrived at the table. Henry had them specially make this for her tonight because it was something no longer on the menu. She smiled at Henry as they shared the desert. He noticed some suspicion growing in her eyes, so he began to talk about work, and Thomas to try to throw her off.

They were soon finished devouring the decadent dessert. Henry helped Anne out of her chair and into her warm coat. They passed by the huge, waiting crowd and back down the steps. He helped her into the car, whispering to the driver their next destination.

"Where are we going now, Henry?" Her voice was beginning to sound very suspicious.

He squeezed her hand. "Just trust me, Anne." He leaned back and lit a cigar to calm his nerves. The city passed as they drove slightly upstate.

Henry felt his stomach jump as the limo slowed to a halt. The driver opened the door and helped Anne out. Henry took a deep breath and followed.

"What is this? Where are we?" Anne demanded.

Henry just grabbed her hand and walked her along a short path. A stream ran along one side of the path in the park Henry had always visited with his parents as a child. They rounded a grove of oak trees and went into a clearing, surrounded by trees.

Anne gasped as she took in the hundreds of white Japanese lanterns hung in the clearing. Red roses and tiny white lights clung to the old, white, wooden arch where his parents had been married.

Henry pulled Anne gently along the rose-petal lined path to the arch. He had his eyes cast low as he led her down the path, his other hand in his pocket, but, when he turned to look at her, she finally understood the purpose of the evening.

Registering her realization, Henry stopped and held both of her hands. He was silent for a moment, bringing her left hand to his lips. He was always so confident in life, but now, in this moment, he was vulnerable, timidly sweet in his approach.

The words he had rehearsed were creeping further and further from his mind as he began to speak. "Anne, you are the perfect woman for my life. I love you. Please make me the happiest man on Earth." He knelt down on his knee, still holding onto her left hand, and smiled up at her. "Will you marry me?"

"Oh, Henry. Yes, of course I will." Anne's eyes were caught in his before they broke away, searching for a ring.

Henry took the box from his pocket and slid the ring smoothly onto her finger smoothly despite his shaking hands. He kissed her quickly and then told her, "Now, we have to go. I have one more surprise."

Anne looked stunned as she still gazed down at the ring, turning it this way and that to fully inspect it. "Another surprise?"

"Come on!" He grabbed her hand and, in his excitement, practically raced her down the path back to the car.

They drove in silence with the occasional gasp of excitement from Anne. Minutes later, they arrived at the Tudor mansion, which was fully lit and obviously filled with people.

Henry helped Anne out of the car and into the main hallway.

Everyone cheered and clapped as Henry announced their engagement. Champagne was poured and passed around by the house staff.

Anne glowed as she discussed the events of the evening with a crowd of listeners, bathing in the glory of attention. She held her left hand daintily in the air for everyone to gasp at its beauty.

Henry shook hands with everyone and looked around for Thomas. He finally spotted him at the top of the stairs, leaning on the banister and staring down at Anne. Henry felt an odd sensation as he watched the sadness in Thomas' face.

But it lasted only a brief second. Thomas caught his eye and smiled broadly as he descended the stairs to shake Henry's hand.

20
HENRY'S JOURNEY
Jackson Hole, Wyoming
August 26, 1992

The sharp sunlight streaming through his cabin window woke Henry from a peaceful sleep. He blinked open his eyes, grinning as he remembered the wonderful day. Stretching his arms over his head, he thought of the satisfying work he had done for Bill, the perfect picnic with Ara, and the way she had wished him good night.

He slowly climbed out of bed, his sore muscles, mainly his arms and shoulders, protesting as he did so. Peering out of the window, he saw it was going to be another beautiful Wyoming day.

In the kitchen, he filled himself a glass of cold water and thought of what he wanted to do with his time this morning. He looked out the kitchen window into the beautiful scenery and decided a hike, slow to start, would be perfect. His stomach growled, and he decided to buy some groceries first, as his fridge was still perfectly bare.

He pulled on jeans and a shirt and headed to town.

Jackson was slow this morning. He guessed it was early, maybe 7:30, but he had no need to rush and enjoyed the feeling of strolling through the quiet aisles of Jackson's grocery store. Henry filled his cart with necessities: bread, milk, assorted meats, vegetables, fruits, and potatoes. He threw some granola bars and trail mix into the cart and grabbed some ground coffee on his way to the check-out line.

The clerk greeted him with tired eyes and a small smile as she rang up his items.

Once back in his cabin, Henry unloaded the items and put them away quickly, eager to hike. He brewed a cup of coffee and made some toast and eggs as he pondered the trails he had seen coming up the mountain.

While he ate and sipped his coffee, he pulled on shorts, a tank-top-style work-out shirt, his hiking boots and a baseball cap. He packed a small back pack with some trail mix and a water bottle. He brushed his teeth and flung open the door, excited for a long walk in the mountains.

Henry spent the morning and a bit of the afternoon exploring a wonderful and complicated trail that started on the far side of his cabin. The trail was skinny by any definition, and he wondered what animal or animals had made this one, as it clearly wasn't manmade. He saw deer and other wildlife, including wild horses, beautiful streams and valleys, and, of course, the Teton mountains. He loved the peace and sounds of nature that surrounded him, and he felt at ease with a quiet heart and mind. He found himself on more than one occasion pausing and taking a deep breath and releasing. Pine was the prevalent smell. He didn't there would ever come a day again when he would smell the scent of fresh pine and not think of this place.

Finally, he returned back to the cabin, looking forward to an afternoon nap to rest his sore body. As he neared the front door, he noticed someone was standing there with her hand ready to knock. He would know that wavy blonde ponytail anywhere; it was Ara!

"Ara?" He asked, smiling as he drew closer.

She turned with a surprised smile on her face. "Henry! I was just about to knock." She explained with her hand falling to the hem of her cut-off shorts to twirl the loose, fraying threads.

"I was just out hiking." He huffed out, breathless from exertion and from surprise at seeing Ara unexpectedly.

She looked him over, smiling. "I can see that. How was the hike?"

He took off his backpack and drained the last of his water. "It was awesome! I mean, I'm pretty much wiped from work yesterday, but I looked out my window this morning and couldn't fight the urge to get outdoors. So peaceful and beautiful."

Ara nodded in agreement. "I know exactly how you feel." She started fiddling with her hands and spinning a ring on her middle finger over and over again in between the small silence that resounded. She hung her head for a just a second before looking up again, like she just gave herself a 5-second pep talk. "So, hey, I was wonderin' if you had any … dinner plans tonight?" Nervously, she turned her head slightly and twirled the end of her ponytail.

Henry thought she had to be the most adorable woman on the planet and gutsy, too. It's not every woman who will ask a guy out. "No, I have nothing planned." His heart leaped in anticipation of her answer.

"Well, I was wonderin' if you wanted to come over ... I was goin' to cook and thought maybe ... It would be nice to visit a little more?"

"Definitely!" He said a little too quickly. "I mean, ya, sure, that sounds great."

She smiled at him and walked off his front step. "Okay, I will see ya in a few hours then? You can head over any time."

"Okay," he managed and smiled, unable to take his eyes off her. "See ya soon."

Ara walked away with grace, her ponytail swinging between her shoulder blades. He thought he heard her softly singing a tune as she went.

He walked inside on nervous legs and decided to shower off before his nap, if he would be able to sleep at all now! As he showered in the freezing water, Henry replayed their conversation in his mind, excited to spend more time with her.

After the cold shower, he tried to lie down for a bit, but he was too nervous and ended up selecting one of the few books on the shelves in his living room. It was a Louis L'Amour book titled *Ride the Dark Trail*. He took the book out to the back porch of the cabin and settled down to read.

The book had a great storyline, and the next few hours passed quicker and quicker with every turn of the page. Soon, it was time to head over to Ara's.

He headed inside and pulled on dark jeans and a white polo shirt. The shirt was from New York, but he wanted to be a little bit dressy since she had invited him for dinner. He pulled on his suede loafers as well and headed out the door toward Ara's.

As he climbed the front porch, nerves fluttered in his gut, and he took a deep breath before knocking.

A few seconds passed and the door opened with a smiling Arabella looking at him. She had her hair tied back in a loose, low ponytail and was wearing a light-yellow sundress. "Hey, Henry. Come on in." She pulled the door back, and he walked inside.

He looked around the cabin. It resembled his own, only it had a definitive feminine touch with white lace curtains in the kitchen windows and several pictures hung on the wall. She had very eclectic taste, but everything fit so well together. A large plank of grey driftwood had black etchings of wildflowers along the edge, and a painting of a woman, elegantly dressed, walking down a dirt path surrounded by thick trees was framed in an antique gold frame. Some family photos were hung here and there with tiny mirrors dispersed through the array of art that made all the pieces fit together as one. The same wooden beams crisscrossed the ceiling.

Looking up, he saw that she also had a loft built over the main floor. Tiny steps built into the wall led up to the loft. The loft was lined with bookcases filled with hundreds of books. A wooden ladder stood perched to the side of one shelf. A small, plush couch and chair filled the space in what he was sure was the living room. Tucked in the corner, on the far end of the bookshelves, sat a worn wicker chair with a giant pillow for cushion in the middle. A deep purple throw blanket sat rumpled and used with a leather-bound book lying open atop it.

Her home smelled welcoming, like wildflowers blossomed in the eaves of each wooden beam that held the structure together.

Henry allowed his eyes to wander to the kitchen to find Ara pulling things out of the refrigerator.

"Do you know how to cook?" She asked, looking a little nervous but happy.

Henry leaned against the counter. "I know how to make a few breakfast-type dishes, including pouring cereal into a bowl." He smiled sheepishly. "So, I guess that would be a no."

Ara smiled back and shook her head. "Well, tonight is your lucky night. I am goin' to teach you to make spaghetti." She pulled a lavender apron over her head and tied it around her waist. She reached into a drawer and found a black apron with girly frills on the end for Henry. She held it out to him and shot him a look that said "you are totally wearing this," and Henry looked at it with apprehension.

He took the apron and said, "All right, but don't get mad at me if whatever I make tastes burnt or raw or whatever other terrible taste there is out there."

She smiled as she filled a pot with water and set it on the stove. "I will take it easy on you, I promise." She turned on the burner and turned to put a fry pan on another burner. She moved with ease around the kitchen, like she had done this exact thing hundreds of times. "Okay, put the beef into this pan." Ara put a wooden spoon into his hand. "Just move the meat around so it doesn't burn and chop it into little pieces as it browns." She grabbed an onion and began chopping it into small pieces before scooping up all the diced onions and dropping the chopped onion into Henry's pan.

"Am I doing this right?" Henry asked as he moved the spoon around the pan in a circle. The meat hissed with heat.

Ara inspected the browning meat. "Um, yes. Just make sure to flip the meat as you stir and chop with your spoon." She placed her hand lightly over his on the spoon, showing him the correct movements. "Like this," she said.

Henry's stomach jumped into his chest as her hand touched his. But he held still and allowed her to demonstrate.

She pulled her hand away and checked the water to see if it was boiling. Henry concentrated on his task, feeling important and special to be allowed in her kitchen cooking with her.

Ara soon poured in a can of diced tomatoes and tomato sauce. She also added a spaghetti seasoning sauce and asked him to stir it all together as she poured in the noodles into the boiling water. She scurried around the kitchen, buzzing with energy.

Henry just kept on stirring and watching her in amusement. She was humming now, swaying her small hips back and forth to her own song.

She scooted up next to Henry and quickly poked her finger in the sauce and taking a taste. She made a popping sound when she pulled her fingertip out of her mouth. "Mmm," she said. "Needs a little salt."

"Can I have a taste?" Henry opened his mouth and waited for her to bring him a taste, playfully grabbing her hand and leading her to dip her finger in the sauce again for him.

She took her big wooden spoon and dipped it in the sauce and put it to Henry's lips.

He tasted it and licked his lips.

Ara laughed and tried it again herself.

"So, when did you learn how to cook?" Henry asked as he went back to stirring carefully.

She walked behind him and began setting her small wooden table with white china plates. "Oh, I don't even really remember when I first learned." Ara grabbed silverware out of a drawer and placed it on the table by each plate. "I do know that my mother taught me, though. She was a great cook." A faraway look came into her eyes.

"Well, by the smell of this dinner, I bet you take after her in that department."

Ara smiled at him and grabbed the pot to drain the noodles. She drained them in the sink, tossed them with olive oil, and poured them into a dish. "Will you pour the sauce into this bowl for me?"

Henry carefully poured the sauce into the designated bowl and placed it on the table. He took off his apron and watched her open the fridge and bend down to reach the already washed carrots inside.

She turned and almost dropped the carrots when she saw him watching her. She pretended nothing happened, took off her apron, and told him to sit down. She scooped a huge helping of noodles onto his plate and added sauce for him. Then she moved to her chair and sat down, laying her napkin in her lap before serving herself. "

Oh, man." Henry moaned, causing Ara to look alarmed. "This is delicious." He flashed a devious smile at her and watched her relax. They both ate in silence for a minute. "I really like your cabin by the way," Henry said in between bites.

Ara spun some noodles around with her fork before asking, "Is it much different than your cabin?"

Henry nodded. "Well, the layout is basically the same, your collection of art and books far outweighs what is at my place. And that loft is great. Did that come in the cabin when you bought it?"

"Oh, no. Mitch and one of his friends added that in for me." She looked up at it. "It is great, isn't it?"

Henry nodded in agreement and spooned more spaghetti into his mouth, trying not to make a mess. He dabbed his chin with his napkin, leaving red spaghetti stains behind.

Ara looked him over. "So, what was it like growing up in New York?"

He thought for a moment as he chewed and set his fork down to speak.

"Busy, always busy," he said. "And lonely. My parents were always gone, and I was home-schooled by tutors. It's funny actually, in a city with millions of people, I felt so alone, and then I came out here, to the wilderness, and technically I'm alone, but I feel … just kind of accompanied by something."

"That sounds hard." She gave him a sympathetic look. "Well, you must have had some fun once in a while?"

"Oh, yes. Like I said earlier, I have traveled around the world. My parents have a summer house in Spain that I really enjoyed. We always went over Christmas, and another family went with us. The weather was so warm as were the people. I picked up Spanish after a few years, along with Italian and French. I ran around the beach with Thomas … It was great times. We felt so free." Henry could not believe he was opening up to her like this. She was just so understanding, nodding and smiling at the right times.

"So, home-schooling, tutors, summer houses, and traveling around the world … I am guessing you did not struggle with money?" She asked and Henry nodded in response. "Who is Thomas? A childhood friend?"

Henry nodded again. "Yes, Thomas and I go way back. All the way back, actually. His parents and mine did business together, and we were born around the same time. We did everything together since then. Now, Thomas and I do business together as well as maintain our friendship."

Ara asked to hear a few stories of the adventures of the two of them, and Henry obliged, telling her some of his favorite times of their youth.

Ara started piling the dishes together, rinsing them off and placing them in the sink. Henry got up and helped her. She turned on the sink water and poured soap into the running water.

Henry playfully edged her out of the way. "You made dinner. I can do the dishes." Ara laughed, seeming pleased with this gentleman act and continued clearing off the table, obliging to his wishes.

"So, what kind of business do you guys share then?" Ara asked him.

Henry rubbed a spot on the plate he was scrubbing. He did not turn around but continued concentrating. "Oh, just corporation, businessy stuff," he answered vaguely as he rinsed off the plate with clean water. His voice must have told her not to push any farther because she just brought him the final stack of dishes and picked up a drying towel.

The window in front of the sink was open, allowing cool night air to stream in. Henry could hear the soothing sounds of the crickets chirping, along with the wind blowing through the trees. He felt so happy and complete standing next to Ara doing dishes. It was so simple, but he loved it more than anything else in the world. New York seemed so far away; it was like a hazy dot off in the far corners of his mind.

Ara began to sing softly as she dried.

Henry listened to her voice as he continued the dishes. The sweet notes were just as calming as the night air. She stacked the dried dishes and put them away.

Henry drained the sink and turned the large pot upside down to dry.

Ara thanked him for helping with the dishes, giving his arm a loving squeeze. "Why don't you go sit on the couch, and I will grab us something to drink." She turned without waiting and opened the fridge.

Henry walked into the living room and sat down on the couch. He noticed the fireplace in front of him and decided a fire would be nice. He looked up as Ara walked over to him, holding two glasses of iced tea.

"Do you mind if I start a fire for us?"

Ara sat down next to him, taking a sip of her tea before answering. "That would be perfect." She set down her glass and hugged a throw pillow to her chest, tucking her knees in.

He walked over to the fireplace and grabbed some kindling from an old wicker basket filled with small branches and newspaper. He rolled a few sheets of paper into the kindling before lighting a match to get it started. He blew on the flames to get them flowing throughout his pile of kindling. Soon, he had a steady flame and added a smaller log to it, jostling it with a metal poker, and then adding another log. Before long, a warm glow was emitting from the fireplace, and warmth filled the cabin.

He stepped back over to the couch and sat down next to Ara.

She turned her body to face him, still holding tightly to the pillow with one hand, sipping tea with the other, seemingly with a strong thought on her mind.

Henry grabbed his drink again, taking a deep swallow. He tried to think of what to ask her.

"I've been married!" She suddenly announced.

He almost dropped his drink. "What?" He said confused, trying to come to terms with this information. He set down his glass before he spilled it everywhere.

She looked so distressed, her brow furrowed and her forehead wrinkled with worry that he moved closer to her.

Henry grabbed one of her shaking hands and held it between both of his own. Her other hand was clamped tightly to the pillow which was still in front of her.

"Oh, Henry. I just had to tell you. It has been eatin' away at me since I met you. Like this deep, dark secret that was just darkenin' everythin' beautiful."

Henry just watched her silently, still stunned by her outburst.

"All I want to say is that it did not end well. And I am livin' in this cabin because of it." She looked down at the couch, shaking her head slightly and playing with the fringe of the pillow.

Henry brushed a strand of hair back from her face, sliding his hand beneath her chin and tilting her face up to him. Her eyes looked so sad, it broke Henry's heart. "Whoever hurt you is a horrible person. How could a man, with any sense at all, ever let a woman as beautiful and intelligent and...," his words rolled off his tongue with passion, "incredibly amazing as you let you get away?" He accentuated the word incredibly as he said it and rested his hand lightly on the side of her thigh.

Ara's lip trembled as she asked, "You think I am beautiful?"

Henry laughed. "Of course, I do. You are the most beautiful woman I have ever laid eyes on. And believe me, I have seen my share of gorgeous women. Nothing compares, I promise you. If you only knew my thoughts for you ..." He looked down into her eyes, ensuring their sincerity.

She stared up at him and managed a tiny smile.

Henry opened his mouth to say something but was cut off when a knock sounded at the door.

Ara looked surprised and startled. "Would you mind getting the door?"

"Of course." He walked to the door and opened it.

"Henry?" Mitch stared at him stunned. Standing next to him, Nicole also looked taken aback. They were both silent as they took in Henry, answering Arabella's front door at nine in the evening.

"Uh, hey, Mitch, Nicole. Come in." Henry stuttered out as he led them into the cabin.

Ara looked up from her spot on the couch, saw the newcomers and turned deep red. "Hey, guys."

"Hey, Partner. Hey, Ara!" Mitch bounded in, pulled off his boots, and plopped down next to Ara.

Nicole smiled and said, "Well, we don't want to interrupt …We were out for a drive and were goin' to stop by to see you, Ara." She slid into the chair on the other side of Ara.

Ara shook her head and smiled. "No, no. It is great to see you guys. Henry and I just made dinner and were just … chattin'." She tugged on the ends of her hair and twirled them around her finger. "Oh, would you both like some sweet tea?"

"Sure!" Mitch said, never one to turn down anything.

"Just some water for me?" Nicole asked.

"All right, then. Ara, you stay put. I can get them" Henry walked over to the counter and filled two glasses before bringing them over to the new guests.

"Ugh, such a gentleman!" Mitch groaned.

Nicole and Ara laughed, rolling their eyes at Mitch.

"So what were you two up to today?" He asked, trying to ease Ara's nerves.

"Not much," Mitch shook his head and winked at Nicole. "We had the day off, so we just … hung around at the ranch, took it easy."

Everyone smiled, and Nicole shook her head good-naturedly at her husband with a light blush coloring her cheeks.

Nicole sipped her water. "So, what about you two? We haven't seen either of you since the bar after the rodeo…"

Ara moved to sip her tea again. "Um, nothing too much." Ara looked up and nodded her head to reassure them, to reassure herself.

"Ara took me to her lake yesterday," Henry said, trying to take the heat off Ara. "Wow, what a place!"

Mitch and Nicole nodded as they thought of the lake. "Ya, that has always been Ara's spot," Nicole said. Her tone sounded as if she was really saying, "We knew her first. Who are you to come inside this family?"

Henry nodded and asked quickly, "So how is everything at the ranch, Mitch?"

"Everythin' is going swell! I am glad to be home. The hands were gettin' restless to see their old boss." Mitch patted his hands on his jeans and sat back in his seat on the couch, looking comfortable and satisfied. If he was upset about seeing Henry here with Ara, like it was his home as much as hers, he didn't show it. It was good old Mitch as usual.

"Well, I bet your workers were happy to see their boss back in town." Henry said with a hint of teasing sarcasm. "I would like to see your ranch sometime. Unless you have another big rodeo to train for?"

"No ... rodeo season is done for the summer." Mitch looked over at Nicole as if for permission to say something. She lightly blushed and nodded. "As far as future rodeos, I am done with those. A father needs to be around for his family." His eyes twinkled as he smiled with sheer joy oozing from part of him.

"A father?" Ara asked confused. She looked at Nicole who smiled at her. "Oh my goodness! Congratulations!" Ara jumped up to embrace her.

Henry jumped up as well and shook Mitch's hand, but Mitch stood up and pulled him in for a big manly hug, bursting with fatherly pride.

"Congratulations, man." Henry couldn't have been happier for them. Even more, he felt like part of their family, and he was warmed with the thought and touched by their openness with him, the new guy.

"Thanks, Henry." Mitch looked around smiling at the others. "We just found out yesterday and couldn't wait to tell you. I just could hardly hold it in any longer! You know me and secrets, Ara. Can't keep my mouth shut, really." He clapped his hands together and almost rolled with laughter onto the couch. "I just can't stop feeling exhilarated by all of this. Let's *do* something, anything. You guys wanna play a game? What do you have, Ara?"

She thought for a minute. "Well, my parents sent me Uno as a sort of gag gift?"

"Uno, it is!" Mitch declared with gusto and ran off in search of the game as Ara pointed to the kitchen. He came back a minute later and began dealing cards with excitement.

They all laughed, positioned themselves in a circle, and picked up their cards. Ara grinned as she set down her first card, and Mitch theatrically had to draw from the pile.

Stories were told, and they laughed so much that Henry often held his stomach as it ached from laughing. As time passed with triumphs and losses, Henry found himself feeling as if he had always known these three people. He smiled around at them and felt as if he finally were someplace he could call "home."

21
SUMMER VACATION
June 21, 1975

A boy sat on the shore of the beach tossing stones and pebbles into the expansive sea. Each stone flew off his fingertips with grace as if he had been sitting on that beach for hours just tossing rocks away along with the day. Each bounced along the surface before landing noiselessly and disappearing into the dark unknown of the water.

The sun was perched low in the sky, and a nightly chill began to fall on the boy. He paused mid-throw and kicked at his pile of rocks next to his sneakers, which lay strewn to the side of his bare feet. He shivered and pulled his hood over his head.

Looking up the beach, he saw a beautiful, young girl. Her sun-bleached blond hair wildly spun with the wind. She was running along the beach chasing the seagulls, wearing blue jeans rolled up above her ankles with a large rip in the knee and a simple white t-shirt that toiled with the wind. She frolicked with the seagulls as they cawed, and she tried to "caw" back.

The boy smiled and laughed to himself, but she heard him and stopped mid-jump and looked over at him. Her cheeks were flushed from the chase.

She smiled at him sweetly and skipped over next to the boy and sat down, grabbing her knees. "Hey..." The girl nudged the boy with her elbow. "What are you doing over here?"

"Nothing." The boy was reserved, shy.

"Nothing?" She looked up at his face and noticed that he looked sad. "What is this pile of rocks for?"

"Skipping."

The girl looked at him quizzically, picking up a stone in her hand and rolling it around. "Huh?" Her nose scrunched up in inquisition.

"You've never skipped a rock before?" The boy was aghast with shock.

She allowed a quirky little smile to sprawl across her face. "Show me?" She stood up and extended her hand to help him get up.

He took her hand in his, and she pulled him up.

"So ... how do I do it?"

The boy bent over and picked up a smooth flat stone from his pile, caught the gaze of the girl, and flashed a bright smile. Never leaving that gaze, he effortlessly skipped the rock across the water. It bounced along the surface four or five times before succumbing to the waves.

She scrunched her nose and pursed her lips, "I didn't see how you did it!"

"Here." He handed her a rock. "Why don't you just try it?"

Glancing at the rock, and then the water, she swiped it quickly from his hand and confidently muttered, "Okay, yeah, I can do this. No problem." Taking a step forward toward the water, she wound up and released the rock with a look of ferocity and determination in her eyes.

It flew from her hands straight behind her, hitting the boy right in the gut. He doubled over, seemingly grabbing at his wound.

She ran over to him, yelling out, "Are you all right? I am *so* sorry ... Wait, are you crying?"

The boy looked up with a smile that went on for miles and burst out laughing hysterically. He fell to his back in laughter.

The girl stood over him with her hands on her hips, laughing in between smart remarks like, "This isn't funny, you know," and "Never would have happened if my *teacher* would have just taught me!"

She finally gave up, and they both just succumbed to the laughter like the stones to the waves.

"Do you live here?" The laughter quieted, and she kept the silence from making its presence known. The beach was surrounded by silence, save for their their fluttering voices of words and laughter.

"On the beach ... uhh no, I do have a home."

She giggled, "No, I mean do you live *here* ... in Spain?"

"Oh, no. I'm here with my parents on vacation, sorta."

"Sorta?"

"Well, we didn't come here for a vacation. My father is here on business, but I'm not. So technically, I am on vacation ... sorta."

"Oh, I get it." The girl nodded in understanding.

"What about you?"

"Same ... sorta" She laughed. "Only, I'm here with my family for the sole purpose of vacation. It's my first time overseas, and I think I'm in love with it." She gazed out at the sea. "I could live here, I think."

They continued on in careless bantering, asking each other basic questions, then silly ones, then serious ones. "How old are you? Can you curl your tongue? Have you ever had a girlfriend?" On and on they innocently talked.

A friendship formed, and they both shared things they had never shared with anyone before. She was from Connecticut, and her parents owned a winery. He was from New York, and his father worked at some big-town business firm.

Before long, the sun began setting on their time together. Longer and longer silences filled the space between their conversations as they realized they soon must part.

"We're going home tomorrow." The girl rested her head on her knees, her face turned to him.

"I wish we had met sooner." The boy looked at her morosely.

A voice echoed from over the hill behind them. The girl turned to look at her mother calling her name, "Ana, come on, it's time to come home, honey"

"Coming!" Ana yelled back. She stood up and brushed the sand off the back of her jeans and then extended her hand again to help the boy up.

He took her hand and stood. She didn't let go of it. Her blonde locks of hair were blowing wildly as if to match the tides, now crashing into shore.

"Maybe I'll see you again someday?" She looked at him expectantly.

"Yeah ... someday." The boy looked at his toes. "Until then, though, I guess I'll just ... miss you?"

"Yes, you shall." Anna smirked with that same confidence she had when attempting to skip the rock. She leaned up and kissed him softly before stepping back. Her cheeks were flushed, and her blue eyes were radiant in the moonlight, like stars glowing in the night sky. She released his hand and ran off down the beach.

The boy stood barefoot and alone at his spot on the sand. He bent to pick up his shoes and began walking down the beach the opposite way of Ana. But he heard her voice and turned around.

"Henry!" She yelled, running back to him on the beach. She sprinted up to him with a silver chain dangling in her hand. She handed him a bracelet with a little round locket dangling from it.

He opened it up and there was a picture of her with her family.

"So you can remember me until someday..." She hugged him and ran back off down the beach becoming smaller and smaller before she disappeared over the top of the hill.

Henry smiled and thought, *My first kiss* ... and strolled down the beach in ecstasy.

22

HENRY'S JOURNEY
Jackson Hole, Wyoming
August 26, 1992

Henry slowly blinked open his eyes as the tiniest bit of light from the sunrise shone through the trees. His thoughts went immediately to the night before, and he remembered cooking dinner with Ara, talking and laughing with her as they ate and cleaned up, and the impromptu "double date" with Mitch and Nicole. He felt content and happy, and maybe even peaceful for the first time in many years. He stretched his arms over his head as he thought of Ara, her kindness, her patience, her genuine love for nature and wanted to do something nice for her. But what could he do?

He thought of the way she had teased him about not knowing how to cook, and the idea came to him suddenly. He was going to invite her over for breakfast! Not just any breakfast though, he wanted it to be special and something that she would remember and enjoy.

He climbed out of bed, hastily throwing on clothes, mentally going over what he had bought yesterday for groceries. Henry decided that he would make pancakes with some of the fresh strawberries he had picked up to top them off, turkey bacon, and fluffy scrambled eggs. He could brew coffee and pick some of the wildflowers around the cabin for the table.

But how should he invite her? He could call over, but that didn't seem very … special. It was rather mundane, actually. She would probably be off on her morning run now anyway. He could drop by and ask. He could write her a note.

A note! Or a series of notes? Henry's mind was churning over the idea in his head. He could leave something like little notes to guide her over like a puzzle, like a scavenger hunt! He'd never done one for someone before, but the idea sounded akin to Ara's personality, her proclivity for poetry and the written word.

Excitedly, Henry found a pad of paper and a pen near the phone and sat down to think. He wished he had thought to do this last night, giving him more time to think of some clever clues. Whatever he could come up with on the fly would have to do. He put the pen to the paper and scribbled several lines before scratching them out and starting all over. He did this several times before he felt satisfied with his four clues.

Clue 1: Often used to describe a mix of delicious peanuts, dried fruit, and the occasional candied chocolate, make your way down this – it's not the road less traveled, as you've been down it more times than one, tut tut Miss Ara or you'll miss all the fun.

Clue 2: All that we see or seem is but a dream within a dream, but know this clue is just what it seems. Go to the place you are most at home, a place fed by the heaven's dews and drops and where poets and sojourners roam.

Clue 3: Further along the trail you go, to the spot in which a crash occurred you know. Near the water's edge it is. Think deeply on it, and you won't miss.

Clue 4: Aw, yes! You have arrived at your final clue. By now, me thinks, you know what to do. Move those feet faster down the trail. Hurry! Something delicious awaits you, if you don't fail!

Henry picked up the notes and headed out the door to leave them in reverse order. He put the last one on his door with a little push pin he had found in a drawer and headed down the road.

At a tree in the bend in the road between his and Ara's, he stuck the next note on the tree at eye level and tied a little toilet paper around the tree and tied it like a bow, leaving the ends loose and dancing in the wind. This was where he had awkwardly run into her the other day and just as awkwardly made conversation.

He grinned at it and moved on down the road until he came to a log that had fallen many years ago. It looked as if it had just been moved to the side, but it would lead her toward the lake instead of down the wrong path. Moss and foliage clung to the log, creating a woven maze of green. It was the perfect backdrop for his next clue, and he placed several flowers around it before moving on down the trail to Ara's cabin.

The last note was placed on Ara's door mat with some flowers around it as well. He smiled at the words and pictured the look on her face as her hurried back to his cabin to prepare breakfast.

He started coffee first and breathed in deeply as the smell filled the cabin. Next, he moved to the fridge to pull out the necessary ingredients and began cracking eggs, mixing pancake batter, and heating up pans.

Soon, the cabin was filled with the smell of a delicious breakfast. He washed and cut up the strawberries and began to set the table, pouring himself a cup of coffee and sipping it in the midst of his work. He dashed outside to grab some flowers for the table and, unable to find a vase, tied some dry grass around a small bundle and set it next to Ara's plate.

He looked around with satisfaction and was just finishing the bacon when he heard a knock at the door.

Grinning with excitement, Henry practically bounded to the door. He flung it open and was greeted with the beautiful laughter and smile of Arabella. Her eyes sparkled with delight as she looked at him, still holding all the notes and flowers in her hand. She wore a soft white T-shirt with worn denim shorts. Her hair looked slightly damp, flowing, loose from the usual ponytail.

"Henry!" She held up the notes, laughing. "Thank you for the lovely surprise."

He found he was speechless again, whether from shock of her gratitude, from excitement at seeing her, or from how breathtakingly beautiful she was. "Oh, that, well..."

She laughed. "It was so fun. Such a nice surprise." She said as she stepped closer to him and gave him a little hug.

Even more at a loss for words, he opened the door wider and motioned for her to come in. "Hungry?" He finally managed to ask.

"Starvin'!" She came in and looked around at his place. "I just got home from my run and saw your note, so I showered and made my way over. Great clues by the way. You'll be pleased to know I never got lost once! Although, what would you have done with all this food if I *had* gotten lost?"

"My plan was held entirely in the balance of your very capable mind. I had no alternative plan, just sheer faith in your intelligence. Would you like some coffee?"

"Sure, that would be great! Thanks, Henry." She smiled down at the table and surveyed the kitchen. "Wow, Henry. I thought you just knew how to make cereal!"

He grinned. "That may have been a comment intended more for comedic effect," Henry laughed. "But, no, I love breakfast, so I learned a little in college as I didn't want to drag myself away from my studies or go out after a long night just for bacon and eggs. But, you know, I still needed my bacon and eggs."

She nodded, and he handed her a steaming cup, motioning for her to sit down. He filled a plate and set it down in front of her.

"Glad to know you did *some* studying in college, Henry, and it wasn't all late-night partying," Ara giggled at her own jab at him. He shook his head at her with a laugh and continued moving foods from the kitchen to the dining room table.

"Henry, really, thank you so much. This is such a nice surprise." Ara's eyes were shining in wonder and gratitude as she looked at him. He could tell he had made the impression he intended.

"Oh, it's nothing." He walked to the stove and filled himself a plate as well. Turning back to the table to sit down, he admitted, "Well, I just kind of wanted to do something nice for you. You know, say thank you."

Her eyebrows rose in disbelief. "Pour moi?" Ara asked, Henry not missing that she spoke in French.

Henry nodded and sipped his coffee while he thought of what else to say. "Mais bien sûr, mademoiselle! I just ... really enjoyed yesterday ... visiting with you and cooking and whooping you at Uno, of course!"

Ara laughed and cut her pancakes into perfect squares before trying a bite. "Mmmm, so good. Breakfast is seriously the best meal of the day." She almost seemed too absorbed in her pancakes, on which she had piled a heaping mound of strawberries, to retort is Uno comment. But she rounded. "And, excuse me, sir! I seem to remember you with tons of cards when I went out every single time."

He elbowed her gently and tried some of his breakfast. "Not every time!"

They laughed together, and Ara looked around at the room a bit, noticing its bareness. "So, I mean, you have a nice place here, but maybe it's a little ... empty? Compared to mine for sure." She corrected.

"Well, I am not here too often. Mostly to sleep." He laughed. "It has been kind of nice to have some space, not so much clutter. People spend so much time filling spaces with things! I want to have adventures and memories, not things, filling my life from now on."

Her eyes widened at his words. "Pretty deep for 8:30 in the morning!" She teased. "But seriously, I love that way of thinking."

They continued to chatter and exchange easy banter as Ara shared some of her favorite childhood memories with him, as well as some ideas of how the cabin could be improved, and not just with added clutter, but with some meaningful things.

After a while, Henry made some more coffee, and they headed out to the back porch to sit on the steps and listen to the sounds of the morning, leaving the entire breakfast, dishes and all, just sitting where they had left them. They sipped the steaming brew in comfortable silence, each in their own thoughts as time slipped gently by.

Sometime later, Ara stood up. "Well, Henry, I have a few things I should do at home." She hesitated, twirling a tendril of hair between her fingers. "But then, would you maybe want to hike up to the lake?" She asked tentatively.

Henry's heart jumped at her last words. "Sure, that would be great." He answered, trying to sound casually excited, even though he wanted to bust out a few dance moves for the fact that she wanted to spend more time with him!

She grinned at him as if she could sense his hidden excitement. "Okay, come over in a few hours? Maybe this afternoon?"

"Perfect."

They moved back inside, and she handed him her cup. "Thanks again for the surprise and the delicious meal." She looked around at the dishes. "Would you like help cleanin' up?"

He waved his hand that it was no big deal. "No way. I've got several hours to burn before anything exciting is supposed to happen anyway. And what kind of surprise ends in washing dirty dishes?"

She laughed and moved to leave. "I'll see ya soon then?"

"I can't wait." He answered honestly.

Ara blushed and opened the door. "Okay, then."

And she was gone.

Henry surveyed the mess, surprised he had managed to accumulate so many dishes in such a short time. He set to work, his mind busy reflecting on the perfect breakfast and the perfect woman who had eaten with him.

****

The lake was beautiful and serene as always. Henry dropped his pack next to Ara's and took a long drink from his water bottle.

"You were a little quieter than usual on our way up here," Ara commented as she settled herself on the grass.

Henry had been thinking about how to tell her who he really was and just who he had waiting for him in New York. "I was a little absorbed in my thoughts on the way up here," he admitted.

Ara patted the grass next to her, motioning him to sit down. "I feel the same way." She admitted. "What were you thinkin' about?" Ara asked as she gently ripped some grass up and fiddled the blades between her fingers.

Henry sat down and rested his hands on his knees. "Just some thoughts ... the last few days..." He hesitated, wondering if he should bite the bullet and just tell her the truth or wait a little longer. "What about you … You said you felt the same way?"

Ara nodded. "Yes, I had some thoughts for sure. I always come up here to sort through my thoughts and just read." She twisted a strand of hair around her finger. "Readin' always helps clear my head."

Henry looked down at the thick, worn book in front of her. "What did you bring to read?"

She held up the book, showing him the Bible. He was taken back for a moment, never having turned to the Bible for answers ever in his life.

"I don't know how you feel about religion or faith. We have a lot to get to know about each other, I guess." She looked down and ran her hand over the worn cover. "But just so you know me, I have faith, Henry. Faith that there is a God out there looking out for us, leadin' us into the arms of those we need and to those we love..."

His tongue felt tied and stuck in silence.

"What do you think about that?" She looked directly into his eyes, her beautiful blues searching his own for an answer.

"I … I'm not acquainted with it, with faith. I've read from the Bible before for scholarly purposes but never for hope or strength or anything like that. I've only ever been guided by myself and my family."

"Can I read you somethin' from it?"

"I would love to hear you read." Henry lay back in the grass and looked up into the sapphire-colored sky.

"'There are three things that amaze me – no, four things that I don't understand: how an eagle glides through the sky, how a snake slithers on a rock, how a ship navigates the ocean, how a man loves a woman.' Proverbs 30:18-19."

Henry was thoughtful. "Yes, those are amazing things. Go on … please." He could listen to her all the way into eternity, if that existed.

She gazed down at him. "Can you read to me?"

Henry sat up. "Me? If you like, I can try. Where should I start?"

"I don't care. I just want to hear your voice; it soothes me." Ara lay back in the grass.

Henry thought he would do practically anything this wonderful woman asked, so he picked up the Bible and opened it up to a random page. He spoke out loud, "'Ecclesiastes 3: To everything there is a season, a time for every purpose under heaven: A time to be born, and a time to die; a time to plant, and a time to pluck what is planted; A time to kill, and a time to heal; a time to break down, and a time to build up; a time to weep and a time to laugh.'" Henry felt himself relaxing as he read the great words, mellifluously rolling off his tongue.

"'A time to mourn, and a time to dance; a time to cast stones, and a time to gather stones; a time to embrace, and time to refrain from embracing; a time to gain, and a time to lose; a time to keep, and a time to throw away; a time to tear, and a time to sew; a time to keep silence, and a time to speak; A time to love, and a time to hate; a time of war, and a time of peace.'" He stopped reading and looked over at Arabella. She was lying in the grass with her eyes drawn and a smile across her face.

Her eyes opened, realizing Henry had stopped reading. "Why did you stop?"

"It's just so poetic … I'm thinking." Henry sat truly pondering the verses he had just read. He was washed over with a feeling of relatability to these words. They applied, and they applied to everyone. Life is never always going to be high, there has to be lows to go with it, making those highs so much more precious. Was this his time to embrace, or to love, or was it his time to refrain from embracing but to still love? He had never known a love without embrace, and it was so natural. Maybe that was the problem: his nature and doing things the same way he always had. Ara was different.

Henry marveled at how wonderful she really was. She was so different, different than any other woman he had ever met. He lay back in the grass and looked up into the sky again.

Ara moved and rested her head on his shoulder, and he put a comforting arm around her.

"Look, Henry." Ara pointed into the sky at a cluster of clouds. "That looks like an eagle."

Henry saw what she was pointing at. "Ahh, yes. And over there, that is, without a doubt, a bear."

They laughed together, pointing out more things in the clouds, each one sillier than the next. Henry relaxed and breathed in the soft, wispy grass around him and bathed in the warm sun all around him. He reveled in the complete freedom of the moment. He felt at peace and at home in Wyoming for the first time in his life. He was in love with this part of the country as it was so serene and fresh, far from the smog of New York. Most of all, Henry breathed in the feeling of the amazing woman next to him. The darkness of Anne was just a small spot in the back of his mind for the moment, and he just bathed in the wonderful light that Ara brought to his world.

He realized Ara had gone quiet and looked down at her, brushing the soft hair off her face. Her eyes were closed, and her face was peaceful. Henry gently felt the relaxing tone of the environment seep into himself as well. He let his eyes close and drifted off to sleep next to Arabella.

****

"Henry? Henry, wake up."

Henry woke slowly, his mind hazy from sleep. He had to think about where he was. He rubbed his eyes and sat up.

The clouds had darkened to a dark, blue-grey, looking suspiciously like storm clouds. His thoughts felt sluggish, and the air was filled with thick humidity. He turned to find Ara's beautiful face just inches away from his. Without thinking, he gently touched her cheek, looking deeply into her eyes, and smiled.

Ara started to say something but was cut off by a deafening crack of thunder overhead. She shirked against Henry for protection. The earth shook as the sound echoed through the mountains fiercely.

"Uh, oh." Henry said as they looked up into the thunderous clouds looming above them.

"That's why I woke you up! A storm is coming, Henry!" Ara started gathering her things, and Henry packed them into her backpack.

He put the pack on his shoulders, and they walked quickly down the path. They had taken about three steps when the sky opened, and cool water poured down over them. The warmth was replaced by a humid chill that overwhelmed the hot earth.

The rain came down, not like sheets, but quilts. He had never seen a rain so thick with moisture in his life, like he would never be dry ever again. He could barely see a foot in front of him as they stumbled down the trail.

He told Ara to let him walk in front. At least if she slipped, he could try to stop her, and if he fell, then he would not crush her. Quickly and not at all gracefully, they made it down the steep slope and onto the main path while the thunder rumbled, and the lightening lit up the sky.

"Henry!" Ara laughed as she slipped and tried to catch herself.

Henry turned and grabbed her arm before she fell into the forming mud. He laughed and tried in vain to wipe the streaming water away from his eyes. Streams of rain water flowed down the curve of Henry's nose, and he buzzed his lips to blow the water off of his face and onto hers. She laughed so hard she slipped again, this time landing her into both of Henry's arms.

It was like he had dipped her after some elegant dance. He brought her back up, and their two faces were inches from each other. Henry could feel the heat from her breath on his lips. She was smiling, and his lips matched hers. He started to lean in, but, just when their lips were about to touch, a loud pound of thunder shook the ground they were on, pulling them from the moment.

Ara ran her hand over her hair, pushing the wet mass away from her face. "Come on, Henry!" She cried and took off toward her cabin.

"Ara, wait!" Henry yelled out. "I need to go to my cabin for some clothes." He waved her over to the right of the main path.

She smiled and ran over to him. As she passed, she shouted back to him about being too slow to catch her.

Henry accepted the challenge and took off after her. They raced through the rain to his cabin with Henry just inches behind Ara.

Just as they reached the door, he grabbed her, turned the handle, and they tumbled inside. "Whew, you really are fast." Henry said to her as he tried to catch his breath.

Ara laughed. "You aren't too slow yourself."

Henry thought she looked adorable as she stood in front of him, water dripping down her face and bright, blue eyes sparkling. He noticed she had started shivering, so he walked into the bedroom and grabbed a couple of towels and a sweatshirt. He came back into the main room to see her shyly looking around his cabin. Henry handed her the towel and shirt.

She gratefully accepted them and pulled the sweatshirt over her head. He smiled at her and toweled his own hair dry. "Why don't you sit down for a sec while I grab some clothes?"

She nodded, and he went back into the bedroom. Looking out the window, he saw it was still raining hard, so he didn't bother to change. Henry threw a pair of jeans, a dry t-shirt, a pair of briefs, and some socks into a bag.

"Ready to go?" He asked Ara as he returned to the main room.

She got up from the couch and looked at him with amusement shining in her eyes. "And just where might we be goin'?"

Surprised, Henry realized they had never actually made plans to do anything tonight. "Well, uh..." It just felt so normal to be with her.

Ara laughed and grabbed his hand, pulling him to the door. "I am just kiddin'. Let's go to my place." She turned and looked at him as they reached the door. "Do you think your car can make it through this mud?"

Henry considered the question. "I think so." He said and opened the door for her. "At least, we can try it."

They ran into the pouring rain and jumped into the car. Henry started up the engine and backed into the muddy road. The car plowed through it like a dream.

In a couple of minutes, they reached Ara's house and ran inside. "Home sweet home," Ara declared and walked around turning on lights and closing some windows. Her lace curtains were furiously flying with the wind, and rain poured through the screens.

Henry set his bag down on the table and took off his shoes. "Your cabin is *much* homier than mine."

Ara came back into the kitchen and looked around. "Yes, I suppose it is quite homey." She got that far away look in her eyes again. Then she shook her head. "All right, so I need a shower. And since you lost the race, I am willin' to let you cook dinner while I shower." At Henry's panicked look, Ara laughed and said, "Just jokin', Henry. You shower. I will whip us up a little something."

Henry shook his head at her and went into her little bathroom. As he got into the streaming hot water, he realized it had been days since he had had a hot shower. He relaxed and breathed in the steamy air. He cleaned his rain-washed body off with the most manly soap he could find in the shower, a pink, flowery bar, and turned off the shower.

As he rubbed himself dry with a towel, the light above him blinked once and then again before going out completely. Henry fiddled for the doorknob in the complete darkness. Just as he was turning the knob, he felt it turn from the other side. He pulled it open lightly, pulling a surprised Ara in with him.

"Whew!" She gasped. She had lit a candle and was bringing another one for him and handed the unlit candle to Henry.

Henry thanked her and guided her hand that held the candle to the unlit candle in his own hand. The room brightened considerably as Henry got the other candle lit. He saw Ara's eyes widen as she saw him standing before her wrapped at the waist in a towel that came only to his mid-thigh. He felt heat begin to burn in his stomach as he looked into her darkened eyes, the candlelight gently radiating their blue depths.

Henry stepped around Ara, managing to murmur, "Hopefully there is some hot water left."

As the door swung shut, he heard her say quietly to herself, "A cold shower is just what I need."

Henry shook his head, thinking the exact same thing. He found his way to the table by candlelight and pulled on his briefs, jeans, and t-shirt. His stomach rumbled, and he remembered Ara saying something about dinner.

He walked over to the stove and lifted the cover on the pot sitting atop it. It smelled wonderful. He put the cover back on and used his candle to try to find others around the cabin to light. Henry found quite a few on shelves and on end tables in the living room. He lit them all and saw the cabin was soon bathed in candlelight. Outside, the rain continued streaming down the windows.

Ara walked out of the bathroom, with her cheeks flushed from the steam. She had put on white capris made out of a soft material and a light blue t-shirt. She smiled at Henry. "I see you found the candles."

He nodded. "And the food. What are you cooking over there?"

She went over to the pot, lifted the cover, and stirred the mixture a little. "Just a little something. It is sorta a hamburger hotdish with a cream sauce made of mushrooms, garlic butter, and milk and some diced tomatoes, too." She stirred a little more. "I am just glad this is a gas stove, or we would have been eating peanut butter and jelly sandwiches."

Henry's stomach rumbled, and they both smiled. "Would you like me to set the table?"

"That would be nice, thank you." Ara handed him a few plates and silverware. "How about some iced tea?"

"Sure. That would be great." He set the plates and silverware out on the table. He grabbed a few, short candles from a nearby shelf and set them on the table as well.

Ara brought over the large pot and set it in the middle of the table. She grabbed a pitcher from the fridge, along with two chilled glasses, and set them on the table as well.

Henry pulled out her chair for her and served them both some hot dish. Ara said grace, and they both dug in.

"Mmm, wow, Ara. This is wonderful."

Her eyes were shadowed, deep blue in the candlelight. Her lips curved slightly, "Yes, my grandmother taught me the recipe when I was very small. I do love to cook."

"Well, it would be a shame for you to stop." Henry scooped up another bite of the meal.

She laughed. "I suppose it would, although I don't really get to cook for many others. Nicole and Mitch and some others in town that go to my church." She took another bite. "They always like me to do the cooking."

"So, you like to read, run, and cook."

Ara looked at him, half-smiling and a little amused. "Yes."

He scraped the remaining bit of hotdish onto his fork. "What else do you like?"

"Hmmmm." She chewed slowly before swallowing as she thought. "I love being on a ranch. Working cattle on horseback is one of my favorite things in the world." The faraway look had returned to her eyes, and she stirred hotdish around her plate absentmindedly.

Henry waited a few seconds. "So ... you are also a cowgirl?"

"Ya, sort of. I am retired at the moment but still help out at Mitch and Nicole's. Which brings me to my next question. How would you like to get your cowboy on again the day after tomorrow?" She smiled playfully at Henry.

Surprised, Henry pondered the question. "Are you being serious?" At her nod, he replied, "Ya, that sounds great actually."

"Great. I think it will be a fun day."

Henry smiled at the thought of spending more time with Mitch and with Ara for that matter. "Wait, so how long have you been a cowgirl? When did you first learn to ride?"

"Since before I could walk!" She grinned at him across the table and launched into the story of her first ride.

By the time she finished, Henry's stomach hurt from laughing at the tale. "Now when did you first meet Mitch? Or did you know Nicole first?"

Taking a sip of her tea, Ara thought for a minute. "Well, Nicole and I have been best friends since grade school, but I knew Mitch since I was a baby! Our parents were best friends." She entertained him with tales of Mitch and Nicole until there tea and food were long gone.

Sighing with contentment, Ara got up from the table, grabbing a few dishes. Henry nodded and piled the rest of the dishes into his hands and brought them to her at the sink. "Did Mitch say what we would be doing?"

Ara turned on the faucet and poured some soap into the sink. "Just workin' on the ranch," she said smiling down at the rising water in the sink.

"All right. I guess I will have to wait 'till we get to Mitch's to find out." He picked up a dish towel and began drying the dishes Ara handed him.

"I guess so." She laughed lightly at Henry's fake pouting face and punched his arm with her wet fist.

He smiled down at her and bumped her with his elbow. "Or maybe I will just have to get it out of you somehow." He set the dried plate in the dish rack and looked down at Ara.

She was looking up at him, shaking her head and smiling. She had taken her hands out of the water and was drying them on his towel. Her shimmering eyes caught his own, and time froze as he looked down into those eyes.

She brushed her fingers through her almost-dried hair, a light blush now coloring her cheeks, and said, "So, let's do something."

Surprised, Henry looked at her. "What did you have in mind?"

"Maybe a movie would be nice?" She suggested and set down the dish towel, carefully spreading it open to allow it to dry.

He nodded, not being able to remember the last one he had seen.

Ara moved across the room and opened the cabinet holding her videos. "Let's see ... what kind are you in the mood to watch? A romance?" She laughed as Henry shook his head quickly. "Maybe a detective story? I know! How about *Pure Luck*?" She held up the VHS for him to see. "Have you ever seen it, Henry?"

He looked at the cover and shook his head, not even recognizing the actors on the cover. "No, I actually have not seen too many movies. I'm just always too busy for movies, I guess … with work"

Ara's face looked sympathetic. "Not even for date nights?"

Henry laughed somewhat dryly. "Date nights where I come from are … quite different."

"You mean the wealthy class dates differently than us modest ranchers?" Ara asked, matching his dry tone and amping it up with a thick country accent.

"Yes." Henry said with a slight smile but a serious tone. "We have such expectations in my world, you know. We have to socialize with the 'right' people and we have to look just 'so.' A typical date is attending a benefit of some sort together or going out to a fancy restaurant. And they are usually expensive, and it is just so impersonal … nothing like this." He looked at Ara with fondness and appreciation, but he was apprehensive to say anything more. Anne came to mind. He thought of all their "dates," as they called them. He never really knew her.

Ara was quiet for a moment. "That sounds … kind of cold. How do you ever get to know anyone's true personality?"

Henry pulled his mind back to the present. He nodded. "Yes. Well, let's watch this movie huh?"

Ara slid off the couch, letting the subject go, and slipped the movie out of its case. He settled into the couch and breathed deeply, trying to relax. His eyes followed Ara as she popped in the video and snuggled down in the couch with a blanket. She smiled at him and started the movie. Henry put his arm along the back of the couch, and Ara rested her head lightly on his shoulder.

They laughed and relaxed together as the movie progressed. Henry realized how much he loved just being around her and how much he enjoyed who he was when he was with her. But he was married, undoubtedly and indubitably so. He needed to tell her before they were in too deep. Or was he in too deep already?

Looking down at Ara, he saw she was asleep, breathing softly. He could feel her exhale on his arm, and it made him quiver in sheer happiness. He laid her down and stretched out his legs before covering them up with the blanket.

Henry kissed her forehead and drifted off to sleep. I *will tell her tomorrow*, Henry thought as deep sleep took his worries away.

****

The beginning edges of sunlight were touching the horizon as Henry slowly woke. He found himself still on the couch, holding tightly to the sleeping Arabella. Her face held an angelic peaceful look as she slept.

He traced his finger lightly along her jawline. Her eyes fluttered open. "Morning," he said quietly.

"Morning." Ara sat up and stretched her arms over her head. "Mmmm. I slept good last night." She yawned and curled closer to Henry.

Henry laughed at her sleepy eyes and tousled bed-hair. She looked so cute. "Me too." He sat up and stretched as well. "That was a good movie, huh?"

Ara laughed. "Ya, it was the perfect night of fun with the perfect guy to spend it with." She pulled out her ponytail and began finger-combing through her hair.

He nodded, smiling down at her. "Well, I am game to make a double feature. That is, if you think you're still wanting to hang out with little old me?"

"I *will* have to check my calendar," Ara mockingly flipped her hand in the air like she was high society and jutted her nose up in the air. It was an all-too-familiar attitude for Henry. "Perhaps I could pencil you in and get back to you" Ara said, fluttering her eyelids but letting a smile spread across her face. She couldn't be an uptight, high-society girl even she wanted to be.

"Then I shall wait by the phone every second until your call," Henry said, holding his hand to his heart with sincerity.

"You better." She gave him a wry smile and winked.

Henry laughed and tickled her lightly.

Ara joyfully screamed and threw herself on top of him, trying to hold down his arms. She failed miserably, finally jumping up and running toward the bathroom to escape. Henry followed quickly and laughed as she shut and locked the door, narrowly missing his fingers. He sighed in feigned defeat. "Well, I suppose I will let you win this one."

"Henry, you just go make us some breakfast!" Ara ordered from inside the bathroom. "And I'll win more than just this one!" He heard her laugh through the door as she turned on the sink.

Grinning, he shook his head and walked toward the kitchen. He pulled eggs and turkey bacon out of the fridge and began pulling pans out to make breakfast. Turning on the stove and spraying the pans, Henry hummed a tune he had heard Ara singing the day before and cracked the eggs onto the pan. They sizzled nicely. He turned, picked up the turkey bacon, and placed it on the second pan. While everything cooked, he opened the cupboard and pulled out a couple of Ara's white china plates, patterned with wild flowers along the edges. Henry carefully set them on the table and turned to flip the bacon and eggs. He popped some bread into the toaster.

"MMMmmm. Something smells great." Ara gracefully walked into the room, combing through her wet hair. She grabbed the orange juice from the fridge along with two glasses and sat down, smiling at Henry.

Her face was completely free of makeup, Henry realized, and she did not look any less beautiful than usual. If anything, she was even more beautiful, even more pure. He turned from her as he pictured Anne's always perfectly made up face. What, of her soul, did the makeup hide?

"Would you like some juice?" She asked as she poured herself a glass.

Her sweet voice helped push away his unpleasant thoughts. "Yes, thanks." He piled the breakfast onto a plate and brought it to the table.

"Eat up!" He said as he set the plate by Arabella.

"Thank you, Henry." She brushed his hand with hers and then added some food to her plate.

His heart jumped at her touch, but he forced himself to remain calm. "You made supper last night, it was the least I could do." He replied as he filled his plate.

"So what would you like to do today?" Ara asked as she picked up a piece of bacon with her fork.

He looked up from his food and smiled, half in surprise and half from happiness that she still wanted to spend the day with him. "Are we doing something?" he asked with kiddish delight.

"Well, sure. Is there anything better to do?" She eyed him mischievously and fiddled with her fork on her plate.

"Well then, did you have any ideas?"

"Not sure yet." She said thoughtfully.

Henry bit into a piece of toast and looked out the window at the sunny day. A cool, morning breeze came through the kitchen window. He breathed in deeply, set down his fork, and pushed his empty plate away from him. He needed to get outside, needed to sweat and work his muscles in the sun. He thought of his so-far-un-climbable rock and found the perfect way to burn off his extra steam. "Have you ever been rock climbing, Ara?"

She looked at him in surprise. "Henry, I grew up here. In Jackson Hole. In the middle of the mountains?" She laughed at the look on his face. "Of course, I've climbed. And I'm not so bad if I do say so myself." She raised her eyebrows expecting Henry to be surprised.

Henry felt like an idiot and apologized to her with a grin. "I was just feeling a little like climbing all of a sudden. Burn off some," he hesitated, looking for the right word to describe how he was feeling, "steam." He smiled, satisfied with his choice of words.

"That is a great idea." She got up and started cleaning the table. "I am actually surprised *you* know how to climb, city boy!"

"Why does everyone call me that?" he laughed. "You are totally going to get it for that!" He picked up the orange juice and put it in the fridge. "I would watch my back if I were you." He stalked over to the sink with a fake malevolence.

Ara stood her ground and started rinsing the pans. "Ooo, I am *so* scared." She pretended she was shaking in her boots, but she had no boots and just looked like she was wiggling around with wet pans in her hands.

Henry couldn't help but smile. "You should be." He put his arms around her playfully. "These dishes can wait. Let's go climb some cliffs." Henry took in her scent and was intoxicated.

"I can't leave a dirty kitchen, Henry!" She set the clean pans on the drying rack and started some dish water. "You go shower, and I will finish up here."

He reluctantly let her go. "All right." He shuffled off, pouting all the way, as he walked to the bathroom. He heard her singing a country tune from the first night they met. He smiled at the beauty of her voice as he shut the door and started the shower. He turned on the hot water and breathed in the steam.

Grabbing the flowery scented bar of soap, he lathered it all over himself and thought about the cliffs. He pictured Muster Buster and its intricately-woven cracked paths. There were so many ways to climb it because Charlie and everybody else never went up the same way twice. There were so many options, so much opportunity, but one wrong move meant failure. He could see himself falling over and over again, but now he was picturing himself making it to the top. He was going to get to the top of that rock. Today. He needed to succeed.

He finished showering, dried off, and slipped back on his shorts. He would need to stop at his cabin and change for climbing. He opened the door and almost ran into Ara.

"Nice shower?" She asked with a tight smile as she took in his naked torso.

He pulled on a shirt and looked at her. She had already changed into her climbing outfit.

"Maybe this way you will be able to keep your hands off me long enough that I can actually climb." Ara looked like she surprised herself with those words, but then recovered, putting her hands on her hips in attitude, as if to say, "Yeah, I said it. What are you gonna do about it?"

Henry played along, "Ha! Okay, let's see whose hands are on who when I take my shirt off because it's so hot. Hard to resist these babies." Henry lifted his shirt and revealed perfectly developed abs that any straight, normal girl would swoon over. He felt a little conceited, but she had asked for it!

"Touché, Henry, touché." A defeated Ara pushed her way past Henry, more confident than ever. Henry never dropped his gaze as he stood there still holding his shirt up, looking like the one who just lost.

Ara turned back around, saw him frozen in the moment still with his mouth open in awe, standing there like an idiot holding his shirt up and smiled deviously. "I win." She shrugged her shoulders like it was nothing.

Henry recovered and dropped his shirt. He pulled on it a couple times just to make sure it was all the way down. Ara laughed until she was rolling on the floor.

Henry came and swooped her up in his arms and carried her out the door. In between her rolls of laughter, Henry made out the words, "You … touched … me first!"

Henry drove down the mountain toward his cabin as Ara recovered from her fit of laughter. He ran in to get the climbing gear that Charlie let him keep from his first climb. He had agreed that he wouldn't climb without an inexperienced climber with him, but Ara said she was pretty good, and he was banking off of that. He checked his bag and saw that there were still a few granola bars left inside from the first trip which was all the food Henry had in his house. He hoped they hadn't gone stale.

He ran back to the car. Ara had turned the radio and was singing softly to herself when Henry opened his door to get in. They exchanged happy glances before Henry started the car. He slipped it into reverse and backed his way out of the cabin driveway. He pushed it into drive, slid his fingers in between Ara's, and they headed down the mountain hand in hand.

They drove in comfortable silence for miles. The road curved on and on. Henry followed signs to lead them back to the spot where he had climbed with Charlie and the gang. When they pulled into the parking lot, Henry couldn't resist a smile. This was going to be fun.

He looked over at Ara, and she was smiling too. "Let's hit the trail and get up there." Henry could barely contain his excitement.

They started up the trail wordlessly. The sounds of their breathing, the grinding of the rocks on their shoes, and the rustling of the leaves were the only sounds. It was an okay silence, though, like the silence one needs after being surrounded by a constant stream of noise for far too long. Henry took a long breath and released as they hit the switchbacks up to the cliffs.

Ara sprinted up the switchbacks, and Henry followed suit. When they made it to the top they were both breathing deeply and loudly. Ara paced back and forth with her hands on her head to catch her breath. Henry bent over with his hands on his knees and took in the view. When their pulses had slowed, and their breathing had calmed, they both looked at each other and exchanged a look of achievement, like they could conquer the world together.

"Well, are you going to help me get these ropes set up?" Ara looked at Henry expectantly.

"Uh, well I could, but I am not so sure I should be the one free climbing. I've never actually made it up this climb before, even with ropes." Henry was embarrassed to admit it, but his embarrassment only emboldened him to conquer this climb once and for all.

"Oh, okay, no problem. I've climbed here before. I will set it up. Be back in a jiff." Ara was on the rocks in a split second, no hesitation in her movement. She had the rope slung over her shoulder with the carabiners attached to the loops on the back of her climbing pants. She eased along the various holds with grace, and Henry stood back and studied her moves. She had a different technique to climbing than Charlie did: she moved with elegance, like it was nothing at all.

Henry remembered the physical endurance it took to just get half way up and then fall. He was beyond impressed by her and frankly, getting nervous about having to follow her climb. His normal confidence was gone.

He shook his head to stop his thoughts in their tracks. Instead, he focused entirely on the holds she was using, to use them himself when he got on the face of Muster Buster. It couldn't have been more than five minutes, and Ara was already at the top.

"Where do you want to set up?" She called down from the top of the cliff.

Henry pointed to the general vicinity of Muster Buster, knowing that other climbs could be done around it, but his mind was set on Muster Buster. Ara disappeared for a few minutes and returned.

She clipped her harness onto the ropes and repelled gracefully back down to Henry's side. "Ready?"

Henry could hear the excitement in Ara's voice, and he was feeling quite the same. "Let's do this," Henry smiled.

"Do you want to go first?" Ara asked.

"Oh right, I would offer you to go first, but I forgot to mention one thing." Henry paused. "No one has really taught me how to belay someone." Arabella looked confused.

"I thought you said you had done this before?"

"Well, I have climbed before, but you know..." Henry wished he had learned or even asked Charlie how to belay.

"Oh. Okay. Well, no worries. It's pretty simple. I will just show you." Arabella seemed happy to be teaching Henry anything. She went through all the steps one by one, repeating a few just to be sure that Henry was sure about the instructions. When Henry felt comfortable, Ara had him do a test run with the ropes and the signals.

Before long, they were ready to start climbing. Henry, like a true gentleman, let Ara climb first.

Ara went straight for Muster Buster. She chose a different route than Henry had ever thought of. Henry sat in awe of her moves. She twisted and contorted her body in ways that Henry was sure he could never maneuver. Before he knew it, she was back on the ground, breathing heavily. The sun reflected off of her sweaty face. She wiped her forehead with her shirt and smiled broadly.

"Nice work!" Henry extolled. "It looked like you did that with hardly any effort at all."

"Do you see my sweaty face?" She pointed at her face with her thumbs. "Obviously there was some effort in there somewhere." Ara bent over and pulled her water bottle out of her backpack. She took a long pull on her water and released with a relieved sigh and then stretched a little before making a motion toward taking over for Henry.

"Okay, you're up, big boy!" Ara started unclipping the rope from Henry's harness and attaching it to her own. Suddenly, Henry was feeling extremely nervous. All of his life he had been the winner, conquering every challenge with finesse and getting the girls to swoon over each victory. Here he was in front of this cliff, this unbeatable cliff that he tried to conquer but failed over and over. And to top it all off, this girl, Ara, just climbed it in a matter of minutes. She climbed it, and he couldn't. Henry stood in front of the cliff and stared at it, perplexed. He felt like a "city boy," as everyone called him, for the first time since arriving in Wyoming.

"Henry, are you ready?" Ara pulled Henry back to the rest of the world.

"Yeah, I just need a minute." He paused and turned back around to her. "I've never actually cleaned this climb before, and I am not used to losing."

"Henry, it's not a competition. I have been climbing my whole life. I wouldn't even expect you to do half of these climbs."

Henry was crushed. "It's not like I'm not good at things. Why would you automatically think I couldn't do it? I've done everything else I shouldn't have been able to, why not this?" He snapped at her. Henry was maybe hurt a tiny ounce, but he lashed out because he was frankly scared to fail. He was raised to be the best. He did not know how to be anything else. Ara couldn't have known these things. Ara didn't know even half of who Henry really was.

This sudden realization made Henry even more panicked. The pressure was causing him to crumble, and the fact of the matter was that he was the only one pressuring himself, not just about climbing but about everything. He realized he was not this great gentleman he always thought himself to be. He had left his wife in New York, met the most amazing girl that he didn't deserve, and she has no clue about his wife, and yet here he was carrying on with her like nothing could be wrong with what he was doing. He felt, at that moment, that he was leading this girl on, lying to her. He literally had told her nothing about his personal life. What was this all based on? He was inexplicably drawn to her, but he questioned whether his feelings could possibly be real.

He realized with horror that he was going to burst into tears at any moment. He started breathing heavier, and he could see the look on Ara's face shift toward worry.

She was reading his face and immediately unclipped from the rope. "I didn't mean that I don't expect you to be the best or extremely wonderful at all you do, I only meant to say that you have surprised me. I wouldn't expect that, but then again, I never expected to fall … either. You are just … full of surprises." She didn't hesitate and pulled him into a hug. "I'm sorry I said that."

Henry melted with her touch. Everything she said felt so right, but everything he needed to say didn't. So he said nothing. He hugged her back, tighter than she initiated, as if to hug away his fears. He didn't know what kind of man he was, but he knew he wanted her. He was content with that, and he feared if he told her what kind of man he really was, he would lose her along with the new man he was trying to be.

"Don't worry about it. I don't know why I was so sensitive," he lied without flinching. This was not who he wanted to be. He stared coldly off into the woods forcing his guilt to the bottom of his heap of problems and chose to focus on what was right in front of him.

He dropped his head next to Ara's, and her scent filled his mind. She was a perfect combination of flowers, dirt, and sweat. He remembered Anne. *Anne would never let me even touch her if she wasn't freshly showered and perfumed to the teeth, even when we first started dating.* Ara smelled natural, rustic, feminine. She was real. He could touch her and know that he was touching a person, not the person she wanted to appear to be.

Ara pulled away from the embrace first and stared up at Henry.

"Are we okay?" She had her best pretend pouty face, which looked like, at best, a frown that wanted to smile.

Henry laughed, "Of course we are. Shall we continue our climbing, my dear?"

Ara blushed at his endearing words, "Yes, let's."

Henry looked at her sweet and innocent face, then turned away from her and looked only at the rocks. A fierce determination to conquer this – the climb, his fears, his turmoiled life – was taking over Henry's body.

Ara reattached the ropes to her harness, and Henry prepared himself to climb. He was angry and in love all at once, a deadly combination for this next climb. Henry's mix of tumultuous emotions were tumbling around inside him like waves crashing along shore on a windy day. He was on belay before he knew it, and he began his climb with fervor and anticipation.

He was finding holds he didn't remember were there before. The world around him was silent. All he could hear was the sound of his own breath rising and falling and the gentle sound of the rope gliding along the carabiner.

He was halfway up the face, guided by a small crack in the rock, when he felt his leg cramping for the first time.

Ara, as if sensing his strain, rang out with words of encouragement, "You got this. Just rest your leg and keep going."

He heeded her words, rested for a moment, and then continued on. He was five feet from the top, and he was stuck. He couldn't find another hold for his left hand and his right foot. His fingertips were beginning to sweat from overuse. He chalked his left hand and rubbed some of that chalk on his right to keep from slipping. He began frantically searching for something, anything to hold onto. This feeling was familiar, like the first time he attempted to climb this. It was the same feeling he had right before he fell. His mind raced for a solution.

"Think, Henry, think! What made you fall last time?" Henry forced his mind to think back to his first fall. He was in a similar position, his fingers were sweating and beginning to cramp from his hold. His legs and arms were all giving out. He remembered being so scared that he didn't think to search.

Henry concluded the only solution was to find a hold and to find it in a matter of seconds. He began running his free hand along the face of the cold rock. He was searching for even the smallest hold that could give him a few seconds to get a hold for his foot. If he could find it, there was a foot hold just at level with his hip on the right. If he could get up to there, he could just about reach the carabiner at the top.

He was frantically searching when his hand slipped over a small groove in the rock. It was small, but it would do. He pinched his finger into the hold and shifted his weight. He felt the strain on his fingers and forearm, but it gave him the height he needed to pull his right leg up to the other foot hold. He swung his foot up and pulled the rest of his weight up too, releasing his strained fingers and bringing him inches from the top. He slid his left foot into one more hold, and just like that he had made it.

He exhaled and let his voice ring out in a victorious shout, "Whooohoo!" It echoed off the mountain sides, and a bird flew out of a tree in surprise. He was breathing heavily, and his adrenaline was pulsing like electric wires through his veins.

"Henry, oh my goodness, I am *so* proud of you!" Ara cheered out below.

Henry looked away from the rock he had been so focused on and looked around him for the first time. He was about sixty feet off the ground, and he could see the whole country side from where he was. The Grand Teton rose into the sky as if looking down on him to say, "I'm still stronger." Henry wanted to shout at the mountain and knock it to the ground. But it was right, it was still stronger and much too beautiful to destroy.

Ara was too beautiful, too. Henry looked down and a chill ran over him suddenly. "Phew, that is really high," he said out loud.

Ara laughed. "Yeah, you don't really notice it until you're done climbing. You wanna come down now or what?" She said, still laughing.

"Yeah, bring me down."

"What do you say?" She looked up at him with her eyebrows raised.

"Oh right, take." As he said it, Ara had him under control, and Henry began bouncing down the cliff.

He soon had both feet planted on the ground. He unclipped himself from the ropes and walked briskly toward Ara, who was unhooking her harness.

Ara was jumping up and down in excitement. "Henry, you did amazing!" She gave him a two-handed high-five, and then she wrapped her arms around him in a tight hug.

He grinned from ear to ear, reveling in the high, and grabbed his water bottle, draining it in three large gulps.

Laughing, Ara handed him her water bottle. He took it gladly and dumped it all over his hair and shoulders. Shaking his wet hair all over her, he laughed and said, "Good thing we packed extra water?"

"Good thing, apparently!"

They walked back to the car to refill their bottles, excitement and adrenaline propelling them forward.

They opened the door and refilled the bottles with cool water. Henry leaned against the car and sipped a little of the ice cold liquid.

Ara sat down on a large rock across from him and sipped hers as well. "Henry, did you know that I met you right when I went on vacation from my job?"

He realized with a start he had never really asked what she did for a living. "Uh, no. But please tell me!" He smiled at her, urging her to continue.

"Okay, so about a month ago, I was working at the church. I run the office there and take care of financial things and pretty much whatever comes up, and I just got this urge to take time off. I had no reason, no where to go, I just needed some time off. And I don't have a particularly demanding job, but everyone needs a break sometimes, right?

"So, anyway, I talk to the pastor of the church, and I ask for a couple of weeks off. Of course, he asked me when, and I was like, whenever. So he says, 'Well, why don't you take off in a few weeks. My wife has nothing going on and can be here to cover for you.' So I say sure. His wife is involved in every charity project on this side of the Grand Teton, so I was shocked she had any free time at all.

"Anyway, my vacation time comes, and my first night of vacation, I go to this rodeo to let loose, have a little fun, and I notice this guy who was just staring at me, not in a creepy way, but like he saw something in me that no one else was seeing."

"On my first night of vacation, I met you, Henry." Ara smiled at the thought. "And maybe it's crazy to think this, but I just feel like I met you for a reason, and that I didn't just randomly take this vacation. No, there was a purpose there, too."

"So I take it you don't believe in fate or destiny then?" Henry was uncomfortable with talk about God and a higher power. He had never been very comfortable with it.

"No, I do. I just don't think it's the same fate or destiny you are thinking of. I just believe that everyone was meant to have someone in their life to lean on, and we are led throughout life facing what me must just to get to that person. Sometimes it's a rough road, but God knows where that road leads." Ara was certain in her words, and she nodded in agreement with herself.

"I wish I had the same confidence as you," Henry spoke softly, his words made him vulnerable, but he knew Ara was the person he could open himself up to. "You know exactly who you are, what you believe. It's like you have no fears."

"Oh, Henry, I have fears. Do I ever! I'm literally terrified that my past mistakes will be punished by eternal loneliness, that I'll never be allowed true love like my parents have because of my previous choices when it came to love. I'm scared that maybe real love doesn't even exist, that no matter how hard we try or hope, something will always go wrong." Ara stopped talking, realizing the fears she was revealing, what her words could mean to Henry. "Oh, and did I mention I am absolutely terrified of spiders?"

"Spiders?" Henry wanted to pull her close and tell her that love was out there for her, maybe even leaning across from her, but how could he? He was on a date with the perfect woman, while his wife is in New York wondering where he has gone to. Who was he to make promises? So he allowed her the topic change.

"Yeah, spiders, Henry." Her eyes bulged at the thought of it. "I mean, I have this recurring nightmare that I buy this packet of Skittles, Okay, and I open the bag because I am just so excited to eat them. Like, it's been years since I've had them, and my mouth is just salivating at the thought of poppin' some ol' skits in my mouth! So, I rip open the bag and dump a bunch in my hands, but, instead of Skittles, thousands of teeny, tiny spiders explode onto my hand and start crawling all over me! And they jump in my mouth before I even have a chance to scream!"

Henry's eyes widen at the thought of it, too. This woman never ceased to amaze him – never a dull moment.

"Well, then what happens?" Henry urged.

"Oh, well, that's usually when I wake up. So, yeah. Terrified of spiders."

"And I should think Skittles!" Henry interjected.

"You would think, but not so much actually. I actually really like Skittles. Dreams and nightmares are funny that way – what you think you would feel, isn't always the reality," Ara said as a matter of fact.

"I've got to say, these are truly revealing details about just who Miss Arabella Bennett is deep down, you know, as a person," Henry joked.

"Oh, I'm deep like that," Ara smiled and nodded, a blush blooming on her cheeks. "Henry … if you could have any candy right now, what would it be?" Ara changed the subject.

Henry was relieved, but he still wanted to know more about her. "Hmm ...Twizzlers," he said.

"All right, I'll bite. Why, Twizzlers, Henry?" Ara sarcastically played along.

"Oh, well I am glad you asked, my friend. I chose Twizzlers, not because I like licorice – I hate it, can't stand it – but because all I can think about is unraveling the mystery that is you." Henry looked pleased with his metaphor.

"Mystery? How am I the mystery? What do you want to know?" She ran her hand over her golden hair and shrugged at him questioningly.

"I can know anything?"

"I promise."

"Pinky promise?" Henry held up his pinky.

Ara interlocked her pinky with his. "Pinky promise." She smiled confidently.

"Wow, now I don't know what to ask." Henry scratched his head.

Ara pushed him playfully, her blue eyes sparkling. "Come on. You had something in mind. Just ask it!"

"I mean, I really didn't have something specific, but I do have one question I really want to know." Henry paused before asking. "Okay, obviously you know that I have never been a religious guy, and you seem to be highly involved with … your faith. Does it bother you that I am not … religious?"

"There is..."

Henry interrupted her. "Wait, let me rephrase that. When you picture the man of your dreams, do you picture someone more devoted to something other than himself, like God?"

Ara looked at him directly in the eyes and without the slightest hesitation answered, "Henry, I picture a lot of things in my life. The answer is yes. I do picture someone more devoted, but you know what else I picture? Someone who loves and cares for me in a way barely imaginable, someone who I could do anything with and tell anything to. And I thought I had the first thing once, the devotion to God, so I assumed the love part had to go along with it, but I was so, so wrong, Henry. And I sort of figured out along the way that if I find someone with all the other traits that I dream of in a man, well, to love like the love I dream of, that can only come from something good. You can't love that way and be a bad person. You may not know God, but I am so certain that He knows you. And that's enough for me."

Henry just looked at her awestruck. "Well … that was the perfect answer." He had no words, literally nothing and smiled shyly at her.

Neither one of them had openly admitted feelings for each other. Sure, they obviously had them, but these words were almost a declaration from Ara, and Henry couldn't say anything to it. He was literally speechless, which rarely happens to him.

Ara laughed. "You don't have to say anything else. I'm pretty sure I know what you're thinking anyway. So, instead of you thinking about something you could possibly say, let's save that for later and get back to climbing. I mean, you did just conquer your climb. I need to see you work some more magic."

"Deal."

Ara jumped to her feet and grabbed Henry's hand with a grin to pull him to her side.

They ran back up the trail together. They made it back to the rock face and paced back and forth to find their next climb. They mutually decided on one immediately to the right of Muster Buster. They took turns climbing and continued climbing until the sun was starting to set.

They drove home with the radio on and the windows down. Ara's head fell gently to the side as she fell asleep against her window.

Henry looked down at her and smiled affectionately, turning the radio down just enough to still hear it. "Lucy in the Sky with Diamonds" played softly as the sun sank below the horizon.

23
HENRY'S JOURNEY
Jackson Hole, Wyoming
August 28, 1992

The rising sun was beginning to light the cabin as Henry awoke, still holding Arabella. He jumped from a sudden cramp in his calf and woke Ara. "Ugh. Man," He groaned, trying not to yell out.

"Oh, Henry." Ara blinked sleepily. "Charlie horse?" She asked sympathetically.

Henry tried to be tough. "It's not that bad." He laid back and yelped, holding his leg.

Ara laughed. "Here, let me rub that for you." She gently reached down and rubbed the hardened muscle until it relaxed.

"Ohhhh. Thanks." He grinned at her. "Taking care of me again."

She laughed. "I am gettin' used to it."

"So am I." He looked down into her eyes and felt a heat rise inside of him. She was so perfectly beautiful as she gazed back sleepily. He was getting used to it, too. But what was he doing? He asked the first question that came to his mind to change the pace of the moment. "So, what time do we need to be out at Mitch's?"

Her eyes flew open. "Soon." She looked at the clock. "Really soon, about a half hour." She stretched her muscles. "Boy, am I sore!" She pulled one leg back and up to stretch her quad. "It is gonna be rough to ride horse after that climb yesterday!"

"It sure will be." Henry agreed as he stretched his sore arms.

She groaned as she stretched her other leg. After some more moaning and groaning from stretching her other sore muscles, she walked to her bedroom, calling over her shoulder, "We can stop quick at your cabin so you can change." She disappeared into her room.

He looked down at his casual shorts and shirt and chuckled. "Probably not the best ranch-working clothes." He said. He heard Ara laugh from inside her room and walked to the kitchen sink. He grabbed a glass of water and watched the sunrise as he sipped.

"Let's go." Ara emerged from her room wearing a brown and white striped button-down ranch shirt with the sleeves rolled up to her elbows. She was wearing Wranglers and brown leather boots with soft pink accents and stitching. Her long hair was tied into a single braid down her back. She held a dark brown cowboy hat and matching gloves in her hands.

Ara laughed at Henry's obvious approval of her outfit and opened the screen door. "Come on, Henry. We are going to be late."

"Can't they manage without us?" Henry asked teasingly, wiggling his eyebrows suggestively at her.

She crossed her arms, and gave him a hard look.

At the stern shake of Ara's head, Henry laughed and followed her out the door to his car. He could read her signals loudly and clearly.

****

They arrived at Mitch's ranch right on time. As he drove into the yard, Henry thought the ranch was absolutely breathtaking. A long, white, wooden fence outlined the front of the ranch. As they entered the driveway, a large blue mail box in the shape of a hummingbird sat perched to his left, its wing up, signaling outgoing mail. To the left of the driveway, a light yellow, ranch-style house with white doors and trim was stretched modestly among lilac bushes and green trees. A large white barn and other white outbuildings were built on the wide expanse of land to the right of the driveway, like speckled white eggs in a nest of green pastures. Beyond them, Henry could see the pasture filled with horses grazing on the grass in the morning coolness. But even beyond that was the most magnificent backyard view of which anyone could ask: the Teton Mountains. One could not see where Mitch's land ended and the mountains began. They were so far away from the mountains, but the high peaks and rising hills still made Henry feel small in comparison.

He parked the car alongside a few other vehicles in front of the house. Together, Ara and he walked up the short flight of white steps. Before they could knock, Mitch flung open the door with a smile. "Well, it is about time, guys! We thought we would have to hog tie all them cattle without ya!" He said loudly as he embraced Ara. He shook

Henry's hand and slapped him on the back before leading them into the house.

A few other men were gathered around the kitchen table eating breakfast. They stood as Ara entered, respectfully saying good morning and nodding to Henry.

Ara laughed as she greeted them in return and told them to get back to their breakfast.

Nicole came around the counter, balancing a pitcher of orange juice, a plate heaped full of biscuits, and a pile of scrambled eggs. "Hey, you two." She smiled at them and thanked Ara as she took the plate of eggs from her. Nicole set the items on the table and waved her hand at it. "Sit down and eat before these three cowboys take it all." She hurried back to the stove to attend to a boiling pot.

Henry pulled out Ara's chair for her, and they sat down. Mitch jumped into his chair and piled Ara's plate full of food before filling his own plate with as much as he could fit.

Ara looked at Henry pleadingly.

Henry scooped half of her plate onto his with a laugh.

Mitch dug right in and chewed a few mouthfuls before introducing the three men to Henry. "Oh, right, I almost forgot … Henry, these here men are my hired hands." He spoke with pride as he continued. "Best cowboys a man could have. That's Jordan over there with the fiery head. Now don't mess with him too much as his temper 'll flare so fast you'll wish you were in Kansas."

The men laughed and shook their heads. Jordan grinned at Mitch with his eyes sparkling. "Then there's Brennen and Cal. They are brothers and can wrangle a calf so fast you can't even blink and it's done." The two men nodded to Henry. "Men, this is Henry. Well, I've told ya'll a few things 'bout him already." The men nodded and continued eating. "And ya'll know Ara o' course." With the introductions finished, he continued eating heartily, thankful that the pleasantries of introduction would stop inhibiting his breakfast consumption rate. He really knew how to "throw down," as some would say.

Nicole brought over some more eggs and bacon, filling Henry's plate first and keeping the platters out of Mitch's reach. She laughed as he protested the inequality of it all before pulling her into his lap and kissing her on the cheek with a grin.

Henry listened to Ara easily chat with the cowboys and took a bite of a biscuit and then one of eggs. The food was delicious, and he told Nicole so.

"Thanks, Henry." She pinched Mitch's arm to escape his embrace and went back to the kitchen to continue cooking.

"So, Henry." Cal said. "We heard about your rodeo skills. Pretty good with them bulls, huh?"

Henry swallowed before answering. "Well, ya, I guess so. That's what I'm told anyway."

"So how do ya think you'll do ridin' horse and workin' cows?" Brennen asked.

Before Henry could answer, Mitch interrupted. "Just fine, guys." He said with confidence and with food still in his mouth. "Henry, here, is a natural cowboy. Just as though he was born in a saddle."

"Well, I don't know about that." Henry protested.

"It's true!" Ara piped up in excitement, then blushed as everyone looked at her with surprise. "Well, I saw you ride, Henry. That was exactly what I thought, too." She looked down at her plate and fiddled with a few pieces of egg.

He looked at her, eyes blazing with wonderment. Henry was touched by her honesty for a moment. He smiled at her and squeezed her leg lightly under the table. "So, what is it exactly we are doing today?" He asked trying to pull the spotlight off her.

Mitch set down his utensils and looked around the table, suddenly all business-like. "We're separatin' cattle in a pasture out there in the mountains and then bringin' a select hundred home for sale. It'll be a full day's work. I really 'ppreciate the help."

"We are glad to help," Ara said as she got out of her chair and began piling the dishes into her arms.

Henry poured himself a cup of steaming coffee and chatted with the other men for a few minutes as Ara continued clearing the table and taking the dishes to Nicole to wash. All the men were either tapping their feet or fidgeting with their hands, anxious to start work. Henry knew he was in for a real ride today.

"Well, let's go," Mitch said, standing up and putting his dusty black Stetson on his head.

Everyone followed suit and walked out the door in a flurry of cowboy hats, worn leather gloves, and broken-in boots.

Henry stopped to thank Nicole for breakfast before following the others out into the bright sunlight and encroaching heat.

They walked to the huge barn where several horses were already saddled and waiting for their riders. The men spread out and began checking the saddles on their individual horses.

Ara ran over to a sleek black Arabian and began talking and rubbing the horse's head. She grabbed Henry and pulled him over to the horse.

"Henry, this is my horse, Cobalt." She rubbed his head, and the horse neighed happily. "I have had him for quite a few years. He is the best horse you will ever meet." She smiled fondly at the horse. Then, she motioned to the horse next to hers. "This is my dad's horse, Boomer." She walked over to him and rubbed the tall horse's cheek. "He is yours to ride today." She went back to checking the cinch on the saddle of her own horse.

Henry looked his horse over. He was a tall quarter horse, a light tan and white paint. Henry ran his hands over his front shoulder, feeling the powerful muscles underneath. The horse eyed him questioningly. Henry rubbed his neck and stroked his long face. "Hey there, boy. You ready to ride today?" He lifted a stirrup and pulled on the cinch as Ara was doing, checking to make sure it was tight before unhooking Boomer and taking him outside to join the others.

She swung gracefully into the saddle as he was still walking and smiled over at Henry. "Here, Henry. Toss me your reins," Ara said from atop Cobalt.

Henry handed her the reins, put his foot in the stirrup, and swung his leg over Boomer. The horse walked a little, impatient to get moving.

Ara threw him back his reins. He caught them easily and shifted his weight to get the feel of the horse.

"All right, men. This way." Mitch waved his arm in the direction of the distant mountains. The men and Ara all followed behind him with the horses moving quickly, their hooves trampling the earth like a vivacious melody being pounded on the drums. The horses took their strides with purpose, each trot adding to their song of the drive.

Henry sensed the horses' excitement, and his heart pounded with adrenaline. Boomer pulled his head against the reins, wanting to run. Henry pulled back firmly and saw the other cowboys doing the same. He looked over at Ara and noticed she was riding easily and barely strained with the reins. He watched as her horse moved his ears backward and forward, waiting for each signal from his rider. She barely moved her hands, and the horse responded instantly. They were almost one being, moving together across the flat grassland.

Ara grinned at him and urged her horse into a trot. With signals from their riders, the other horses also began trotting and then loping across the land toward the mountains. Henry much preferred the smooth lope to the trot. He pulled his hat down lower over his forehead to help keep out the dirt. The drums of the horses' hooves played smoothly but rapidly onward.

Before long, they came to the base of the first mountains and slowed as they moved into a single-file line to ride into the hills. The air was cooler and kept cooling as they wound their way deeper into the land. At the start of the slope, it was dense with dark green pine trees and small spruce trees that shaded the horses and the riders. Henry filled his lungs with the scent of fresh pine and hints of moisture from a creek nearby and relaxed his back slightly. He looked back and saw Ara taking a deep breath as well. It was irresistible.

She smiled at him and rubbed her horse's neck, murmuring words to him. The horse nodded his head a few times as if taking her words to heart.

"Hold up." Henry heard Mitch say. He pulled back on the reins to stop Boomer. They all watched as Mitch dismounted and walked around the few cattle paths that branched in different ways. Mitch looked carefully at the ground, touching it in a few places before mounting his horse again. "Okay, boys. This way." They all followed behind him on the cattle path to the farthest left.

Henry shook his head in wonder, not believing Mitch could track the cattle by touching the ground. He supposed he would find out soon if Mitch was right.

After a few minutes, Henry heard Ara say, "It's the best, isn't it?" Henry looked back and nodded as they continued riding. Her eyes burned brightly with fiery excitement and passion. He had never seen her look quite so intense before, so focused yet excited.

The sun rose higher in the sky as they followed the path deeper into the mountains. They passed a few lakes and streams, stopping once or twice to let the horses drink for a few seconds. At one lake, Henry spied two deer drinking across the water. The graceful deer bounded away gracefully into the woods. He took his water bottle from one of the pockets in his saddle and took a small drink before slipping it back inside.

Just as he was buckling the strap of the pocket, he heard a loud noise and saw a few pheasants flying noisily into the air. Boomer shied to one side underneath him, almost slipping Henry off. He grabbed onto the saddle horn and pulled himself back into balance. He pulled the reins tight and rubbed Boomer's neck to steady him.

Up two horses in line, Henry saw that Brennen was having trouble settling his horse down. The horse bucked up twice and stomped his feet, neighing angrily. The cowboy spun him in a tight circle to try and regain control. The horse shied to the side to try and throw his rider off. The cowboy pulled back hard on the reins and talked to the horse in a low voice to soothe him. The big horse finally calmed down, but his nostrils were still flaring and snorting uncomfortably.

"Everybody all right?" Mitch asked, looking back. Everyone nodded, and they continued on the trail.

"Brennen's been workin' with that stallion for about a year. He is still pretty young. Starts at every little noise." Cal turned and told Henry.

Henry nodded. "Looks like quite a handful."

"Ya. He sure is a fine horse, though."

The trail opened up to a flatter, wider area. Ara rode up beside Henry. She grinned at him and pushed back her hat to let the sun warm her face. Henry returned her smile and relaxed as the horses moved quickly over the short plane. "So do we have quite a ways to ride still?" He asked her.

Ara shook her head. "No, the herd should be close around here." She pointed down to a cow pie. "Look how fresh that is."

Henry nodded and looked around for some more signs of recent activity from cows. The plain slightly narrowed up ahead, and the trail wound around a high mountain peak. He listened carefully and thought he could hear the unmistakable sound of cows mooing to one another. A gentle breeze blew by him, and he wrinkled his nose, now certain that the cows were close. Ara laughed at him and shook her head. "I am still not used to that smell." Henry said grimacing dramatically.

Ara breathed in deeply. "Mmmmm. I love the smell. My dad used to always say it was the smell of fresh money."

"Well, he sounds like quite the business man. I would love to meet him." The words rolled off his tongue before he realized the depth of his words, but Ara just laughed and trotted ahead of him.

Up ahead, Mitch directed the three hands to a different trail to sneak behind the cows and move them the way the group had just come. He then waved Ara over to block a gap in the foliage and rock. Mitch then told Henry to follow him to the other side of the trail where a large gap in the trees showed a cattle path lined with cow pies. "That's their path to water." Mitch told him. "We need to block it because their first instincts will be to run that way."

Henry nodded and guided Boomer over to stand in front of the gap.

It was not long before Henry heard some whooping and yelling in the distance. Suddenly, the ground seemed to shudder as tons of cattle came running around the mountain and into the plain. Boomer stomped his foot and blew air out of his nostrils, impatient to start moving.

Mitch yelled as some cows tried to sneak between his horse and his side of the gap to the water hole. He expertly rode, twisting and turning with his horse to block each cow.

Henry mimicked Mitch's moves and blocked the cows coming to his side. He felt as though he barely had to tell Boomer what to do as the horse had obviously worked cows for years.

As the cows found the trail that Mitch wanted them to be on, they moved steadily after the other cows in the lead. Henry watched them run past and looked over to see Ara expertly blocking her path. She twisted and turned her horse as Mitch had, whooping and yelling to scare the cows. He had never seen anyone look so graceful and completely at ease while working so hard. Women did not work like this in his class of people.

Finally, the endless line of cattle seemed to dwindle with a few stragglers bringing up the rear, and Henry saw the three cowboys close behind them. They yelled and slapped their saddles to keep the cows moving.

"Come on, Henry!" Ara yelled and urged Cobalt into a gallop to keep up with the cows.

Henry kicked Boomer in the sides, and together they blasted up to Ara and the rest of the group. He yelled and slapped his leg with his reins.

Mitch and Brennen moved to the side of the cows, driving them into a closer line. They then urged their horses faster until they were in front of the cows, pulling the horses to a trot and effectively slowing the cows down for the trail out of the mountains.

After a few minutes, the cows slowed to a fast walk, and Henry breathed deeply, trying to calm down. His blood still pumped quickly, filled with adrenaline.

"I thought bull riding was a rush!" He said to Ara, who was riding quite close to him now as they descended down a trail, bringing up the rear of the group.

She laughed and adjusted her cowboy hat. "Ya." Her eyes sparkled as she smiled at him. "You look like such a natural cowboy. I almost forget you were a city-boy when we are out here."

Henry chuckled and breathed deeply. Boomer reached out and nipped a straggling cow in the tush. The cow jumped and moved up to join the herd. Henry rubbed Boomer's neck fondly.

"He is a good horse, isn't he?" Ara said and reached over and rubbed Boomer's neck as well.

"Ya, he is. Does your dad come home and ride often?"

Ara bit her lip. "Not really. He hasn't been home in a few years. My mother gets anxious if he leaves her alone." She loosened the reins and scratched Cobalt's ears. "But I ride Boomer quite a bit when my horse needs a rest. Or I lead them both out into a valley over that way," Ara pointed southwest. "And they eat grass while I suntan or read."

"But don't they just run away?"

"Well, if they would, the horses would just run back to the barn. But they love to be out in the open. And Cobalt, well, he loves me. Horses are even more loyal than dogs to good owners, you know."

Henry took in this information and adjusted his reins, giving Boomer some more free rein. "That sounds wonderful actually."

"Mmmm, yes, it is."

They rode in silence for a bit, just enjoying the beautiful day and the company. Henry watched Jordan and Cal working on the sides of the cattle line. They rode up and down pushing the cows together when some stopped for grass or to find their calf. A cow got behind a tree to eat some grass. Cal pulled back on his horse and rode a wide circle around behind the cow. He whooped and scared the cow back into line. Then he rode ahead to keep pushing the cows. The whole thing was like a dance, wild and yet highly organized. Henry thought his own job pushing the cows from the back was much easier but still exciting.

The trail declined some more, and Henry leaned back to help Boomer balance down the hill. He looked up ahead and saw Mitch waving signals to his group. Henry was confused as he saw the cowboys turning the cows. They were still about a half hour away from the ranch. He glanced over at Ara. "We have to sort the herd. There is a small corral fence just around that hill." She took off to help turn the cows. "Stay at the back and make sure they don't turn around but just turn right." She yelled over her shoulder.

Henry watched as the herd slowed and turned slightly in the direction Mitch wanted them to turn. But then a few in the herd turned too far and began making a wide circle back toward Henry. The rest of the cows followed the ones in the lead. Hundreds of cows began running full bore toward him. Henry saw the others yelling and kicking their horses to come help him. He let instinct kick in and let Boomer have his head. The horse knew what he was doing.

Together, horse and man trotted back and forth in front of the oncoming stampede. Henry yelled and whooped to scare the cows. They barely hesitated and kept barreling toward him and Boomer at full speed. Henry looked up and saw the other cowboys were still seconds away. He guided Boomer to the far left and, when the cows were almost close enough to touch, he kicked the horse hard in the side and Boomer leapt forward at a gallop. They shot in front of the cows and in the direction they were supposed to turn.

Looking back, Henry was shocked to see that the cows had slowed and were now following him. He galloped straight for the trail Ara had pointed out earlier. He heard the other cowboys whooping and yelling to keep the cows following him. Henry saw the fenced-in corral and charged to it on his willing horse. At the last second, he turned and pulled Boomer to a stop right before entering the corral. The cows poured in, and Mitch rode up, jumped off his horse, and shut the gate.

"That was some nice ridin' there, Henry!" Mitch told him as he jumped back on his horse. "I thought we were in some real big trouble there for a minute."

"Ya, well I just let Boomer take over."

"He is a great horse, but it takes a cowboy to ride like that." Ara said as she rode up next to them. Her eyes shone with admiration as she smiled at Henry.

"All right, now that we have established the rodeo champion can work cows, let's get movin'!" Brennen said with mock sarcasm.

"Good idea." Mitch looked off into the distance. "'Cept I see my beautiful wife is right on time in bringin' us a late lunch. Men, I guess we get to eat quickly before gettin' back to work!"

The men whooped and hollered in excitement, and the herd of cattle mooed loudly in the corral. Henry still could not believe that all the men had to do was tie the reins loosely around the saddle horn, and the horses just grazed on the grass around the corral. He followed their example and watched as Boomer took a few steps away from him and began eating grass.

Nicole pulled up in a dusty red pickup and climbed out. She reached into the cab and pulled out a large bag.

Mitch walked over, kissed her with a smile, and grabbed the bag from her which he tossed to Jordan. She pointed to the passenger side of the truck, and Mitch pulled out a large cooler filled with water bottles, fresh vegetables, and fruits.

He set down the cooler by the group, announcing, "All right, men. We have a ten minute break for lunch, and then we gotta sort them cattle to get 'em where we need 'em by dark. There is no way we can let that ol' sun set on us before we are finished. Those cows are goin' out on the train in the mornin'."

Everyone nodded and filled the thick paper plates Nicole had provided with the sandwiches and fruits and veggies. They all ate the thick roast beef sandwiches quickly without stopping to take a breath. They ate in silence. Henry realized his body was feeling slightly drained of energy, but he was still having the time of his life. The adrenaline from the rush of the adventure kept him going full throttle. He was surrounded by great people including, most essentially, Ara, in the middle of one of the purest forms of nature.

He surveyed the land and all these wonderful people around him that had welcomed him most ardently. Suddenly, he remembered his promise to himself to tell the unbearable truth to Ara. He was dizzy, and he could hear his heart pounding in guilt. He forced it away like usual, leaving a scar on his conscience for keeping something so crucial from his Ara. But would she be *his* Ara when she knew the truth? His heart was in turmoil, but now was not the time to deal with these contentions of the heart.

Nicole came around and collected all the garbage, and she gave Henry a quizzical smile as if she could see into his heart before taking his plate from him. She also handed out bottles of sunscreen, urging everyone to reapply.

Henry slathered some more on as he could feel the hot sun beating through his skin, not that it would fix the handprint left on his chest from before. He remembered his nickname affectionately. "Burns."

He felt Ara tap him on the shoulder. She was sitting cross-legged next to him on the grass and applying sunscreen as well. "Did I get it all rubbed in?" She asked with a white streak down her nose and a smear on her forehead.

Henry laughed, his stress melting away with just one word from her. "Just about." He said teasingly and reached over and gently rubbed in her remaining sunscreen.

She scrunched her nose in girlish delight. "Thanks. Oh, and you have a little somethin' right ... about ... here." She reached over and placed her hand on the side of his neck and gently rubbed in the white streak.

Henry reached up, caught her hand, and squeezed it affectionately. "Thanks."

Ara blushed and looked down at her water bottle shyly. She opened it and took a small swig before standing up. "Looks like break time is over." She said as she dusted off her hands on her jeans and put her cowboy hat back on.

"All right. Back to work." Mitch called. He kissed Nicole and helped her back into the truck.

She drove off with a wave to the group, leaving a winding dust trail back to the main house.

"Jordan and Cal, you boys are on splittin' duty. Brennen, why don't you and Ara drive 'em to their sides once cut. And to help me cut, Henry, you are my man."

Everyone mounted up and went to their assigned sections.

Henry climbed on Boomer and rode over to Mitch. "So, you want to explain real quickly what "cutting" means?" Henry asked.

Mitch nodded. "Oh right … so, we are splitting some of the herd off to sell tomorrow at the station. See the blue tags on their ears? I'll tell you a number, and then we'll separate or "cut" each one from the herd. Got it?"

"Ya. I think so." Henry said trying to sound more confident than he felt.

Mitch smiled reassuringly as though sensing Henry's wariness. "Boomer will do most of the work. He has done this thousands of times and is a real good cow-sorter. Just point him straight at the cow we want, and he will pretty much do the rest."

Henry thought Mitch's words over for a few seconds. It sounded like he would figure it out and had a great horse to help him. "Okay. Let's get started."

"Good." He pulled a sheet of crinkled paper from his pocket and looked it over closely. "Okay. The first one is 922." He yelled it to Jordan and Cal who nodded.

Ara opened the gate and all four entered the fenced-in area. Henry saw that Ara left the gate open, mounted Cobalt, and then guarded the gate with Brennen a few yards behind her. He turned his attention to the blue tags on the cows: 845, 864, 969, 801, 945.

"922 here." Cal said.

Henry and Mitch closed in on the cow. The other cows moved out of the way as they approached, moving closer to 922.

Henry pointed Boomer straight at her, so he would know which one to cut from the herd.

The cow suddenly tried to dart to the right past Mitch, but he swung his horse over quickly to block her. She then decided to run straight between Henry and Mitch.

Boomer leapt forward and blocked her path. Finally, 922 ran down past Cal and Jordan who helped guide her toward the gate entrance.

Ara moved Cobalt to the side to let just 922 through. Then, along with Brennen, Ara chased the cow out a ways back, the way they had come with the herd.

Mitch called out a new number, and the whole process resumed again.

About two hours later, Mitch announced there were only two left on the list. Henry was relieved as his arms, legs, and hands were beginning to ache from the rigorous work. He wiped his arm across his forehead to catch the sweat dripping from his brow and adjusted his hips in the saddle. The next two were standing right by each other and went out the gate easily.

Mitch announced, "The remainin' cows are goin' to the ranch." He tipped his hat back and wiped his brow. "Whew. It is just easy goin' from here."

They whooped at the cows to get them moving out of the gate. Ara and Brennen blocked the way on both sides of the gate so that the cows would not run to the rest of the herd. Soon, they got them moving in the right direction.

Henry sneakily maneuvered his way to the back to join Ara. He could not believe it had only been just over two hours since he had last talked to her, and he missed her already.

She smiled as he approached. "Hey. You did some good work today."

"You think so? I think it was mostly Boomer."

Ara laughed. "Always so modest."

They listened to Brennen and Cal discuss the herd Mitch had cut out to sell for about half an hour. As they neared the ranch, Ara motioned to Henry to slow Boomer a bit. He pulled back on the reins, and Cobalt and Boomer slowed as the herd kept moving away. "I want to show you something."

Henry did not recognize the look in her eyes. It was urgent and sad and excited all at the same time. "All right. But, doesn't Mitch need us?"

Ara shook her head. "No. I already told him what we will be doing." She tossed Henry a water bottle that she had stowed in her saddle bag. "We are going to come back for the bonfire in a few hours." She pointed toward the right to a faint trail in the grass. "This way."

Henry heard Mitch call out to them. "Bonfire at eight, guys. Don't forget!"

They urged the horses into a smooth lope and rode through a long valley in between the mountains. He sensed that she did not want to talk and focused on the ride. The horses threw their heads back and ran with a sense of freedom Henry knew they had not had during working cattle. It was as if they knew the work was over for the day, and now they could play.

They came to the end of the valley and ascended up a short trail. After winding through the mountainside for a short time, they came to a clearing in the trees. Ara dismounted and tied Cobalt's reins to a large tree branch before walking to the edge of the short cliff. Henry followed suit and joined her.

Below him was one of the most beautiful scenes he had ever witnessed. Nestled in a small valley was a ranch. The buildings were white as the ones on Mitch's ranch but were lined with blue trim. He saw white fences holding sleek horses. The scent of the flowers filled the valley with an almost dizzying scent. Henry could see blue dahlias and asters in fuchsia and lavender in bloom, and bright yellow sunflowers were sprinkled around the edges of the clearing. Bluebells and golden asters filled the spaces in between countless rose bushes. Roses in white, light and dark pink, and deep shades of red surrounded the buildings. It was like its own little sanctuary tucked safely in this fortitude of beauty.

From the cliff, Henry could also see the charming two-story main house in matching white with blue trim. A little stone pathway lined with Little Bluestem grass led up to swirled glass doors. A large willow tree stretched across the backyard, covering the grass with a wide, cozy shadow.

After taking in the view for another minute, Henry realized that the paint was beginning to peel and fade on the buildings. The trees were in need of pruning as well as the flowers. He could see that the white fences also needed some work. He couldn't imagine letting a place like this just wastefully rot away.

Ara still had not said a word since they had arrived. Henry patiently waited for a few minutes, but he felt fairly certain he knew what was in front of him. His stomach clenched painfully at the expression on her face as it was filled with longing and heartbreak. She had wrapped her arms around herself as if to keep herself from crying out in utter pain. Henry could not help himself; he moved behind her and wrapped his arms tightly around her. "So this is your ranch."

She turned in his arms and looked up at him with pain-filled eyes. "It was." She moved out of his embrace and sat on the ground facing the ranch with her arms wrapped around her legs. "It is a terrible story, Henry. But I just need to share it to help you understand me."

Henry sat down next to her with one leg dangling over the edge of the cliff and rested both arms on his bent knee. He looked down at the ranch and waited for her to continue.

"Do you remember when I told you I was married?"

Henry nodded silently, waiting, his stomach wrapped into a tight ball of dread and sadness. He wanted to lift the heartbreak from her, free her of the terrible look of pain on her beautiful face.

"My ex-husband had been cheatin' on me, with multiple women actually, during our short, little sham of a marriage."

Henry felt her need to confess, and he felt a sharp twist of guilt for not sharing himself.

"I was young, incredibly naive, and blinded by what I thought was love. I was like his pet, followin' him around beggin' him for scraps of affection." She was shaking her head as if she was in disbelief that she would ever allow herself to be that way.

Henry wanted to reassure her that everyone does things for someone that they just can't explain. He wanted to tell her that the past is the past, and that is where pain and mistakes should stay. But he let her continue.

"Anyway, I finally had had enough and confronted him about the cheating, and he tried to hit me. I ran out of the house, *my* house, the house I had grown up in and ran to Mitch and Nicole's and stayed with them, terrified of him coming after me. They protected me and helped chase him out of town while the divorce was processed. You see, people around here do not take kindly to hittin' or tryin' to hit women around here." She paused and fiddled with the string of her hat. "My parents gave us the ranch as a wedding present. We had to split it in the divorce. I could not buy his half with the amount of debt he had racked up, debt which we also had to split ..." She trailed off and looked down.

"So you had to sell it." Henry's voice twisted in anger. His heart hardened with pure and unadulterated indignation for the man who had caused her to lose everything. "I guess he's pretty lucky he's not still in town, or he would be getting a visit from me. I just want to smack the jerk right out of him."

Ara laughed somewhat bitterly. "Ya. Me too."

He put his arm around her shoulder and pulled her closer to him. "Do you know who owns it now?"

"Oh, yeah." She rested her head on his shoulder. "You know him. His name is Joe, Joe Davis. You were talking to him at the rodeo when I first saw you."

Henry tried to remember, then it hit him: Joe, the guy with frozen blue eyes. "Ugh."

"Exactly. I have tried countless times to buy the ranch back, now that I have saved up enough." She stretched out her legs so they dangled over the edge. "Joe won't have it. Not unless I ..." She made a terrible face, like she was embarrassed even to say the words. "Marry him." She hung her head in her hands.

"What!" Henry felt even more enraged, and, he realized, jealous. "You would never marry that man ... would you?"

Ara shook her head sadly. "It is such a ludicrous idea! Like, how does someone have the nerve to even suggest that. It's so ... medieval. You just don't bribe somebody into marriage. Ugh! I just wish I could have my ranch back. I mean, look, he doesn't even take care of it!" Her hands splayed out in front of her as if to showcase the decrepit sight before them. "My family planted the flowers and grasses and built that house, and, if you think this is beautiful, you should have seen it when

Amber Duran & Talia Johnson

we took care of it." Her frustrations were coming to a boiling point, and tears started to well up in her eyes.

Henry wanted so much to tell her that it will all work out, you'll get it back, you have nothing to worry about. But no words came out. He couldn't promise anything, but he knew for sure that he was going to do everything in his power to get that ranch back for her.

"When I came here, I came because I had lost myself. I was so ... lost in what people call life, and what I call a lie that it took just turning my back on everything I had ever known and driving off into the unknown."

He looked into her blue eyes, eyes sparkling with unshed tears. "And I ended up ... here, with you. *You*, this unexplainable force, who inspires me and knows what I'm thinking without me saying it, and I believe in all these different things that I have never thought of before, like destiny and a sort of predetermined purpose for life. For the first time in my life, I am passionate about things besides work and how people "see" me, about life and enjoying life and looking forward to the future."

"And I know it's not even close to the same thing, but I know the loss you feel, how it is fraught with sorrow and misery. I understand your pain., and I am sorry these things have happened to you in your life." He took her hand, hoping to ease her pain in any way he could.

Tears were rolling down her pink cheeks, which were hot with emotion. She let them roll freely, not embarrassed in front of Henry, and she whispered softly, "Thank you, Henry." She leaned into his chest, and he wrapped his arms around her in a tight embrace.

Henry felt connected and vastly lighter in spirit just holding Ara close. He could feel her ragged breathing, and her wet cheek dampening his shirt with her tears. His thoughts drifted to his own sorrow, his own marriage that he knew could not go on. He could not go back to New York and resume the person he had been. He was forever changed.

He was even more confident of his decision to end it with Anne. He decided he needed to start that process as soon as possible. He needed to call his lawyer in the city to have him draw up divorce papers. Surely, Anne would be expecting it after not hearing from him in days and his abrupt and depressed departure.

Maybe that would mean something to Ara, if he was planning to leave his wife all along. There was no way to avoid hurting her at this point, but anything to soften the blow was what Henry was searching for. He couldn't bear the thought of hurting the already scarred Ara, but he knew that he already had, by not telling her. And there was no going back now. One way or the other, Ara had to know, and he would hurt her, deeply. He hated that he would be the one causing her tears as her ex-husband and Joe were causing her now.

Fury built up in his chest as he thought of him. His anger toward Joe was accentuated by the guilt he felt about hiding from Ara. He hadn't even begun to reconcile the shared moments of laughter, conversation, and adventures to the fact that every single special moment was tainted by his lies. They were wrong, each and every one of them. He had no doubt Ara would believe that once she knew the truth. It all felt good and right, but it wasn't. Not really. She would never see it any other way. He remembered what she said about how he was good and how God knew him.

His thoughts churned, making him even angrier, at himself mostly, but he knew that if he saw Joe right now, he would not be the gentleman that Ara knew.

Ara parted their embrace and took his hand to get him up off the ground. "We better get back, huh? Mitch will throw a fit if we are too late for the bonfire." Ara laughed and brushed away the last of her tears, sniffling slightly and using the sleeve of her arm as a tissue.

Henry paused and looked at her casual release of her anger and replacing it with a loving smile. He wished he could just let go like her. His tendency was to hold onto anger and grudgingly seek revenge until everything was justly made right. Since being here, though, he realized he was letting go and giving in more often and more easily. "Yeah … yeah, we better get going." Henry got up and patted the dirt off the butt of his jeans, offering a final sympathetic smile.

"Thank you for being here." Ara whispered as she traipsed over to the horses, affectionately squeezing his hand.

Henry climbed on his horse slowly with sore muscles while Ara mounted hers with grace. "There is literally nowhere else I would rather be," he said, trying to keep from wincing.

They rode off into the mountains, back the way they came. Ara kicked the pace up with Henry following suit, and they were back just as the bonfire was starting, and the sun was setting on the day.

A large group of people had gathered at Mitch's house, certainly more than Henry had expected. A cluster of women were in the house banging pots and pans. Henry hoped they were making food. He was starving, and his stomach growled angrily.

A cacophony of laughter echoed through the countryside as folks passed around drinks and shared stories. Two little blond boys with sun-kissed freckled faces were chasing the dog around the yard, while a red-faced little girl cried out in protest, "Leave her alone, or I...I'll...I'll call the police!"

Henry smiled, and Ara concurred with her eyes that the exaggerated threat was indeed, passionate, something to take seriously. "Wow, an activist at such a young age. She's going to take the world by storm someday, if she hasn't already," He winked at Ara.

Ara nodded and bit her lower lip, raising her eyebrows in trenchant nervousness. "Let's get these horses put away."

They headed to the barn where they had help in unsaddling and brushing down their sweaty horses. Henry gave Boomer a loving stroke down his nose and thanked him for the ride before they walked back toward the still gathering crowd.

Henry put an arm around Ara and kissed her on her cheek, before grabbing her hand and moving into the crowd. "Let's go." They made their way through the meandering people, hand in hand. He caught the hesitant stares of people analyzing the clear display of affection. Some scowled while others smiled. Henry didn't care, and Ara didn't seem to even notice.

A couple of guys were sitting around the campfire strumming away on guitars, while a couple of girls sang a country tune in a perfect two-part harmony. The brunette, who was singing alto, was tapping her thigh with her hand, keeping the beat, and the redhead to her left sang a boisterous soprano, her hair tossing about as she wildly sang the lyrics of some upbeat love song Henry didn't recognize. A young teenage boy with shaggy brown hair and a Sex Pistols t-shirt joined in, beating a bucket with his hands for the drums.

Ara clapped her hands excitedly and started dancing then, completely free. Lines started forming around her for a line dance.

Everyone started whooping and hollering their cheers of approval as they made their way over to the dance party that was starting by the campfire. Tiki torches were lit and scattered throughout the yard, casting playful golden shadows on the dancing people.

Ara pulled Henry into line and fell right back into step with the music, flicking her feet with rhythm and grace and swaying her hips sensually with the beat of the concocted drum. She looked like she was letting the music take over her body, and her blissful smile overwhelmed Henry with desire, longing to take her home right then and there.

But he shook off the dizzying thoughts and played along, trying to keep step. Everyone seemed to know exactly what to do, and Henry watched Ara carefully to pick up the steps. Eventually, the moves began to repeat back to the beginning, and Henry recognized each step, now keeping up with the line of people exuberantly kicking up dirt with their boots.

Mitch and Nicole came up beside Henry, joining in on the festivities. When the song ended with a final and sudden pounding of the drum, the whole crowd threw up their arms in cheers.

Ara ran over to Henry and jumped on him, wrapping her legs around him and laughing with delight. She knotted her hands around his neck and threw her head back before grinning at him.

He smiled at her and spun her in a circle, his hands softly splayed across her lower back. Their eyes met as they spun, and the people, the music, the entire world seemed to disappear. Hers were dark blue in the light of the fire, sparkling and filled with warmth. Their lips were inches apart, then centimeters.

Ara tilted her head down, bringing her mouth close to his. She brushed her lips against his own confidently. There was no fear, no nervousness. She knew what she wanted, and she went for it. He loved that she wasn't the type of woman that felt like he had to initiate this, their first kiss.

He moved his hand to lightly cup the sides of her cheek and met her lips again, this time applying a light pressure. Their mouths parted slightly in their kiss, and her tongue played softly with the inside of Henry's lip.

Ara pulled away all too soon, and they momentarily gazed at each other before Henry dipped Ara back like they were still dancing. She laughed heartily, her head tilted backward, and strands from her long blond hair fell out of her loose ponytail, swaying softly back and forth in the gentle evening breeze.

She was pure joy in that moment, and it was infectious. Everyone around her fed off her energy. Couples were embracing while others cheered for another tune.

Ara brought herself back up from Henry's dip and smiled brightly. "I need a drink. You want me to get you one?"

Henry set her on her feet, "Ab-so-lutely!"

"Great, I'll be right back." Ara quickly darted off to one of the large white buildings and disappeared in the multitude of people. It seemed like more and more people had arrived by the minute. The numbers had almost doubled since Henry and Ara had arrived.

Henry sat down on a log around the campfire, next to the young drummer, impatiently awaiting Ara's return. He couldn't get enough of her.

"How's it goin', man?" The young boy stuck out his hand, thrusting himself into Henry's restlessness. "I'm Lewis."

Henry shook his hand, "Henry." He smiled at him. He didn't want to be rude so he set out to have a conversation with him. "That was some nice playing, Lewis."

"Oh, that? Yeah, that was nothin'. I was just playin' off the energy of the crowd. It's easy to get lost, isn't it?"

Henry remembered the look on Ara's face when she let herself go with the music. "Yeah, it really is. Is every get-together around here like this?"

"Naw, every night is different, sometimes it's more mellow, with casual conversation ... but there is always music..." Lewis continued talking, but Henry saw Mitch headed in his direction, looking determined.

He stopped in front of him curtly, removed his hat and stared Henry straight in the eyes.

"So you and Ara really hit it off, huh?" Mitch said bluntly.

Drummer-boy Lewis excused himself awkwardly and went over to another circle of people.

"Wow, Mitch. You cut right to the chase don't you?"

Mitch shook his head. "Well, look, Ara is a grown woman and can make her own decisions. But she hasn't looked at a man the way she is looking at you since ... well, in a long time, and I know what she showed you today. She doesn't do that for just anybody."

Mitch took a second to rub his beard and think about his next words.

"Look, you seem like a great guy, Henry. I like you, I really do. Just do not hurt her, Henry. Don't be that guy. That's all I'm going to say." Mitch held up both hands resolutely.

Henry got quiet for a moment and then, looking down at the ground as he spoke, he softly answered, "I'm not going to lie, Mitch, I'm inexplicably drawn to her. There's no getting around that." He looked to Mitch for some sort of reassurance and found no offering. "I don't know how to explain it, but with us, I just feel like it was ... all out of our hands, like there is some cosmic reason I came to *this* place and met *this* girl. And sometimes that doesn't seem right. Like, it's unfair that the fates would choose us, but who am I to deny it? I couldn't even if I tried. I would lose because I'm drawn to her like ... like I was this dead planet before I met her, and she entered my galaxy, a shining star, more beautiful than the sun, and now everything orbits around her. And now I just feel to lose her would be to like losing the sun."

"That's a nice speech, man, and I hope it's true. I'm just tellin' you right now, man to man, if you break her heart, I will never forgive you. There will be no 'I'm sorry's' to say."

His insides churned as he realized that he would inevitably end up hurting Ara, and, in the same foul swoop, losing a good friend – Mitch. He thought, *You are married, for Pete's sake. This has no future; it can't.* But Henry realized that at this point in time, he could not give her up. She was a light in his dark existence, and, for now, he had to take all the light he could get. Just thinking it, he knew how selfish he was being, but it didn't matter because, in his heart, he knew there had to be a purpose to seeing this through. He was hopeful that if the fates really were the cause of their coming together, then maybe the fates had a way of taking something so wrong and turning it right again.

He was about to say something to reassure Mitch, but his attention was pulled away as he caught a glint of a man walking through a group of people.

Joe, arrogant and vain, was eying a girl with tight blue jeans and an equally tight yellow tank top that revealed a tan midriff. The girl looked like she was sixteen, if that, and was giggling with her equally young friends. He nudged one of his buddies and pointed over to the girls, saying something Henry couldn't hear. They laughed crassly. Joe was practically drooling all over himself.

Henry felt his face get hot with rage, and, before even being aware of it, he found himself getting up and making his way over to Joe.

Mitch, a few feet away, saw where Henry's angry eyes were going, and he stepped in front of him. "Henry, do *not* go there."

"What? I just want to talk to the guy," Henry lied. He knew very well he did not want to talk, and Mitch knew it, too.

"Those are not talking eyes I see. Look, fighting Joe will not get Ara's ranch back. In fact, fighting him might make it even harder for her. So just back off."

Unconvinced, Henry pushed forward. He had never been one to run into a situation looking for a fight. Maybe it was the guilt racking up on his conscious for the lies and deceit, but Henry wanted to fight tonight, and Joe, after all he had done to Arabella, had it coming. Henry could kill two birds with one stone: pound the guilt down a little bit further so he could continue blissfully getting to know Ara, and teach arrogant Joe a much-needed lesson.

Mitch stopped him again, "You think I haven't wanted to take a swing at the bastard's face? I have. Trust me. But it won't do no good." Mitch sounded defeated knowing he had failed at convincing Henry.

Joe looked up just then, and saw Henry intently staring him down. He smiled slyly and sauntered right on over with his tall buddy.

Almost intuitively, the crowd parted, making a crooked circle around the four guys, sensing the tension between Joe and Henry.

"Well, if it isn't Mr. City Boy out playing cowboy. Boy, How-dee! Woohoo!" Joe mockingly whooped and guffawed to try and get the crowd riled up with him. Only his friend played along.

Everyone else seemed uneasy, the mood of the evening tapering to an eerie silence with dispersed whispers rising from the crowd. Mitch was the only thing standing between Henry and Joe.

Henry could smell the blue-eyed man. He stank of whisky and stale tobacco. It looked like his teeth were stained yellow from years of using chew, or maybe he was just imagining a nastier appearance to go with his hideous personality and character. He stared Joe down without speaking, his eyes hard and filled with anger.

Joe was laughing under his breath and glaring at Henry. "Boy, I don't like that look in your eye. What's chappin' your hide anyway? I ain't done nothin' to you." Joe persisted, irritated by Henry's intentional silence. "But if you wanna fight, you better think twice cuz I don't play nice. I'll warn ya now." Joe got up real close in Henry's face and muttered fiercely, "I don't think you could take me on even if you had the guts to, ya chicken!"

Henry had had enough and pushed him back away from his face.

Joe's face held a satisfied look, as if to thank Henry for initiating the fight.

"Just stay away from me, man. Stay away from me and stay even further away from Arabella." Henry sounded controlled in his voice, but inside he was shaking all over, He wasn't scared of Joe, but rather what Henry would do to him if he did not control his anger.

"Arabella? What are you her boyfriend?" Joe looked displeased and puzzled, no doubt disgusted by Henry's protectiveness over Arabella.

"Yeah, I'm her boyfriend, and I would appreciate you revoking your *bribe*!" Henry's voice dripped with disdain.

A flash of anger rose in Joe's eyes, and he took a step forward. "You have no right barging in on my business." His voice was low and rigid.

"If it involves Ara, I have every right." Henry retorted crisply.

"What? She needs a city boy to come play businessman for her, just to get her precious little piece-of-crap ranch back? Ha! She couldn't take care of a potted plant if she tried. You should have seen the crap I had to fix when I bought that 'ranch' off her. If it weren't for me, the place would be in shambles. It takes a man to run a ranch, not some washed-up divorcee!" Joe looked pleased with himself, sneering at Henry and then turning to look at the crowd to see if they were entertained by his display of masculinity, if you could even call it that.

Henry's rage boiled over, and he could no longer contain himself. He lunged forward quickly, passing Mitch, who now looked ready to punch Joe as well, and braced for contact against Joe's face. As Joe's face turned back toward Henry, his fist made contact with Joe's upper lip and the end of his nose.

Joe wasn't prepared for the blow and was knocked to the ground, his nose bloodied. The crowd gasped, and Henry saw Ara running up out of the corner of his eye. He was immediately filled with remorse even as anger and adrenaline thundered through his veins.

She had two bottles in her hands, and she dropped them straight away when she saw a bloody-faced Joe on the ground and a fuming Henry standing ready for a fight. "What is goin' on here?" Arabella's cheeks were flushed red, and the look in her eyes was confused and scared.

No one answered her, waiting to see what happened next.

Joe was pushing himself back to his feet, ready for a fight now. "That was a cheap shot, city boy," he snarled.

"Yeah, well those were cheap words, pretty boy. You deserved it. Never talk about Arabella like that again, ya hear me?" Henry said assertively, his tone never wavering.

Joe raised his hand to his nose to see if he was bleeding, and he wiped the liquid on his sleeve. Henry could recognize the embarrassment on Joe's face. He had been knocked down in one blow. His ego had taken a nice blow as well.

Finally, Henry looked over at Ara, and his heart tightened as she did not look pleased.

"What did you do, Henry?" Her voice was restrained.

Joe began walking toward Henry, clearly looking for a return hit.

Mitch stepped between them and told Joe angrily, "Get your lousy butt off my property, Davis." He then signaled his cowboys to get Joe.

Brennen, Jordan, and Cal, along with several of Mitch's friends, surrounded Joe and forcibly walked the angry cowboy and his friends off the ranch.

Nicole stepped out from the crowd and grabbed Henry and Mitch. She pushed them to the ranch house, while Ara followed close behind. Henry glanced at her as they stepped into the kitchen. Ara's face was pale. She had wrapped her arms tightly around herself and was avoiding meeting his eyes.

"Why don't you two sit down." Nicole said, motioning to the table.

Henry felt way too worked up to sit down, but he did not want to be rude to Nicole. He grudgingly sat down and leaned back, resting one arm heavily on the table.

Mitch slumped into a chair with obvious fire flooding his veins. "Nicole, I am sorry but, man alive. You shoulda heard what he was sayin' 'bout Ara." He took off his hat and turned it around in his hands.

"I know, Mitch." She rested a hand on his shoulder as her face twisted painfully. "It was just awful." She turned to Henry. "But violence is never the answer."

Mitch rubbed his neck. "Oh man, Henry. That man was just lookin' for trouble as always. He has had a vendetta for you since Cheyenne."

Henry rubbed his temples before putting his hands in his lap. "Ugh. I know. I tried to keep cool." He looked at Ara, mentally pleading with her to meet his eyes. "I really did, Ara."

She finally looked up, blue eyes clashing with his own. "I know." She dropped her gaze, then gave him a tiny smile. "I understand why you did it."

His heart leapt into his chest with hope. "Really? Will you forgive me, Arabella?"

She looked into his eyes and grabbed his hand under the table. "No." Henry felt his chest tighten until she added with a hint of a smile: "Because I have wanted to hit him forever, and you got to first."

They all laughed, and Henry felt his chest relax a little.

"I actually have wanted to hurt him for a *long* time, too." Mitch said with a chuckle. "He is a no-good, self-important jerk."

"Can I get anyone something to drink?" The men nodded while Ara asked for some water. Nicole walked to the fridge and pulled out a pitcher of iced tea and chilled glasses. She set them on the table along with Ara's water before taking a chair next to Mitch.

They all sipped the beverages for a few seconds until Mitch burst out: "Oh, man! Joe's face when ya punched him! Priceless!"

Henry smiled as he remembered the moment. "Even though it was wrong, it felt great."

"So, how was your first cow chase, Henry?" Nicole asked, delicately changing the subject.

They reminisced about the day, each taking turns discussing different events. Mitch tactfully left out the part about Ara's ranch.

Finally, Ara let out a huge, adorable yawn. Henry decided it was time to take her home. He felt exhausted as well. "Well, thanks for a great … eventful day, guys."

They laughed and walked Henry and Ara to the door. Outside, the party was still going. The music had resumed, and people were joyfully kicking their feet to the new tune.

He held Ara's hand and guided her to his car. He tucked her inside before walking around and swiftly getting in his door. He then drove them carefully through the people and out of the ranch. Ara yawned again and dozed as they drove up the mountainside to her cabin.

Henry walked around to her side and gently pulled the sleeping Ara out and carried her into her home. He opened the door with one arm and switched on the kitchen light. He carried her through the cabin to her bedroom. Carefully, he laid her onto the soft bed.

Her hair spilled across the pillow, and her lashes swept across the top of her cheeks. Her mouth rested peacefully, and he truly thought she looked as beautiful, if not more, than an actual angel. He whispered what he knew in his heart to be true, something that had grown in his heart since the moment he had seen her at the lake, "I love you, Arabella."

She whispered something lightly in her sleep and grabbed his hand. He leaned his ear close to her mouth. "Stay." He finally heard from her tired lips.

"All right, I won't leave." He promised her as he pulled off her cowboy boots and set them softly on the floor. He pulled off his own boots before climbing into bed next to her and falling fast asleep curled next to his love.

24
HENRY'S JOURNEY
Jackson Hole, Wyoming
August 29, 1992

Henry woke up and yawned deeply. He looked at the clock next to Ara's bed: 5:03 a.m. He pushed his bare feet onto the wood floor and shivered. The room was icy cold from the cool of the night. He stood up and felt his muscles ache. His whole body twinged in pain. His back rippled and cramped as he tried to stretch out his tender body. All he wanted to do was go back to sleep, curl up next to Ara's warm soft body, and let the day just pass by without a care. He felt tired but knew he couldn't sleep now that he had gotten up.

He shuffled off to the bathroom and splashed some water on his face, staring at the man reflecting back at him in the mirror. He had a steady and refined stubble across his chin, under his neck, and climbing along his jawline. He clenched his jaw. His muscles flexed and pulsed. He rubbed his stubbly chin and then grabbed the hand towel to dry his face.

His dark eyes looked back at him in the mirror. They looked happy and tired, but most of all, he saw guilt. His conscience was weighing on him. Ara had shared every detail of her life with him, and he felt like he had barely said a word about who he was. Today, he needed some alone time to sort through some of this. He told Ara he loved her. Just thinking about saying those words to her made chills run up and down his spine. He really loved her, and he was feeling more and more stuck in an endless black hole with his situation. How had he let it get this far? Today, he had to visit his old life to move onto to his new life.

He left the bathroom and saw Ara still fast asleep on the bed. He fought the urge to join her one last time and quietly made his way to the living room. He found a pen and paper and began to scrawl Ara a note:

"I'll tell you how the sun rose, a ribbon at a time, E.D."[4]
I woke before you and couldn't bear to wake you. So peaceful.
I am heading back to my cabin to get cleaned up and run a few
errands. Get together? Leave a message on my answering
machine, and I will give you a call when I get your message.
Miss you already. Love, Henry."

Henry set the note on the kitchen table and headed out the door, his every thought hanging on his last words, "Love, Henry." As he stepped outside, he saw a patch of wildflowers. He walked over and picked just a few and bound them together with a loose stem. He went back inside and set the flowers on the note. He smiled, touched the note in passing and headed out towards his cabin, ready for a day of change.

****

As he opened the door to his cabin, Henry realized how very often he was not there. A dusty haze was in the air with the sun dancing along with the dust particles in the air. The cabin looked just about the same as when he had first arrived. Except, the first time he had opened the front door, he had been so lost and had felt helpless and destitute with his collapsing marriage.

Now, he was so full of life and energy, filled with love for Ara and Wyoming. For the first time since he was a little boy, he felt like he knew who he was and what he wanted. He was determined to never let go of this new person that he had become, the person that maybe he always had been but kept locked away out of fear and conformity. His very soul had been kidnapped and held for ransom most of his life.

He set down his keys and walked into the bedroom. Digging far into the dark recesses of his suitcase, Henry pulled out a black, leather-bound journal. It was so tiny and insignificant, but Henry shuttered as it sat in the palm of his hand. Staring at it in dread, he took a deep breath and opened it, cringing at the thought of all the messages that awaited him. He picked up the phone and dialed his office extension and entered his password to receive his voicemails. At the sound of Anne's frantic voice, he put the phone under a pillow until the thirty-three messages finished playing.

He stared at the wall, his composure like the cold, blue stones of the creek outside. He heard a faint beep and the sound of a computerized woman's voice proclaimed the end of his messages. Henry's heart beat frantically in his chest as he dialed the number of his personal lawyer.

He knew his marriage was over, but it was still difficult to step back to his old life, even if it was only for a few minutes this time. It wasn't his reality anymore, and he felt like he had stepped into another dimension just hearing Anne's voice clamoring in his ear. With just this one step, he felt hollowed out and yet so full. At the conclusion of all this, no matter the struggle, he would be with Ara and that filled him with courage to proceed.

"Hello, Mr. Tudor." His lawyer's voice resonated with concern and curiosity through the phone.

Henry took a deep breath. "Mr. Jacobs. I need a favor."

"Well, certainly Henry. Always happy to help my boss." Henry heard the lawyer's familiar deep chuckle. "But where have you been these last few weeks, Mr. Tudor? You have certainly caused a stir in your family and colleagues."

Henry ignored the tight pit in his stomach. The workaholic in him wanted to take over and ask about business and other goings-on in the company, but he choked it back. He would catch up with work soon enough. "I need you to draw up divorce papers. It should not be too difficult as Anne signed a prenuptial agreement."

Silence resounded on the opposite end for a few seconds. "Are you sure, Mr. Tudor? Perhaps some marriage counseling could be of some assistance? I personally know a few great counselors..."

Henry was straightforward and firm, just how he was with every business deal. "Just the papers, please. I will be checking in in a few days to deal with work-related questions. For now, I am sure Mr. Cromwell has been doing his share of the work?"

"Yes, Mr. Tudor. Would you like me to fax the papers to you or perhaps you will stop in the office?"

"Call me when they are done. I will give you a fax number at that time." Henry hung up the phone. He laid back on the bed and let his body and mind go free to search in his memories. It was the end. He knew this was for the best, for both him and Anne, certainly the best for Ara as well. But it was the end. He knew that any end brings a certain kind of sadness: the end of summer or any season for that matter, a good book, the last drops of coffee in your mug, the end of a parting kiss, certainly the end of any relationship.

Henry thought of his wedding day and the possibilities it had held. He had had dreams for Anne and himself, dreams to be happy, to be certainly better than what they had become now. He thought of his parents and the way they still looked at each other after thirty-five years of marriage. He could never forget that look. It was a look he longed for with Anne and had never obtained. Everything with them was always strained or forced.

Nevertheless, he lay there, saddened. A single tear rolled softly down his stubbled cheek. He wiped it away and thought of Ara and about his new happiness. His old life couldn't even compare. He let the past melt away. This was a natural progression. He didn't go searching for anything but himself. He was led here though, he knew that. By what, he was not sure. Fate, God, time and circumstance, his mind tangoed with each idea. He remembered rock climbing with Charlie and their talks that helped him so much. Henry had been looking for a muse, for a purpose to live passionately. Arabella, his muse, was the one.

Henry pushed himself up, pulled off his shirt and headed for the door. The creek was calling, and he was in need of an invigorating shower.

****

Back at the cabin after his cooling wash, Henry dug around through his bags trying to find a clean shirt and shorts. When he realized that he had no clean clothes except a sweater which would not suffice in the middle of summer, Henry decided to do some laundry before meeting up with Ara.

He grabbed some change from inside his suitcase pocket, shoved all the dirty clothes into a garbage bag, and headed out the door, car keys in hand. Henry threw the bag into the front seat and started up the engine of his car.

He smoothly guided the car down the side of the mountain while deep in thought. How should he tell Ara this terrible truth? How will she react? Will she hate him or try to understand a little? Henry sped up the car as his thoughts turned more and more anxious in his mind. His brain was buzzing.

No, she will definitely be angry. He had had way too many opportunities to come clean, and he just hadn't. Something had always stopped him: the moment, the look in Ara's eyes, or pure and utter fear. How could he soften the blow? Henry decided to try to keep the evening light, humorous, and romantic before telling her he had something terrible to say. He should get some flowers for sure, really, really nice flowers.

At this last thought, Henry was so deeply engrossed in his plans that he did not notice the rabbit darting out from the trees in front of his car. He looked up just as his front right tire was about to slam into the furry animal.

Slamming on the brakes, Henry swerved slightly to the right in an effort to try to save the rabbit's life. At just the last second, the little animal jumped to the side and back into the dark green safety of the trees. Henry gripped the steering wheel tightly and stared intently at the road. He breathed in deeply through his nose and released the air through his mouth, letting a loud sigh of relief come with it. He tried to pay more attention as he continued down the mountains.

Driving into town, Henry passed the now-familiar buildings and tried to remember where the laundromat was he saw at one point. He turned a few corners before finding it. He parked his car and hauled his clothes into "Miss Nancy's Laundromat." Henry nodded and smiled to the white-haired, older lady behind the counter, obviously running the store. She smiled at him briefly before going back to helping another disgruntled lady with a stain on a yellow blouse.

Henry realized just then that he had *no* clue how to wash clothes. He had hired help in the house for this his entire life. *Well, it can't be all that hard.* Henry decided, literally scratching his head as he went forward with his first attempt at washing clothes.

He took a deep breath and walked over to a pair of machines and loaded quarters into the one that dispensed detergent and then loaded more coins into the washing machine itself. He threw all his clothes in and dumped three packets of detergent in with them. *That should do it,* he nodded with satisfaction and closed the lid, reaching for one of the buttons.

"Young man! Don't start that machine!"

Henry turned and saw the tiny, white-haired lady running with all her might, which was actually quite a slow pace, toward him with her arms flailing.

She peeled to a stop in front of his machine and peered inside. Her face was bright red, and she had pink lipstick forming the shape of her wrinkled lips. "Young man!" She looked up at him with utter disbelief and shook her head. "Do you have *any* idea how to wash clothes?"

He laughed and shook his head. "Well, no," he admitted.

She tisk-tisked her tongue and waved her finger at him. "Well, that is not acceptable at Miss Nancy's," she said sternly.

Henry felt his stomach clench tightly in despair. How was he going to clean his clothes?

The lady curved her lips into a bright curvy smile with kind warmth reaching from her eyes. "Well, luckily for you, young sir, Miss Nancy will gladly wash these right up for you. For a small fee, of course."

Henry was relieved and returned her smile. "Oh, I would appreciate that!"

"Now, just come back in about two hours, and I will have those all finished right up." She walked back up to the counter and grabbed a white slip. "And what's your name, young man?"

"Henry. Henry … Michael."

"All right, Henry. See you in a bit."

"Thank you so much." Henry told her, but he saw that she was already bustling back toward his washing machine.

He walked out the door and wondered what to do next. As he walked by the laundromat window, Henry caught sight of his reflection. He rubbed his hands over his unshaven face and the shaggy length of his hair that he usually kept so short. Tonight was going to make or break the rest of his life. So Henry decided to get gussied up to see Ara.

He continued down the street a ways until he found a barber shop with a spinning red, white, and blue striped pole adorning the front door.

He stepped inside, and bells tolled his entrance. The shop was bustling with activity. Men were telling stories while getting shaved and trimmed. An older gentleman sat in a small cushioned folding chair in the waiting area and read the daily news while gnawing on a toothpick.

Henry walked up to the counter. A short man with a dark beard looked up at him. "What can I do for you, sir?"

"I need a cut and a shave, please."

"Right you are. Jim here will fix you up. What's your name, son?"

"Henry Michael," Henry said without flinching. He didn't like that living a lie was getting easier and easier for him. At some point, it had to stop.

The short man gestured to a tall man sweeping around a barber chair. "Jim, got a live one for you!" He said and chuckled, returning to his magazine.

"Come have a seat, sir."

Henry walked over to Jim and sat down in the chair. The barber briskly tied a long, black salon cape around Henry's unshaven neck and spun the chair around to face a large mirror. "So, a cut and a shave today, sir?"

"Yes, please. Just need to shorten up this hair a bit."

Jim grabbed his barber shears and began snipping away at Henry's hair. "So, Mr. Michael, you enjoyin' your time in Wyomin'?"

"So far, yes. There are some great people here." Henry thought of blue-eyed Joe. "And some not so nice people."

Jim chuckled and efficiently combed Henry's hair up to make sure the length was even as he snipped. "So I have heard," he murmured.

"And what might that be?" Henry asked, meeting the barber's eyes in the mirror.

"Most stories I hear are local goings-on. But what I have heard about you intrigues even an old barber like myself." He snipped some longer strands by Henry's neck. "You have done pretty well for yourself in Wyoming so far. Winnin' rodeos and makin' friends and enemies all in about two weeks."

Henry watched his hair being trimmed into his usual style. "I guess barbers really do hear everything." He said a bit dryly as he saw his old self appearing in the mirror. His eyes were different. Henry saw a sparkle inside them he had never seen before. It was Ara and her love reflecting back at him in the mirror, and he was so grateful for her at that moment.

Jim carried on, "So you and Miss. Arabella, eh? I gotta say I'm a mite bit surprised … She never dates. How did you manage that one?"

Henry's curiosity was aroused. "What do you mean she doesn't date?"

"Well, she turns every guy down who approaches her. She got hurt pretty bad. Nobody ever thought some out-of-towner would pull her out of that rut." Jim checked the lengths of Henry's hair on the side to see if they were even. He dropped the hair and made a few more cuts before turned on the shaver to trim his neck and sideburns. They didn't speak any further.

Henry sat silent in his chair thinking about his last statement, "pulled her out of that rut." He had felt in a rut too, as if he was a stranger in his own life. He couldn't expect anyone else to know his internal struggle. But Ara had been there; she knew destitution and fear and that burning desire for something greater. He knew the need for a search for one's true self. But she had known the search longer. Henry was fortunate to have found Ara so soon on his journey. They were complete together, and, as two halves of the same whole, they were strangers in a world of others: other people, other lives, other stories. Their story was perpetuated by fate and it was their own. Henry never wanted to share it with anyone else. Rather, he wanted to bundle it up, raise, grow, and hide it away from the ruthless world. He was scared of its youth and impetuosity, scared to be swallowed up by the evil hindrances of someone else, someone not part of their story. Their love was young, but very true.

He remembered his impassioned self in high school and college, every detail in his life up in the air and never settled down. He tried to think of words to describe his youth: frivolous, free, fleeting, anything but lasting. He was enveloped in fear for a moment but was calmed by the memory of a song he once listened to over and over again during his British punk phase. The words meant something different to him then, which amused him now. He used to think it was a revolutionary cry to the youth of the world, to stand together, united, and against society's norms and expectations, against all that was thought true. To free one's mind of thoughts of worldly success because youth is now: embrace it, rebel. The Kinks were never as big as the Clash or the Who, but they were, in Henry's mind, better than them both combined because he was moved to action by them:

"So we will share this road we walk
And mind our mouths and beware our talk
'Till peace we find tell you what I'll do
All the things I own I will share with you
If I feel tomorrow like I feel today
We'll take what we want and give the rest away
Strangers on this road we are on
We are not two we are one..."5

Henry sighed and smiled. Oh, how far he had come. The same youthful passion he had bridled years ago was surfacing inside him once again. Not for idealistic revolt or rebellion, but for love and for life, a life worth living because he was not alone in his memories, but he walked a stranger.

"All finished up here." Jim brushed the locks of hair off of Henry's neck, and Henry blinked himself back to the present.

Jim removed the black smock from him as Henry got up from the chair.

He rubbed the back of his neck and ran his hands through his new haircut. The freshly cut ends felt like the stiffness of an unsoiled paint brush, soft but rigid. His rugged unshorn look was gone, and he gazed at his reflection. He looked like Anne's Henry and, for a small moment, he regretted getting a haircut. Then he gazed into his own eyes and saw that the changed Henry still lived and would keep living as the self he had found in Jackson Hole, the self that Ara had helped show him.

He turned to Jim and slipped him a ten-dollar bill for a tip. "Thanks."

Jim smiled and began sweeping up the dark hair that dusted the floor around his chair. "Good luck, Henry."

Henry paid up at the front of the store and walked out of the shop. He knew his laundry would not be done yet, so he tried to think of how to pass the time.

He realized that he already knew where he was going as he walked to his car and drove out of town. He headed in the general direction of the ranch Ara had pointed out to him from Mitch's. He tried not to think about how Joe would react to seeing him, knowing nothing good could probably ever come from it, but he hoped otherwise. He pictured Joe's angry, bloody face as he was escorted from Mitch's property. Henry probably should have stopped and brought Mitch with him. But it was too late now, and he wanted to try talking to Joe on his own. He hoped his instincts were right.

Soon Henry turned the corner into a valley and pulled into the breathtaking ranch that had once belonged to Ara. He drove up the winding drive to the beautiful main house. He did not have a plan of what he wanted to say to Joe; he just knew he needed to see if he could get Ara her ranch back.

As he looked around the breathtaking property, it hurt him deeply to see how much she had lost. The ranch was even more astounding down here as it was from up above.

He took a deep breath, turned off his car, and climbed out. The scent from the flowers lining the driveway and surrounding the property mixed with the fragrant smell of horses and dust filled him with an intense longing to stay right where he was. It felt like it could be home to anyone who stood at that spot. But he knew he had better find Joe before Joe found him. Since it was mid-morning, Henry decided Joe was most likely outside working and not in the ranch house.

He walked down the driveway and over to a long white building with three large garage doors as it appeared to be a shop. He walked slowly, casually, and took in his environment carefully. He noticed wear and use on fence posts and on the siding of the building, like it was somewhat neglected.

As he walked closer, he heard voices and knew he was right. He took a breath to steady himself and opened the door slowly. He saw Joe working with another man on a tractor.

"Move that there to the right." Joe said to the man. They both heaved and set the piece into place. "Okay, good there." He twisted the nut into place and looked up as Henry closed the door and walked inside.

"Morning." Henry said, nodding to them both.

"What the hell are you doin' here?" Joe wiped the grease off his hands and stood up, snarling at Henry. His nose and left cheek were swollen and bruised.

Henry held his ground. "I came to apologize. My temper got out of control, and I should have just walked away."

Joe seemed a little unsure of what to do next. He clearly had expected Henry to want to fight. "Well … I suppose I went a little far with what I said about Arabella. But it didn't warrant a fist in my face. … Well, maybe it did." He grinned arrogantly.

Henry found it hard not to put another fist into his face. But he resisted the temptation and nodded. "Again, I apologize."

"Hey, Joe, John needs me over at South B," the man that had been helping Joe with the tractor said as he walked toward the door. He paused and asked, "Will you be all right here, boss?"

"Okay, fine, see you in a bit." Joe walked over to the window and grabbed his jug of water sitting on the windowsill. He took a swig, never taking his eyes off Henry and set it down. He pulled out a pack of Marlboros and lit up a cigarette. "So we done here or what?" He leaned back and surveyed Henry with his cold eyes as he took a long pull on his cigarette.

Henry was curious. "Why do you ask?"

"Well, usually a man don't come willingly into a man's home when he knows that man hates his guts. But you came and "apologized," so I just assume you are lookin' for somethin' else too."

Henry was surprised at Joe's calculating mind but tried not to show it. "Yes, you are right. I am not just here for that." He took out a business card from his wallet and handed it to Joe. He knew that Joe would now know his real name, but he had already decided to tell Ara everything tonight, and he had to lay all his chips on the table and let them fall where they may. "As you can see, my name is Henry Tudor, as in Tudor Industries." He saw a recognition flash into Joe's eyes, so he continued. "I'm the CEO of the company. I would like to buy this entire ranch and am prepared to offer you well over the value." He handed Joe a folded paper with with just the number $5,500,000 written on it.

Joe took the paper with a skeptical look on his face. He opened it and stared down at the figure before looking back at Henry. "For a little over 550 acre ranch? In these times?" He asked Henry in disbelief. "I know you are a Tudor but jeez." Joe was looking quite satisfied with the turn of events and even went so far as to put out his hand to shake Henry's in agreement.

"There is a catch." Henry said with a firm look on his face, and Joe's hand fell to his side. "You will sign a contract that states you are entitled to that amount if and only if you sign the deed to the entire ranch, property, cattle, horses, along with everything else over to Arabella Bennett. You will also leave Jackson Hole and move at least three hundred miles away. You are never to visit this town or this ranch again." He paused. "And you are never to tell Arabella any of this. I would like to remain anonymous. Failure to obey any of those rules to the full extent of their wording or meaning will result in you losing everything the sale has given you. *Everything*, and the ranch will not be returned to you." Henry looked out the window. "And I will take the deed and see to it she gets it from a different source." He paused to let Joe think the deal over and let his demands sink in.

Joe looked down at the paper and lit another cigarette. He breathed out a ring of smoke as he considered his options. "Well, this would set me right up down south a ways." He looked at Henry with his icy eyes. "You sure are willin' to do a lot for this woman." He took another pull at his cigarette. "Don't understand quite why."

Henry smiled coldly. "I think you do. Now, do we have a deal?"

"I have family here, ya know. What am I supposed to just never see em' again? I can't visit?" Henry could tell that Joe was milking whatever he could get, but his weak attempt at negotiation wouldn't work on Henry.

"With five and a half million dollars, I think you could fly your family to visit you wherever you choose to vacate to. Now, do we have a deal?" Henry was calm and collected, never conceding an inch.

Joe glared at him silently and exhaled smoke into Henry's face. "Ya." Joe put down his smoke and shook Henry's hand. "Do I have to go and meet somebody to sign this contract or what?" Henry could see the greedy excitement in Joe's eyes.

"I will send someone here to meet you. She is my accountant and real estate agent and will be out in a few hours. Ms. Mortinson is her name." He walked briskly to the door. "Just sign the contract and get it over with. Any attempts to change the agreement will be firmly denied. Ms. Mortinson will inform me when it's done." He turned his back on Joe and walked out the door. "For what it's worth, thanks … Have a nice life, Joe."

Henry strode to his car, climbed in, and drove back toward town. He could not believe he had succeeded! He never doubted himself ever when doing business, but when it was this personal he couldn't help but fear the worst. He took a moment to celebrate and shimmied in his seat to the song playing on the radio.

After he had calmed down, he called his Ms. Mortinson and told her the news. He informed her of her task and that it needed to be done as soon as possible.

"I will jump on the first plane out to Jackson," she told him. "Is this a company account or a personal one?"

"Personal. Book the flight from my own personal account, too, please. Thanks, Ms. Mortinson. You are the best."

She laughed. "Job security, Mr. Tudor. I will call you when it is all done."

Henry hung up the phone and drove around Jackson Hole until he found what he was looking for: the florist shop. Henry walked into the door and was instantaneously surrounded by the scents of hundreds of flowers combined into one exquisite smell.

Fresh flowers arranged into beautiful bouquets filled fridges that lined the walls. Exotic plants and potted flowers took up the middle of the store along with gardening tools and other flower bed essentials. Vines blooming with white flowers hung from the ceiling and clung to the store's supporting pillars.

Henry stepped to one of the bouquet-filled fridges and tried to decide what Ara would like the most. He saw ones with brilliant colored lilies mixed with numerous pin cushion mums. He eyed a bouquet with two dozen perfect red roses and shook his head. *No*, he thought. *That would be more perfect for Anne.* Ugh, Anne. Henry's stomach twisted, and he forced himself to focus on the task at hand. He saw a pretty mix of soft yellow and white roses that still were not right for Ara. He tried to think of her personality: sweet yet smart and witty, hard-working, fragile yet determined, beautiful on the outside and even more on the inside, and … just perfect.

His eyes dropped to the lowest shelf. Filling a simple glass vase was a beautiful variety of wildflowers. He opened the door and pulled the vase out, admiring the perfect mix. Breathing in deeply, Henry smelled the sweet blend and was reminded of his and Ara's lake.

He walked up to the counter and set the bouquet on it.

"Oh, that's a special bunch, isn't it, sugar?"

Henry smiled at the lady, a blonde woman in her mid-forties. "Yes, it is different but perfect."

"Well, I will just get these all made up for you." She bustled around behind the counter. "Would you like a card for inside the bouquet?"

Henry nodded. "Yes, please." She handed him a little blank card, and Henry thought for a moment before writing a stanza from one of his favorite love poems, "The Passionate Shepherd to His Love" by Christopher Marlowe:

> *"The shepherds' swains shall dance and sing*
> *For thy delight each May morning:*
> *If these delights thy mind may move,*
> *Then live with me and be my love."* [6]

Henry tucked the card into the bouquet and asked the florist to add a rose of each color into the bouquet with one red rose in the center.

The florist added the flowers as requested and loosely held the stems, deep in thought before lifting her finger and triumphantly murmuring, "Uh-huh!" She scurried to her back storeroom and returned a moment later with an off-white lace ribbon and a single pearl-tipped pin. After loosely wrapping the stems in lace, she fastened the note to the stems with the pin. She smelled the flowers before tenderly handing the flowers over to Henry as if she were parting with her own child.

Henry grasped them gently, thanked her for the exquisite additions, paid, and exited the store. The bells on the door rang out, announcing his exit, and he made his way down the street, flowers in hand, and Ara on his mind.

He opened the door to the laundromat and smiled at the tiny, white-haired lady at the counter.

She beamed at Henry and waved him up to the counter. "I have your clothes perfectly clean and ready for you!"

"Thanks." Henry brought out his custom-made wallet his father had had made for him in France.

"My! What a wallet! My late husband had one wallet for most of his life. The ol' thing was in pieces when he died, God rest his dear soul." She handed the bill to Henry and began pulling the laundry bags up from under the counter.

Henry nodded and smiled as he wrote her a check. He finished signing the bill with a flourish and handed it to her.

"You have a good day now." She placed the check in her drawer and handed him his bags.

Henry walked out of the store to his car. He threw the laundry inside and slid into the front seat. He decided to surprise Ara with a picnic, maybe see if she wanted to go to the lake to eat. He started the car and drove to the grocery store. Henry knew he had to find something for late lunch/early dinner to take to the lake. He tried to brainstorm during the short drive to the store. What would be delicious, easy, and romantic at the same time? Dinner had to be perfect tonight.

Henry's mind was blocked. He could only keep seeing Ara's face crushed with despair and disappointment as he told her he had not been truthful with her from the beginning: who he really was, his reason for being in Wyoming, his marital status. That last part killed him. He did not feel married, not in the least. Henry knew he hadn't told her he wasn't married, but he also knew that Arabella would think not telling the truth was a lie. A lie by omission is often worse than a straight up lie. At least, it felt that way to Henry.

He pulled into the parking lot of the store, locked his car, and he walked inside. First, he checked with the store manager to see about the store's fax machine number and policy. Henry wrote down the information carefully and placed it deep inside his pocket. He then wandered around the grocery store trying to select the perfect meal to take to the lake. He paced up and down aisle one, two, three. He stopped at the end cap and anxiously rubbed his temple. This was not like him, anxious, nervous, or rather scared to death.

Suddenly, the deli case caught his glance, filled with meats, cheeses, and salads. His stomach growled as he moved closer.

"Can I help you?"

Henry looked up to see an older gentleman in his mid-fifties smiling at him from behind the counter. "Yes. I would like some of everything!"

Henry's over-excitement made him a fun customer. The deli man laughed. "I get that a lot. Is there any particular occasion for some deli selections?"

"Actually, I need some for a picnic, slash, sharing scandalous secrets about my not so great life with the woman I love ... anything for that?" The man blankly stared at him, his mouth agape. Henry smiled quickly, "Just kidding, man. Well, I am having a picnic, though. What do you recommend? Oh, and do you have some sort of a cold compress pack I can use?"

The man smiled and nodded. "Well, we have the ever-popular roasted turkey breast. Can't really go wrong there. And I have just the thing to keep it all cool." He went into the back for a moment before returning triumphantly with a small cooler made of Styrofoam. "This will do the trick."

"Oh, that will be perfect." Henry looked down into the window. "I will take a fourth of a pound of the roasted turkey breast and another fourth of that chicken breast." He looked at the selection of cheese. "And a few pieces each of the Swiss, the Wisconsin Muenster, and the Colby-Jack." He walked down by the salads. "And what salads would you recommend?"

"The traditional macaroni salad is superb. The German potato salad is excellent as well. You also might like to consider the strawberries and cream salad for dessert."

Henry smiled at the helpful man. "I will take eight ounces of each of those."

The man skillfully sliced, measured, and scooped for a few minutes before suggesting that Henry select some bread and bring a small bag of ice over.

Henry walked quickly to grab a fresh loaf of whole wheat bread and ice. He also remembered to grab plastic silverware and cups and paper plates.

He handed it to the deli man who priced and efficiently packed the cooler for Henry. He told Henry his total and handed the cooler to Henry.

"I really appreciate all your help." Henry told him as he handed the man cash with an extra ten dollars for a tip.

"Anytime, sir. Have a great day and a delicious picnic. Oh, and I hope your talk goes well too." He nodded at him and gave a look of encouragement.

Henry walked out of the store with a shy smile on his face. He thought Ara would enjoy the food he had picked out. Once in the parking lot, he set the cooler on his trunk and opened the backseat door. He carefully slid the cooler onto the floor and checked the flowers. The bouquet practically took his breath away.

Everything was in order. Now if he could only organize the words to say the words he had to say.

He gently shut the door and climbed into the driver's seat. He smoothly drove the car out of town and up the mountain toward his cabin.

****

"Arabella!" Henry called, pausing to catch his breath. Holding the temporary cooler, he walked the last few steps up the trail and looked around for Ara. He saw a poetry book, backpack, and a water bottle laying in the grass in Ara's usual spot. Henry set the cooler down next to her things on the grass and looked toward the lake. "Ara?"

"Over here, Henry!" Ara's sweet voice rang out from the top of a large rock. She waved at him and squeezed the water out of her long hair. The yellow and white polka dot swimsuit she was wearing glowed in the sun's bright light. "Jump in, the water feels so refreshing." She put her hands over her head and gracefully dived into the water.

Henry laughed and began pulling off his shirt and shorts. He quickly climbed to the highest rock and dived into the lake. The cool water really was refreshing. He swam up to the surface and breathed in deeply. "Ah!"

He heard Ara's sweet laughter as she swam toward him. "I told you it feels great." She swam next to him and reached over to kiss his cheek lightly. "I missed you." She said those words like she enjoyed saying them, like she appreciated just having someone to miss. "Did you get my message to come here or did you just guess?"

He laughed. "I got the message … But I also guessed!" He looked into her eyes and smiled. "I missed you too."

"Your hair," she reached out to touch it. "It looks so different."

"Good different?"

"Well, you always look handsome. But, ya, it does look nice too." She blushed and splashed him gently before taking off through the water, shrieking as he swam quickly after her.

He caught up to her in a few strokes, but, just as Henry reached for her, Ara dived under the water and swam in the opposite direction. She pulled herself out of the water and looked at Henry with a triumphant grin. He shook his head at her and swam with speed similar to a bullet out of a fired gun over to shore and climbed out.

Ara shrieked and ran to her things in the grass.

Henry laughed and ran after her. He picked her up and fell down onto the grass with Ara landing on top. They both caught their breath for a few moments, still laughing.

Ara rolled off Henry to her side and rested her head on her hand. "So what did you do all day?"

Henry stretched out on the grass and looked into the clear sky. "Oh, I had some errands to run. I realized that I was out of clean clothes, so I went into town and found Miss Nancy's place."

"Miss Nancy? Oh, she is quite a character, isn't she?" Ara rolled onto her elbows and began picking at the grass. "Such a sweet lady."

"Yes, she is. While she was doing my laundry for me, I went to the barber shop and the grocery store before coming up here."

"Ah, and of course she did your laundry for you?!" Ara teased but then was distracted by the rest of his sentence. "Mmmm, yes." She eyed the cooler presumptuously. "What did you bring us, Henry?"

Henry sat up and opened the container. "I hope you like it all." He pulled out a few containers of the meats, cheeses, and salads along with the soft bread and plates.

"Oh, it all looks wonderful, Henry!" She looked into container. "Macaroni salad!"

Henry laughed. "Well, dig in." He pulled off all the covers and dug out the plastic silverware from inside the cooler. "Here ya go."

"Thanks." She took the silverware and scooped some macaroni salad onto her plate.

Henry handed her two pieces of bread. "Turkey or chicken?"

Ara contemplated for a few seconds. "Mmm, a little of both." She wrinkled her nose and pursed her lips to the side, as if questioning herself, and then nodded in agreement with her initial choice.

"All right." He laughed and handed her the containers. She was so darn cute; he could not get enough of her. "I bought three types of cheese since I wasn't sure what you liked."

She looked over the types and decided on a slice of the muenster. "Yeah, we really need to know more about each other, like, little things: favorite color, drink, movie, you know, just everythin'. And thanks, by the way, for all this, Henry."

He smiled. "You're welcome." He started to make his own sandwich: turkey, a small slice of Swiss, and Colby-Jack. "And blue, but mostly because I've never seen more beautiful eyes than yours, a Shirley

Temple, but only if it comes with a cherry, and *Jaws*; it was the first scary movie my dad ever let me watch with him." After taking a bite, Henry smiled a big dorky smile and laughed with his mouth full.

Ara playfully punched him in the arm and cracked up, laughing too. "My turn. Okay, my favorite color is blue also but not because I love my own eyes ... weirdo, but because it's serene and reminds me of here: this lake. My favorite drink is iced tea, you might have already known that, and my favorite movie is *Rebel Without a Cause* mostly because I had a huge crush on James Dean when I was a teenager and totally dreamed of living in the '50s. I even had one of those dresses that looked like something Grace Kelly would wear in *Rear Window* or something, which is weird because Grace Kelly doesn't seem like James Dean's style." She giggled. "You know you're kind of like him in *Rebel Without a Cause*, not that you had a troubled past or anything, but you are new in town, makin' friends, and well, unfortunately, enemies."

He smiled at her, bemused and continued eating his delicious sandwich.

She bit her lip. "What?! Come on like you never had a celebrity crush when you were young."

A smile crept on Henry's face. "I knew it! Who was it?" Ara sat up on her knees in excitement.

"All right, you won't be nearly as impressed by mine as I was with yours."

Ara nodded.

"Okay, are you ready?"

Ara pushed Henry, and he swayed backwards.

"Okay, okay, I always had a thing for Marilyn Monroe for no reason other than I thought she was hot ... I couldn't even name one movie she was in." Henry mockingly cringed and covered his face with his hands.

Ara leaned over on Henry, laughing in his ear, each hand on one of his shoulders, "You are such a cliché, Henry. Every man loves Marilyn." She continued to laugh.

Henry retorted, "Hey, you're no better! James Dean! He was practically a pin-up boy."

Ara dropped her jaw in shock, "Take it back, Henry." She pointed at him fiercely. "How dare you talk about my James like that! My precious James ... he was a wholesome man, by God." Ara stood up and defiantly put her hands on her hips and struggled to not smile.

Henry sat cross-legged, his knees raised a bit with his elbows resting on them, holding his wrist. He shook his head at her and smiled. "Well, who am I to judge you for your pin-up boy when mine was a pin-up girl. Tie for worst cliché?"

Ara practically tackled him in a hug, giggling. "Okay, deal." She kissed him quickly on the cheek with her arms wrapped around his neck. She put herself back in sitting position, caught her breath from laughing, and continued eating off her plate. "Have some of the salads." Ara said to cover up being flustered from the little kiss she had just given and pushed the containers toward him.

Henry piled some of each on his plate with a knowing smile.

"I love hearing about a little version of you, Henry. Every detail of your life is just … juicy to me. So please … feel free to dazzle me with yourself anytime." She smiled as she took a big chunk out of her sandwich.

Henry nodded and took a bite of his own. They ate for a few minutes and talked about what she had done that day, the weather, and the people Henry had met that day. He carefully avoided the encounter with Joe.

Ara brushed her hands off, set her plate back in the cooler, and took a long drink of water. "Delicious." She lay back in the grass with her backpack as a pillow and closed her eyes.

"Oh, I am stuffed." Henry threw the remains of their lunch back into the cooler and lay back in the grass as well. He breathed in deep and tried to relax the nervous pit in his stomach. He knew it was not the right moment to talk to Ara about Anne, so he gazed into the clear sky for a moment and closed his eyes. He listened to Ara's breathing, the leaves of the trees rustling, and the water slapping against the rocks. There was nowhere else in the world he would rather be at this moment, or ever for that matter.

After a few minutes, he heard Ara roll onto her stomach. He turned his head and saw she had opened her poetry book. "In the mood to read aloud?" He asked her with a smile.

"Hmmm. I suppose, just for you." She met his eyes with a teasing look for a moment and opened the book and paged through for a few moments:

"O wild West Wind, thou breath of Autumn's being,
Thou, from whose unseen presence the leaves dead
Are driven, like ghosts from an enchanter fleeing,
She continued reading the rest of the rather long, yet enchanting poem, finishing:
"The trumpet of a prophecy! O Wind, / If Winter comes, can Spring be far behind?"[7]

Ara paused and looked into the sky. "As August comes to an end, I always think of this poem. Autumn crawls up on summer so quickly.

193

Even in this heat, I can feel the fall descending from the sky to cover the earth, especially once night falls."

Henry sat up and swung his arms behind him. "I do love that poem. Shelley just has a way with words. I actually wrote a paper on his work in college."

Ara looked over at him thoughtfully. "How fascinating. I would love to read it sometime."

"It was not that good."

"I highly doubt that, Henry. And besides, any paper on the work of Shelley would be wonderful to read." She gazed back into the sky. "Today, I just feel as if my life is the end of summer: like it is about to change into something colder … But that sounds silly."

Henry knew it was the moment to tell her everything. He took a deep breath and grabbed one of her hands in his own. "Ara-"

"Hey, guys! Thought we might see you both up here!" Mitch's voice rang through the clearing.

Startled, Ara and Henry jumped to their feet to see Mitch appearing at the top of the path. He turned and helped Nicole up the last, steep steps.

Henry and Ara exchanged a quick glance. Ara's brows furrowed lightly together in confusion at the previous, serious look that Henry had given her.

Henry took her hand and squeezed it in reassurance and walked over to meet the newcomers. "How is it goin', you two?" Ara asked as they got closer to the couple.

"Just wonderful," Nicole breathlessly stated as she took a swig of water. "What a beautiful day for a walk!"

Mitch took the bottle from her and sloshed some into his mouth, getting most of it on his face and clothes. "Ya, we were walkin' and decided to ask you guys out for dinner tonight. When you weren't at Arabella's cabin, we just knew you would be here." He put the cap on the empty bottle and threw it to Nicole, who laughed and stashed it inside her backpack. "So what do you guys say? Double date in a few hours? Down at the bar?"

Ara and Henry exchanged a questioning look. "Well, I don't think we had anything planned tonight, did we, Henry?"

"No, I think it sounds great." Henry knew he would not have another chance to talk to her about Anne until after their date now. He thought that at least he could think of what exactly he wanted to say to her between now and the end of the night.

"Great. Well, we will meet you about seven then, all right?" Nicole asked.

Ara smiled at her, "Perfect."

Mitch grabbed Nicole around the waist and kissed her cheek. "All right, we will see you guys soon then. And bring your A-game for once, Henry! I am gonna whoop ya in pool." He spun Nicole playfully around, and they took off down the path.

Henry and Ara watched them go, shaking their heads and laughing. "What a couple." Henry said fondly.

Ara nodded her head in agreement, smiling up at him.

He moved in closer to her until he had wrapped his arms tightly around her waist. Looking down into her sparkling eyes, he felt his chest go tight as his heart pounded fiercely.

She looked down for a moment before meeting his eyes. "Thank you, Henry."

"For what?"

Ara touched his cheek softly with her fingertips. "For showin' me how perfect life can be at times."

He felt his stomach twist with guilt. "Well, you're welcome," he said in a teasing voice. "Now, let's get outta here and shower up for this date tonight. If I am gonna bring my A-game, I gotta get this lake water out of my ears!"

Ara laughed and began picking up her things. "Good idea. I better help you get warmed up!"

"I like the sound of that." Henry said slyly.

She punched his arm. "Not that kinda warming up! I meant intellectually."

"Oh, I see." Henry laughed and picked up the cooler. They started down the path together. "So more along the lines of twenty questions?"

"Yes! How about we guess authors or works?"

Henry raised his eyebrows and concentrated on maneuvering a tricky part of the path before looking back at her. "So we are really warming up then?"

She playfully pretended not to hear him. "All right. I have one."

"Is it a person or a thing?"

"Person."

"Male or female?"

"Female."

"Well-known or relatively unknown?"

"Pretty well-known." Ara smiled, trying not to reveal her secret.

Henry thought for a moment. He turned and watched her face as he spoke, "'My river runs to thee: / Blue sea, wilt welcome me? / My river waits reply. / Oh sea, look graciously!'"[8]

Her face gave it away as she recognized the lines. "Emily Dickinson!"

"Henry! Haha, that was an easy one. All right, your turn."

Henry smiled and shook his head at how much fun he was having. Life was just pure simplicity. He thought for a moment. "Okay. I got it. It's a 'work/author.'"

"Hmmmm. All right, when was it written?"

"Let's see." Henry walked carefully around a large tree branch in the path and held it back for Ara to pass through. "Early 1920s."

"Ugh, I just cannot think. Give me a hint."

Henry smiled teasingly at her. "'I have been one acquainted with the night. / I have walked out in rain – and back in rain. / I have outwalked the furthest city light.'"

Ara jumped up so excitedly that she nearly twisted her ankle on the way down. Henry reached out to catch her as she began reciting back to him: "'I have stood still and stopped the sound of feet / When far away an interrupted cry / Came over houses from another street.'" She paused and stepped down around a rocky section in the path. "'But not to call me back or say good-bye; / And further still at an unearthly height, / A luminary clock against the sky.'"

They rounded the last bend in the trail and could see her cabin in the now gently fading sunlight. Henry joined her for the last stanza:

"'Proclaimed the time was neither wrong nor right. / I have been one acquainted with the night,' 9" they said in unison.

Ara slipped her hand into his. "Robert Frost, eh?"

"One of the greats," Henry answered. "I have always just felt the words of that poem."

"Mmmm. Me too." Ara turned and beamed up at him. "So I guess we tied then, huh?"

Henry pretended to be surprised at her suggestion. "Excuse me, lady. I did not need a hint."

"Well, yours was much harder than mine."

He grabbed her around the waist and swung her in a circle. "All right, it's a tie." He added under his breath. "Miss. Competitive."

She teasingly shrieked and punched his arm. "So why a poem about the city? Tryin' to hint you're gettin' hungry?"

Henry shrugged as he felt the guilt ball up hard in his stomach again. "I guess the city is just on my mind today."

"Gettin' homesick on me?"

He smiled. "You are my home," he said and turned his face away from hers. He didn't mean to say it so matter of factly, but it just slipped out.

Ara's cheeks flushed deeply, and she looked down. He placed his hand under her chin and slowly pulled her face up toward his own. She met his eyes, and Henry felt himself drown in the resplendent color of her eyes. He slowly kissed her left cheek, then her right, and then barely brushed his lips against hers. "All right, let's get ready to hit the bar. I am starved!" He smiled fiercely to cover up his desire for her.

Ara laughed and pulled him toward the cabin. "Let's go then."

They walked up the front steps and stepped inside. "I am goin' to change quickly. Then we can run to your cabin." She walked gracefully into her room, humming like usual.

Henry sat down on the couch and looked around the homey cabin. He felt so at home in this place that he wondered why he had not just moved all his stuff over here. He supposed he should wait until after he told her the truth, the gut-wrenching truth that was killing him. She might not want him in her life, let alone in her cabin, after she found out. He sighed and tried for the hundredth time to decide how to tell her.

Ara emerged from the bedroom with her hair loosely pinned to the crown of her head. Soft trendles framed her face and moved with her as she turned to face him. "What do ya think? Okay for a bar date?"

Henry's breath caught as he took in her beautiful face, now lightly made up for an evening out, and sapphire blue cotton dress. The dress fell gently to swirl above her knees and came in at her waist to show off her stunning figure. The halter top tied into a soft bow behind her neck. He found he had no words to describe how perfectly gorgeous she really was. "Perfect," he said quietly, standing and placing his hands lightly on her waist.

She gazed at him for a moment, seeming to sense that he could not say more. Even Ara seemed at a loss for words. She did not even hum a melody as they walked out to the car.

He opened the car door for her and climbed in on his own side. Henry turned up the radio lightly and drove the few seconds to his own cabin. "Be right back." He told her with a wink.

He walked quickly inside and to his bedroom. He pulled out a pair of his freshly washed Wranglers and crisp black t-shirt and pulled them on. He had to keep the cowboy look tonight, especially when going to the bar. With that thought, he found his champion belt buckle from his first rodeo and slid that on his belt. He pulled his boots on, surprised to find he was actually growing quite fond of the cowboy clothes. His entire life had been fitted and pressed into stuffy, uncomfortable business suits. Even on his days off, Henry had always worn dress pants and polos.

He dabbed on some cologne as he checked his reflection in the mirror. He brushed his teeth with water from his water bottle and spit out the bedroom window. He carefully picked up the wildflower bouquet resting in water in a bowl, grabbed a jacket in case Ara got cold, and quickly walked out of the house and jumped in the car.

She gasped in wonder at the bouquet as he held it out to her. "These are breathtaking," she whispered and turned the bouquet slowly to admire all of the flowers.

"Not quite as breathtaking as you." He told her with a wink.

Ara set the flowers next to her carefully and looked at him, smiling appraisingly. "You look good, Henry."

"Thanks. I am really starting to like the whole country look."

They both laughed quietly to themselves, and Henry put the car into drive and took them down the mountain.

They were both quiet as they drove into town, each in their own thoughts. Henry parked the car next to Mitch's truck. "Looks like they beat us here."

She laughed. "If Mitch is as hungry as we are, I bet ya breakfast that he is already eatin'."

"I'll bet you are right. But I'll still make you breakfast in the morning." He helped her out of the car, and they walked hand in hand into the bar. There was a pulsing sound of laughter, and voices with a tangling of music oozing from the building. Ara squeezed Henry's hand in excitement, and they each quickened their step as they walked through the door.

People were pocketed throughout the bar, in swarms and in scattered madness. Music was playing from a Jukebox from the other end of the bar. People were dancing, while some were just talking, and others stood on the sidelines drinking beer and talking.

Henry and Ara caught sight of Nicole and Mitch. They all waved like silly children with overexcitement and met in the middle, Nicole and Ara with a girlish hug and Henry and Mitch with a firm, manly handshake.

"You guys wanna get a drink while me and my lady take the dance floor?" Mitch pushed right past them, hand in hand with Nicole, both of them already shaking their hips and laughing at each other.

Henry cast a waving hand at the pair as if to mockingly say, "Good riddance," and Ara and he made their way over to get drinks. They toasted to nothing particular and took a sip of their respective drinks. Smiling all the while, Ara shook her head to the beat of the song, her shoulders matching the off beats and her eyes lit up like fire. Music made her wild, and Henry was lost in watching her.

Henry felt as if he had not a care in the world. He was in a beautiful area, surrounded by great people and his new friends, and the love of his life. His world was so much bigger than it had ever been. He smiled and gazed at Ara with a momentarily guilt-free heart. She met his gaze and smiled back. He took her hand and kissed her on the cheek.

"You two are the cutest." Nicole said as she took Mitch's hand. They had finished dancing and rejoined them at the bar.

Henry smiled at them. "Well, you and Mitch are just about as cute as we are," he teased.

"Nicole and I are going to freshen up. You two all right here without us for a minute?" Ara asked with a smile.

"I don't know …" Henry said with a laugh.

The ladies went off toward the restroom with resounding laughter. He took a sip of his drink and discussed the ranch life a bit with Mitch. After a few minutes, his pager went off and he knew exactly who it would be before looking at it. "Excuse me a minute, Mitch."

He walked out of the bar, went to the nearest pay phone, and dialed his lawyer.

"Mr. Tudor, I have the deed. The contract is also signed and air-tight, sir. Where would you like me to meet you?"

Henry thought for a minute. "I will leave the passenger door of my car unlocked. Please place the deed inside the glove compartment and lock the door as you leave. Take the contract to the safe in New York. Oh, and Ms. Mortenson?"

"Yes, sir?"

"Please take your usual commission on this deal, plus double the extra hours you worked tonight."

"Oh, Mr. Tudor. You don't have to do all that … But you know I never question you, so I will take it. Thank you, sir!"

Henry told her the location of his car and went back inside, thankful and excited that Ara would soon have her beloved ranch and home back.

He weaved his way through the crowd and back to their table. Ara and Nicole were back, listening to a wild story Mitch was telling. They laughed.

"Did I miss a good story?" He asked with a mock disappointed look on his face.

"Well, I was telling it, so of course you did." Mitch launched back into the story for Henry's benefit.

Ara gave Henry a questioning look, so he mouthed, "Tell you later." He turned back to listen to the rest of Mitch's story. But Mitch had stopped and was looking at the bar's door.

Henry froze as he saw Mitch's face, which was turned toward the bar's door. It was a mixture of amusement and confusion. "Who is it, Mitch?"

199

Mitch shook his head. "I have no idea. But she is definitely not from around here." The girls turned their heads to see first.

Henry turned sideways to see the door, and his blood ran cold. His heart pounded in his ears, and alarm bells blared in his mind.

The woman who had just walked in the door had caused the entire place to go silent, save for a few drunken cowboys playing pool. She wore a silk, black knee-length skirt with four-inch heels that showed off her long legs. A dressy black tank top showed off her perfectly toned arms, and the green silk scarf around her neck emphasized the intense emerald color of her eyes.

She looked around the bar coolly. As she spotted Henry and began slowly and purposefully walking toward him, her perfect, dark hair curled at the ends did not move an inch.

Henry was unwaveringly frozen in the spot until his mind blinked back to reality, and he remembered Ara. He quickly turned to her and grabbed both her hands in his. He hung his head in guilt as he spoke, "Arabella, I am ... so sorry." His voice tapered off at the end of his words, and he clenched his jaw in agony.

Confused, Ara searched his face and did not understand. "Henry, I-"

"Ah, Henry. There you are. I have been searching much of the day for you, Mr. Tudor."

Henry turned to face his wife with as much dread and hate as he had ever felt. "Anne," he said coldly. He could smell her signature perfume and cringed.

Anne slid a hand smoothly onto Henry's shoulder and squeezed it. "Hello, darling."

"Tudor?" Ara asked confusedly, looking back and forth between the two of them.

Anne walked past Henry and stood face to face with Ara, staring coldly into her blue eyes. "Yes. And I see you are the woman who is, oh, how was it the postman put it, head-over-heels in love with my husband?" Anne arched her eyebrows in mock inquisition.

Ara shook her head slowly at Anne, not quite understanding the horrible truth to her words. She looked at Henry with a pleading glance, "Husband?"

Henry could not speak. Everyone in the room faded, and Henry could only see the terribly cold face of his wife smiling slyly at him and the beautiful and confused face of his love. He closed Anne out and tried to hold Ara's hands. "Ara, I was going to tell you. I just, I couldn't. The time was never right. I didn't want to lose you." Henry was frantically trying to find the words to make it right, to make everything okay. But those words didn't exist. Nothing could make this right.

She stepped back away from him and shook her head, tears welling up in her eyes. She grabbed her purse from her chair and silently stalked out of the bar. Mitch and Nicole ran after her. The look the two of them gave Henry as they walked out was almost as gut-wrenching as the one Ara had just given him; they were glaring at him with the intensity of a thousand suns.

The silence broke as everyone in the bar began whispering about this latest development.

Henry turned toward Anne. "What are you doing here, Anne?"

"Well, I came to see my husband, of course." She set her Chanel black leather purse on the table, sat down on Henry's chair, and crossed her legs. Everything about her was so fake, he missed Ara and longed for her.

"Don't get too comfortable. We are leaving. Now," he said menacingly as he grabbed her arm and pulled her to her feet.

Anne had a look of confusion, obviously surprised by Henry's physical force.

His pager blinged as he guided Anne firmly out the door. He reached down and checked it. "Papers faxed this evening," the page read.

"You must be here to sign the divorce papers," Henry said as he opened his car door and half-shoved her inside.

"I have a car and driver, Henry." She tried to get out of his car. He glared darkly at her. "Just wait right here. I will inform him to return to your motel and get the jet ready to fly back to New York."

Henry walked quickly to her driver, spoke just as fast, and returned to the car. He opened the door, got inside, and slammed his door.

Starting the car, he asked, "How did you find me? Was it my lawyer?"

She laughed, the sound hard and without any sense of humor. "I hardly need to resort to bribing your personal lawyer." She smoothed her already perfect hair. "I hired a private detective."

"Oh, really." Henry matched her cold laugh. He drove the car out of the parking lot and toward her hotel. As his thoughts raced, he accelerated faster and faster. "I don't suppose you used your own allowance for that?"

"Henry, you have been gone for over three weeks. I had to do something."

"Well, if you would have stayed put, you would have seen that I did something. I sent you divorce papers."

"Yes, I received that message. Mr. Jacobs contacted me. As I was already in Jackson, I told him I would talk to you instead of going through him. But don't worry, Henry, Mr. Jacobs had no idea how soon I would be talking to you."

"That is great to hear," Henry said sarcastically. "So you will sign the papers then?"

She sighed, showing Henry a slight break in her coldness. "Henry, are you really willing to throw away our marriage so quickly? What is everyone going to say?"

He parked the car abruptly in front of a hotel and turned to her. "Anne, our marriage was some fairy tale image our parents wanted us to portray: the perfect, rich, party-going, sexy couple, that smiles for the cameras. We don't even know each other. In a year of marriage, I barely saw you. I thought I would know everything about you, and I think I actually know less. We both have changed, and I think we both expected different things from this marriage." He ran his hands over the steering wheel and thought of his Arabella. His voice was raised with passion. "I have found something here that I have never had. I found real, can't get enough of, bare your soul love, and I found a part of me that I forgot even existed, a me that you have no clue about. Arabella knows more about me in three weeks than you do in a year of marriage."

"You are still married, Henry!" Anne's eyes flashed with anger.

Henry knew she could not stand to be upstaged by any woman in beauty or wealth, but she was also right. He was married. He sighed and walked around to help her out of the car. "I just want out, Anne."

Anne stepped out of the car, flashing her long smooth legs, and looked Henry pointedly in the eye, "Did you sleep with her, Henry?" Her face was stone, marblesque.

"No." He answered honestly. He kept his face stoic as he stared right back at her and added simply, "I just want out." He turned to walk back to his side of the car, but she was unscathed.

"Are you sure you have thought about everything you are giving up, Henry? What about your business, your empire? How will you run that while you're traipsing around here in some fantasy in the middle of nowhere?" She followed close behind him, breathing down his neck with her malice and contempt. "And what about your little mistress? She will want nothing to do with you again. I took care of that tonight. There is nothing here for you."

"Fortunately, we signed a prenuptial agreement." Henry replied mechanically. He just wanted to get away from her and find a way back to Ara, to fix things.

"You think divorce will make this right? Wrong! So stop trying to play some victim, like I forced you to marry me or forced you into the arms of another woman," Anne spit out.

He could feel a small part of himself, himself before Ara, stir inside him, like a familiar enemy looming in the corners of himself waiting to go back to the way things were.

Fearful and determined, Henry pushed that part inside him away. "You will have more than you need every month to be sure." He grabbed her purse out from under the seat and handed it to her without looking at her. "So my business and my life are no longer your concern." He walked her to the revolving doors of the hotel. "This is goodbye, Anne."

"Henry."

He turned and began walking away.

"That is all fine. But is that the sort of life you want for your child?" Her voice quivered, revealing her desperate fear for the first time.

He froze. "What did you say?" He spun on his heel and looked at Anne.

"You heard me." She smiled sinisterly at him. "Think about those 'papers' you want me to sign and call me. I am leaving on the jet in the morning, and I would like to know before then." She pivoted and entered the revolving doors of the hotel before disappearing among the crowd of people in the lobby.

Henry shook his head. "You are lying." He whispered in disbelief.

25
NEW YORK, NEW YORK
August 6, 1991

"For as the eyes of bats are to the blaze of day, so is the reason in our soul to the things which are by nature most evident of all."
-Aristotle

"Henry, look at that."

Henry followed her gaze and looked into the shop window. "Just what am I looking at, ma' chère?" He moved to stand next to her.

"See that crystal bowl on the the white shelf over there." She pointed and turned to look at Henry's face, pleading with her green eyes.

"Mmm hmm, yes." Henry looked into the shop. "Would you like me to buy it for you?"

Anne laughed. "Just one? Henry, please." She grabbed his hand and pulled him toward the door leading into the shop. "I need at least three hundred of that exact bowl. I have been looking for this same piece for months now."

Henry barely looked at the bowl before digging into his pocket as his pager was blinging. "Looks great, Anne." He kissed her cheek quickly and handed her his credit card. "I have to get back to the office."

"Thanks, my darling." Anne said without much gratitude as she turned to talk with the eager salesman.

Henry walked quickly out the door and climbed into his sedan. "Office, Hanson."

"Yes, sir."

26
HENRY'S JOURNEY
Jackson Hole, Wyoming
August 28, 1992

He practically ran to his car and slid inside. He slammed his door shut, and everything was silent, too silent. Putting it in drive, he sped the car out of the hotel's parking lot, screeching his tires as he turned to head back to his cabin. He started breathing intensely; this was more than he could handle. He thought of the look on Ara's face, and his face went hot with anger and he could feel tears welling up in his eyes.

He rolled down all four windows and let the cool breeze envelop him. He inhaled deeply and tried to exhale everything. He looked at his hands; they were shaking. He clenched his fist in an attempt to stop the tremors. How could he have done this? He felt like screaming in agony. Never, had he ever been this passionate about anything or anyone in his entire life. Arabella was this impossible dream. He would give, do, be, anything for, to keep her from harm. And, yet, he had left her with the same agony and despair he swore he would never let befall her. He never would have fought for a woman before this, not even his wife. He wished he could be the one feeling her pain instead.

As Henry drove into the mountains, he knew he needed to collect his thoughts and calm down before he could confront Ara, before he tried to make it all better. The task felt daunting, impossible.

He parked his car abruptly at his cabin, threw on tennis shoes instead of his boots, and sprinted up the trail to the lake. His pulse pounded and the cool night air whizzed by him. He breathed heavily, pushing his sprint as fast as he could until his legs went numb in resistance. But he kept running, faster and harder. Beads of sweat formed on his forehead, and he could feel his shirt clinging to his chest and back.

The yellow-orange fall moon was the only light needed to light his way. His muscles and chest burned from the incline, but he kept moving.

His thoughts whirled around inside his head. He saw flashes of the last weeks as he walked: the first time he saw Ara diving into the lake, the rodeo when he first heard her voice, riding horse next to her while working cattle, when she told him she loved him, dancing with her at the bonfire, holding her in his arms while she fell asleep.

He slowed to a stop as he reached the top of the climb, breathless and full of whirling thoughts of memories of Ara. The beautiful lake was in front of him once again, bathed in the soft light of the moon, but all he saw were his thoughts, playing out in front of him. He collapsed to his knees and hung his head. A tear dripped from his eye to the crisp grass below him. He clenched the grass in his hand, and he uprooted handfuls of blades. Twisting the grass into a tangled pile, a mirror of the agony of his heart, he looked up at the sky. "What did I do?" He desperately asked the stars, already knowing the terrible answer, and strew the grass down in front of him. The stars did not reply but a soft sweet voice whispered his name.

"Henry?"

Henry thought his mind was playing tricks on him as he looked up and saw the beautiful silhouette of Arabella moving towards him. He shook his head and sadly whispered:

"'And neither the angels in heaven above,
Nor the demons down under the sea,
Can ever dissever my soul from the soul
Of the beautiful Annabel Lee.[10]'"

"Henry?"

He got to his feet as the graceful figure drew nearer, her flowing blonde hair now visible. He blinked hard and looked closer. It really *was* Ara. Henry's heart dropped, and his throat seemed to twist shut.

"Henry, what are you doing here?" Arabella crossed her arms coldly and averted her eyes to the ground, her face clearly tearstained.

"Ara ... I ... " Henry hesitated. He reached out to try and grab her hand, but she pulled away. He winced in pain. "I am just here ... to think. What are you doing here?"

"If you remember, Henry, this was my sanctuary before you even came to town. Why do you *think* I'm here?" Arabella was obviously devastated, rightfully so. Her voice tapered off with her last words. He could hear the anger in her tone but hidden in her words was still a sense of love, or at the very least, concern, concern for Henry. There was a long silence before anyone spoke.

"I just don't know how to form the words to express how deeply sorry and, and just, so wrong I was and am, Ara," he said. Henry hung his head as he spoke but brought his gaze to meet Ara's as if to silently plead for her forgiveness, for her love.

"How sorry you are? Really, Henry. How many opportunities did you have to tell me you were married?" Her voice shook with anger and hurt. "While we were walking together? While we were cooking dinner in my cabin? While we were lying up here reading poetry or talking at this very lake? Or hey, maybe before you said you loved me! 'Hey, Ara, by the way, I am married.' It doesn't seem that hard of a sentence to say." She turned away from him to hide the tears that began falling from her eyes.

"Ara." Henry stepped toward her hesitatingly. He hadn't known she had heard his whispered words the night before. All he wanted to do was wrap her tightly into his arms and take away all the pain he had caused her. He touched her shoulder tenderly.

She turned to face him. "Henry, I trusted you, I trusted you with every ounce of my soul. I thought you would never hurt me." As she looked into his eyes, the anger faded and sadness and despair took over. "You were supposed to be different."

He took her hands and held them close to himself. "Ara, I know I messed up. I am so sorry for hurting you. I did have the divorce papers drawn up ... I was going to tell you about Anne ... I was just working up the courage. So many times, I was about to tell you, it was on the tip of my tongue, but something always happened and the moment passed, and I couldn't imagine hurting you. I thought I could take care of it." She let him pull her closer. "I just didn't know how to tell you."

"Henry."

Henry held up a hand. "Wait. Ara, you need to know, I didn't know what real love was before I met you. I came up to Wyoming with no clue, who I even was or what I was looking for, and I found you, the most wonderful, beautiful, smart woman I have ever met. And you brought me to life. I was dead before, Ara, you don't even know." Tears were quietly falling from Henry's eyes as he continued his plea. His voice was steady and certain in what he was saying, but the tears were steady, too.

"Arabella, you are ... the love of my life. And I'm so stuck." He looked deep into her eyes and knew he had to tell her everything. He took a deep breath. "Anne just informed me this evening that she is pregnant with my child. She has done this before, pretending to be pregnant to get my attention. So I don't really know what to believe. I don't really know what to do at this point."

Ara's eyes widened. "Henry..."

He squeezed her hands tighter. "I never intended for things to happen like this, but here we are, and we both have a choice to make. I have so much I still want to share with you, and I yearn for so much more of you, but what I need to know is if you still want anything from me?" Henry stopped speaking and realized he was breathing heavily, his chest rising and falling like waves crashing on an ocean shore. "I know I have no right to ask anything of you, especially to decide in these painful moments whether you can look past that pain and see love for me again. But I am. I am asking you to tell me right now, to give hope to a hopeless man. Please."

She stood there blankly, her mouth slightly agape, dried tears being drowned by the moist new ones that fell consecutively, as if they were counting each second that passed in silence. Drop. Drop. Drop. The silence was excruciating. Her chest rose and fell vigorously.

Henry remembered the first night he saw her at the lake and swam through his memories to calm his heart.

Ara took a deep breath and looked down before answering. "Henry, I realized even before you whispered those words last night that I love you. And, despite all of this, love, real love just doesn't disappear when someone does something wrong. In time, I could forgive you for not telling me about your wife." She met his eyes and tears filled hers once again. "But you know what you need to do. If you have a child or not, you already know what I would tell you to do. My forgiveness and my love shouldn't change the decision you have to make now."

Henry's initial hope at her first words were crushed, and now he didn't know what to say. This was not how he envisioned this conversation, or how he envisioned his relationship with Ara, or even how he envisioned his life. How had everything changed so much since just this afternoon?

He looked beyond her toward the peaceful tranquility of the lake. Henry tried to drink in the calmness of the water to calm his heart. "You are much too good of a person for me, Arabella. I do not deserve either your love or forgiveness." He took her hand and walked with her toward the water. "I need to find out if there is a baby and make the divorce final. As you also found out tonight, I have Tudor Industries to take care of as well. I have neglected my duties there for too long."

"You have to go back." Ara stated with finality and regret combined together. She let go of his hand and put some distance between them.

"But … every ounce of my being is screaming, 'Stay, don't turn your back on this!' If there is one thing that has always worked out for me, it is my instincts. They have served me very well, and right now they are pulling me to you, Ara. Am I supposed to ignore it, just because it seems like the right thing to do right now?" He closed the distance between them and wrapped his arms around her. He felt her hesitate, but then she gazed at him in such a way that he could not resist bending to kiss her.

Their lips touched for a brief moment, and then Ara broke the kiss. Pulling away, she said firmly, "Yes, Henry. You need to leave. Leave me to go back to my life and you to yours. That is where you belong." She pushed Henry off her with tears and sprinted off into the darkness of the night.

"Ara!" Henry yelled after her. His feet remained planted in the cold dirt, still stuck in his enormous mess of decisions.

****

Henry began his sorrowful trek back to his cabin. He apparently had to pack, and he had not yet come to terms with where he was headed, away from Ara, away from his new life, away from happiness. He was about to willingly walk away from everything he had discovered in the last few weeks. His mind was tormented with the thought of it. But then he entertained the thought of the possibility of his child never knowing his father. He could never be that guy. Ara would never love a man who would do that to his own child. He sighed in defeat.

In the sharp light of the moon, he made up his mind right then and there. Henry looked into the stars and vowed to go to New York to straighten everything out, and then he would come back here as a man worthy of Ara's love to see if they could make things work. He was acutely aware of the total possibility of Ara not wanting him back or anything to do with him for that matter. But he would try to the utmost of his ability.

He began to walk more quickly down the dusty trail, the night chill suddenly overtaking him, causing a shiver to spread from head to toe. He crossed his arms around himself in an attempt to ward off the cold. His mind, though, was still hot with the smoking embers of his choices.

If there really was a child, Henry would fly back and forth from New York to Wyoming. He would bring the child to Wyoming for his time with him/her and raise the child to be a good person, a better one than he or Anne ever was. He would do whatever it took to be with Arabella again. He just knew he could not live without her. She was part of him now, and he knew she would never be able to forget him. Their connection was far too strong. This kind of love only efflorescences once in a person's lifetime if they are even fortunate enough to experience it.

Henry reached his cabin just as the crickets finished their song and began another. The night air had a winter chill, and it felt as cold as snow.

He marched inside, determined. He pulled out his suitcase and began emptying his drawers, carelessly tossing his various garments into the case. He went to the bathroom to collect his toiletries. He once again caught a glance of himself in the mirror. He had that strained, intense look he first had when he left New York. He gritted his teeth and finished packing.

When he was done, he just slumped himself into the soft chair in the corner of his room and remained motionless. A single lamp illuminated the left half of his face, the other half hung in darkness. The cabin fell silent, eerily so. He could vividly hear his intake and the slow release of each breath. He glanced at his watch: 10:30 p.m. He let out a long sigh of annoyance. He couldn't just sit here until he had to leave. He would talk himself out of doing what was right. The only place he wanted to be right now was making things right with Ara. But she was not going to talk to him now anyway.

He tried calling her number. It cut straight to her answering machine. His last words to her were so pitiful, not fitting of what he truly felt. He had more to say before he left. His eyes glanced around the room. A small, blue notepad sat on the side table. He grabbed it and went to sit on the porch.

Flying bugs hovered intrinsically around the warm porch light, causing a steady hum of the bugs' wings. He tapped the pen in his hand steady against his jeans, his pace quickening as he sought the words he wanted to share with Ara. Poets always said the words he could never think of in tough times. He swore to himself that one day he would write his own poem for her, his own words, his own heart, expressing his love. But for tonight he was drawn to the words of Robert Burns and "A Red, Red Rose:"

"Till a' the seas gang dry, my dear,
And the rocks melt wi' the sun:
I will luve thee still, my dear,
While the sands o' life shall run[11]."

Henry flipped the small paper to the other side and wrote: "Arabella, I will be back. Forgive me for everything. I love you, I hope you never forget that."

He slipped the paper carefully into his pocket. He dialed the operator and had her direct him to the number for a cab company. Once Henry had arranged for a cab to pick him up, he set the phone in front of him on the porch railing and tried to think of anything else he should do before he left. He had nothing, and the more he sat around the more he ached inside.

Since he was going to be returning shortly anyway, Henry decided it would be better to fly home rather than drive the long way. He wanted to get back to New York, take care of everything and return to Wyoming as quickly as possible. He had decided there was no way Anne was pregnant and forced that idea completely out of his mind.

He grabbed his phone and dialed the pilot for his jet. "Trace? Hello. I apologize for the late hour, but I would like the jet to leave tonight, instead of tomorrow. How soon can it be ready? … Perfect. Please let Mrs. Tudor know. Thanks. See you soon."

After hanging up the phone, he grabbed a fresh piece of notepaper and wrote a note to his landlord that he would continue renting the cabin until he had returned and decided what he was going to do with his life. He completed the math quickly in his head and wrote out a check for six months' rent. Even if he returned within the month, Henry did not want to lose this cabin so close to Ara's. He attached the check to his note and placed it in plain sight on the kitchen table.

Checking his watch, he saw that he still had a few minutes before his cab was due. He made sure Ara's note was still in his wallet and walked out the door toward her cabin. Henry quickened his strides to get there faster. He just wanted to deliver the note, get back and into his cab, and to New York to take care of this mess as soon as possible.

As he neared her cabin, Henry noticed that her living room lights were on as well as the back bedroom lights. He walked quietly up the steps to her front door and pulled the note out from his pocket. He bent down and slowly slid the note under her door. He heard footsteps behind the door in the kitchen, so he quickly turned and hurried down the side of the driveway in the shadows.

As he walked away, he thought he heard her cry his name. But he most certainly could have imagined it in his distressed state of mind. Why would she cry after him after all he had put her through? So, Henry shook his head and kept walking.

He saw headlights down the winding mountain road and hurried inside his cabin to grab his bags. He decided to check around the rest of the cabin one last time. He did not see anything else, and, seeing that the cab had arrived, he picked up his bags and walked outside.

The cab driver greeted Henry as he got out of the car to help him load his luggage into the trunk. "Evenin,' sir."

"Evening." Henry said as he lifted his heaviest bag into the trunk. "I just need one thing from my car." Henry walked quickly to his car and opened the glove compartment. He carefully found the deed to Ara's ranch and took it out of the car. He locked and closed the door before walking to the cab and letting himself into the back seat.

The driver slammed the trunk and climbed in. Starting the car, he looked at Henry in his rearview mirror. "Where to, sir?"

"First, I need you to drive to this address." Henry said in a firm voice as he handed him a note with the address written on it. "Then, I will need to go to the airport, please."

"Yes, sir." The driver slowly drove the car away from his cabin and away from Ara, away from happiness.

As they drove down the mountain, the driver turned and handed him a note. "Sir, a lady gave me this note for you as I pulled up to your cabin. She paid me to wait to give it to you until we drove away."

Henry took the small note and opened it. With the light of the moon shining into the cab's windows, he read the note. In beautiful, graceful handwriting, Arabella answered his note with the remaining lines of Burns' poem:

> "And fare thee well, my only Luve
> And fare thee well, a while!
> And I will come again, my Luve,
> Tho' it were ten thousand mile$_{11}$."

He sighed in relief and was filled with the overwhelming sensation of hope. They would be together again. He just knew it. His whole body was warmed with the thought, and he allowed himself a small ounce of joy.

As the car steadily made its way down the mountainside, Henry gazed out the window at the familiar scenery. He watched as the trees thinned and the ground leveled as they drove out of the mountains. He turned and looked back into the dark forest, and wanted, with all his being, to jump out of the cab and run back up the mountain. Henry resisted the temptation and faced forward.

They drove through town and turned at the road to Mitch's ranch. Once they reached the ranch, Henry instructed the driver to turn off the headlights and stop at the mailbox. He opened the box and slid the deed in carefully. Closing the mailbox, he hoped Mitch would know what it was right away. He also hoped it would help Mitch to understand his real love for Ara.

With one final glance at what he was leaving behind, Henry committed to his choice. "All right, let's go." He said to the driver.

The driver drove back into town and down the straight and narrow highway that led to the airport. The highway followed the mountains, and he noticed dark clouds rumbling behind the mountains. Bad weather was approaching. *How fitting,* he thought, *that the night should match the storm that has erupted across my life.*

A couple of hours later, he saw a dark sedan pulling to a stop just in front of them as they arrived at their gate. He saw Anne walk with her familiar air of condescension and pride and cringed at the thought of what he was about to embark on with her. Getting out to join her was the very last thing in the world Henry wanted to do at that moment.

He paid the driver and got out of the cab. The jet's glaring lights lit up the runway, and Henry watched as Anne was helped up the steps into the jet. The whirring cry of the plane's engine silenced every sound around him. He pulled his luggage from the trunk and set them on the pavement. The jet roared louder as the pilot warmed the engine.

Two baggage carriers picked up his luggage and stowed them safely under the jet. Henry stood for a moment just staring at the plane. He saw Anne was now taking her seat next to a window. She looked at him and smiled shyly. He realized she was nervous. She was never nervous.

Henry dug his hand in his pocket and felt around. He caught the edges of Ara's last note to him with his fingertips and traced the edges of it as he took a deep breath and boarded the jet. The cabin door was shut and sealed: his fate in the same manner.

The air inside the luxurious jet was cool. He breathed in the scent of leather and coffee as he stepped up the two indoor steps.

A tall man in a dark uniform and pilot hat stood in front of the door leading to the cockpit. "Welcome aboard, Mr. Tudor." The pilot said as he stood at attention with his hands clasped together behind his back.

Henry nodded curtly. "Evening, Trace." He shook the pilot's hand. "Thanks for getting her ready to leave on such short notice."

The pilot smiled. "Anytime, sir." He opened the door and looked in at the cockpit. "She is a pleasure to fly. Tip-top shape, sir."

Henry smiled and turned to walk into the cabin. He pushed aside the thick curtain to reveal the cabin's lush, khaki-colored carpet and light gold walls. Four wide, dark brown leather chairs sat in a semicircle facing a matching couch and glass coffee table. Anne was curled up on the couch, her usual seat. Dread filled his stomach, and he walked firmly to the chair furthest from her.

"Evening, sir." The jet's flight attendant, Sherry, greeted him. With softly curling grey hair and slightly wrinkled skin, she smiled up at him with her light blue eyes sparkling.

"Hello, Sherry." He was genuinely pleased to see her. Sherry had been working for the Tudor's for years. Over the years, she had cooked, cleaned, nannied, and done pretty much any other job the family had needed her for in between. Lately, Sherry had preferred being on board the jet. She claimed she wanted to see the world but could not stand to leave the Tudors. It was the only life she had ever known.

"It is good to see you, sir." She took his briefcase from his hand and set it next to his chair. "Your usual drink, sir?"

Henry was thankful she did not comment on his disappearance from New York. Sherry always knew what to say and, in this instance, what not to say. He smiled gratefully at her and sat down into his seat, "I will take the usual, yes, please."

"Right away, sir." Sherry bustled back up to the front of the plane and closed the curtain behind her.

Henry reached down to click the lever that turned his chair to face the window instead of Anne. He knew he would have to talk to her eventually, but this flight he was going to ride in silence. New York was where the old Henry was from, but, as long as he was in Wyoming, he would be the Henry he liked best. That Henry was not speaking to the old Henry's wife. It was childish, but Henry relished every last moment he had away from his old life. Henry looked out into the sky and saw a flash of lightening in the distance. A chilly storm was brewing.

"Here you are, Mr. Tudor." Sherry handed him his drink.

"Thank you." Henry said absentmindedly as he stared out the window at the gathering clouds.

"Sherry, I need you over here." Anne commanded.

Henry heard Sherry bustle over and respond to Anne's wishes. She walked quickly to the back closet and pulled out a blanket, pillow, and Anne's CD player. He wanted to tell Anne to get those things herself but decided against talking to her.

"Please prepare for takeoff." The pilot's voice came over the speaker.

Henry buckled his seatbelt and nodded to Sherry, who was waiting to see if they needed anything else. She smiled at him and went up front to her flight attendant's seat.

As the curtain closed, Anne tried to speak to him. "Henry?"

He ignored her and continued to look out the window and sip his scotch in silence.

The plane started moving, rolling to the runway. It was a short drive before the pilot pushed the engine speed up, and the plane sped down the runway. It lifted up in the air a little roughly.

Sherry came on the speaker after a couple minutes of rough turbulence. "Mr. Trace says we are experiencing a little turbulence because of the little storm that is developing. He believes it will be over in a few minutes."

Henry watched the lights of Jackson fade below him. He formed his clearest image of Ara and wished he was not in this plane but down in Wyoming with her instead. The words of E.E.Cummings came to his mind, and he silently read them in his mind's eye, wishing them fiercely toward Ara, hoping with all his being that she could hear the words he felt so deeply. The plane continued to take him farther and farther from her until the clouds enveloped his view completely until he was alone:

"i carry your heart with me (i carry it in
my heart) i am never without it (anywhere
i go you go, my dear; and whatever is done
by only me is your doing, my darling, i fear
no fate (for you are my fate, my sweet) i want
no world (for beautiful you are my world, my true)
and it's you are whatever a moon has always meant
and whatever a sun will always sing is you

here is the deepest secret nobody knows
(here is the root of the root and the bud of the bud
and the sky of the sky of a tree called life; which grows
higher than soul can hope or mind can hide)
and this is the wonder that's keeping the stars apart

i carry your heart (i carry it in my heart)$_{12}$"

27
NEW YORK, NEW YORK
June 26, 1992

Henry walked next to Anne, holding her hand tightly in his. His thoughts were elsewhere, thinking about business as usual.

"Henry?" Anne smiled up at him. It was cool for July, and Anne was wearing a tight-fitting blazer with her khaki skirt.

"Yes, Anne?" He asked distractedly, while deep in thought, trying to figure out what error there could possibly be in the Hamilton contract and could not focus on his wife. His gut told him there was something wrong with that contract, but he could not think of what.

"Hen-r-y." Anne said a little louder.

"What, Anne?" He said with a little irritation.

She had stopped walking and had dropped his hand. "You walked by the restaurant. Cromwell and his new floozy are meeting us for dinner, remember?"

"Cromwell. Dinner. Yes, I remember and don't call her a floozy." He waited for the doorman to open the restaurant entrance and then helped Anne inside.

The Maitre d' smiled and welcomed them, "Good evening, Mr. and Mrs. Tudor. Mr. Cromwell is right this way." He showed them to their table.

"Cromwell." Henry shook his hand and sat down. He nodded to Cromwell's newest lady, a blonde with Barbie-like proportions and looks, and helped Anne into her chair.

Cromwell nodded to Henry and then to Anne. "This is Angela. Angela, this is Henry and Anne Tudor."

"Pleasure to meet you, Mr. and Mrs. Tudor."

The waiter greeted them and took their drink order.

"Did you two have a nice day?" Anne asked Angela politely.

Henry listened to the small talk, while gazing out the window and waiting until their waiter brought out their drinks before launching into business talk. "Cromwell." He took a small sip of his drink and leaned forward. "What is wrong with the Hamilton contract? Something is telling me they are pulling the wool over our eyes."

Cromwell shook his head and sipped his drink. "Henry, the contract is airtight."

"I just have a feeling … Well, it is probably nothing." He took a deep sip and tried to relax.

"Ugh, Henry, I know your gut." Cromwell made a face and took a deep drink before saying, "Man, just get out the contract." He said with a grin and slapped his hand on the table.

Henry leaned over, pulled the papers from his briefcase and laid them on the table between them. He bent his head in, and Cromwell did the same. "Good, let's look this over."

He heard Anne's sigh of frustration as she rolled her eyes to Angela but ignored her. She took a long pull on her water having not ordered her usual glass of wine, leaving a deep red lipstick stain on the rim or glass and leaned in to talk closer with Angela.

Henry pulled out the first page of the contract and scanned every word. He had to make sure the contract was perfect. Tudor Industries stood to make millions out of this contract. They could not afford any loopholes. But he could not get Anne's reaction out of his mind. She should see that he did all this to support themselves and their future children. His mind stopped short. Children? A pang of longing hit Henry. He had wanted children, not to raise himself personally, he was much too busy for that business, and they would use the family nanny anyway, but Anne was never ready. He resented her slightly for this, but they had not been together very long yet. He cocked his head slightly at the thought of it and was even more at ease ignoring Anne's complaints.

Cromwell put down the papers, "I just cannot see anything, Henry."

He put his hand up to stop Cromwell as he finally found the answer to his feeling. The wording was off in section G. He read through it one more time to be certain. "Here it is," he said triumphantly and pointed to the section.

Just as Cromwell bent over to look at the section, Angela excused herself to the restroom, and Anne joined her.

The two men were deep in discussion and hardly noticed. Henry explained the problem with section G to Cromwell for several minutes. As they were deciding what to change in the wording, Cromwell's pager chimed.

"Excuse me, Henry, I need to take a call. I'll be right back."
Cromwell excused himself, and Henry sat by himself combing through
the pages of the contract to make sure the rest was perfect, barely
noticing Cromwell's absence. He grabbed a calculator from his briefcase
and started calculating figures. He was immersed in the projected
spending figures when Angela returned to the table.

Henry looked up and nodded to her, acknowledging her presence,
then realized she was alone. "Where is Anne?" He asked with his mind
on the figure currently on the calculator.

"Oh, she was fixing her makeup. She said she would be right out."
Angela's voice was lower than he personally liked, but something in her
tone made her seem kind. She smiled at Henry and asked him how he
had met Anne.

Henry tried not to show his irritation at the distraction and began
telling her a shortened version of the story. He was almost finished when
he saw Cromwell heading back to the table looking irate. Henry was
instantly worried that something had occurred with the contract and cut
off mid-story.

"What happened?" Henry asked without hesitance.

"Happened? Whatever could you mean?" Cromwell played coy, but
Henry knew worry in his face better than anyone. It was the same look
he had had back in college when he got drunk the night before a final and
woke up late pretending not to care.

"No need to play coy, Thomas. I know you better than you know
yourself, I think." Henry gave him a look like, "You know better than to
try that trick."

Cromwell challenged his gaze without flinching. "Absolutely
everything is fine, Henry. And perhaps you don't know me as well as
you think."

Cromwell's jaw was clenched, and Henry knew something was
putting him off. He was about to say something further when Anne
returned to the table, her cheeks flushed with pink embarrassment.

"Is everything all right?" Angela asked, her kindness ringing in her
voice.

"Everything is great." Anne said curtly flashing her prettiest smile.

Henry stopped thinking about the contract, and Cromwell's
behavior momentarily and eyed Anne curiously.

Anne's eyes darted to each person at the table and tried to reassure
everyone with another debonair smile.

"Really, I'm fine." She looked at Henry, her eyes begging him to let
it go.

Henry stared at her silently. A strong feeling that he was missing something gripped him.

Cromwell broke the awkward silence. "Well, that's enough business for now, Henry. Put those papers away and let's show these beautiful ladies a fun evening." Cromwell lifted his glass in a toast before Henry could protest.

Anne exuberantly accepted the gracious change of subject and thanked Cromwell with a nod. "To living in the moment." Their glasses clamored in a syncopated chime, and Cromwell downed the rest of his scotch.

Henry noticed Anne eyeing Cromwell curiously before she broke her gaze and looked back at Henry. She set her glass down again and declared, "I'm starving ... where is the waiter?"

Cromwell signaled the waiter for them.

The man came over. "What will the ladies be having?"

Henry ordered Anne the chicken special, and Cromwell ordered the same for his lady.

"And for the gentlemen?"

"I will actually have the chicken as well," Henry said and handed back the menu to the waiter.

"Really, Henry." Cromwell said disapprovingly but with teasing in his eyes. "A man needs a steak to help keep his lady satisfied." He winked at Angela, who laughed lightly in return.

Henry took a drink and felt the liquid spirit lift his own a bit. He smiled wryly, "I don't need a steak to help me with anything."

Cromwell nodded and laughed. "All right, you best give me the chicken as well," he said to the waiter.

Anne cleared her throat. "So what were you two talking about over here?" She asked, looking from Henry to Angela.

"Well, Henry was just telling me about how you two met before you and Cromwell returned. It seemed like it was just getting good." Angela smiled. "I would love to hear the ending."

"Oh, well, the rest was sort of just history ... and now we have been married for almost a year." Henry smiled at Anne and squeezed her hand.

She pulled her hand away to drink a sip of water. He looked at her with a questioning gaze but did not say anything

Cromwell said with slight annoyance in his tone, "Yes, it is a wonderful story." He grinned devilishly. "Now, let's get on to something a little more interesting. Like the trip my lady and I are taking to Paris next weekend!"

Everyone at the table exclaimed excitedly, especially Angela. "I had no idea, Thomas!"

"And how many trips to Paris will this be for you, Cromwell?" Henry asked dryly.

"Oh, just a few. I suddenly found myself craving *vin* and *fromage!*"

"You can have wine and cheese here." Henry said smiling.

"Ah, but I am also craving Paris herself!" He laughed and, seeing that his glass was empty, motioned to the waiter to bring him another drink.

Henry laughed and sat back in his chair. "Not me. I am happy to be staying in New York next weekend for once."

Anne, who had been unusually quiet during their conversation, suddenly complained, "Well, it would be nice to go on an *actual* trip for once, Henry." She turned to Angela. "All we ever do is travel for business."

Henry felt his temper rise slightly as he looked down at her. "Anne, we just got back from Spain. You shopped and hung out with friends the whole week."

"While you were working."

"I work so hard, so I can support you. If you haven't noticed, Anne, you fly through your allowance every week and still need more." He regretted saying it all as soon as he said it, especially in front of Cromwell and Angela.

Her green eyes flashed with anger. Dramatically, she stood up, threw her napkin on the table, and walked out of the dining area.

Henry apologized to Cromwell and Angela and went to talk to the waiter about packing up their meals. He was used to Anne's dramatic exits but grew tired of her theatrics.

The Maitre d' retrieved Anne's jacket for him and carried their packed meals out to Henry's car. His driver had already brought the car around and was waiting with the door open for Henry. Anne was inside, lying dramatically on the seat with her arm across her forehead.

"Thank you, Clive." Henry said to the driver and nodded to the Maitre d' as he climbed inside next to Anne.

"Where to, sir?"

"The mansion, please. And put up the partition, Clive." He slid his arm across the seat and looked down onto Anne's face. "Anne." He gently pulled her hand from her eyes and placed it in his own. "I apologize for saying what I said in there. It was not right of me to do so, especially in front of others."

She opened her eyes and looked at Henry with an exaggerated hurt in her expression. "I do not *fly* through my allowance."

Henry laughed and nodded his head. "Of course you don't."

Anne sat up and looked down into her lap. "But there is something I need to tell you, Henry." She continued to gaze at her hands in her lap. "I am pregnant."

He did not think he had heard her right. "What?"

She met his eyes then. "I took a test at the restaurant. It tested … positive." She said with a slightly sour expression. "You know I don't want kids, Henry."

Henry was overjoyed. He smiled down at her. "Well, I guess we can't do anything about that, Anne."

She took the test out of her purse and handed it to him with disdain. "You are going to have to make this up to me, Henry."

"And how will I go about doing that?"

She looked defiantly into his eyes with her chin set. "For starters, I would like that diamond necklace I showed you in that little shop over on 47th Street."

Henry was too ecstatic to refuse. "We will go over first thing tomorrow." He kissed her cheek.

They rode home in silence while Henry thought about teaching the little girl or boy how to throw a baseball and, eventually, how to run the business.

28
NEW YORK, NEW YORK
July 2, 1992

Henry whistled as he walked into the mansion. He had gotten off work a little early, so he could buy Anne, his beautiful wife and mother-to-be, a little surprise. Ever since she told him about being pregnant, Henry was practically living in a good mood. He greeted Francis, the home's butler, and handed him his briefcase and hat with a cheerful smile and a nod. "Please put those into my office, Francis," he said as he climbed the large, sweeping staircase that led to their private wing of the mansion.

He held the gift behind his back and quietly opened the door, hoping to catch Anne off-guard. But he heard voices coming from the sitting room. He walked passed the entryway and stood to the side of the door to the sitting-room. He listened intently to the angry conversing of his wife and her maid.

"Priscilla. I wanted you to buy me the Kotex brand of tampon. Honestly!" Anne stomped to the bathroom and began throwing boxes at the maid. "It was on the list I dictated to you yesterday. Can you do anything right?"

"I-I'm sorry, Mrs. Tudor. I must have mixed up the directions. I will go back to the store right now."

"Don't bother. You are fired." Anne said coldly. "Now leave my house at once."

Henry stepped around the corner just then. "Priscilla, please go downstairs and put on a pot of coffee and help yourself to a cup. And ignore my wife's previous statement. Your employment is safe." He turned to Anne as Priscilla, with a grateful smile, walked quickly past him toward the door.

"Thank you, sir." She said with relief as she closed the door to the Tudor's suite.

"Is there something you need to talk to me about?" Henry said firmly as he stood tall with his hands in his pockets. He kept his eyes averted to the ground, and his tone was one of deep concern. A horrible feeling that he had been tricked settled into his gut, and he said icily, "I guess your doctor's appointment didn't go the way you planned? Or did you even go at all?"

He picked up a box from the floor. "Why would you have sent Priscilla to bring you tampons. You certainly will not need them for at least a year." He walked purposefully toward Anne.

"Henry, don't overreact." Anne turned away from him and looked at her reflection in the mirror vainly, pretending to smooth down her perfect hair.

He reached out and took her wrists firmly in his hands and asked her to look at him, his eyes no longer averted and now fierce with anger.

She struggled against him and defiantly met his gaze. "Well, Henry, I wanted you to pay more attention to me. And frankly, being pregnant was the only way … well, let's just say, you have been more than attentive in the past few days than you have our whole marriage." She laughed cynically, as if her words were weightless feathers that were casually tossed away with the winds of consequence. "So I think my lie was perfectly warranted." She turned back to the mirror with a victorious smirk.

Henry was filled with a boiling rage. Releasing her from his grasp, he glared into her cold, green eyes through the mirror. She didn't appear to care or was very good at hiding it. His dreams of what the two of them could have had vanished with the realization that was what they were – just impossible dreams.

He silently stalked out of the room. He walked quickly down the stairs and into his office.

"John," he yelled to his assistant as he entered. "Get Cromwell on the line and tell him to meet me at the bar."

He barely heard John's answer of "Yes, Mr. Tudor," before he was out the door, letting it slam shut behind him.

Thoughts ran together through his mind as he walked quickly to the bar he and Cromwell frequently met at together: *How could this woman be his wife? Was she really that selfish? How could he have believed her so completely?*

He walked faster down the street and turned the corner. His heart felt ripped in two as he realized how much he had wanted that child. He had already developed an unfailing love for someone who apparently never even existed. He had loved, with all his heart, a lie. He felt as though something inside him had died, and he could do nothing. He was also so angry at Anne that he could hardly think anymore. Numbness began to overwhelm him, like the chill of downing a shot of whiskey, or two. Henry wanted the real thing.

He opened the door to the bar and walked inside, fuming. He sat down at the bar and ordered a shot of whiskey along with his usual. He took a sip of his scotch and felt the spirit burn his throat and settle warmly into his stomach. He focused on that warmth and forced himself to calm down as he stared into his drink.

"What's the trouble, Henry?" Cromwell said as he burst into the bar.

Henry motioned for Cromwell to sit down next to him and shook his head.

"What's up, man?" He cajoled, always ready for a trip to the bar.

Henry sighed deeply, "Thomas … let's get drunk."

29

WYOMING TO NEW YORK
August 30, 1992

The plane hit a small bit of turbulence, jolting Henry from his thoughts. He sat up and looked around the quiet cabin. Through the darkness, he could make out the shape of Anne lying on the couch listening to her music. His stomach knotted up as he remembered why their marriage had begun to fall apart in the first place, not that it was altogether very strong to begin with, but at least it was honest up until that point. Or was it? Anne had pretended to be pregnant to get his attention. He was sure she was capable of lying about much worse. She had wanted his attention before, and she certainly wanted it again. He remembered how livid he had been at her and couldn't imagine her pulling the same act on him again. She must think him smarter than that. But then, how desperate was she? He had been gone almost a month, maybe she had had to do something so desperate that he couldn't ignore again. At this point in their relationship, he knew as well as she did that only a baby would keep them together. After that stunt she pulled in early July, he had not been able to forgive her, and that was one of the reasons he had left New York. What she didn't realize was that even a baby could not change his experiences in the past month. And everything had changed because he had met Arabella, baby or not.

He watched the dark sky out the window and allowed his thoughts to drift back to Ara. He saw her walking up the path to their lake, looking over her shoulder at him and smiling softly. She tried to hide her smile behind her shoulder, like she held the greatest secret of humankind. When she finally revealed her smile, it dazzled, and it reached her eyes as they met his own. Her wavy curls bounced and moved with the light breeze. The sun flashed behind her as she threw her head back and laughed before punching him playfully in the arm. She exuded complete ease around him, and he felt the same around her.

He would grip her hand lovingly as he spun her around before gently kissing her lips. As he set her down, Henry remembered a look in her eyes he could not place until just now. She had been perfectly and incandescently happy but scared that it would not last. It was kind of like that moment in any relationship where a person had to decide whether they were in the relationship for all or nothing, but then the person would realize that he/she was all in already, and that realization was unnerving.

Henry felt a twist of guilt and longing for her. That same day, Henry had woken from a little afternoon nap to see Ara picking wild flowers a little ways away from him. She had hummed to herself like she always did, like every moment was worthy of song and carried on without a care in the world. He remembered how he never wanted to forget that moment. Everything had seemed so perfect, so wonderful with her.

Anne jostled him from his memories as she turned to lay on her side on the couch. He looked down at his watch. Two hours had passed since they left. They would be landing in New York in about forty-five minutes. Henry tried to imagine what it would be like to step back into his old life, but looking back at those memories was not as easy as thinking about Ara was. All he wanted to do was forget the New York part of his past.

Knowing there was nothing he could do about that for the moment, he downed the rest of his scotch and settled back in the chair. He let his eyes rest for just a moment and fell into a light sleep.

****

When he woke up, the roar of the plane's engines had quieted, and they were on the ground in New York City.

Henry rubbed the sleep out of his eyes and turned his chair to look around the cabin. He glanced over to see Anne still fast asleep on the couch.

"Mr. Tudor?" Sherry walked over and put a hand on the back of his chair. "It is safe to exit the plane, now." She smiled down at him kindly, but Henry could see concern in her eyes. "Clive is here with the car."

"Thank you, Sherry." He looked over at his sleeping wife. "Please wake her for me," he told Sherry, who nodded in response.

Henry grabbed his few things and walked down the steps of the jet. The New York skyline was picketed with tall buildings much like mountains only cold and unfriendly. His neck stiffened from the cool chill in the air. It felt like winter was setting in early this year, or maybe

Henry was chilled by the thought of what the next few days and weeks would hold.

He wished desperately that Ara was here with him, but he knew that would never happen. He had messed so many things up.

He gritted his teeth as the baggage men began retrieving their luggage and loading it onto rolling carts. Henry heard Anne from inside the plane asking Sherry for an umbrella. Henry looked up at the sky and saw the reason why it was so a cold. The storm had followed them, and the sky looked like it was about to break open with rain. He pulled on his jacket and began walking briskly towards the waiting car.

Small drops of rain hit Henry's face slowly at first but then steadily until the drops were large and thick with moisture. He held up his hand over his eyes to block the rain from obstructing his vision and climbed into the dark sedan.

"Hello, Mr. Tudor."

He nodded to his driver. "Clive." He ran his fingers through his hair and shook the moisture from his clothes. He glanced through the window and saw Anne approaching with two men holding her bags. A third followed with Henry's.

Clive climbed out into the pouring rain. He helped Anne into the car and then directed the men to load the luggage into the trunk.

Henry ignored Anne pointedly and continued to stare out the window. She sat a little ways from him and did not try to converse with him which made him extremely relieved.

They rode in silence to the mansion with only the sound of the rain spattering against the car and sunroof, like a metallic orchestra playing a tune of misery fitting of Henry's internal struggle. Henry looked out to see the familiar sites of New York City as they drove. He found himself comparing each site that had once given him such joy to the beauty of Wyoming: the mountains, the lake, the ranches. Nothing in New York would ever compare now that Henry had seen true beauty; beauty not created by man's hand. He knew he had seen beautiful things before – he had travelled to all areas of the world. But Wyoming was special for one reason and one reason alone. She was Wyoming; she encapsulated all of its beauty and more.

They arrived at the gate of the mansion, and Clive entered the gate code before it creaked open, allowing them entrance. Clive then pulled smoothly into the long, curving driveway of the mansion. Henry looked up at his expansive home which now looked cold, unfriendly, and filled with despair. He longed for the warmth of Ara and her cabin.

Clive walked around to help Anne out of the car. Henry felt her look questioningly at him, but he continued to ignore her and climbed out of his side reluctantly. Walking to the trunk of the car, he pulled out his own bags and walked to the mansion.

Once at the huge glass doors, he dug into his pocket and slid his key into the lock. He turned it with dread, not wanting to unlock the door to his "home" any more than he wanted to walk into it, to walk back into any part of his old life. The familiar feeling of turning this key made his gut ache. He took a deep breath, turned the key, and slipped inside the house, hauling his luggage in tow.

"Mr. Tudor." Francis said as he walked quickly out of his quarters. "I must have dozed off!"

"Well, it is the middle of the night, Francis." Henry said with a tired smile. "Will you call Mrs. Wile over, please?"

"Right away, sir. She should be in, sir." Francis bustled away just as Anne walked in the door, followed by Clive, who was carrying her luggage.

Anne glanced at Henry coolly and began to walk up the stairs toward their master suite. Henry couldn't understand her intentions. She seemed indifferent to him even now being home. *Why is she playing this game?* Henry wondered.

Mrs. Wile and Francis walked quickly back into the entryway. Francis grabbed Anne's bags from Clive and followed Anne up the stairs.

"Hello, Mr. Tudor." Mrs. Wile smiled and brushed her greying curls out of her face. "What can I do for you, sir?"

"Please make up the guest suite in the far side of the mansion for me. I am sorry for the hour of night, but I would appreciate it very much." Henry was angry at Anne, but he refused to take it out on his loyal staff.

She thought for a second and nodded. "It should be very close to ready, Mr. Tudor. You may come right up with me if you like." She bustled up the sweeping staircase, her soft house slippers causing a whirring whisper to echo through the empty hallways.

Henry picked up his luggage and followed her, thankful his staff did not ever question his requests. He walked into the suite and set his luggage down in the entryway.

Mrs. Wile was running around, quietly muttering to herself as she turned down the bed and checked the towels in the bathroom.

"Everything should be fine for tonight, sir. I will check back tomorrow and have the ladies finish the rest."

"Thank you, Mrs. Wile." Henry slipped off his shoes and walked inside the bedroom.

She slipped out the door with "Good night, sir. It is nice to have you home again."

Anne had probably been wreaking havoc on the house staff. He felt terrible for leaving them under her authority.

As the door closed, Henry realized he had not felt so alone in quite some time. The room fell silent, and he rushed over to the window, suddenly needing fresh, crisp air. The night was chilled, a sure sign of the imminent winter approaching.

The cool air chiseled away at his thoughts. His eyes widened, and he released his breath. Almost unaware, Henry let out a deep and agonizing shout that lurched through the New York night. His mouth closed and the sound of his voice dissipated with the wind. There was no response echo, his voice was just gone. He was gone. In Wyoming, he had felt surrounded by the silence. It comforted him. Here he was just another hopeless mess in a maze of emptiness. No one heard his cry. No one would rescue him from this nightmare. Was this really his life? It had to be a dream.

He took a small step back from the window and shut it tight. He hung his head, grabbing the back of his neck, as he crawled into the bed still fully clothed. Before drifting to sleep from exhaustion, he pictured Ara's beautiful face and closed his eyes, pretending for the moment that he was still with her, pretending he was still home.

30
NEW YORK, NEW YORK
August 30, 1992

Henry woke with a start from the noisy sounds of traffic outside his frosted window. He put his hand over his startled heart, and he remembered he was in New York. His life was different once again, but his true life was not here. He knew he would have to cope with this eventually. Devastation filled his slowing heart as he recalled the course of events of last evening.

He rolled over and grabbed the small clock on the night stand. It was just after 6 a.m.; he had only slept for about two hours. He remembered how the sounds of traffic used to put him to sleep. Now the sounds jarred him awake, resounding the terrible moments he knew lie ahead of him for at least the next few days.

He pulled the covers over his head and tried to block the dark thoughts from his mind but the street sounds outside rang out like a cacophony of hysterical laughter. The joke was on him. After a few minutes, he finally drifted into a sleep with nightmares sinuously tormenting him with thoughts of losing Ara forever.

****

A few hours later, he woke up in a cold sweat from his most recent nightmare. Arabella had been trapped in a closet, and he could not get to her. Every time he took a step, he sank further into the ground like it was quicksand. He could hear her screaming his name, and he tried to call out to her but no sound would come out of his mouth. He sank further and further, helpless. It felt like if he could just reach out with all his might he would reach, but, just as his hand would graze the handle, the quicksand pulled him deeper.

Henry sat up and shook his head, trying to forget the sound of her screams. He imagined it all, but it felt so real. Looking around the unfamiliar bedroom, he realized he had gotten out of one nightmare and into another: his current life. How could he have made such a mess out of his life?

He put that thought and other dark thoughts that loomed near the surface aside and walked into the bathroom to shower. He stumbled from sleep as he stepped into the walk-in shower and turned it on to the hottest temperature, full blast. He pulled off his clothes from the night before and threw them to the side. He walked into the shower and breathed out a deep sigh. He put his hand on the shower wall and let his weight rest on his hand. The showerheads on the side of the shower soothingly pulsed water onto his tanned skin as the giant square shower head above gently rained down hot water. Steam quickly filled the room and soon Henry's muscles relaxed.

How long he showered, Henry had no idea. He only knew that when he finally turned off the water and walked out, he felt a tiny bit better. With hot, clean skin, his problems seemed a little easier to handle for the moment. He toweled off and heard a knock at the door of the bathroom.

He wondered who could be bothering him already as he tied the towel around his waist. Henry's first thought was Anne, and his stomach twisted in dread. He put his hand on the doorknob and turned it slowly.

"Henry, you old dog!" Cromwell exclaimed, grinning at Henry.

"Thomas," Henry said with a faint smile and rolled his eyes. Of course Thomas would be knocking at his private bathroom door at eight in the morning. He was not quite ready to talk to anyone just yet, but oddly Thomas was the one person Henry could always handle. Plus, he knew Thomas would never leave even if he asked him to. "Do you mind?" Henry said to him mildly, gesturing toward the towel around his waist and the bedroom. "I am in the middle of getting ready."

Oblivious to Henry's hint or just ignoring it, Cromwell stepped back into the bedroom to let Henry through. "I cannot believe you just disappeared out of town for nearly three weeks without a single word to your best friend and business partner," he said as he reclined on Henry's bed, propping up a pillow behind his head. "And then you come back in the middle of the night without telling me!" He said indignantly and straightened his black Armani tie and ran a hand over his immaculately combed, short, dark brown hair.

Henry rifled through his luggage for something to wear. Not one stitch of clothing was free of the smell of fresh pine and, worst of all,

Ara. He clenched a plain white shirt he had worn a few days earlier with Ara at the lake. He threw the shirt to the ground before answering.

"Thomas." He sighed and tried to think of what to say. He wondered why telling Thomas the truth felt wrong and oddly too personal. They were closer than brothers, best friends for years, but he still didn't know how to say what he wanted to, at least not to him. "Well, I just had a few things to take care of out of state." He said, looking down at his suitcase. Lying to him was easier than he thought.

"Really? And are you telling me those 'things' also led you to sleep in the guest suite once you returned?" Thomas asked dryly. "C'mon, Henry … you can't fool me with a lie. Especially a lie like that. I know you better than you know yourself."

"Uh huh." Henry said mildly and dug out a clean dress shirt and dress pants. *Then how do you seem to know so little about who I really am?* Henry thought to himself. His clothes were wrinkled, of course, from the rushed packing and flight. He walked over to the intercom and called down to the household staff room. "Mrs. Wile. I need someone to iron my clothes for the day. Sooner rather than later. No, I want to wear this. Patricia? Yes, send her up." He strode back into the bedroom and faced Cromwell. "Thomas, I will tell you more later. Right now, I just want to get dressed in peace and get caught up on everything."

"Henry..." Cromwell's eyes darkened in concern but broke off the rest of his sentence as a knock sounded at the door.

"Come in." Henry said.

"Mr. Tudor." Patricia smiled and held up and iron and a few other essentials. "What shall I work on for you?"

Henry handed her the clothes. She nodded and averted her eyes from Henry's naked torso, her cheeks bright pink as she hurried to the entryway to iron them.

"All right, Thomas. It seems I have a minute." Henry grabbed a pen and small notebook from the bedside table. "Why don't you brief me on work … just the most important business for now, please."

Thomas sighed and dug out a small electronic planner from his pocket. "I suppose. Well, for starters, Wallace Chan from …"

Henry nodded and took quick notes as Thomas talked. He had never missed a day of work, let alone three weeks. He realized it was going to be a lot of work to get caught up again.

After a short while, Patricia laid his clothes on the bed. Henry nodded his thanks and kept taking notes from Thomas as she left the room.

He had filled five small pages with writing when Thomas finally said, "Well, that should be enough of a briefing to get you started." He put the planner away, stood up, and looked at Henry. "Will you be coming into the office today?" Thomas asked, straightening his suit and moving toward the door.

Henry shrugged his shoulders. "Maybe later on." He offered no other information as to what he would be doing the rest of the day.

Cromwell opened the door. "Well, I will see you later then. I sure am glad you are back." He said with a smile that did not quite reach his eyes and shut the door.

Henry sighed with temporary relief at being alone for a bit longer. He pulled on his pressed clothes, swiped on some deodorant, and a spritz of his cologne.

He walked into the bathroom and ran a comb through his short hair. Looking into the mirror, he took in his black silk designer shirt and pants. He breathed out, determined not to think of Ara or Wyoming. He needed to focus on getting things taken care of here. Only, then could he allowed himself to think of his real home, when he had an actual chance of going back. Henry reached over and grabbed a dark silver and black tie. He breathed in and tied his tie with practiced expertise.

His stomach growled. Henry thought for a bit as he tried to remember the last time he had eaten. It had been the picnic with Ara yesterday afternoon. The last time he had waited this long to eat he had been leaving this very place behind him, not knowing where he was headed. He had a very similar feeling today. His stomach twisted, in misery this time, not hunger. It felt like months had passed since he had been with her at the lake. He pictured her blue eyes filled with joy, and her golden hair moving gently with the breeze.

No. He put his hand on the counter and pushed her from his mind. That was who he was, always pushing, pushing forward and pushing away, never in one place for very long. He had to *focus*.

He strode out of the bathroom, slipped his notepad into his pocket, and left his room. He walked quickly to the end of the hall and down one side of the curving stairway. He headed toward the kitchen to find some breakfast waiting for him on a silver tray. He noticed a second tray at the other end of the counter. *Hmph, even our breakfast is separate ... we have a really good waiting staff*, Henry chuckled to himself. It was the first laugh, or resemblance of a laugh, he had allowed himself since yesterday. This was the joy he had left, the pitiful leftover crumbs of the joy he once knew. Henry was resilient, though; he just had to give his soft heart a chance to get accustomed to the city air. Stony his heart once was and to the stone it would return, unless he could get away before that point.

His goal was going to be to take one small step at a time. Finish one task and complete another until he was finally ready to head back, back to his Arabella. He felt his heart beating inside him for her. She would keep him soft. He smiled and touched his hand briefly to his heart before letting his hand fall into his pocket.

The moment passed. He took his tray, turned the corner, and strode through the gigantic dining room.

"Why, Mr. Tudor!" The house cook, Nicolaus, said as he rushed over and shook Henry's hand. "I am glad you are back, sir. Will the breakfast be sufficient?" He motioned toward the tray with a questioning look.

Henry smiled and his stomach growled loudly in answer. "Yes, thank you. Maybe some coffee, please." He set the tray down as Nicolaus bustled out. He knew that Anne would never come into this room, not with the staff. Henry was sort of thankful for their cheery voices. He was glad he didn't have to sit in complete loneliness in his own house.

The morning paper was open on the table. Henry sat down and turned it to the front page to catch up on the world news scene.

"Here you are, sir." Nicolaus said as he set a cup in front of him and poured steaming coffee into it; no cream and no sugar, just the way he liked it.

"Thank you, Nicolaus." Henry took a sip of the hot liquid and smiled. It burned his tongue slightly but he swallowed. It was too good to waste, rich and nutty in all the right ways. He remembered comparing good coffee to a good looking woman, too good to waste. That was in his college days when Thomas was much too great of an influence on him. He had always enjoyed his morning brew, though, that was timeless. The coffee settled into his stomach like it was finally home and warmed him up slightly.

He continued reading the news for a few minutes. Nothing too interesting seemed to be happening in the world. He turned the page and read some local news and continued to sip freely on his now warm coffee.

Henry dug into the heaping plate of turkey sausage, scrambled eggs, and breakfast potatoes in front of him. Nicolaus was a great cook, and he never disappointed Henry. He loved nothing more than to make people happy with his food. He knew he was good at it, but he always acted surprised when someone swooned over something he made. Henry put another piece of sausage in his mouth and turned to the next section of the paper.

"Everything all right, sir?" Nicolaus asked.

"Yes. Perfect as usual, Nicolaus."

Henry finished eating and drained the last bit of coffee from his cup. He walked his plate and cup to the sink area. "Thanks again." He turned to leave the kitchen.

"Sir, will you be joining Mrs. Tudor for lunch?

Henry looked over his shoulder. "I think not, Nicolaus."

He walked out of the kitchen, back through the dining room, and into the large entryway. He nodded to Francis who was hanging out by his post as the butler.

"Good morning, Mr. Tudor."

His footsteps echoed off the glossy marble floor like an unchained melody sung with solemnity. It carried up the stairs as if the sound were rising and falling with each step it climbed before silencing itself suddenly, no more stairs to play its echo song.

As Henry dug into his pocket for his office keys, slid the key into the lock, and walked into the room., he whistled the rest of the song his steps played, the soundtrack to his current situation. The office was where Henry spent most of his time, when he was actually in the mansion. He slipped his keys back into his pocket and walked to his huge oak desk.

He breathed in the familiar smell of wood and a faint scent of scotch as he sank into his chair. He slid his hands across the smooth desk. He set his notepad on the desk and pulled out a fountain pen and a sticky pad. His dad always said that using a fountain pen was like signing even the most meaningless of documents with class. "You can never go wrong with a fountain pen."

What do I need to do today? He thought and drummed his fingers on the desk in deep thought. He read over the list that Thomas had given of work-related issues, but he couldn't focus on one thing except Anne. Obviously, he needed to make an appointment with their doctor to see if Anne really was pregnant this time. He hoped with all his being the test would be negative. He flipped through his Rolodex and pulled out the doctor's number. He wrote down the number and put that card back.

He should see his parents as well. Henry knew they had to have been very worried about him while he was gone. Nobody had any clue where he had been. He wrote that down and decided to see them tonight for dinner if they didn't have plans. That way he would get out of having dinner with Anne, too. One more day to put off the inevitable.

He also needed to stop and check in at Tudor Industries. No doubt that would be even more overwhelming than the encounter with Thomas this morning. He wrote that on his list that seemed to just get longer and longer, and he wanted nothing to do with any of it.

Henry also remembered that most of his "office" clothes, his designer suits, were inside his room – the room he shared with Anne. He decided to have Patricia move all of his clothes into the guest room. This would also show Anne that he was done with this marriage. Done.

Reaching for his phone, Henry called their family doctor. "Hello, Dr. Olson. Henry Tudor, here."

"Hello, Mr. Tudor." Dr. Olson rumbled slowly in his deep voice. "What can I do for you, sir?"

"I need you to test my wife. She says she is pregnant, and I would just like to double check, you know, make sure. Will you come to the mansion to administer the tests?"

"Certainly, Mr. Tudor. I can be there in about an hour. Are you both available then?"

"Yes. See you soon, Dr. Olson."

Henry hung up and called Francis to wake Anne before dialing his father's number. "Mr. Tudor, please." Henry said to his father's secretary.

"May I tell him who is calling?"

"It's Henry."

"Oh, Mr. Tudor! Of course, I will put you right through."

There was a slight pause. Henry suddenly dreaded telling his father where he had been and what he had been doing. His fingers tingled as he heard his father's concerned voice on the end of the line.

"Son?"

"Hello, Father." Henry paused, unsure what to say next.

"Back from your ... trip, I take it?"

"Yes." He answered simply. "Are you and mother free for dinner? I would like to catch up with you two."

There was a slight pause. "Henry, I will clear our plans. Your mother is dying to talk to you. We really missed you. Your mother was worried sick. Is everything all right?"

"Yeah, well, I'm back so ... want to meet at our usual place? I will have Francis make a reservation."

"That will be fine, Henry," Henry could hear the sound of disappointment in his father's voice already. "See you about seven?"

"Yes. See you soon then." Henry hung up the phone.

Henry looked at his watch and saw that he had time to discuss the clothing situation with Patricia before Dr. Olson arrived.

He rang down to the staff phone and discussed it quickly and quietly with Mrs. Wile. He also asked her to check if Anne was in her room still.

After he hung up the phone, Henry crossed the completed items off his list and swiped his hands in a quick, satisfied motion. In his short time back in New York, Henry already felt like he had accomplished a few things. The thought made him fill with a heartsick anticipation. The sooner he was done here, the sooner he could leave "here" behind and return to his real home.

Henry heard the echo of the doorbell ring out through the house: the doctor. Henry's heart jumped as he realized that the doctor was going to find out if Anne was truly pregnant. The result would not change his decision about getting back to be with his Ara, but it would alter Henry's life considerably if she really was with child. He hoped Anne was awake.

Taking a deep breath, he opened the door and stepped into the large entryway. Dr. Olson was talking quietly with Francis. He was holding a black doctor bag with a black stethoscope around his neck.

Spotting Henry, the kind doctor lifted a hand in greeting and walked towards him. Dr. Olson was in his mid-fifties with dark hair speckled with grey and of medium height.

"Mr. Tudor." Dr. Olson said as he stretched out a hand.

"Thanks so much for coming, Dr. Olson, on such short notice." Henry shook his hand vigorously and motioned toward the sweeping staircase. "Anne will be upstairs in her room."

They headed up the stairs. "How has business been going?" He asked the doctor.

"It has been very steady, thank you for asking. And your business is doing well, I hear?"

They stepped onto the second floor and headed toward Anne's room, Henry's former master suite.

"And who have you heard that from?" Henry asked politely with curiosity.

"Why, your father. I have been seeing him on a regular basis ..." Dr. Olson broke off as he saw the confusion in Henry's face. "I am sorry, Mr. Tudor. I thought you knew." Henry was mixed with confusion. His eyebrows furrowed, and he opened his mouth to inquire.

They were interrupted as Anne stepped stormily out of the suite. "What is going on here, Henry?" She demanded. Fully dressed for the day in a deep orange designer dress and matching Jimmy Choo heels, she put her hands on her hips and glared at the two of them.

His stomach wrenched at the sight of her, not from guilt, but dread. "Dr. Olson is going to confirm your pregnancy. Aren't you going to say hello to the doctor?" He said firmly in a cold tone.

The surprise showed in her face. "Really." She said coolly and folded her arms across her chest. "You can't make me take any test, Henry."

"Will you excuse us, Dr. Olson?" He said to the doctor, who was beginning to look quite uncomfortable.

Dr. Olson nodded and walked back from the doors a few steps.

Henry grasped Anne by the elbow and steered her into the suite. He turned her around to face him and put his face down closer to her own. "You wanted me here, I'm here. This is what you wanted, right? You fly yourself to Wyoming to announce this child, and now you don't want to take a pregnancy test? Why should I possibly believe you are carrying my child, Anne? After what you put me through last time?" He loosened his grasp to make sure he wasn't holding her arm too tightly. He was angry, yes, but that didn't mean he should hurt her. "You are going to take the test with Dr. Olson, or I am going to forcibly move you out of the Tudor mansion."

Her green eyes widened, and she tried to hide the fear from her eyes. Henry couldn't stand that the only thing that mattered to her were things, no one's happiness, no one's feelings, just material things. "Fine. Tell him to come in so I can *get on* with my day." She said frostily, wrenching her arm out of Henry's grip.

He walked to the door and asked Dr. Olson to come in. The doctor came in slowly and looked from Anne to Henry.

"Anne has agreed to the test, Doctor." Henry shot a glance at an apathetic Anne.

"Very good. Will you please take a seat, so I may draw some blood?" Dr. Olson asked politely as he set down his bag and began pulling things from it.

Anne rolled her eyes and sat gracefully down in a chair. "This is so unnecessary."

"Anne." Henry warned. He leaned against the wall and watched her with darkened eyes.

She "huffed" and held out her arm.

The doctor began to draw her blood. Once finished, he then asked Anne to head into the bathroom to fill a cup with her urine.

She sighed with annoyance but grabbed the cup from his hand and stomped to the bathroom.

"I apologize for her behavior, Doctor." Henry said with a tight smile.

Dr. Olson chuckled. "Don't you worry, Mr. Tudor. This is not my first interaction with your wife." He put a few things back into his bag. "She is … something else. If she didn't make a fuss, I might be concerned."

Henry nodded and obligingly chuckled. This was the woman he married, the woman apparently others also saw as conceited, selfish, and horrid. "Yes, she has been quite a handful."

Anne called the doctor into the bathroom. A few minutes later, they both emerged with Anne wearing a triumphant look.

Henry's stomach plummeted as he waited for the doctor to speak. "Well, sir, it appears from the initial urine test that your wife is indeed pregnant." He picked up his bag and put a few things inside. "But I will run the blood test and let you know if I get a different result." He put a hand on Henry's shoulder. "Not to worry though, sir. The urine tests are almost always correct."

His blood ran cold, and he felt dizzy. He cleared his throat and led the doctor to the door. "Thank you again for coming, Dr. Olson." He said without feeling. His whole body was numb as he turned and walked toward the stairs in a daze.

Anne stood at the top of the stairs towering over him with unadulterated pride. Her arrogance was sickening. She was so pleased with her victory, and Henry directed his gaze away to avoid her childishness. Anne was really pregnant. He shook his head in disbelief. He realized he had seriously doubted there would ever be a baby the entire time. He was going to be a father. The thought sunk in with shock and despair, but, was there also a shimmer of joy inside the dark thoughts? Henry had wanted a child for quite some time...but not this way. It was not with Anne that he now wanted to have a child. He wanted to have a baby with Ara, Arabella Bennett, who was the love of his life. How had everything become so convoluted?

Anne said nothing before turning and walking back to her room, her head held high.

Henry suddenly found it hard to breathe. He gasped in air and pulled at his tie and collar. Pulling his tie loose, Henry stumbled quickly out the mansion's doors in a desperate need for fresh air.

He stopped a few paces outside of the house on the plush, green grass. Putting his hands on his knees, he gasped and breathed in the warm air. It was New York air, however, and therefore not the fresh, clean, crisp air of Wyoming that he craved. He let his head fall between his knees and focused on his breathing for a few minutes, trying to slow his heart and lungs down to their normal pace.

Traffic steadily sounded noisily in the distance, reminding him just how far from *her* he actually was. No, he needed to clear his mind, especially from thoughts of where he wanted to be. He listened to the car honks and the noisy squealing of brakes awhile longer, focusing on the grass below him.

Slowly, he stood up still listening to his breathing to hold off the major panic attack that threatened to come. The late August sun warmed the top of his head. He looked up, closed his eyes, and let the bright light warm his face. How could anything be wrong when the sun was shining? His heart slowed as he calmed down.

Finally calm, he opened his eyes and glanced around at the familiar surroundings. He had grown up here among the pruned hedges and manicured lawns. As a young boy, whenever his family was home and not traveling on business, he had explored among the many trees down a ways from the house. There was one tree in particular he remembered asking his dad to build a tree fort in. Of course, his mom disapproved outright and that was the end of that. But he remembered dreaming about having a tree house anyway.

This place, this home, held some of Henry's most precious memories. His wild and adventurous mind always kept him busy. He would read until the sun went down outside, next to the treehouse that was never built, almost every summer. His parents always trusted him alone outside because the grounds were so well protected, but he rarely was given the free time away from school work. Thomas had been there on all his adventures too, of course, although when Thomas went home, that was when Henry read. It was in those rare moments when Henry was alone, away from Thomas, away from school work, that Henry developed his love for poetry. Thomas never knew about his love for words.

Henry stepped onto the stone path that wound its way around the grounds and headed toward the grove of trees at the edge of the property.

It was not long before he passed the mansion's garden and entered the cool shade of the thick trees, a place he had named Utopia, after reading Thomas Moore's *Utopia*. He had named it other things, like Nanook, when he was deeply enthralled with living in Alaska with the Inuits, and Amore, when he was enamored with his first grade English tutor. Utopia was the last thing he had named it before he became too cool for the shady trees. Thomas told him that anyway. *How long has it been since I have walked down among these trees?* Henry thought as he looked around at the long-forgotten "forest" of his youth. He remembered picking this spot because it was as close to the outside world he could get without being in trouble.

He followed a faint trail until he came to the fort Thomas and he had made a very long time ago in thickest part of the trees. They built it so deep in the trees, so their parents couldn't climb in and pull them out. Now the trees were trimmed so the fort could be openly seen by anyone who entered the shady nook. He remembered working on it during the years of his childhood, years when Henry would sneak away to the fort with Thomas with any spare time he had in between his extensive studies. This fort had been his sanctuary from tough school work, demanding parents, and other time-consuming duties Henry had had as being heir to the Tudor empire.

At the top of the two-story fort, faded pieces of their flag still clung to the pole, waving in the light wind. He remembered the wood being golden brown before, but now it was greyed from years of weathering and age. He ran his hands along the branches they had woven through the trees to form strong walls. The fort had held together well in the last twenty or so years it had been since they had last been here. He brushed leaves off the dusty door and pulled it open.

Henry laughed out loud as memories of his youth washed over him. In the corner of the fort, sat the "chairs" Thomas and he had made out of large rocks they could barely carry. Some, he remembered with a rueful grin, they had had to use an old wheelbarrow to haul the rocks into the fort. Their "weapons" area, which consisted of homemade slingshots, sharpened rocks, and a BB gun Henry had gotten for his eighth birthday, filled the front right half of the fort. Of course, the gun was rusted and dusty, as were the rest of the weapons.

He lifted his old, child's size bow and arrow off its rack on the wall and shook his head as he remembered his father teaching him how to use it. His father had told him, "A Tudor man must be able to hit a moving target with a bow and arrow." When Henry had gotten frustrated while learning to shoot, his father had pushed him constantly, as he had throughout every aspect of Henry's life. "A Tudor man does not give up, son." His father had told him sternly. "He finishes every task that he has set out to do. And, not only does he complete each task, but a Tudor finishes it *perfectly*, with excellence." This had been only one of many "Tudor" rules his father had taught him.

He had resented his father's methods many times throughout his life, but now, thinking back, Henry knew his father had made him into a Tudor man, through and through. Whether that was a good thing, Henry did not know. All he knew was that he had found a Henry in Wyoming that he wanted to keep. He had pretended to put aside his "real" personality and actually found his true self in the process. Well, he had had the help of Ara. His stomach twisted horribly, and he pushed her out of his mind yet again and focused on looking up into the second story of the fort.

The far side of the fort consisted of a large tree with a solid trunk. Henry and Thomas had carved footholds into the trunk for stairs to get to the second story. This was where they had made up beds for themselves with stolen blankets and sheets from the housekeeper's section of the mansion. Henry remembered concocting a foolproof plan with Thomas as to how they would "acquire" the bedding. He had distracted the house staff with a long story about something or another while Thomas had snuck into the laundry room and grabbed all the bedding he could carry. Henry had excused himself from the staff and snuck away after Thomas to the fort. The success of their mission had resulted in quite comfortable beds. He grimaced as he could only imagine what they looked like now.

He had many great memories from his childhood with the happiest formed in this very fort. But now, in a few months, a child, his child would be born and soon would be making its own childhood memories, maybe building his/her very own fort. Would he be around to see that happen? To help and parent this child as his father had helped and parented him?

The footholds they had carved for themselves no longer seemed to be able to hold Henry. The second story would remain entombed in the remains of its last adventure, never to be disturbed. Henry slid back down the trunk of the tree and let his body hit the soft dirt with a thud. A faint puff of dirt billowed around his legs and ankles. He noticed a dark blue stone across the expanse of the fort floor. It seemed oddly familiar and somewhat out of place to him. But it was rather in place, and Henry suddenly remembered the significance of that rock. He crawled on his hands and knees over to the rock, too tall to stand. He lifted the blue rock, and in a small leather pouch was his most prized treasure as a little boy. He pulled out his tattered journal and blew fragments of dirt and rock off the cover. He smiled and traced his fingers along the rigid edges of the paper, stained with dirt and age. He opened the pages to the scribblings of his little self at varying ages. He flipped to the last page and read his last entry:

"Thomas says we can't hang out at Utopia any more. It's just not becoming of 'lads' our age, apparently. I think I might still come by myself every once in a while. I like this place, and I don't mind the dirt as much as Thomas. He had his first date last week. Maybe when I find a girl I will be ready to leave Utopia for good, when I'm a man. I leave for Spain next week with my parents. I'm trying to think of it as a vacation, but they are going for work. I don't know what I'm going to do with my time. I'll be by myself most of the time, but at least it's on the ocean. I can spend time there, do some reading for myself. Who knows ... maybe I'll meet a girl then, but, if not, I guess I'm not too worried about it. I don't get the big deal with having a girlfriend. Since Thomas got a girl, I've seen him maybe once a week. We used to spend every free minute together here at Utopia or on some other adventure. I think when I find a

girl, whoever she is, she will be the kind of girl who wants to get to know me and my life, just as much as I will want to get to know her world, and we will equally share our time with our friends. She would want to come to Utopia and make believe about things with me. And I will trust her to be off without me, and she will trust me. Trust. I think that's pretty important. Thomas just wants a girl to make out with. That's all I ever hear him talk about anymore, in the rare times I see him. Somehow the image of tangling tongues with some girl doesn't sound as appealing as Thomas makes it out to be. But who knows. I'm a pretty patient guy even if Father says good things come to those who take them and not to those who wait. I'm ok with waiting. I can't help but recall Robert Frost's words. I think about his words right now, 'Why abandon a belief merely because it ceases to be true? Cling to it long enough and it will turn true again, for so it goes. Most of the change we think we see in life is due to truths being in and out of favor.' I will cling to my belief for as long as it takes. I will find myself in this world and someday, whenever that day, whether tomorrow, or in Spain, or 30 years from now, I will find her, the girl I clung to with belief, the belief in something that was not until she was. I will cling. Signing off, Henry."

Henry sat clutching the worn book and smiled at himself. He marveled at his young, youthful maturity. He remembered Thomas's first girlfriend pretty vividly: Vivian Thomas. They hit it off right away because they said, "By the name of Thomas we are united. Destined to be together." Henry never got it, but they seemed really into it. They dated for three months, but after she dumped him for an older high school boy, Thomas was never as committed to a girl again. After that, Henry saw him more when he had a girlfriend than he did when he was single. It was a confusing flip flop of Thomas. Henry knew Thomas was heartbroken after that first breakup. One night, a few weeks before they broke up, Henry remembered Thomas coming to his bedroom window late at night. He had rapped and rapped until Henry came to let him in. Thomas crawled impatiently inside, shivering from the crisp autumn air of New York. He said almost nothing, but as they sat in silence, the moonlight casting playful shadows on their faces, Thomas turned to Henry and just smiled and said, "I love Vivian, Henry." Henry remembered not knowing what to say, having never known this love he was speaking of, so he patted him on his back and told him how great it was. Thomas left moments later, and Henry went back to sleep wondering whether that was just a dream or real life. A few weeks later it ended, and Thomas came around again. He was different, though. Maybe he just put up an impenetrable guard against women getting to him ever again. He seemed happy with his life that way, but Henry wondered if he really was happy.

Henry stopped his thoughts and looked at his watch. He had been in this little fort for nearly an hour. He felt strangely calm and at ease. The words of a much younger Henry encouraged him. He could cling, he could wait. Good things come to those who wait; he really believed that even if it never seemed to be how he did things. He didn't wait for Ara. He settled for Anne. Look how that worked out for him. If only he had just waited. But he couldn't help but wonder if he would have ever met Ara if he had never left Anne so impulsively. Maybe, people are all intended to go against their initial beliefs, if only to see that it's the belief they should have clung to in the first place. But one would never understand that need until one could look back, and see the need for it. "Why abandon a belief because it ceases to come true?"

Henry felt ready to face the world again and the unbelievable reality his world now held, Henry softly treaded out and closed the door of the fort. He left in silence and didn't look back. He needed to get the rest of his list for the day accomplished. As much as he dreaded it, he had to get to work and face his family before he could move forward, before he could be where he belonged.

He turned and strode quickly toward the mansion. As he neared the front door, he spied Anne making her way quickly down the front steps toward her waiting car. He stepped closer to the house to stay out of sight and observed her to guess where she might be headed. Her glossy, dark hair was smoothly hung down her back, curled at the ends, and she wore the deep orange ensemble she had had on earlier. Dressing immaculately was nothing out of the ordinary, though. She slid gracefully into the open car door and spoke in a low voice to the driver. Henry was struck at how beautiful she was. He felt nothing toward her, but she was absolutely radiant. He was thoughtful for a moment about the idea of the baby, not the idea of Anne, but his child. The thought of his child made him radiant. But then he wondered what Anne was doing? Who was she meeting?

Henry checked his watch: a little after one. She could possibly be meeting someone for lunch. He hoped she had other things going on so she would be away from the mansion for as long as possible and away from him. He loved the idea of being a father, but the idea of sharing that experience with Anne made him sick to his stomach.

He waited until the black sedan had driven away before walking back into the mansion. Keeping his thoughts neutral, he focused on "next step, next step, next step" as he walked to his office. *What is my next to-do on the list?* He thought as he picked up the list on his desk that he had made earlier. Work. He needed to head into the office and catch up a little on business before having dinner with his parents.

The now-familiar empty pain in his stomach, from stress and everything that had happened in the past twenty-four hours, deepened slightly, and Henry realized he felt mildly hungry now that he had calmed down. He pushed down the call button on the intercom and requested a small sandwich with some ice water.

"Nicolaus will whip something right up for you, sir!" Mrs. Wile told him cheerfully.

"Thank you, Mrs. Wile." Henry clicked off and started looking around the office for his briefcase. He found it resting by the side of his desk.

That's odd. He mused to himself. *I always keep it in front of the desk, not to the side.* He lifted it up and set it on his desk. *Maybe Mrs. Wile or Priscilla moved it while cleaning.* Running his hand over the worn leather, he typed in the combination to unlock it and lifted the cover. He rifled through the papers, struggling to remember what he had been working on three weeks ago. It felt like a lifetime had passed.

A knock sounded at the door. "Come in."

"Here is your lunch, sir." Priscilla set a filled plate and glass of water on the desk and stepped back with a smile. "Anything else you would like?"

"Well, will you find my business brain for me?" He joked with a wry smile.

Priscilla laughed. "I think you were born with that, sir." She curtsied slightly and walked out of the room.

He took a bite of his sandwich, a BLT with turkey bacon, crisp lettuce, and a juicy tomato with a little ranch dressing, and sipped his water. It was his favorite sandwich. If there was one thing he missed about here, it was Nicolaus's cooking. It was normal human food, nothing fancy, just good. The papers closest to the top seemed to be in a strange order; he always kept the contracts in order from most important to the finer details. He shrugged off the nagging feeling of suspicion and dug out his notes from Thomas's briefing this morning. Taking another bite, he sat down in his leather chair and compared the notes to the contracts and other forms inside his case. He swallowed a little more water and made notes as to what was still relevant and what had been resolved while he had been … gone.

After a while, he thought he was caught up enough to head into the main office. He replaced the papers and added his own notes before shutting the case. He brushed crumbs off his shirt and looked into the mirror inside a closet door in the office. Cutthroat, professional business

Henry looked back at him. *Old Henry is only going to be here for a while*, he thought. *I might as well get used to it.*

He noticed that he did have a little dust and dirt on his pants from crawling around in the old fort. He decided to clean that up before he left the mansion. Sighing, he straightened his tie, shut the closet door, and picked up his briefcase. He opened the door to his office and stepped out onto the glassy marble floor, closing the door behind him.

"Are you headed out, sir?" Francis asked as Henry stiffly approached.

"Yes. Francis, would you mind finding me the keys to the other sedan? I see that Clive has taken Anne out in the usual car." He gestured to his dusty clothes. "I'll be right down as soon as I clean up these clothes."

"Yes, of course." He walked into his quarters next to the door and emerged a few seconds later, keys in hand. "Shall we expect you home for dinner tonight, sir?"

"No, Francis and thanks." He took the keys and headed upstairs to the guest suite.

He returned to the main level a few minutes later, dust free and as office ready as he could be. He gave Francis a wave goodbye and walked out the side door to the mansion's garage. He started the dark Lincoln sedan and said aloud, "Tudor Industries, here I come." He half-smiled and pulled out of his long driveway and out the gates that enclosed this home.

Henry followed his old familiar routine. He was headed to the office later than he usually would be on a typical day, but he stopped and got a coffee and bagel at his favorite local coffee shop. The girl who normally greeted him by name with a big smile, Charity, was not working. Her shift was probably over for the day. A teenage boy named Rob greeted him instead with a half-hearted smile and sent him on his way nonchalantly. Henry lifted his drink slightly as if to say "good day," and turned to the door shaking his head. He got back in his car and started driving into the heart of the city.

Before long, Henry could see Tudor Industries. It was easily spotted even from a few miles away. The forty-eight-story building with sleek, black windows and even darker steel, pierced the New York City skyline like a steel blade striking an unbreakable glass surface. The feeling of pride surprised him as he looked up at this immaculate structure of architecture. He especially loved the dark blue lights under the different spires and roof edges that shown even more clearly at night. He walked up the smooth, stone steps to the main doors of the building. "Tudor Industries" glowed an ominous dark blue above the large black doors. He smiled faintly up at the words before heading inside the building he had entered so many times before.

The expansive lobby was bustling with activity as usual. Men and women in expensive business suits entered and exited seamlessly, like the steady flow of a stream. A long row of small rod iron tables lined the lobby hall. Each table had a small fountain in the center with water spilling over the sides that recycled itself back into the fountain. The splash of the water echoed through the corridor along with the sounds of shoes tapping rhythmically on the marble floors.

"Mr. Tudor!" The security guard straightened up and stood at attention as Henry drew near. He held up his briefcase to activate the clearance security gate – his card was inside the pocket of the case – but the guard was already waving him through with a smile.

Henry nodded his thanks and walked through the open gate toward one of the waiting elevators. He watched as the numbers lit up as the elevator descended floor by floor. The shiny black doors opened with a ring, and Henry stepped inside with a few other employees that Henry didn't recognize. He reached over to push the floor to his CEO office, but a man in a dark grey suit stepped over to assist him with a smile. "What floor, sir?" The man's fingers hovered over the top button.

"You know the one," Henry said with a wry smile. How had he never noticed all the people in his life trying to please and impress him? He felt like a jerk, plain and simple. He made a point in his mind to learn these people's names.

They soared up to the top of the building within seconds. The door slid open, and the other workers inside the elevator stepped aside to let him through. He smiled curtly in thanks and stepped onto the smooth, black, polished stone floor of the top floor.

In the middle of the expansive room, a large white marble fountain softly cascaded water as large windows facing the city and the skylights above showered the fountain in golden sunlight. The base of the fountain was wavy, forming the shape of Greek-like clouds. Atop the base, a graceful and beautifully carved angel held out a hand in triumph with his face tilted toward the heavens, a determined smile upon his set lips. If he got close enough to examine the fountain, he could see that under the wavy clouds was the shape of the Tudor building, towering above smaller buildings in triumph. Water dripped soothingly all around the base, pouring over the Tudor motto, which was carved below the angel and above the fallen men: "Non est ad astra mollis e terris via." This translated from Latin to English was "There is no easy way from the earth to the stars."

The room was quiet, save the soothing sound of the water and his steps as he crossed the floor to stand closer to the fountain. Henry put his hand through the cold, flowing water and touched the carved motto. His father had always harped the motto at him while teaching him how to run the company. Henry had always thought of the "stars" as the stars of success: the stars of closing a deal, the stars of running a multi-billion dollar company, the stars of filling the large footsteps of his powerful father.

Henry splashed the water around the words and thought of how many times he had said the Latin phrase in his mind during a tough decision or a trying time. But he remembered reading the Bible with Ara that one day in the meadow. The words could mean so much more if he only thought of it from a different perspective. *Possibly,* he mused silently. *One could think of it as the trials we face on earth, the difficulties one must go through to achieve true happiness. Ara would think of this to mean that the difficulties of a life not lived as our own, but the life lived for a higher power, the Lord, were the "stars" one reached in the end: Heaven.*

His stomach twisted, and he knew he had not led that sort of life yet, but he wanted to learn. He wanted just one person to teach him how: his Arabella. Startled, he realized he was looking for a phone, having her number committed to memory.

He snapped out of it and stood up. He cleared his throat as if it would clear his muddled mind as well. Turning his head away from the fountain towards his office door, Henry began walking. The rest of the floor consisted of offices that surrounded the center room, the one he was in right now. Thomas, the CFO of the company, Thomas's secretary and assistant, and a few other of Henry's right-hand people occupied the offices on the right half. On the left side of the floor, Henry occupied the main office and adjacent to his office was his secretary's.

The door to his office opened, and his secretary walked out, expertly holding a stack of files as if they were the most important possible thing she could be holding. Her chestnut hair was pulled into a tight bun at the back of her head with straight, no-nonsense bangs covering her forehead. The beige pencil skirt and matching jacket were free of any wrinkle or imperfection as usual, he observed, as she stepped toward him in beige Mary Jane heels.

"Mr. Tudor." With her free hand, she straightened her dark, wide-brimmed glasses, which were already straight, and smiled professionally. "Hello, sir. We have missed you around here."

"Jennifer." He walked toward her with a slight grin, his hands held up in a "so what" motion. "You only missed bossing me around for the last few weeks." He joked, genuinely happy to see his secretary, a lady whom, for the past ten years, had spent eighty to ninety-hour work weeks with him.

"Really, Mr. Tudor." Jennifer said disapprovingly but with a tiny hint of a smile on her lips. "The CEO of a profitable company cannot just disappear without even a note to his secretary or CFO!" She shook her head at him, and Henry could see the tired stress lines around her eyes.

He suddenly realized how ignorant it had been of him to just leave town without a word. Of course, Jennifer would have had most of the burden of the company fall on her. He felt awful and told her so.

She smiled professionally. "I forgive you." She good-naturedly shook her finger at him and said, "But you have a lot of work to make up, sir! And I need your signature on..." She sighed, "A LOT of things," and motioned for him to accompany her inside of his office.

He smiled and walked inside the large three-room office with one hand in his pocket. The first room that opened once through the double, dark wood doors was a conference room of sorts. Of course, there were many conference rooms in the Tudor Industries building, the forty-seventh floor held the largest conference room in New York, but this room was where Henry's top clients would be invited to work out business deals while casually conversing and sipping drinks made from the wet bar that ran alongside the front left-hand side of the room. The entire office was floored in dark Brazilian walnut with dark leather couches and chairs. Black, modern lamps rested on end tables while tasteful paintings decorated the walls. Each painting had been given by various clients or purchased by his art advisor, and Henry was considered quite the art collector by his colleagues and clients. A plush, deep blue rug warmed the center of the room looking very presidential for an office space.

Henry walked down the side of the "conference" room and through a dark colored stain glass door into his personal office. The office mirrored that of his office at home with a large, dark walnut desk and various filing cabinets and closets. This office, however, had one of the most amazing views in the city, save the view from the Empire State Building. He had had the window custom built once his father had given him the office. The window was a "bump-out" style so it extended about a foot from the side of the building, giving the viewer a 180-degree view. The entire bump out was bullet-proof glass with the floor, sides, and ceiling entirely clear. Standing in the glass window had always given him a thrill and rush of adrenaline when he needed to clear his head.

"So what have I missed?" He asked as he walked with her into his office and set down his briefcase on his desk.

Business as usual, Jennifer stood in front of his desk, set down the large stack of files, and took a little notepad from her inside pocket. "Just from today? Well, Christopher Dane called and needs to speak with you asap. 'It is of the utmost importance.'" She quoted.

Henry rolled his eyes and wrote down "Dane" on a sticky note on his desk. "Of course, it is." He said cynically. "Continue."

She rattled on in order of most importance to importance. He took notes and felt more and more overwhelmed. "And these," she said as she motioned toward the files she had set down on his desk, "are notes and information from when you were gone. Each file is a separate day and crossed out items have been resolved." She closed her notepad and straightened her glasses which had not moved since she last corrected them. "Fortunately, Thomas really stepped in while you were gone, sir. So it should only take a few long days to be fully caught up." She brushed her hands down the front of her thighs, straightening her skirt, and looking up at him with a look that told Henry she was very pleased with herself.

"It sounds like you need a bonus." Henry smiled approvingly, and the slightest curve of a smile played out on her lips, accepting his appreciation.

The phone rang in her office which was on the opposite side of the conference room. She pretended not to be anxious to answer it. Her face had reddened during her last statement about getting caught up and curiosity struck him. He stared inquisitively at her. What would have embarrassed this unflappable woman?

"Will there be anything else?" She asked with a hint of impatience as the phone rang again.

"No, thank you." He waved her away and thought over her last remarks. *"Thomas really stepped in while you were gone."* He sat down in his leather office chair and sighed. He had *forbidden* Thomas from having any sort of sexual interactions with any of the staff as they had had many lawsuits for sexual harassment once Thomas had slept with practically every woman in the building from secretaries to interns and never called them again. This was why Thomas's assistant was required to be male. He went through almost a secretary a week before that rule was in place. At first Thomas was outraged by it, but, when he realized how much more productive the workflow was, he conceded his complaints.

Apparently, Cromwell did not think rules applied to him when I was gone. Henry mused with a touch of anger and annoyance. He jumped out of his chair and stalked across the floor to Thomas's office. He opened the door to the office without knocking. "Cromwell." Henry said with a slight, dangerous undertone in his voice.

Cromwell looked up from conversing with the two men seated in front of his desk. They were obviously in the middle of a business deal. "Yes, Henry?" He asked with a matching edge to his voice, clearly annoyed to be interrupted.

"I need to speak with you. How long until you are finished here?"

"We were just finishing up, Mr. Tudor." One of the men said and stood up to shake Henry's hand. "Mr. Cromwell has been working with us on the Curie Industry contract, but we are pleased to see you are back in town, sir."

"Yes. Nice to see you, too." Henry said with a tiny smile as he showed the two men from the office.

"What *is* up, Henry?" Cromwell inquired as he casually leaned back against his desk. His lips over pronounced the "p" and he made it pop. "You disappear for three weeks and then burst into my office in the middle of a large business deal?" He shook his head and looked Henry over. "You sure you're all right, man?"

Henry shut the door and walked closer to him. "It seems you have slipped back into old habits while I was away." He folded his arms and glared at Cromwell.

Cromwell seemed taken aback for a moment but quickly regained his composure. "I don't have any idea what you mean." He said nonchalantly and walked over to the windowsill where he kept liquor and glasses.

"You can't fool me, Cromwell. You have some nerve, sleeping with my secretary!"

Pouring Scotch into two glasses, Cromwell walked back over to Henry and tried to hand him a glass, which Henry refused. "Well, the secretaries downstairs don't light me up near as much as Jennifer can." His eyes glittered mischievously as he took a drink.

"Jennifer is highly valuable to the company and to me personally!" Henry was used to Cromwell's numerous conquests, but he was very fed up with it all at this moment. He paced around the office and tried to calm down. Cromwell was, after all, his closest friend. He wouldn't talk this way with the other employees. "I just have … a lot to deal with, Thomas."

Suddenly feeling exhausted, Henry sank down in the chair opposite Thomas's desk. "Please make everything right with Jennifer and *promise* me you will not, under any circumstances, sleep with any more employees of Tudor Industries from this moment on?"

Thomas sighed and nodded. "All right, Henry. You don't have to throw a holy fit your first day back." He handed him the untouched glass. "Have a Scotch and let's get on with the day!"

Henry flung back his drink and finished it in one, clean drink before standing up. He set the glass down on Thomas's desk and walked toward the door. Opening it, he paused in the doorway and looked back at Thomas. "Oh, and Thomas, thank you for taking care of things here while I was away. I appreciate it."

Cromwell smiled wryly. "Oh, it was no trouble at all."

A strange, unsettling feeling gripped Henry as he returned Cromwell's smile, but he shook it off and walked back into his office. He had a good couple of hours to begin catching up on work before dinner, and he intended to make the hours count.

****

Henry walked into Delmonico's, his parents' favorite restaurant for cozy, catching up times with him. It was a restaurant that dated back to the late 1800s and was known for fine dining, excellent cuisine, and, of course, upscale clientele. Crystal chandeliers trimmed in gold, other golden fixtures, and gold-toned, plush carpet, along with soft-toned, live singers, made the atmosphere feel like taking a sip of a good cognac.

Henry was shown to their regular table and found his parents were already there.

"Henry!" His mother jumped from her seat to embrace him. Her hair was a shining chestnut with a reddish tint that hung down between her shoulder blades. Tonight, she had it loosely curled and wore a cream, knee-length dress suit that showed off the slim figure she had had to work hard to keep now that she was in her early fifties. She was as radiant as ever, and Henry couldn't help but smile warmly at the love she exuded. She was a mother to the core.

"It's good to see you, Mom." Henry told his mom as he reached down to embrace her and kiss her cheek. He got his height from his father, as his mother was about 5'7" with 3-inch heels on, which she wore practically all the time.

Elizabeth pulled back and searched his face, her light brown eyes full of concern and love. "How are you, darling? We have been so worried." Her hand brushed his cheek lightly. Henry let his face rest in her palm for a moment, as he always did, knowing it made her feel like the wonderful mother she was.

Henry turned from his mother and shook his father's hand without responding to what his mother said. His dad was a perfect, older version of Henry. Although, tonight, Henry thought his hair seemed to hold a little more gray than when he had seen him a little over three weeks ago, and his dark eyes were tired and filled with concern as well. "Henry." His father said with a relieved smile. When he said it, it was like he let out a long sigh of relief, and the tension he held in his shoulders released.

Henry felt a pang of guilt as he had caused all this needless concern and worry for his parents. He had never seen his father look this tired.

"Anne couldn't join us?" His mother asked.

"No," he said simply and suggested, "Why don't we all sit down?"

They took their seats around the table, set with a shimmering, light gold tablecloth, white roses set in gold-tipped, crystal vases, and candles. The waiter appeared for their drink order. His father ordered a fine Merlot for the table.

Henry tried to relax in the soothing atmosphere but felt on edge. He knew his parents would demand answers to his absence, in the nicest way possible of course, which only made it worse. He took a sip of the ice cold water in front of him to calm his nerves. Either his hands were wet from the condensation of the glass, or Henry was sweating.

His parents exchanged a glance. "So what did you do today, Henry?" Elizabeth asked gently, trying not to force the conversation to where everyone knew it was headed.

The waiter returned and poured them all a glass of wine. He passed out menus and informed them of the excellent beef bourguignon as the special before departing.

Henry swirled the deep red liquid in its glass gently and said, "Well, I did a few things around the mansion and went into the office for a few hours." He took a sip of the wine and waited for the questions to begin. His wine settled placidly in his glass.

"And how are things at the office?" Mr. Tudor asked casually as he perused the menu.

Henry picked up the menu and pretended to peruse it as well. "Everything seems to be in order." He said carefully. His father would no doubt lecture him on the responsibilities of being a Tudor before the night was out. "We have a few contracts to follow up on, and the Curie Industries buyout is going well."

"Thomas must have had to work very hard the last few weeks?" His father asked as he set down his menu. His insinuation was loud and clear.

"Shall we order?" His mother interrupted and waved the waiter over.

Grateful for the interruption, Henry gave her a small smile and nodded.

"What will we all be having?" The waiter asked professionally.

His mother ordered the broiled fish with lemon seasoning and a small salad.

"I will take the special," Henry said, hardly remembering what the waiter had said the special consisted of, and his father ordered the special as well.

"Excellent choices." The waiter said with a slight tilt of his head. He picked up the menus and walked away.

"So what is new with you both?" Henry asked to shift the conversation from himself. He took another sip of his wine and smiled at his parents. He genuinely was happy to see them.

"Well, we had just returned from Paris when you ... first left." She paused and took a sip of her own wine. "It was a relaxing trip. We attended the art exhibition, and I did a little shopping."

"And I played a few rounds of golf with some of my old business friends," Henry's father added with a smile.

"Then we relaxed a little together before flying home. It was a fine trip."

"Of course, your mother's suitcase weighed about twenty pounds more than when we arrived!" His father gave his mother a teasing smile.

His mother laughed and shook her head. "The autumn collections were coming out," she protested.

"I'm glad you enjoyed your trip." Henry said and poured them all a little more wine as he continued steadily sipping from his.

"Yes, your father pulling away from the business has been wonderful." She smiled at Henry's father. "And how is Anne doing these days? We have not heard from her in quite some time." She remarked. Henry was not sure what he expected from Anne when he left, but he thought at the very least she would have the guts to tell his parents that he had left. Evidently, she remained in her own little world the entire time he was away.

Mother had never liked Anne, and Henry could now see why. If only he had been more attuned to anyone but Anne a year ago, he wouldn't be in his current predicament. His soon to be ex-wife was spoiled, self-centered, and, well, not Ara. He smiled tightly. His mother would fall in love with Ara as fast as he did. She would fit so perfectly into his family. "She is doing just fine. Busy as always."

Henry changed the subject and got them chatting about a charity event his parents were hosting in a few weeks until their food arrived. He had relaxed while his parents talked, so his appetite had crept up again. His dish looked amazing, and his stomach rumbled in response.

The waiter stood by until they had all deemed their first bites to be delicious.

"So, Henry." His father said as he sliced his tender beef. "It's time to tell your mother and me what is going on. No more dancing around the subject any longer."

Henry's stomach turned slightly, and he focused on slicing his beef as well. He took a bite of the seasoned vegetables to bide for time. It was delicious. He wished his father could have held out until he could eat a good meal. *What should I tell them?* he contemplated silently. Nothing would ever be a good enough excuse for his father, but his mother would maybe understand the marriage strains from the way she felt about Anne.

"I just had to get away."

"Away from what, Henry?" His mother asked, not touching her meal. Her brow was furrowed in deep concern. She reached out to hold his father's hand. She always reached for him in all her times of need. Henry noticed this movement of pure love between them and smiled fondly, thinking of Ara. He would reach for her hand right now, if only she were here.

"Well, you both know Anne and I have had some problems ... I just cannot see her the same since she lied to me about our child ... or, rather, the child that never was." Henry took a breath and focused on his word choices. "I just needed some time to try and forgive her ... Time to remember why I married her ... There were a few reasons." He took a sip of his wine to decide what else to tell his parents.

His parents faces contorted with rage. They were still upset with Anne's lie as well and were just as excited as Henry to have their first grandchild, to not only carry on the Tudor name, but to shower with love.

"So, where did you end up, son?" His father asked with clenched teeth, still angry from the memory of Anne's lie.

"Jackson Hole, Wyoming." Henry said with a wry grin. He knew that would confuse his parents.

"*Wyoming?*" His mother asked, astounded.

His father asked incredulously, "What on Earth gave you the idea to go there?"

Henry laughed at the looks on their faces. "I said I needed a change!" He urged them both to eat a little so their food would not grow cold. He took a bite of his delicious beef dish and a sip of his wine before continuing. "I ended up learning quite a bit about myself and really gained an understanding about marriage and life while I was there."

His parents took in his words and nodded, encouraging Henry to keep talking.

Taking another bite of his meal to buy some time, he chewed slowly and swallowed before saying, "Well, I rented a cabin in the mountains, learned how to rock climb, rode in a couple of rodeos..." His parents gasped, and Henry laughed before continuing. "And won ... twice." His parents' faces were priceless. "It was fun, mom. Don't give me that look!"

"Henry, you rode on a wild bull?" His mother asked looking pale. "That is so dangerous!"

He refilled her wine glass and pushed it toward her. "It was fine, mom. They have cowboys that circle around and keep it safe."

She took a sip of wine and looked slightly reassured.

Looking impressed, his father asked, "A real bull, son?"

Henry laughed and launched into an account of his first rodeo, including Joe and his friend taunting him into competing in the rodeo, a brief description of Mitch, and the excitement and terror of riding a bull. He left out any mention of Arabella, not sure if he wanted to bring his parents in on her quite yet.

His parents were quite entertained by his story, laughing and gasping at the right parts. His father waved the waiter over to bring another bottle of wine and to clear the table. The waiter poured them all a fresh glass of wine and retreated.

"Oh, Henry. That does sound like fun." His mother said, wiping tears of laughter from her eyes.

"Oh, it was a good time." Henry said with a grin. Encouraged, he told them the story of his first rock climbing experience with Charlie and the gang.

His parents seemed to enjoy hearing about his rock climbing moments and triumphs and about the people he met. HIs father seemed quite impressed with Charlie's work ethic and sympathized with his loss of his parents. He found it commendable to take up the family business. Mother said she would love to see Lucy at some point and suggested taking a trip to visit all the places Henry's story told of. The three of them laughed and smiled and drank wine for the next hour or so as Henry told them a little more about Wyoming and the sights. The more Henry talked, the more he opened up about everything. It felt natural to tell them everything, and he flirted with the idea of mentioning Arabella.

Henry couldn't remember the last time they had gotten to talk like this. Anne was always with him, and she could hardly stand to make it through dinner with his parents, let alone visit afterwards. He felt yet another surge of anger toward her, but pushed her from his mind to enjoy the carefree visiting with his parents. Arabella was on the tip of his tongue as the conversation began to taper off. But he never got the words out.

Finally, his parents waved the waiter over to pay the tab and stood up. "Well, Henry, it has been wonderful." His mother said and hugged him tightly.

His father shook his hand with a smile. "We are glad you enjoyed your trip, son, but we are happy to have you home again. Don't go running off without at least telling us. We will always understand." Henry knew it was true, but he also knew they would have talked him out of it. He was confident that the choice he made was the right one for him.

He walked them both out of the restaurant and told them good night. Watching them get into their chauffeured car, Henry felt a sudden urge to climb in with them instead of going to the lonely mansion where his pregnant wife resided. He shook off the feeling, knowing he was a grown man, capable of dealing with a little loneliness, and waved goodbye to them as they drove off into the New York night, never knowing about the most important part of his trip, the reason everything he just told them was profound. Maybe he *should* have said something about Arabella.

He turned and walked to his car, driving home with the radio off, lost and alone in his thoughts. He snuck into the mansion, climbing the stairs stealthily to the guest suite and crawled into bed. Henry fell into a deep sleep, not to be awakened until the harsh ring of the telephone sounded at two in the morning, the call that would change everything.

31
APPALACHIAN TRAIL
July 8, 1978

"Henry, don't stand so close to the edge!" His mother yelled hysterically. She was always paranoid that the worst things would happen to him. He couldn't even walk to school because she was sure he would be mugged, shot, kidnapped, or a combination of the three. But Henry liked that feeling he got when he was doing something he was not supposed to. He pushed the limits, and the limits had never let him down before.

His foot was dangling over the side of a rock, and a soft mist of water dampened his t-shirt and face. The sun was shining brightly, bouncing endless beams of light off the water's constantly changing face. Henry sat mesmerized at the top of a wide six-foot high waterfall waiting for his father to get the fishing poles ready.

It was the middle of July, and Henry had just turned sixteen. Every summer they took a camping trip along the Appalachian trail. Henry's parents loved hiking since their own parents introduced it to them. Henry was just as in love with it as they were. The air here was nothing like the air in New York. One could inhale and flood one's senses with the scent of pine and earth. The smells were so vivid; it was like they accentuated even the sights and sounds. The birds chirped a little louder, and the wind jostled the trees and bushes. One's eye could wander endlessly. It was Henry's favorite time of year. It was an actual vacation as opposed to the business trips they frequently took throughout the year. His father had taught him how to fly fish a few years ago, and this year Henry felt like a pro. They were heading out for an afternoon of catching dinner, and Henry could barely contain his excitement.

"Dad, I think I see some giant trout just *waiting* for me to catch them!" Henry exclaimed aloud, no doubt scaring away any trout that may have been swimming near him.

Henry's father smiled broadly from their campsite. He adored the childish delight Henry still had for these trips, even at age sixteen.

"Just about ready to head downstream," Henry's father called out.

Henry lifted himself from the rocks and brushed the dirt off his khaki shorts. He stole one more look over the falls before turning back to where his father was just about ready to go.

"Do you remember how to flick the line?" Henry's father quizzed him about fly fishing as he grabbed his tackle box and handed the poles to Henry.

"Dad, I have been doing this since I was thirteen. I could do it in my sleep, I'm pretty sure." Henry held his head high and scoffed sarcastically at the preposterousness of his father's statement.

"Careful, Henry, confidence is one thing and arrogance is another. Never let something you're good at become a detriment to you." His father was always a fountain of statements like that. There was always some lesson to learn or some way to grow as a person.

They waved to Elizabeth; she was staying at the campsite to rest as they fished.

Henry was sure of his skill. There was nothing wrong with that. His father didn't know it, but Henry had practiced his casting in the yard at home. Mother had bought him a subscription to a fly fishing magazine, and he had been studying up in preparation for this trip. He wanted to see the shiny glint of that rainbow trout and the proud smile his father gave every time he did so. He never got tired of pleasing him.

Henry just nodded at his father's advice and paced himself equally with him as they walked silently down the river to go fishing. Henry was sure he would stun his father with how well he had retained fly fishing in his memory. He knew the movements so well, but he had a feel for it, like it was an art form. He knew just how long to study the drifts and when to cast. He was patient and was careful to never rush a cast and spook away a good trout. Henry was a natural.

It was still early, and the sun was yawning on the horizon from its night sleep. The grass was wet with morning dew, and Henry slipped a few times and had to catch his balance a couple of times. His father held perfect footing. Henry was determined to not slip again.

They got to a spot in the river where the water was flat and flowing swiftly. They both had on their fly fishing boots and looked like true men of the sport. Henry handed his father his pole and began preparing his own. They stepped carefully into the water being as quiet as possible.

The smooth stones below Henry's feet shifted slightly with each step until he came to a spot in the river he felt comfortable with. His father waited close by for him to send out his first cast. He always waited, making sure he got into the swing of it before heading down river himself, always careful to not tangle lines or scare the fish.

Henry, at first cautious, followed the routine he had made for himself. Before long, he was flicking his line seamlessly, and his father began his retreat to his own fishing spot down a bit further on the river. He gave Henry a salute gesture as he moved out of the water. He settled about thirty feet down river, just in Henry's eye sight enough that if he turned his head to the left slightly he could see the glare of his wet line flying on and off the surface of the water.

Henry was flowing now and focused. Everything else around him just kind of swirled into nothingness. There was no wind, just the sound of the river raging, and little creatures flitting about in the trees around him. His fly was skimming the water gently, and Henry could see the trout in the water teasing him and flirting with the idea of nibbling. He was eager to feel the pull of a fish on the end of his line, his pulse racing with excitement. But he held himself at bay, a feeling he was very familiar with. Patience was one of Henry's strengths. He never had angry outbursts or lashed out on anyone. He felt the anger and the desire to react, but he had this weird satisfaction in being in control of everything he felt. So he waited, patiently. Before long, his patience paid off.

Just as he was pulling the first trout of the day, Henry turned to show his father the first catch. But he couldn't see him. *He was just there*, Henry thought. He put his hand up to shield his eyes from the blinding sun that was now awake and starting its day. Nothing. Henry began exiting the water. He reached the shore and tossed his pole, fish still dangling from the end, onto the grass. A strange feeling began pushing its way to the surface: panic. He wouldn't just walk away or leave without telling Henry.

Henry quickened his pace as headed over to where his father was moments earlier. He came upon the bucket for the fish they had caught and the tackle box. Henry crouched down and looked at all the supplies that had no supplier.

He stood and, just then, he caught a glint of what looked like a boot in the water. He darted towards the water, surging as fast as he could, his fastest run not being fast enough.

"Dad! Dad, answer me!" Henry yelled out. There was no reply. He came to the boot he had seen in the water and found his father submerged in the water, not moving. Henry felt like he had just run into a wall. He felt like his breath was taken from him, but his chest still rose and fell.

He quickly picked his father's limp body up out of the water and pulled him to shore.

He placed both of his hands on his face and tried to shake him awake. His face was cold and white, and Henry got no response. There was a large bump on the side of his head with a small stream of blood trailing down the side of his face.

"Dad, please, wake up." He began shaking him harder. "You can't do this ... Dad, I need you." Henry began to weep.

32
NEW YORK, NEW YORK
August 31, 1992

The phone next to Henry's head rang loudly, noisily breaking him out of his deep sleep. Picking up his watch on the bedside table, Henry squinted to make out the time: 2:30 a.m. His heart pounded fiercely as he picked up the phone, no idea who would call him at this time of night.

"Henry?" His mother's voice frantically asked.

His heart dropped into his stomach. He felt his face get hot, and his pulse quickened. "What is it, Mom? Are you in trouble?" He jumped out of bed and began throwing clothes on, the phone still attached to his ear. He grabbed the first things he saw, his blue jeans from Wyoming and a white V-neck t-shirt.

He could hear that she had been crying. "I need you to come down to the hospital, Henry. Right now."

"What's going on?" Henry asked again as he threw on his boots one at a time. He was bouncing around in a circle with the phone in one hand and his boot in the other.

"Just come right away." He could practically see tears running down her face. "Henry, I can't lose him. I just got him back."

Henry's heart pounded as he grabbed his wallet and burst out of the room. "Francis!" He yelled from the top of the stairs.

"What is it, Mr. Tudor?" Francis exclaimed with concern as he opened the door to his quarters, dressed in a robe and striped pajama pants. His bedroom slippers made a swift shuffling sound on the marble floors.

Henry ran down the stairs. "Call for Clive immediately. I need to go to the hospital."

"Yes, sir. Are you okay, sir?" Francis asked.

"I'm fine, just get me the car."

Francis opened the front door and ran outside to Clive's little cottage.

"Henry?"

He turned at the sound of Anne's voice and saw her descending down the stairs, scantily clad in a lace nightie and see-through robe.

"Why are you going to the hospital?" Her eyes were filled with concern and worry, which shocked his already shaken self. He was sure his face was contorted with confusion at the site of her.

"My mother just called." He told her as she reached the bottom step and stood in front of him. His voice was shaky, and it cracked at his last word.

"I am coming with you." She declared, turning and running back up the stairs.

He shook his head in confusion and walked to the front door. His mind ran with different scenarios of what had happened. His mother had called, not his father, so it had to be about him, especially from the way she sounded. She had said, "I can't lose him." Him could only mean his father. He was the only one for her to lose except, of course, Henry.

It was growing harder to breathe, and he felt idle just standing at the door waiting. He began pacing back and forth as he waited for Clive to pull up. He left the front door ajar so he would know the instant he pulled up. His father had had a little trouble with his heart in the last few months but was on medication and had stepped down from the company to alleviate stress. "This can't happen," Henry sighed.

Clive pulled the dark sedan out of the garage and parked by the doors. Henry looked over his shoulder. He heard the click-clack of stilettos on marble. He turned only to see Anne running down the stairs in jeans and a solid black top with high heels.

She touched his shoulder and smiled grimly as they walked out to the car. "It will be all right, Henry."

Although he was confused and a little annoyed at this pretend concern she suddenly had for anyone other than herself, he found himself a tiny bit glad to have her with him, if only to have a little company. They drove quickly to the hospital. During the short drive, Henry's mind continued running with the possible scenarios of what had happened. He started thinking about everything he could and couldn't do.

Clive pulled up to the hospital with a screech of his tires, jumping out the instant the car was in park. He opened the door and helped them both out of the sedan. "I hope everything works out, sir." He said and patted Henry on the back. "I will be in this parking lot when you need me."

"Thanks, Clive." Henry tried to smile, but his mouth was frozen. He turned and walked into the hospital with Anne by his side. She grabbed his hand firmly and resolutely as if to say, "I know you hate me, but right now I'm here, so suck it up." Henry couldn't wrap his mind around this situation. Everything was spinning, and it took everything he had not to pass out. He focused on his breathing as he walked down the hospital corridor hand in hand with Anne. He could barely look at Anne, but he was thankful he was not alone at that moment.

They approached the receptionist desk in the emergency room. Henry scanned the waiting area for his mother, but she was nowhere to be found. *She must be with Dad*, Henry thought. They reached the receptionist, and Henry's throat closed. How was he supposed to say the words he didn't want to be true? He hesitated, and Anne stepped in without flinching.

"We are looking for our father, Henry Tudor. We got a call that he was here." Anne was still holding his hand with her other hand on the counter in front of her, as if it were some display of power. She knew how to handle herself. Henry was hung up on the words, "our father." Anne had never called him her father before.

"Yes, we do have Mr. Tudor here." The receptionist asked a few short questions and then buzzed them into the back.

"He is the third room on the left, behind the curtain," she said comfortingly.

"Thank you," Anne replied before leading the way down the hallway.

The sounds of the hospital were a cacophony in Henry's head. Buzzes and beeps from various medical machines and voices speaking in hushed tones behind the different blue curtains in the emergency room made Henry uneasy. The blue curtains and the brightly painted white walls with light blue trim and tacky wallpaper made it impossible for him to forget where he was. The walls were lined with plastic clipboards in front of each curtained room. A nurses' station was at the center of all the rooms, and employees moved about like a well-oiled machine. The countertops were blue and speckled with bits of what looked like microscopic snowflakes. Henry felt cold. Whoever thought that blue was the best color choice to be seen in every direction the eye could wander should be fired. Henry felt like he was drowning in pastel blue water.

They reached the curtain. Henry saw the clipboard hanging outside it. His father's name was typed into a field at the top of the page. This was real. Anne pulled back the curtain enough for them to walk through.

Henry's mom was hunched over the bed holding Henry's father's hand and whispering something. Henry saw her lips moving but couldn't make out any words until he got closer.

"You will make it out of this, you will make it out of this, you will make it, make it..." His mother noticed them in the room and turned to Henry with dried tears and mascara running down her cheek. Henry had never seen her look so distraught. She reached out to him instantly for a hug. He pulled her into his chest and held her close and tight and never wanted to let go. She had both of her hands on Henry's chest, and her tears began to fall, staining his white t-shirt.

Henry rested his chin on the top of her head and then drew one hand off her back and held her head. He kissed her forehead and whispered, "Everything will be all right, mother. Shh, just try and relax." Anne stood behind them silently holding her hands together.

Henry pulled himself away from his mother to stand beside his father. He grabbed his father's hand and bent over to hug him. His mother just stood there. Anne came up behind her with a tissue to offer. She took it willingly, and Anne then dabbed the corners of her mascara stained eyes and began to clean her up. Henry was touched by her warmth at that moment. He turned back to his father.

He smelled like a hospital but a faint scent of his cologne wafted off of him. Henry kissed his cheek and whispered, "I love you" and looked at his pale, ashen face. He didn't look alive attached to all these wires and tubes, but he could hear the beeping of his heart monitor and felt his heart beat in time with his father's. His eyes were closed. His lips held no color, and Henry just sat there.

Anne came up behind him and placed her hands on his back to comfort him. "I am so sorry, Henry," she whispered softly.

Henry felt the tears welling in his eyes. He wiped them away quickly and turned to his mother. "What ... what happened?" He asked exasperated. "He was fine this evening."

The doctor entered the room just then in his white coat, looking tired like it was the end of his shift. Henry didn't like the look of him and was ready to request a new doctor.

"Mrs. Tudor, we have the results of his ECG, and we have confirmed that what your husband experienced was, in fact, a heart attack, but it was mild one." His name tag read: Dr. Greg Larson, MD. "We also took a chest x-ray and are awaiting the results of his angiogram. From the x-ray, his heart appears to be enlarged slightly, but there is no fluid in his lungs at this point so this is good news. But the next 24 hours will tell us a lot as far as recovery." The doctor was holding his clipboard between both his hands and looked at Henry's mother the whole time but glanced at the new faces in the room at the close of his words.

His mother caught the cue and introduced them. "This is my son Henry and his wife, Anne. They just arrived a few minutes ago." She told the doctor in a quiet voice.

Henry's professional side was kicking in. He extended his hand and shook the doctor's hand firmly.

"I figured you were his son; you look just like him." The doctor sent him a reassuring smile.

Henry attempted to smile politely in return. "So, where do we go from here?" He questioned the doctor. "Treatment? More tests?"

Dr. Larson shook his head. "We have to wait for the results of his angiogram." He looked over Mr. Tudor's chart and made a few notes. "We will keep him in the hospital for a few days, mostly for observation and to see the effects of the new medications on his heart. Like I said, the next 24 hours will tell us a lot about what is going on with your father's heart." He set down the chart and nodded to the family. "I will check in first thing in the morning."

"Thank you, Doctor." Elizabeth said with a tiny smile that did not reach her worried eyes.

The doctor nodded again and left the room. Henry helped his mother into her chair before opening the room's closet to find two folding chairs. He set them down opposite his mother and sat down tiredly. The last forty-eight hours had been an immense change from the previous few weeks in Wyoming ... with Ara. He pictured her face for a split second and imagined her clearly. She smiled at him with her beautiful blue eyes and reached over to hold his hand. He could feel her presence so strongly as if her hand was actually squeezing his hand to give him comfort and support. He looked over and jumped, realizing it was *Anne* who was holding his hand.

"You okay, Henry?" Anne asked, her green eyes narrowing slightly in concern.

Henry shook his head, clearing Ara out to focus on his family. "I am all right, I guess." He told her. "I just can't believe ... I just hope he is okay," he whispered.

His mother reached out across his father to grab Henry's hand. He reached out and held tight to her hand, both of their hands resting lightly on his father's abdomen. As if finally sensing their presence, his father opened his eyes. "Henry? Elizabeth? What happened?" He asked, looking back and forth between the two.

His mother gasped and tears ran down her face in relief at seeing her husband open his eyes. She reached down and kissed his cheek.

"You had a heart attack, Father." Henry said as he grabbed his dad's hand. "We are waiting on a few tests, but the doctor thinks you will be all right for the most part."

His father smiled grimly, "I guess this means more 'relaxation' time, huh."

They all laughed. Henry felt his heart and stomach loosen a tiny bit with relief. His father was going to be fine. *He has to make it through this*, Henry thought. *He just has to make it.*

33
APPALACHIAN TRAIL
July 8, 1978

His tears kept falling, and he sat with his unmoving father, helpless. Henry's mind was going a mile a minute, and it didn't seem ready or willing to slow down enough for him to think of anything to do to help the situation. He looked at his hands and then looked at the ghostlike face of his father. And then his mind stopped.

"Okay, you are going to be just fine," Henry's voice shook but his hands were steady. Confidence not arrogance. He had learned CPR in Boy Scouts and in his wilderness survival books. He told himself over and over again, "Okay, you can do this." He began reciting that over and over out loud as he proceeded to attempt to save his father's life.

He tilted his father's head back slightly to clear his airway, and he opened his shirt to feel on his chest where to begin chest compressions. He found the spot and, without further hesitation, he began. One. Two. Three. Breath. One. Two. Three. Breath. He found a rhythm and followed it.

"You. Will. Live. Breath. You. Will. Live. Breath." Henry kept at it. Time slowed. He heard nothing but his own heartbeat.

Then suddenly his father turned his head and began furiously coughing and spewing water and spit from his mouth. Henry gasped as if the air he breathed would fill his father's lungs for him. He still had his hands resting on his chest and feeling the rising and falling of his lungs brought him the greatest comfort he could ever ask for. He was alive, he could feel the life moving inside him. His face was no longer white and ghostlike but a fire engine red. And a giant smile of relief sprawled across Henry's face.

"Never scare me like that again." Henry said as he leaned in and hugged his father, who raised his hand and placed it on Henry's back as he continued to cough the water from his lungs.

Henry let the tenseness in his neck release. The rush of adrenaline was making him somewhat dizzy. He sat back on his knees as his father began pushing himself back up again. It had all happened so fast; Henry began replaying everything out in his head moment by moment. His father had almost just died. He had never been more scared or utterly useless at that realization. But something made him snap out of it. He couldn't figure it out, but he felt a strong urge to say something to him. "Dad." He paused, catching his breath. "I love you."

34
NEW YORK, NEW YORK
August 31, 1992

"Henry?" Anne asked as she shook him awake.

Henry groggily sat up, rubbing his neck. Apparently, he had fallen asleep in his folding chair after his father had drifted back to sleep. He looked at the time: 8:30 a.m. His mother was still asleep in her chair, resting her head and arms on his father. Henry could hear the sounds of the hospital outside his father's room: nurses walking around checking on patients, hushed whispers between doctors, various machines, and occasional crying. Not a pleasant place to wake up.

Even though it was morning, the room was still dark. He looked out the window and saw dark storm clouds and pouring rain. "You need to eat something." Anne whispered. "And we should also bring your mother some food."

It was so unlike Anne to worry about anyone other than herself. He looked at her in disbelief and was about to ask her what was going on, but exhaustion took over. He couldn't eat at a time like this, but he did need to stretch his legs at least. "Okay. Let's go." He whispered detached and slightly groggy. He stood up slowly without another word.

Stealthily, they snuck out of the room and out into the brightly lit hospital hallway. They found an elevator and rode down in silence to the main floor, Anne leaning up against one wall, Henry the other. As they neared the cafeteria, Anne pointed out some restrooms. "I need to freshen up quickly, Henry."

Henry decided he could use a little freshening too. He walked in, used the bathroom, and looked into the mirror as he washed his hands. Dark circles made his eyes look even more tired. His face was lined with stress and worry. He sighed and splashed water onto his face to try and look more awake. He looked again, and he just looked tired and wet now. He dried his hands and face and walked out to wait for Anne.

She emerged after a few minutes, face and hair completely made up, looking like a Paris runway model, even in the clothes she wore all night. She gave Henry a ghost of a smile that did not quite reach her eyes. The look struck him as odd for split-second, but his thoughts were far too preoccupied to bother with his wife's smiles. He pointed the way toward the cafeteria, and Anne led the way.

The hospital cafeteria was busy as well. The thought made Henry cringe. All these people here meant that many people were hurt or sick somewhere in the hospital. It was the one business Henry thought should never thrive: the hospital cafeteria.

Henry and Anne examined the selections, Henry mostly looking to find something his mom would eat. He decided to bring her a bowl of fruit and some dry toast, a breakfast he knew she would like and could stomach right now. He grabbed two cups of coffee as well — with lids — and paid for Anne's dry English muffin, plain yogurt, and juice and his own selections at the register.

They headed back upstairs with Anne quietly commenting on various people or paintings they passed to fill the silence. Henry ignored her. He was in his own world, hoping for his father's tests to come back clean so they could all go home, and he could go back to hating Anne. Right now, he almost could stand her, and it was making him sick to think about it. Who was this woman, acting like she cared? The more he thought about it, the angrier he got, so he pushed it from his mind. He thought only about his father and what it would take for him to be better, to be himself again. The man he saw lying in that bed was not his father; it was a shell of him. He was eerie to look at.

The elevator opened. Anne stepped out, turning to look questioningly at Henry, who was still thinking about his father. "Henry?" She said with a touch of impatience.

"What? Oh, yes, sorry." He walked out the elevator door and toward his father's room. Once inside, he noted that the machines were all beeping regularly, a sound he was growing used to. His mother appeared to have just woken up.

Elizabeth stretched and brushed the light brown hair away from her face. "Morning," she said in a hoarse voice and cleared her voice timidly. Henry had never seen her looking so tired, worn, and scared to death. As long as Henry, her husband, was with her, she never looked scared. But this was a whole new situation for her to be in.

"I brought you some coffee." Henry set a steaming cup down on the bedside table. Steam was sneaking through every orifice in the lid teasing everyone with the warmth it offered.

She smiled tiredly. "Thank you, Henry." Putting the cup to her lips, she took a sip of the hot liquid. Her eyes closed, and she took a deep breath of release.

He set down the fruit and toast next to her coffee. "I also brought you a little breakfast." He placed a hand on her shoulder. "You should eat something."

She thanked him and sipped her coffee while still tightly gripping her husband's hand.

Anne had taken a seat in her usual chair and was eating her breakfast.

Henry stood with his hands behind his back and looked down at his father. "Does he look a little better to you?" He asked his mom, hopeful.

Elizabeth nodded. "I think so." She glanced over at the clock. "The doctor should be in soon."

Henry picked up his coffee from the hospital table in front of him and took a deep sip. The hot liquid burned a path down to his stomach, but it left a familiar taste in his mouth that comforted him slightly. He took another sip, smaller this time to protect himself.

His father's face looked less lined with a little more color in his cheeks. Henry hoped he would wake up soon. He suddenly felt the need to tell his father every single thing that had ever happened in his life, especially about Arabella. His stomach twisted at the thought of his father never meeting the most amazing woman on Earth, or at least the most amazing woman in Henry's world. He thought about going right up to his ear and telling him the whole story right then, but Anne was right there, and, although she knew where he had been and who he had been with, he did not want to share the joy that Ara brought him. He didn't want her to know the love he had for her. So he stood there rigid and bitter toward Anne's presence.

"Why don't you sit down, Henry?" Anne suggested and took a delicate bite of her English muffin.

His annoyance at her flared up. "I am fine here, Anne." She was always trying to control his life.

A nurse walked in to check on Henry, Sr. "Hello, hello." She said with a big smile. She checked his vitals, humming to herself as she noted them in the chart.

"How is everything looking?" Henry asked.

The nurse just clicked the pen and smiled. "The doctor should be in soon." She left the room.

His father opened his eyes and yawned slightly like he had just woken up from a short nap. "What's new?" He asked in a cracked voice.

Henry jumped and looked down at his father with a relieved smile. "Nothing much. Uh, Anne and I just brought Mom coffee and breakfast from the cafeteria downstairs."

"And where is mine?" His dad asked hoarsely, genuinely offended.

Elizabeth smiled and picked up his hospital water cup, holding it up carefully to her husband's mouth. "Only water for now, darling." She said sympathetically. The tension in her face had already begun to ease, and the couple's general demeanor shifted toward each other again. Henry remembered seeing them on his own wedding day, and how they seemed to have this gravitational pull towards each other. He had wanted that with Anne, but now that was a distant dream that he had long let go. He looked at his parents with love and let his shoulders relax.

"What are you still doing here, Henry?" Henry Sr.'s voice was not crackling anymore, and it was back to its normal, advice-giving timbre. "It must be about time to head to the office."

"No." Henry had very few words to say, but that was because he was thinking too fast to translate his thoughts into speech.

"You know what I say about going into work early, don't you?" Henry Sr. always had this look on his face when he was telling one of his "you know what I say about this" statements. It was a look of pride and humor at the same time. It was part of the reason why Henry could sit there respectfully so many times as his father rolled another one off his tongue. Everyone did. One couldn't help but listen to what this man had to say.

"No, what do you say, Dad?" Henry was glad to play into it, although he knew exactly what he was going to say.

"A great leader leads by being first to the job!" Henry Sr. looked pleased with himself as did everyone else in the room. Everyone was just way too happy that he was awake and talking right now; they just wanted him to keep on talking.

Henry sat there looking at his father, who was acting like nothing had happened at all, and he wondered whether he even knew. "Dad, do you know why you are here right now?"

"Well..." Henry Sr. hesitated for a moment before continuing. "I remember being at home in bed, and I felt sharp, stabbing pains in my chest, and your mother called an ambulance. I assume as a result of all that, Henry, I am here, in a hospital bed, hooked up to these machines and wires and things."

"You had a heart attack, Henry." Anne chimed in.

Henry shot her a glare and was extremely irritated that she felt she even was at the place in his family where she would speak at this moment.

Gradually removing his devilish glare off of Anne, Henry shifted his eyes back towards his father and tried to control himself. "You had a heart attack," Henry repeated, as if Anne's words were worthless and needed to be restated. "The doctor says right now you are doing okay, by which I mean you are awake and talking, so that's great. And they say you may even be able to go home this afternoon. So, so far the tests look good." Henry smiled encouragingly. "It's really great to hear your voice." Henry's voice broke off slightly, and he cleared his throat to disguise it. He was unsuccessful.

"Oh, don't worry, Henry, the doctors are really confident at this point," his mother came over by his side and put her hands on his back. She rubbed his shoulders back and forth soothingly, something she used to do when he was younger after a game he lost or a tough day of school.

Henry tried to shrug his mother off like he was fine and didn't need it, but he gave in almost instantly and hugged her back.

Anne cleared her throat and tossed her hair over her shoulders. "Henry, I need to go home for a bit to change." She stood up and waited for him to answer, but Henry was engrossed with his parents.

"Fine," he said without looking at her.

"Well, will you take me?" She asked impatiently.

The doctor entered the room suddenly looking upbeat and much better than he had last night.

"Good morning, all. How are we doing, Mr. Tudor?" He turned his attention immediately to Henry Sr. with a friendly smile.

"Well, Doc, I heard I get to go home soon. That sounds like a good morning to me." Henry's father was surprisingly upbeat for having just woken from the sleep of a heart attack.

"Well, you know what they say about rumors, don't you?"

Henry Sr. perked up even more, intrigued by the doctor's similarity with himself. "What do they say, Doc?"

"Well, if I told you it would just be another rumor now, wouldn't it." The doctor smiled broadly at his small, albeit not so funny joke. Everyone laughed, but Henry Sr. louder than the others. He had a taste for dry humor. Henry Sr. could befriend anyone with the same sense of humor as himself.

"No, but in all seriousness, you may in fact be going home this afternoon, but we need someone to fill out the paperwork, which is somewhat hefty – my apologies in advance. And then after that we can do a final check-up. If everything is still stable, I see no reason to keep you here. But he must be on bed rest for at least a week, and he will have to return for routine check-ups for a while." The doctor wrote something on his chart and looked around at the family with a curt smile this time, and they all returned his smile with an even bigger one, even Anne smiled.

"Doctor, thank you so much," Elizabeth was practically in tears over his words. They were happy tears, though. Anne looked at Henry with glad eyes. She looked genuine at that moment, and Henry even gave her a smile. She squeezed his hand briefly and then turned toward Henry Sr.'s bed. They all looked at him and smiled sappy, tear-ridden smiles.

"All right enough of that; everybody, just act normal, would you? Doctor, thank you for the great news. If my son here doesn't mind, I will have him take care of the paperwork if you will direct him accordingly."

The doctor nodded and looked at Henry, "Would you care to follow me?"

"Hold on, girls, did you want to head home and get things ready there? I know Anne is desperate to change, but you all know that don't you?" Anne rolled her eyes at Henry. Henry ignored her. He really only cared what his mother wanted.

"I should probably get things prepared at home, you're right." His mom still had mascara slightly staining her eyelids, and he could tell she wanted to look right for her husband, although Henry knew he didn't care. It would be good for her to freshen up before he got home. She would be more attentive that way.

"All right, well, Clive … Oh crap, Clive has been in the parking lot this whole time." Henry sort of felt like a jerk, but Clive would understand his reasoning for forgetting about him.

"Anne, page Clive and let him know to meet you guys out front. And give him my apologies for me. I will do it myself later, but just do that for me. Please."

Anne smiled coolly. "Of course, Henry." She reached over and touched Henry Sr.'s hand, a gesture of kindness not often seen from Anne. "Feel better, Mr. Tudor." Anne turned to pick up her pager to let Clive know they would be coming down.

Elizabeth stepped close to her husband's side and bent down to kiss his cheek. Henry knew she did not want to leave his side. "I will see you soon, darling." His mother said while squeezing his hand tightly.

"Clive is ready for us, Elizabeth." Anne stepped toward the door.

The doctor had left the room, but a nurse returned and was ready to direct Henry toward the discharge papers.

"Sir, are you ready to begin filling out this paperwork?" The nurse uttered kindly.

Henry gave his mother a hug and kissed her cheek goodbye before turning back to the nurse. "Yes, I will follow you."

Anne grabbed his hand suddenly and turned him back to her. She gave him a short peck on the lips and said, "I will see you at home," her eyes locked in on his. Her eyes were fierce and determined, the same look she got when she was competing for something she wanted. Henry didn't know what to say. They had not kissed in weeks. It felt odd on his lips. She was so different from Ara. He was shocked at how comfortable and familiar Ara had felt on his lips. Anne's touch was not familiar, or no longer familiar, and that puzzled Henry.

"Good bye," Henry said with befuddlement. His eyebrows were raised in curiosity, and he stared at Anne a moment longer. The nurse tapped his elbow to get his attention, and he hesitatingly broke off the stare and turned to walk away.

"Follow me, Mr. Tudor," the nurse smiled warmly. Her voice was birdlike, hushed, but it had a ring to it that made her sound like every word she spoke was actually a song. Her voice eased him into following her and forgetting about the moment he just shared with Anne.

His apprehension appeased, he took the clipboard the nurse passed to him and began filling in his father's information. It was such a cruel joke, to be filling in hospital papers for his father. The reversal of roles, young child dependent on his parent to the older parent dependent on his grown child, had come too quickly. Henry had not expected this to come for twenty years, at the very least. His stomach twisted as he pictured his father lying in the hospital when Henry had first arrived: pale with shadows and age showing on his face. He looked down at the papers and remembered they were taking his father *home*, so he took solace in the fact that these were discharge papers and that his father was all right.

Henry was knee-deep in paperwork when something caught his attention out of the corner of his eye. He turned his attention away from the paperwork, and he caught a flash of it again. His heart beat quickly as he questioned whether it really could be what he thought he had seen. He would recognize that rich blonde hair anywhere, wavy and streaked with various shades and tones of blonde from days in the sun.

The wisp of blonde hair disappeared around the corner. Henry dropped his pen without realizing it and followed the blonde as if in a trance. *Why would she be in New York?* He found that it mattered not why she was here, but that she was here at all.

Reason fell away as he picked up his pace until he was running around the corner, frantically searching for her. He yelled out her name, and it echoed down an empty hallway. She was gone, or simply had never been. He leaned against the wall, needing support from the disappointment and to catch his breath.

Henry knew in that moment that he truly loved Ara, above all else: above what was honorable, above his very life. He wanted to see her more than ever, to hold her beautiful face in her hands and tell her how much he loved her. Mostly, Henry wanted to tell her how sorry he was about everything. Distraught with sadness, he took a few deep breaths and turned around to head back to his paperwork.

What he saw took his breath away. His heart dropped, and his blood ran cold. A name formed on his shocked lips...

****

August 31, 1992
10:00 P.M.

The rain had barely let up before the sky parted once more to rain down on him. He had been wandering around the streets of New York for a few hours, unsure of how he was going to face everyone again. He needed time alone to remember, time to reminisce about every moment they ever shared, time to savor each memory. His clothes clung to him as if drowning from the rain, and his shoes made a slapping sound with every step, so soaking wet that they weighed him down.

He saw his reflection in a large glass storefront. Although strong and healthy, he almost looked emaciated. He shoulders were slumped and dark circles under his eyes were so thick it was if they were painted. Nothing was going to make this easier. The sun had fully receded into night, and Henry knew the time had come. He needed to go home, to his home and do what he had wanted to do from the moment he arrived back in New York.

He hailed a cab and instructed the driver to take him to his home. They pulled up, and he saw that the windows were dark. He thought nothing of it and headed inside, his head hanging pathetically, like the rain was pushing him down further into his depression. There was nothing but eerie silence on the inside. No butler, no maid, no human being in sight.

He began slowly removing his soaked t-shirt. He ruffled his hair with the shirt, attempting to remove the excess moisture. He shed his boots and his pants as he walked, until he was left only in his boxers. He entered his office, picked up his phone and sat on the ground with his legs bent and his chin resting on his knees. He was cold and wet still and began to shiver. His back was leaning up against the smooth wooden grain of his desk as his teeth began to chatter.

He set the phone on the ground between his legs. He sat there for a moment soaked with a melancholy soul. He didn't know what he was going to say, but he hoped he would have words as soon as he heard her voice. Picking up the phone, he began dialing the number he could never forget. He took a deep breath when it started ringing, and his shaking stopped.

It rang and rang until Henry heard her voice and melted. He was a mix of joy and sickness at the sound of her voice. Tears began to fall from his eyes. He wiped them away furiously.

"Hello, you have reached Arabella Bennett. I am sorry I missed your call, I'm probably rounding up some cattle or some shenanigans like that, but if you leave me a message, I'll be sure to get back to you as soon as possible." Her voice tapered off with a little giggle, like Mitch had put her up to leaving this as her answering machine message. Henry smiled fondly remembering all of them, but the sound of the beep on the other end pulled him back from his memories.

He cleared his throat awkwardly trying to buy some time to think of what he could possibly say that would mean anything to her. "Arabella..." He paused. "I, uh, it's Henry. I was just calling because, well, honestly I thought just to hear your voice, but your answering machine, although very sweet, just isn't what I had in mind." He was silent for a moment longer before continuing. "I miss you and I... I hope..." He hoped for so much he wasn't sure what he hoped for most and didn't know what else to say to a machine that would spit this message back to Arabella whenever she got home. Where was she anyway? It was pretty late. Was she on a date? A sick feeling fell over Henry, and he was determined to make this message count. He continued.

"That's all, I hope. It's all I have left really. So, I hope every day for you, for us, um..." Henry's voice broke off, the tears starting to sound through his voice now. He knew he couldn't speak much more before he broke down completely.

"Anyway, I just want to hear from you, see you really. A lot has happened in just the short time that I have been away from you, and I want nothing more than to share every detail with you. I... I love you, Ara." He slammed the phone down and could hold it together no longer. He began to weep. All day and all night, he had held his composure, not even really sure what he was feeling if anything. Just numb. But now he wrapped his arms around legs and hugged them close to his body. He rocked back and forth alone and falling apart. Every emotion came ripping through his body, and he felt dizzy. His hands were shaking, and his head felt almost swollen from the rush of tears and thoughts pouring out of him.

He cried out loud in utter agony. "Why?" He screamed. Why?" He kept asking and asking and each time his voice tapered off quieter and quieter until he was at a barely audible whisper. "Why? Why are you gone? Why did you leave me? Dad … please … come back." His tears fell steadily still, but he released his legs and lay flat on the ground facing the ceiling now. His breathing steadied. He laid and cried silently to sleep, whispering a call for his father every so often.

"Dad..."

****

August 31, 1992
11:30 A.M.

"Dad?"

As he turned around, he saw the lights above his father's door blinking rapidly while an alarm sounded. Nurses and a few doctors rushed into his father's room. A few nurses quickly pushed in a crash cart, while a head nurse barked orders. Henry was frozen in fear. He wanted to run to his father's side, but his feet were cemented to the ground. His heart pounded wildly into his ears and shock numbed his body. *Why are they in my father's room? I was just filling out the discharge papers.* He thought in numb confusion. *He was supposed to be all right. I was taking him home.*

Dr. Larson, his father's cardiologist, ran past Henry and darted into the room. Seeing his father's doctor was enough to temporarily shake Henry's confusion, and he followed the doctor into the room.

"He is in V-tach!" A nurse yelled as Henry entered.

Filled with doctors, nurses, and machines, Henry could barely see his father. He tore toward the bed but was blocked by a few employees.

"Sir, we need you to step out of the room." Henry didn't acknowledge the words. He saw the machines beeping wildly and saw Dr. Larson holding an AED to his father's chest. Hands pushed and pulled at Henry, but he fought back with all his might.

"Clear!" Dr. Larson yelled before he pushed electric current through Henry's father. Henry saw his father's body rise upward before falling back onto the bed. "Charge to two hundred," he said in a hurried, yet calm voice.

"Sir, we need you to *leave,* so we can help your father." Stronger hands pulled at Henry. He resisted and watched the doctor.

"Yes, doctor." The nurse pushed the button. "Charged to two hundred."

"Clear!" Dr. Larson yelled again. Henry watched as his father's body rose and fell again. The machines slowed their beating, and everyone watched the monitor with baited breath.

"Sir." The incessant hands pulled on him.

Henry ignored them, his eyes glued to the monitor. Suddenly, the steady rising and falling of the lines fell to a single, straight line.

"And he has flat-lined."

Henry's body froze, his veins pouring ice into his heart, his heart that was still beating, a heart that he wished he could rip out and give to his father.

"Start CPR." Machines and carts were pulled out of the way as a doctor started chest compressions.

After a short while, Henry heard someone ask, "How long has he been down?"

Henry felt wetness on his cheeks and realized he was crying.

"Four and a half minutes, Doctor."

"Move," Dr. Larson said to the doctor giving chest compressions. He took over, pushing with all his might onto Henry Sr.'s chest. "You are not dying on me today, Henry! I promised your wife you were coming home to her." He pumped his arms steadily, sweat beading on his brow as he tried to pump life into the silent heart. He continued pumping until his breathing grew labored, twenty minutes had passed in merely seconds to Henry's frozen mind.

"Check the monitor." The head nurse said steadily, as if this horror happened every day.

Dr. Larson stopped, breathing heavily. Time froze as everyone stared at the monitor.

The incessant, unforgivable sound of the heart monitor flat-lining, the sound of his death, was almost palpable. It hung in the air until a nurse turned off the heart monitor, and the room fell silent.

A doctor checked his watch and waited for Dr. Larson to call it. When Dr. Larson said nothing as he looked down at Henry Sr. with a tear rolling down his face, another doctor cleared his voice and said, "Time of death: 11:57."

35
SCOTLAND
July 5, 1972

"Henry!" Thomas cried, frisbee in hand, as he ran up the steep, rocky hill after Henry.

Henry laughed as he looked back at Thomas. "I can still beat you, even in Scotland!" He leaped over a large rock, balanced between two sharp boulders, and pumped his fist into the air. The wind caught his hair and tousled it lightly. He turned and looked down into the valley far below. He shaded his eyes from the bright sun and followed the little stream that flowed between the hills and disappeared around a bend.

"Henry!" Thomas exclaimed again with a hint of anger in his voice. "You cheated back there."

Henry turned to look down at Thomas, amusement lighting his gaze, not from beating Thomas to the top of the hill but from *not caring* that he had. "Really?" He said more as a statement than a question. "Look down there!" Henry pointed down to the stream where he could just make out a turtle crawling alongside the shore.

Thomas stepped up next to Henry and looked down. "Pretty cool." Thomas said and put his hands in his pockets. "I still say you cheated." Thomas said quietly.

"Winning, winning, winning," Henry said and punched Thomas's arm playfully. "That is all you think about!"

"Is not." Thomas retorted, returning Henry's punch.

"Is too." He punched Thomas a little harder.

"*Is not!*" Thomas cried, now angry and punched Henry with all the might a ten-year-old can muster.

Henry, still balancing on top of the two sharp rocks, lost his balance and tumbled over the top of the hill, falling fast toward the stream, lined with jagged rocks and trees.

36
NEW YORK, NEW YORK
August 31, 1992

"I am so sorry, Henry." Dr. Larson said as he turned to Henry. He reached out and placed both hands on each of his arms just at the elbow.

He was genuinely sorry, Henry could tell, but there was nothing Henry could say to him to make Dr. Larson, or himself, or anyone feel better about any of this. He was speechless and stood frozen, staring at the black, powered-down monitor. He felt only a horrifying numbness and disbelief. His father could not have died; he had just been talking to him only minutes ago. It had to be a terrible, awful nightmare. He closed his eyes and focused on waking himself up. But he realized how backwards it was to close one's eyes to wake up. It couldn't be a dream. He could wish and pray and close his eyes so tight that he could never open them again, but it would not change the fact that he was still powerless. Maybe he just wanted to close his eyes to hide away from everything, but he couldn't even do that. He couldn't just block this out like he did his other feelings. No, he could feel his heart simmering in fear and anger and at some point it would boil over. He just wondered when.

"Henry?" That nurse with the sing-song voice pulled his thoughts back to earth, where the pain was even more real.

Henry didn't like this place and suddenly got the urge to run, run to the farthest corner of the earth and never have to face the next few hours.

The nurse grabbed his hand firmly, with a sudden ferociousness, and forced his face to stare directly into hers.

"You will be okay, Henry. You will be okay." She brushed one hand across his cheek and hugged him motherly. Henry had a feeling this wasn't hospital protocol, in fact probably against it. He appreciated her care, though. She gave his arm one final squeeze before turning around to leave him with his father.

The doctors had removed the wires and contraptions and things that were on his body, and his body lay there, almost peaceful looking. Henry remained at the foot of the bed, statuesque. He felt cold and useless, but he noticed something on the bedside table that he didn't see before all of this happened. This made him break his standing paralysis, and he walked over to the table. It was a small leather book that was opened already to a page, like someone was just reading it. Henry touched the pages and then looked at his father.

His mouth opened to say something, but he closed it and pulled up a chair to his father's bedside. He put the book in his lap and read the passage that was highlighted.

"Be anxious for nothing, but in everything by prayer and supplication with thanksgiving let your requests be made known to God. And the peace of God, which surpasses all comprehension, shall guard your hearts and your minds in Christ Jesus. Philippians 4:6-7."

Tears began to well up in his eyes. He grabbed his father's cold hand and squeezed it as he hung his head between his knees. He closed the Bible and noticed how worn the binding was from use. It must have been the hospital's copy. Henry thought of the countless number of people who probably turned to this title for some sort of comfort or inspiration in a time of fear. His father must have been one of them, which took Henry by surprise. His father was never scared, and the Bible was just for education, or that is what he had told him, and that is how Henry had grown up. But something, despite the the positive diagnosis from the doctors, had scared his father, and he turned to this book for something.

Henry rubbed his stubbly chin and wiped the tears from his eyes. He reread the words in his mind searching for meaning. His eye kept falling on the word "prayer." Henry had never said a prayer before, not that he could remember anyway, but he felt compelled to say something to someone for his father, whether or not someone was listening.

He clasped both of his hands now around his father's and closed his eyes, but not to hide this time. He bowed his head and began to quietly say a prayer for his father, for his family, and for himself. He wasn't really sure if he was praying right. Sometimes he would say things out loud, softly, but audibly and then other times he silently let his words leave him just in thought. How long he prayed, Henry wasn't sure. But, for just a few moments, he felt a calm peace seep through the numbness as he sat with his father's lifeless body. He let himself remember all the good experiences he had with his father and all the things his father had taught him. He already missed him, and he wished he could tell him things he had never had the courage to before. He said them to him now. He couldn't hear and he would never know, but Henry needed to say them out loud for his own peace of mind.

The door opened quietly. "Henry, your mother is here." The nurse said softly.

Henry broke himself out of the thin bubble of peace he had created and stood up, walking to the door. He took a deep breath, wiped away his tears, and stepped out of the room. He had to be strong now.

37
NEW YORK, NEW YORK
October 30, 1992

"And right there," the doctor pointed to the screen, "is your baby."

The sounds of a steady heartbeat and a tiny, faster heartbeat filled Henry's ears as he looked at the shaded blobs on the screen. He couldn't make out anything, let alone a baby.

Anne squeezed his hand anxiously. "I'm sorry, Dr. Kay, I just can't see it."

Henry was grateful Anne had said it, because he felt like a good father should be able to see his own baby. He squeezed her hand back and leaned over her a little, closer to the screen.

Dr. Kay smiled. "That's all right. Most parents can't either." She pointed again. Her finger outlined the tiniest shape. It was similar to the shape of a little walnut. Their baby was just a little walnut baby, and it couldn't be more precious. It took Henry's breath away, and the look in Anne's eyes reminded him of seeing a movie for the first time as a child: sheer joy.

"So, I will send you home with a copy of today's sonogram and a few more dietary directions." She wiped Anne's lower stomach to clear the ultrasound gel and threw away her gloves. "Any other questions?"

Anne pulled her top down and sat up. "When should we sign up for Lamaze classes?"

"Oh, you have a little time, but you can take the classes any time that works." She stood up and took Anne's chart with her. "You two will be great parents, don't worry." She smiled and left the room.

Henry's cheeks flushed with fear. "You will be a great father." The words loomed over him like a storm cloud. He felt very overwhelmed with becoming a father as he had just buried his own a few weeks before.

How could he be as great of a father to this child as his own father had been to him? How could he be a father without his own father to help him? He had so many questions, and the only people he could ever ask them to were either gone or halfway across the country not speaking to him.

"Henry?" Anne said and held out her hand to be helped down from the table.

"Yes?" Henry asked distractedly. "Oh, here." He helped her down, and they both left the room.

At the main desk, Dr. Kay's nurse handed Anne a copy of the sonogram. "You two have a lovely day." The nurse said cheerfully before calling another patient into the office.

"We should show this to your mom." Anne proclaimed as they walked to the car. "I think hearing about the baby would really lift her spirits."

Henry looked at Anne in surprise. It was true that she had been less selfish since the passing of his father, but it still shocked him when she genuinely cared about someone other than herself. "It would help, but do you think it is too early?" He asked her. "Remember, we wanted to wait until the second trimester in case anything happened. My mother could not handle it if anything were to happen." He thought of how his mother had been struggling with deep depression since his father died. He had even had to move her into a guest room at the mansion so he could keep a close eye on her. He cringed at the thought of another loss in their family.

He opened the car door for her and helped her inside the passenger side door.

Anne waited until Henry had started the car and drove out of the parking lot into NYC traffic. "Henry, you heard the doctor. She said the baby is healthy, and everything is on track." She looked down at the picture clutched tightly in her hand. "I think it would really help her."

"And you are really tired of keeping it a secret?" Henry asked drily.

Anne pouted slightly and flipped her long dark hair. "Well it isn't fair that I can't talk about it to *anyone*, not even my parents. But I still say we do it."

Henry furrowed his brow, still not sure about telling everybody, partly because he wasn't sure how his mom would react and partly because he was still not sure where his life was headed either.

"Come on, Henry, it couldn't hurt anyone." Anne pleaded with finality. She knew she would get her way, she always did. Henry knew Anne did not realize how untrue her last words were.

"Okay I guess, but only family for right now, okay?" Henry was defeated.

"Does that mean Thomas? He should know, you know ... because I'm sure it will affect your hours at work and what not."

"Of course, Thomas has always been family." Henry retorted with slight annoyance. Anne knew that. It was odd that she brought him up.

"Oh, Henry. I am just so excited! We should get announcements made up! What do you think..." Anne continued talking about colors and who had the best card stock.

Henry tuned her out like he normally did when she went on and on about something that seemed totally pointless to him. He wanted their announcement to be more intimate, a face-to-face conversation with the people he loved and cared about.

Henry stopped Anne mid-sentence. "Anne! Just take a breath. I want to tell my family face-to-face. No announcements, no shows. This is a child. A human person that is ours. It's not a party you're throwing. It's very serious and incredibly daunting. I mean we are going to be parents: a mother and a father." He stopped to let his words sink into her mind. "I mean, do you grasp what it means to be a mother or a father?"

Anne stared at him, puzzled and slightly bewildered. She was no doubt confused that Henry would stand up to her.

"Henry, I mean, of course I realize..." Anne shrugged her shoulders casually. "Announcements and parties are just part of it all."

This angered Henry. "Anne, we will be responsible for this child, his or her life, how it turns out, who they become, everything. We are going to be molding a person's *life* and how we go about this can change this baby's life forever. You and me. Even that is incredibly complicated right now. We haven't even begun the discussion of what is next for us let alone another human person. How can you be so ignorant as to brush that to the side and think that won't have a profound effect on how this child will be raised?"

Henry felt like he could go on and on, and she would never understand. She would never understand his pain. She would never understand what he left in Wyoming to raise this child he had fathered. She would never understand the debilitating fear that took hold of his heart every time he imagined raising a child.

"I'm sorry, Henry, but I still don't see the big deal. I mean, it's not like we will be raising this child ourselves." She paused and tossed back her hair arrogantly. "There are nannies and tutors for that."

Henry turned his attention to the road instead of screaming at Anne like he felt like doing. He tightened his hands on the steering wheel until he felt sure it would bend from the pressure. He inhaled and exhaled until he felt calmer. Of course, Anne would believe a child should be raised in this manner. Is this not how he was raised himself?

He thought of the kind of parent he wanted to be and found himself imagining taking the child on hikes in the mountains, lifting him or her up on his shoulders when the child was too tired to walk. He imagined his and Ara's lake, teaching the child how to swim in its calm waters. His mind wandered to Ara and thought of the warm mother she would be if she ever had children or helped raise his child. He thought of her sparkling eyes and kind smile.

The thoughts lulled him into a peaceful mood until the honking of a car broke him from his daydreams.

"Henry! Pay attention," Anne said exasperatedly. "All this talk of responsibility and a baby coming, and you almost kill all three of us!" She crossed her arms and shook her head in disgust.

He straightened the car without comment and drove on with an intense longing for Ara filling his already broken heart. Wyoming had changed him. Even a year ago, he would have agreed with Anne's announcement parties and child-raising theories. But, a year ago, he had not understood what real love was and what was most important in life. He hadn't known what he wanted, and, now that he did, he couldn't have it. It certainly wasn't fair to him, but it most definitely was not fair to Ara. He wanted to be in this scenario with her and being in it with Anne made him feel like a traitor. He did not know how he was going to keep his new self in tandem with his wife, a woman who lived in a way that felt foreign to him now. They were foreign to each other. Henry knew that he had put off talking about the future with Anne since his father had died, and he would need to talk to her about it soon, especially before she started making announcement plans.

They soon arrived at the gate to his home. Henry guided the car to the front of the house and parked. He walked around to help Anne out and walked with her into the mansion.

She pulled out the sonogram picture and began to walk up the stairs, most likely headed to the guest suite where Elizabeth would be.

Henry was filled with apprehension and decided to prolong the announcement as long as possible. "Anne, wait."

She turned around impatiently. "Yes?"

He walked to the stairs to join her. "Let's tell my mother tonight at dinner. You both can get all dolled up, and we will make a night of it." He tried to smile persuasively, but the most he could manage was raising the corners of his lips.

He need not have worried. The promise of going out was enough for Anne. "Oooh, Henry! Can we go to Chaterelle?"

"Yes, of course! Now go invite my mother to dinner tonight and don't spoil anything."

Anne rushed up the stairs without another word.

Henry shook his head and walked wearily to his office.

****

Henry was nervous. His palms sweaty and his knees weak, he held the door open for Anne. She walked into the restaurant with her usual air of confidence, handing her jacket to the doorman and leaving Henry to wait for the ticket while she made her way to the table.

His mom was certainly already here. She had so much free time now that she arrived everywhere at least thirty minutes early and tried to make everything go on longer than typically comfortable. He understood that she needed to fill her time with something other than grief. That's what today was all about, helping her with her grief.

The door man thanked him for waiting and handed him the ticket for their jackets and had the maitre'd lead him to their table.

Before he could take two steps, Henry felt a hand on his shoulder.

"Wait for me, would ya?" Thomas sounded out of breath, like he ran here from somewhere.

"And what have you been doing?" Henry asked with a smile. Thomas seemed nervous too, obviously for reasons different than Henry, but whatever the reason it made Henry relax a bit. Thomas always put him at ease anyway, and he was glad his best friend was here.

"I ran here because traffic was … just ridiculous and my taxi driver didn't know how to drive." Thomas shrugged off his black pea coat and passed it to the door man as he talked. He was still slightly out of breath. "And I didn't want to be late for the big news." Thomas turned all of his attention toward Henry as he was handed his ticket for the coat check.

"What big news?" Henry asked, surprised.

"Come on, big boy, how long have we known each other? We don't get the family together in the middle of the week for nothing short of 'big news.'" Thomas put his arm around Henry, and they followed the now impatient maitre'd to their table.

"I guess you will find out soon enough," Henry tried to feign some sort of smile, but he wasn't sure how it came across.

"Well you're nervous, so that makes me nervous." Thomas released his grip on his shoulder and they both walked with their hands in their pockets, side by side, like brothers, brothers who turned the heads of every single lady in the place.

When they reached their table, Anne had already shimmied her chair closer to Henry's mother and was laughing out loud as she shared a story about one her trips to the Cayman Islands. His mother smiled politely and sat quietly listening but pivoted her position as soon as Henry made it to the table. He smiled warmly. He knew she saw his father in him.

Thomas greeted each lady with a kiss on the cheek before taking his seat, and Henry did the same.

The waiter arrived almost instantly to get their orders. Thomas ordered a scotch, as did Henry. His mother ordered iced tea, and Anne ordered water.

"Water?" Thomas had a quizzical brow. "Since when do you order just water?"

"Since I started worrying about my health is when," Anne responded defensively, jabbing him in the arm with her finger.

"Hmm," Thomas sat back in his chair, and Henry's mother perked up in hers.

"I guess we sort of gave ourselves away," Anne chimed in with a big smile, clapping her hands together in joy.

Henry knew he needed to chime in. He wanted to be the first one tell his mom. He grabbed her hands and formed his words in his mind.

"Mom, we actually do have some news that I wanted to be the first to share with you and with Thomas." Henry shot a glance at Thomas and returned his attention to his mother. Henry's hands were clammy, but his mom rubbed his hand with her thumb as if sensing he needed calming, and he felt better. He kept his eyes diverted to their hands and spoke quietly.

"We are ... having a baby." He felt his mother's hands tense up around his, and he raised his eyes to see her reaction. Tears started falling from her eyes, and he was was worried the news upset her, but then a giant smile or pure joy spread across her face.

"A grandbaby?" She reached out to pull Henry in for a hug.

He embraced her back, his eyes wide in shock. He glanced at Anne who was watching for Thomas's reaction. He looked at Thomas who seemed unaffected.

Henry was released from his mother's embrace, and she let out a laugh. It was the first time he heard her laugh since his dad died. Anne was right. This news truly lifted her spirits. Her face had life in it again. He never expected such an instantaneous reversal like that, but there it was in front of his face. He was in a state of shock but was broken out of it when the waiter returned with their drinks.

Thomas began to raise his glass in a toast, in haste to drink, but Elizabeth stopped and ordered the waiter to bring their finest champagne.

"We are going to toast to this news the proper way," she said as she wiped away her tears, as if she were wiping away her sadness with them.

Henry marveled at her attitude, and, in that moment, he felt a shred of happiness swell inside of him. He smiled wholeheartedly for the first time since he came back to New York. But although he had always wanted to be a father, that wasn't what was bringing him happiness now, it was the joy that it brought to his mother. Family was everything to her, something she and his father always agreed on. She had lost someone very dear to that family and was left with this void in her life, but Henry's child would help fill that void, it would make her feel whole again.

As he smiled, the waiter brought the champagne, and Henry poured everyone a glass and led the toast.

"To new beginnings and to family." They all clinked their glasses together, and everyone drank accept for Anne, who laughed.

"I think this is the first time I've turned down a drink!"

They all laughed and Thomas and Henry downed their drinks in unison. As they slammed their glasses down on the table, they embraced in a short hug.

Henry sat back in his chair and crossed his legs, finally allowing himself to relax, but something kept him tense. His smile faded slightly. *Why am I still tense?*

He looked up from his table to the window outside and saw a faint click of gold blow past the window and fresh remains of breath on the window. There was a handprint slowly fading away.

"Arabella," he whispered to himself. He lowered his head, finally understanding his tension. In all of this, the baby, his father dying, he left out a very important piece in his life. That was why he was nervous. That was why he felt guilty. Guilty because he was having a baby with a person, not the love of his life. This entire moment was about bringing joy back to his mother. But he realized that now was the time to find the joy in his own life again.

Henry and Anne needed to talk. Tonight.

****

Henry let Anne chat about his mother's and Thomas's reaction to their news for a few minutes on the way home. He had his thoughts fixed on what he had to do. He turned the car into a well-lit grocery store parking lot and killed the engine.

Anne paused her happy chatter. "What's going on, Henry? Do we need something for home?"

Henry sighed and unbuckled his seatbelt, gathering his thoughts. "Anne, we need to talk."

Her green eyes filled with fear, the same fear he saw the day he drove off to Wyoming. He cringed, but his face remained adamant that this conversation must continue.

"Henry, this is silly. We need to get home!"

"Anne," He took her hands into his. "This is serious. I have put this off far too long, and I apologize for the false hope this has given you." He looked down at the center console and tried to think of the best way to explain his decision.

"Anne, you know that when you came to Wyoming, I was with another woman." He paused and waited for Anne to yell or scream, but she stayed frozen in fear. "I know … I know it was wrong to be with her, but I was. Her name, which I suspect you already know, is Arabella, and I love her with my entire being." Just saying her name aloud gave him courage, and Henry kept talking, this time with more conviction. "The baby and my father's death does not change the fact that I have found my true self and real love. I know where I want to be and who I want to be with for the rest of my life. I sent you divorce papers last August, and I would like you to sign new ones that I will have drawn up. I am going back to Ara, Anne. We can have shared custody of the baby, or I can have full custody, if that is how you feel."

"Henry, stop!" Anne cried, freeing herself from her frozen terror. "This is ridiculous. Think of how you sound? You are married! With a baby on the way! Your father just died. This is the grief talking." Clearly agitated, she shook her head and threw up her hands. "And what about your business? How will the CEO control a company from across the country?"

"Anne, I am quite serious..."

"Henry," she interrupted hysterically. "Think of what this will do to your mother! A divorce in the family after she lost her husband! How will she make it while you traipse around with your whore in the mountains?"

Anger rose up in Henry. "That's enough, Anne!"

"No!" She screamed. "I will not let you destroy our marriage! I will not let you do this to me!" Tears began to fall down her cheeks. "What would your father think of you, Henry?" She threw this at him, desperately knowing how it would affect him. "What would he say if he knew you were divorcing your pregnant wife to be with another woman?"

Henry paused for a moment, even though he knew Anne had only said that about his father to get him to reconsider his decision. What would his father say? He thought back to his wedding day. His father had questioned his choice of marrying Anne from the beginning. "'I just hope you are sure about Anne, son. Is she the absolute one?'" What would he say about going back on his decision? Henry furrowed his brow. What else had his father said? "'I only want you to be happy, Henry. The love I feel for your mother is so strong, so undeniably true. I never second guessed it. She completes me, son. I want the same for you." His father had put a hand on his shoulder. "I just hope you are not doing this out of obligation to me, so you can live up to some imaginary expectation you think I have for you? The only expectation I have for you … is your happiness. And that is all I want for you.'"

Henry knew what his father would say. He wouldn't say he was proud or tell him "Good for you, son!" No, his father would tell him to find happiness in life because, really, what else mattered? Henry's decision was made, and he was firm in it.

"Henry?" Anne questioned angrily, awaiting a response.

He turned to her. "Anne, my father wanted me to be happy." He said firmly, now without a shadow of doubt. "He told me so the day I married you, when he questioned my choice as you for my wife."

It was cold of him, but why shouldn't she know? If anything, her knowing made his decision even more resolute. She was never really meant to be his. Their marriage was never anything but a mistake.

Anne's look of fear dissipated and a look of anger took its place. Her eyes burned, like the fear she had was burned up, turned to ashes from his words. "You have no idea who you're messing with, Henry," her words came out like a hiss. "You think your happiness is all that matters. Well, you're selfish and so was your father!"

Anne got out of the car marched over to the street. She hailed a cab, got in, and was gone before Henry could catch his breath.

Henry exhaled with relief, glad to have that conversation over. Now, all he had to do was work out the few hitches here in New York with his plan to return to Wyoming. He felt like his new start was just around the corner. He started the car and drove toward the mansion, deep in thought. What were the unresolved issues? He started a list: leaving his mother alone while she was in a fragile state, his company, obviously, and the upcoming birth and life of his child. Solutions or at least plans to all three would be needed before he could leave for Wyoming. But it all felt doable because doing so meant finally seeing Ara again.

He realized with slight surprise that he had arrived at the gates to his home. He punched in the number and drove in to park his car. His mind reeling with thoughts, Henry decided he needed to burn some energy while he worked out his plans. He quietly opened the front door to the mansion and snuck up the stairs to the guest suite to change into his running clothes, being careful not to waken or alert anyone to his presence. He did not feel like talking to anyone right now, especially Anne. Once changed, Henry snuck back down the stairs and quietly slid out the side door leading to the expansive grounds. He bent down to tie his shoelaces a little tighter and then took off running into the night at a brisk pace.

Okay, he thought as he ran over the perfectly trimmed grass, now slick from the dew of night. He fell into his stride and began unraveling all of his thoughts as his breath became steady with his steps.

Obviously, I will fly back and forth to see my child and bring him/her back and forth to Wyoming, unless Anne gives me full custody. Henry doubted that would be the case. He felt like Anne would want to keep as much of a hold over him as she could manage, or at least the hold on his checkbook. So he would be flying a lot, which was nothing new. Would that be enough for his mother? Maybe she would like to be around her grandchild and stay in her home in New York. He pictured the crisp, clean mountain air of Jackson Hole. Maybe the scenery would be soothing to her, so he could set her up with a house. She could fly out there whenever she wanted.

He stopped at a tree to stretch out his calves, catching his breath. *Two problems solved,* he thought. *Now what to do with Tudor Industries?* That thought was the most troublesome for Henry. Now that he would be with Arabella, Henry would like to step down from CEO or even sell the company altogether and take a simpler job in Wyoming, like working on Mitch's ranch or something. But he knew Tudor Industries was his father's dream for Henry, and that dream had always been non-negotiable. Henry did like the company, and he would not want to disappoint his father.

Frustrated, Henry jumped back on the grass to continue running. He ran harder, trying to come up with a solution. He needed to stay the CEO, but did he need to stay as busy? What if he hired a few extra operation officers to pick up more of his work? He would still be in control, but the extra employees could do much of the work Henry had preferred to take care of himself. Did he need to be in New York then to run the business? Henry did not see why he could not be in Wyoming for much of the business week. He could conference call and do his computer work from anywhere. He could fly to New York when he had to and even fly clients out to Wyoming if he needed to. He could try this solution out for a while, at least. If it didn't work out, he could cross that bridge when he came to it. What was most important to him now was getting back to her. The thought made him sprint for a good thirty seconds.

He slowed back down to a jog, satisfied with his planning, Henry decided to brainstorm any other issues that might come up for the remainder of his run. He wanted to get back to Ara as soon as possible. After a few more loops around the grounds, Henry snuck back into the mansion and crept up the stairs to his room. He quickly showered and climbed into bed. His mind happy with thoughts of Arabella and Jackson Hole, he drifted peacefully off to sleep for the first time since he had left Wyoming. He was going home.

38
NEW YORK, NEW YORK
October 31, 1992

"What is goin' on in that tiny, little head of yours?!" Henry had just woken up, or rather, been woken up by the words of an enraged Mitch.

Henry was so excited just to hear his friend's voice that he ignored his actual words. "Mitch, buddy ... is that you?" Henry yawned between his words and stretched his hands above his head and held the phone to his ear with his shoulder.

"Buddy? What world are you livin' in, pal? This here ain't a friendly, buddy-buddy chat, amigo!" Mitch howled.

Henry could sense his anger but chuckled in his mind at Mitch's conflicting words and a smile crept across his face anyway. In a normal situation when things weren't on hostile terms with Mitch, Henry would have told Mitch that amigo means friend, and then he would laugh until he rolled. But from Mitch's tone, Henry knew he couldn't laugh, he had to remain stoic and refrain from friendship, at least for now.

"Sorry, I guess I didn't realize my first phone call from Wyoming would be at three in the morning and so, so incredibly hostile." Henry laughed sarcastically in the phone and rolled his legs out to the side of his bed. He ran his fingers through his hair, which was starting to get long again, like it was in Wyoming. Of all people, he thought he would hear from Ara first, so this phone call was coming as a surprise to him.

"Sorry to disappoint, but I need to know why you're the way you are?" Mitch fell silent on the other end, waiting for his reply.

"The way I am? What do you mean?" Henry was confused by this: his call, this question, everything. Something felt off about the whole thing.

"Yeah, the way you destroy something you claim to love. How do you get that way? And why, for the love of God would you put on this whole show of buying Ara her ranch, promising to return, only to move on with your life in the opposite direction, prancing around in your little city-boy suits and having a merry old time while Arabella sits here waiting and waiting until she can't wait anymore. You must think you can buy your way out of a life of guilt, and I could just punch you straight to China right about now..." Mitch kept talking and yelling and then mumbling things Henry couldn't even hear. Henry couldn't wrap his mind around any of it. Where was this coming from?

"Mitch...MITCH!? What are you going on about? I am not moving on without Ara. I just told my wife to sign divorce papers, my pregnant wife!" Henry was exasperated. Yes, this was a crappy situation, but he was trying to make it better or at least make the best of it. He was making every effort in the world he could. "Mitch, I am coming home to her. I always was, but you know this isn't a black and white situation. Unfortunately, I was married, and my wife *is* pregnant. You have no idea what I have been going through and why, of all times, did you choose to call me out on this now?"

"Why of all times, Henry?" Mitch had stopped yelling but a barely controlled rage still lined his voice. "Because Arabella went to New York to find you, you blockheaded jerk! Because she saw you last night at some fancy-schmancy restaurant, happy as can be, celebrating with your rich, perfect little family. Because you blew it, pal." Mitch sounded worn and truly defeated. He didn't want things this way anymore than Henry did. Henry suspected that was the reason he called instead of just ignoring him altogether. The both of them only wanted happiness for Arabella. Henry was just obviously the worst at making that a reality. In fact, he was probably *the* worst.

Henry's world came to a stop as he took in what Mitch was saying. Arabella had been in New York last night. She was so close, and he had missed it. She had seen him celebrating with his family, with his wife, the wife he had told Ara he wanted to divorce. With horror, Henry finally understood what had brought Mitch's call on.

"Now, don't ya hang up on me." Mitch warned. "I am not through yellin' at you!"

Still holding the phone but otherwise completely motionless, Henry was frozen still in fear as he realized what Ara must have thought.

"Henry?" Mitch questioned with impatience.

He thought of how devastated Ara must have felt. How long had it been since he had left her in Wyoming, promising to come back once he had straightened things out with Anne? It was already the thirtieth, no, the thirty-first of October. Two months had passed! So much had happened in that time. He had to explain things to Ara; he needed to make her understand everything, including how much he loved her. "I need to fix this." Henry finally whispered, more to himself than to Mitch.

"Fix this?" Mitch asked angrily. "You are NOT going to fix this, Henry. I told you not to hurt her, and, what did you do? Your broke her heart TWICE!" His voice broke as he yelled out the last word, reflecting the anger, hurt, and betrayal felt by himself and Ara. "You are not allowed to see or speak to her again, you hear me, partner? You try, and I swear, I will rip you into pieces. I would wish you luck for the future with your pregnant wife, but you don't deserve it, and Ara agrees with us." Sadly with defeat, Mitch dejectedly said, "I really thought that I knew you, Henry. But I didn't. Not even close."

"That's enough." Henry's heart jumped as he heard Arabella speak through tears on the other end of the phone before silence ensued and then the droning tone of the dial tone as Mitch had hung up with two final words that cut his heart in two.

39
NEW YORK, NEW YORK
November 1, 1992

In his office in the mansion, Henry reached into his briefcase for the divorce papers. His expression aloof, he took them out and tore them in two. He looked at each half. Cleanly cut in two in one fowl swoop, the papers were just like him.

Sliding the papers into his shredder, he opened the door and strode out of the office without a backward glance.

40
NEW YORK, NEW YORK
November 10, 1992

"Jennifer, bring me the Henderson contract, please." Henry said into his intercom. He sat back in his chair and rubbed his tired eyes. One look at his watch told him that Jennifer should have been sent home hours ago.

She opened the door and walked in, looking about as tired as he felt. "Here you are, sir." She laid the papers on his desk, straightened her wide-brimmed glasses, and stepped back with her hands folded in front of her. She was a great sport.

"That will be all for today, Jennifer. You should go home." Henry looked down at the contract, trying to remember what he wanted to do with it.

"Thank you, sir." Jennifer turned to go, her heels clicking lightly on the floor. "Henry," She said, using his first name to catch his attention. "You really should go home as well. You've hardly left the office for the last few days." She rested her hand on the door and looked back at him with concerned eyes. As far as assistants go, she certainly had to have been among the best.

"Hmmmm … What?" Henry looked up from the contract. "Ah, yes. Well, work is work." He turned on the lamp at his desk to see a particular line better. "Good night." Henry said without looking up from the document.

Jennifer sighed, her voice full of worry, and left the office, closing the door behind her.

A few hours after she had gone, Henry set down the completed contract — just one in a pile of hundreds — and walked over to his "bump out" glass window. He looked down at New York City with a passive glance before leaving the office to catch a few minutes of sleep. A few hours and he would be back to work again.

41
NEW YORK, NEW YORK
November 12, 1992

Henry poured fine scotch for the two clients debating at his conference table. Thomas lifted his drink slightly to Henry with a twinkle in his eye as he listened to the two debate. He slid the drinks onto the table and sat down across from them. Lifting his own scotch, Henry sipped his drink and interrupted the debate. "Might I suggest you gentlemen read this line of the contract?" Henry pointed to the line he knew they would both agree upon, a line that would seal the deal.

The men, including Thomas, poured over the section Henry had pointed out. The murmurs of approval soon filled the room. "Ah, yes, this will work out perfectly for us."

Thomas smiled calculatingly. "Perfect. Please sign at the bottom, and we will be in contact with you in the very near future about dates."

The men signed the contract with gumption before standing, preparing to depart.

"Pleased to do business together," Thomas said, shaking their hands firmly.

Henry nodded and shook their hands as well, moving his lips to mimic Thomas' words.

The men left, and Thomas clapped Henry on the back. "Well done, man! That simply never gets old."

Henry nodded without victory, feeling only the drive to stay busy, and looked at the time. "Should we be going to meet the women at the Anderson's?"

"Ah, yes! Dinner awaits!" Thomas handed Henry his coat, and they walked out of the conference room toward the elevator. As the elevator "dinged" and opened, Thomas declared, "I just love dinner parties after closing a big deal. Actually, I love *anything* after closing a big deal!" He continued to chatter on about how Henry and he had really worked those men for some big money as they descended to the main floor.

Henry nodded along, not really listening to Thomas, but keeping his mind focused on the work to complete tomorrow. The elevator opened. "How far is it to the Anderson's?" He said mildly as they walked to Henry's car.

"Oh, about twenty minutes. I can give you directions." He slid into the passenger seat and started discussing the list of invited people, people Henry didn't care to know.

Henry turned the key in the ignition to start the car, looked straight ahead, and let Thomas carry on.

42
NEW YORK, NEW YORK
November 15, 1992

"The baby is looking quite healthy." Dr. Kay stated as she looked over the ultrasound. "Everything looks great." She wiped the ultrasound gel off Anne's slightly growing belly and smiled at the two parents.

"And how is the mom doing?" She asked Anne.

Anne sat up and pulled her shirt down. "I have been feeling a little tired."

"Well, naturally." Dr. Kay said and then launched into a nutrition talk. Anne nodded along and wrote down a few notes. Henry pretended to be listening but ended up making a few mental work notes in his head.

"And does the father have any questions?"

"Henry." Anne nudged him.

"Oh, no. As long as the baby and mother are happy, I am satisfied." He turned up the corners of his lips into a smile and helped Anne off the exam table.

"Well, we will see you in a few weeks then."

43
NEW YORK, NEW YORK
December 20, 1992

Garland and white lights swirled around the banister as Henry walked down the stairs in his winter running gear. He heard voices coming from the living room and walked towards his mother and Anne, who were supervising the staff while they decorated the gigantic tree in the mansion's living room. Anne and his mother were sitting on a sofa, surrounded by paint samples and fabric samples. Once in a while, his mother or Anne would hold up a swatch of color and nod excitedly. Henry watched his mother delightedly clap her hands over a choice they made together. The women set the selected choices on the table in front of them.

"Now for a bassinet," Henry's mother said and turned to select a magazine from the pile.

"Oh, I do like that one." Anne wrote something down, and his mother agreed. "What else do we need?"

"Changing table? Those are over here, in this section, dear."

"Oh, thank you. Yes, I see them."

They pointed and discussed several options before writing some more notes down.

Henry watched the scene for a few moments before slipping out of the mansion for another winter run.

44

NEW YORK, NEW YORK
January 10, 1993

"As for the baby's sex, did you two want it to be a surprise?" Dr. Kay looked up from her chart and waited for the couple's response.

"Oh, no. We want to know right away." Anne said with slight impatience.

Henry would have liked it to be a surprise, but he did not care to argue with Anne at the moment. "Yes, please tell us, Doctor." He said without feeling or excitement.

Dr. Kay smiled. "All right. Well, you two are having … a … boy!"

"Oh, my!" Anne clasped her hands together. "That is just what we wanted, isn't it, Henry?"

"Yes, of course, Anne." Henry smiled and helped her down from the exam table.

Anne brushed a hand over her perfectly smooth dark hair. "Thank you, Dr. Kay." The two turned to leave.

"Now I can finally get that nursery done, Henry." Anne told Henry as they walked out of the office. "I know it has been just a weight on both our minds."

Anne spoke like Henry was so worried about the nursery getting completed. He helped her into the car and drove her to her next destination, tuning out her endless chatter.

45
NEW YORK, NEW YORK
January 15, 1993

Breathing.

It's something one can easily take for granted until they think about it, the in and out and the out and in. It's all so rhythmic and soothing, but it is also so sensitive. If one takes a breath at the wrong time, it can throw off one's whole run, one's whole state of mind.

Henry breathed in and out. The sight of his breath told him he was still breathing that he was still alive, and, so, he kept running. He ran every day before the sun came up. It was when the air was still bitter cold from the darkened night, the sounds of the city were at a minimum, and the voice in his head, his voice, would stop talking.

Every day he ran around the city to avoid thinking about his life, and every day he was still alive, but he felt lifeless, like his heart had quit beating even though he felt a steady thump in his chest.

Thump. Thump. Stop. He had reached the top of the stairs and was facing his front door like he did every day. It was the worst part of his run, those last steps toward home. He opened it and stepped back into his life.

46
NEW YORK, NEW YORK
January 30, 1993

Anne had asked Henry to come home during lunch. She had a surprise for him, but he already knew. After all, he paid the bills; he knew where his money was being spent. Anne had been working on the nursery, and she had a lot people working very hard.

Henry took a cab home. His driver was one the few great conversationalists left in the world, but lately Henry wasn't up for much talking, so he felt the driver's services were better utilized by his wife.

The cab driver pulled up and spouted off how much he owed. Henry wasn't listening and threw him a twenty before slamming the door behind him. Henry propped his collar up around his neck to block falling flakes of snow from melting on his skin.

Anne opened the door for him before he had the chance. She had a very genuine smile on her face, like she was really happy at that moment. It puzzled Henry. She grabbed his hand and pulled him up the stairs. This is the first time they held hands since ... He shut out the thought.

She opened the door to the room just down the hall from the master suite, and Henry stepped inside. His insides melted as he saw where his future child would sleep and play.

A simple white crib was illuminated by the natural light flooding in through the French doors that led to a small balcony. Blue curtains lined the windows and soft, matching blue rugs lay strategically on the floor. On the wall to his right, he saw three large pictures in a line. The one on the left was a picture of Henry's parents and a little Henry, the one on the right was a picture of a little Anne with her parents. The center picture was empty. His family would fill it.

"I thought we could take a picture with our son after he was born ... together." Anne tenderly touched Henry's shoulder.

It was all too much for him. "I think ... I need to go." Henry bolted out the door.

"Henry?!" Anne cried out to an empty hallway.

47

NEW YORK, NEW YORK
January 31, 1993

The sun was just setting, and the city was very much awake, but the bitter cold was out in full force as Henry ran to the cemetery. His breathing wasn't even, and his hands were shaking from more than just the cold. This wasn't like his morning runs.

The entrance to the cemetery was frozen and slippery, and Henry slid to a stop before slowly walking toward his father's plot. He had not been back since the day of his funeral. He missed his father.

As he came upon his gravestone, Henry dropped to his knees. The snow began to melt and dampen his pants. Henry's hand fell on the gravestone and used the other to wipe the tears from his eyes.

"Dad … I just … I'm sorry that it took me this long to come, and I'm sorry for the reason I'm here now." His words came out in sobs at first, but he calmed himself and got control of his breathing. He was breathing. He put a hand to his heart: still alive.

"I'm gonna be a father, like really soon." Henry laughed at the thought. "And I'm panicking, and I know I'm not ready for a family. Neither of us are. And my life … my life," He gave a grim chuckle. "What life? What would you do, Dad, if you were in my shoes? Why can't you be here to answer that for me?"

Henry knew what his father would do, and he knew what he needed to do now. He had been avoiding this choice this entire time. But the time had come to face facts. He had a family to take care of, despite everything else, his pain, and despite *her*.

****

Henry sat in his office in the mansion. Opening the center drawer, he saw his wedding ring, laying right where he had set it before leaving New York. He picked it up gingerly, the gold cool against his skin.

Turning it over in his hands, the black onyx stone set in the center glittered darkly as it caught the light. With a grimace, Henry slid the gold ring onto his wedding finger. He flexed his hand, remembering what the ring stood for and why he now would wear it once again.

With a sigh, Henry closed the drawer and left the office.

Upstairs, Anne called, looking for him.

48
NEW YORK, NEW YORK
February 3, 1993

Henry piled his belongings into his suitcase and looked around the guest suite for any additional belongings. Not seeing any, he opened the door to the suite and pulled his suitcase behind him. Dread pushed the usual feelings of numbness out of the way as Henry closed the suite's door and walked out into the hallway. He pulled his belongings behind him and took measured steps down the hall, past the main staircase, and toward his old room. He stopped in front of the master suite and took a deep breath. There was no going back after this.

Taking a deep breath, Henry opened the door to the suite.

"Welcome back, Henry." Anne purred from her place on the bed, her baby bump very much noticeable.

Henry walked in, pulling his suitcase behind him, and closed the door.

49
NEW YORK, NEW YORK
February 10, 1993

Tea cups and pastries lined every table in sight. Anne had hired a wait staff of thirty men and women to cater to the guests. Elizabeth was in charge of the theme, and she chose to put on a formal tea party. It was for the ladies only, as was traditional, so Henry was not invited, although he was still witness to the giant spectacle that was being put on before him.

A pile of gifts had already arrived from guests who were unable to attend the baby shower. Henry recalled Anne's earlier snarky comment, "Seriously, who doesn't attend a Tudor party?" He rolled his eyes thinking in retrospect but smiled at the sight of Anne with one hand draping tulle on a table and the other on her baby bump.

He walked over and lightly kissed her cheek before wishing her a wonderful time. He opened the door and headed to Tudor Industries with only new business deals on his mind.

50
NEW YORK, NEW YORK
February 12, 1993

"Henry, if we keep up the deals like we have been these last few months, you and I can retire next year!" Thomas slammed his glass onto the bar happily. "Bartender! Another round, please!"

Henry laughed lightly. "While that may be true, my friend, you and I will never retire." He brought his glass to his lips and sipped his scotch.

"Here, here!" Thomas laughed and held up his glass. "We love making those deals more than we love how much money those deals make us!" He clapped Henry on the shoulder and firmly shook him. "We make a great team."

Nodding a response, Henry ordered another shot for Thomas.

"Thank you, fine sir!" Thomas yelled, holding up his glass. "To a great team," he toasted.

Henry clinked his glass with Thomas and threw the rest of his scotch down his throat. "Another round?" He asked Thomas with a small smile.

"Of course!" Thomas held up his empty glass. "Bartender!"

51
NEW YORK, NEW YORK
March 25, 1993

The wail of his baby entering the world for the first time resounded in Henry's ears.

Anne cried out, exhausted and elated as Dr. Kay quickly checked over the baby. "Well, what does the baby look like, Henry?" She demanded, struggling to see around the nurses and doctors crowding around her baby.

Henry cautiously walked to the end of the bed, closer to where his son was being held. His skin was bright red, and he was crying furiously. Henry reached out without thinking and touched his finger to his son's foot. The baby kicked and continued to fuss before the doctor wrapped him up in a blanket and carried him over to Henry.

Henry held him, so fragile and small, close to his chest, to his beating heart. The feeling of holding his son was like holding Arabella: it was love. Before Henry could think to stop, he was crying.

"Henry! I need to hold my baby, please bring him to me now!" Anne's arms were already frantically outstretched to receive him.

He walked over, slowly bouncing him, and placed him in her arms.

"Asher," Anne whispered tenderly. Henry brushed a strand of hair out of Anne's eyes. She looked up and smiled at him and returned her gaze to her new baby boy.

Henry wiped the tears from his eyes, grabbed the bag of blue-tagged cigars, and walked out the door to the waiting room filled with family and friends, all awaiting news on the baby.

"Well, we had a boy!" Henry cried out, feeling an emotion somewhere close to happiness, at least the closest to happiness he had gotten in the last five months, and held up the cigars in a victory pump.

Cheers and congratulations surrounded Henry as he passed out the cigars to all the men.

Thomas reached over to clasp Henry's hand, shaking it and shouting his congratulations.

"Asher Michael Tudor." Henry's numbness melted slightly at the sound of his baby boy.

52
NEW YORK, NEW YORK
March 31, 1993

The scent of dark, oak wood smoothly enveloped the office where Henry sat, deep in his thoughts. The letter in front of him was minute compared to the massive, wooden desk it lay upon, but the contents were dauntingly larger than anything in the room; everything revolved around that piece of paper.

In the soft light of his desk lamp, the truth was written in the folds of the expensive paper, parsed with a known, spiky handwriting. Henry's stomach fell to the floor as he took in what he had already known in his heart to be true, just had not yet confirmed until this moment. The letter was from Thomas, his best friend, to Anne, his wife. At least, she used to be his.

Scratched in Thomas's notorious slanted cursive, he read a note of devious intentions, detailing a secret rendezvous they were to endeavor upon. "Tell Henry you are going to the Hampton's with some friends, whatever you find most convincing." Henry felt a flash of anger at Thomas's carefree demeanor, as if every word weren't like gunshots to the heart. "Wait for me by our park, where we first kissed. I'm sure you remember it. I can't wait to feel your lips on mine. Until then, Arrivederci, my love." Love.

Henry turned his head away in twisted agony. His lip quivered slightly as he fought back the urge to scream at the top of his lungs. He heard a soft knock at the door.

Anne slowly opened the door to his office. Her dark hair was piled on top of her head with little tendrils gently falling down to frame her face. It reminded him of his wedding, the way her curls framed her face so elegantly. The formal, satin, emerald-green dress accentuated her delicate olive skin, and her opera length gloves hid her beautiful long arms, a shame to hide them. *A pure hand needs no glove to cover it*, thought Henry, remembering one of his favorite authors, Nathaniel Hawthorne. Henry had only seen her look so beautiful on their wedding day. But he remembered her betrayal and thought grimly, *Beauty appears pure until the ugliness within is made evident.*

She smiled slightly. "You ready to get out there?"

Henry looked into her green eyes, knowing the truth hiding in their depths. He did not want to look into those eyes any longer. He forced the image of betrayal away as silky, blond waves suddenly swam into the forefront of his lucid mind. Her blue eyes glistened as the sun set, casting shadows onto the smooth skin he stroked beneath his fingertips. She was more than beauty. She was the epitome of love, something so foreign to Henry back in this city. What he knew of love was for the lost, but the love she shined with was for the gods. His love was a lie, and he wasn't fit for her, for Arabella.

Thinking back, Henry could see that the evidence had been lain before his eyes, subtly, but all the more infuriating now that he knew. If he had paid attention, the truth would surely have been so obvious. His wife had bewitched him into a false sense of happiness, a dishonest form of love. If it's dishonest, can it even be love? He thought of Arabella and what he had given up to come back to this shamble of a marriage.

The anger was building in his chest. It was like a sudden roaring fire, consuming his entire body as he thought of his best friend and his beautiful wife together – making love. Henry wanted to throw up and, at the same time, cry out in pure agony. In his whole life, he had never hated anyone as he did now his own wife. And Thomas. What was worse about the entire situation was that he wasn't so upset at his wife's betrayal, but, rather, for being taken away from a woman far more pure, honest, and filled with a brimming hope that he longed for. He left her lighted presence for this dark pit of lies that he now faced, lies that surrounded his life completely.

Her cool hand on his burning cheek chilled him. Surprised, he realized Anne had moved from the doorway to his side while he had been deep in thought. Her dark eyes glittered down at him while she inquired whether he was feeling ill. Anne touched the back of her slim hand to his forehead, trying to decide if he had a fever.

Henry reached up and caught her hand, pulling her down into his lap. Her wedding ring caught the light as she moved, casting a quick glow about the shadowed room. One of his hands held tight to her left hand while his other examined the ring. Despite the churning fire of his insides, Henry felt eerily calm. He slowly slid the ring off her finger, allowing the expensive diamond to glimmer in the quiet light of his desk lamp as it rested on his open palm. His heart pounded so fiercely that he could not even hear his own thoughts; he was now solely relying on his instincts.

"Henry? What are you doing?" Anne asked hesitantly. She sat frozen on his lap while Henry closed his fingers tightly around her wedding ring. "Henry?"

He gazed coolly into her eyes. "Anne, what does marriage mean to you?"

The question stunned her. Unmoving, Anne stared at him while the seconds crept by. It seemed an eternity before he could speak again.

"Answer me, Anne." He commanded with a calm firmness. He was fueled with a flaming fury that burned within himself, trapped within his bones, fighting to set itself free. His countenance displayed this internal struggle and revealed the utter agony he was plagued with at that moment.

Bewildered, Anne looked around the dimly lit office, trying to avoid his piercing gaze. Her eyes fell upon the impervious letter, resting casually on his desk. She quickly scanned the words scrawled across the page, written in the hand of her lover. Fear flushed her face as she read word after devastating word.

Breaking his hold on her, she clamored to her feet, knocking her wedding ring from his hand. As if stalled in time, the ring flew through the air, both with grace and purpose, as the oblivious couple before it tumultuously feuded breathlessly. With every turn of the light, the diamond, eternal and resolute, shone brightly. Each face of the stone mirrored the many failures that plagued their souls. But as the ring met coldly the stone floor below, a chiming echo resounded, breaking the frigid silence in the room. And the couple stared blankly at the ring, forever frozen in destitution, lying still on the stone slab floor. They were both very still, almost placid, for what felt like hours but just two seconds passed before their eyes turned to each other again.

Henry watched as Anne's face twisted into a confused web of fear and shame, and her green eyes pleaded with the victim of her secret vice.

She began to move away from Henry, knowing her only escape was the door, an opening that was still much too far from her.

Henry's long swift legs enabled him to easily step in front of Anne, causing her to stop and retreat backwards until the wall was behind her. Henry watched his usually confident wife shiver with terror as he stalked toward her, the anger and fear in his eyes causing them to appear blacker than ever before as his dark gaze practically pinned her against the cold wall. His jaw was clenched as she quivered in fear. Every ounce of his being wanted nothing more than to hurt this woman and, for that feeling, he was very scared.

A single tear swelled and collapsed, falling ever so smoothly down his cheek onto Anne's shoulder. His deep sense of severity was something he had never revealed to Anne before now.

The look on Anne's face as she fearfully realized just how defeated and torn he was reminded him of a look she had had once before. A terrified look that had haunted him the entire time he was away.

His heart was on the floor, limp and seemingly unrevivable. The whole time he had been gone from New York, he had had this pit in his stomach that was filled with guilt every moment that he drew further and further away from Anne and drew closer to another. His hands trembled as he thought of the love he fought back to abstain from unfaithfulness out of honor and integrity to a woman who he had thought felt abandoned, alone, and confused. But she certainly was none of those things. He had been a fool to think of her as this consummate being.

Things became very still as he sat there despising her malevolent secrecy, and he stepped aside to let Anne go. He floated above it all with everything coming full circle in his mind. She was never the one with whom he wished to live forever. His ill-educated and youthful will was what led him to this precipice with which he now hung, fingertips just barely holding on. He used to struggle with validity and self-worth and valued each of them as society around him valued them. He never allowed himself a single idiosyncratic thought. There was never room for an individual to form. He used to think that he had to be married by a certain age to be a normal, successful person, and indeed she must be a gorgeous and flawless bride. But of course, no one ever really is flawless, are they? No matter how hard one tries to see them that way.

The world around him let these misconstrued ideas about life and love blind him about what is real and pure. He had been living in this world surrounded with a hazy atmosphere of false concepts, and, for the first time, he saw clarity, a clear view of who he was and how he had become someone that he was not. He missed Wyoming, and the mountains, and, most of all, he missed her.

Anne had slowly moved around the massive desk and away from the wall while Henry immersed himself in his thoughts. Henry did not even notice the absence of his wife until he allowed himself a moment outside his thoughts. She must have crept out among the shadows, a familiar place for her. After what he had just learned, she was no longer worth his concern. She was just a mistake full of heartbreak. He could not help but yearn for her to be gone and once she was ... he would be free, free from her and from Thomas, but never from what he had done to Arabella.

Henry pulled out a battered, leather bound journal he had kept for years. Only one other person besides himself knew what he had written about, and only one other person had ever read it. He opened it to a blank page and began writing furiously. He wrote for hours, pouring his heart and soul onto the pages. His pride and love was written "with a pen of iron; with the point of a diamond, it was engraved on the tablet of his heart" (Jeremiah 17:1).

He pictured her face as he wrote, felt her warmth as he held her in his arms and ran his fingers through her silky, blond hair. Henry finally sat back to read what he had written. He moved the words around, shifting them into the shape of a poem.

Alas, my love, you do me wrong,
To cast me off discourteously.
For I have loved you well and long,
Delighting in your company.

Greensleeves was all my joy
Greensleeves was my delight,
Greensleeves was my heart of gold,
And who but my lady greensleeves.

Your vows you've broken, like my heart,
Oh, why did you so enrapture me?
Now I remain in a world apart
But my heart remains in captivity.

I have been ready at your hand,
To grant whatever you would crave,
I have both wagered life and land,
Your love and good-will for to have.

If you intend thus to disdain,
It does the more enrapture me,
And even so, I still remain
A lover in captivity.

My men were clothed all in green,
And they did ever wait on thee;
All this was gallant to be seen,

And yet thou wouldst not love me.

Thou couldst desire no earthly thing,
but still thou hadst it readily.
Thy music still to play and sing;
And yet thou wouldst not love me.

Well, I will pray to God on high,
that thou my constancy mayst see,
And that yet once before I die,
Thou wilt vouchsafe to love me.

Ah, Greensleeves, now farewell, adieu,
To God I pray to prosper thee,
For I am still thy lover true,
Come once again and love me.

*** It has been said that Henry VIII was the author of "Greensleeves." However, the author remains anonymous and the poem shown above is a copy of that author's work. 13

Henry looked over the words filled with pain and love in the depths of his soul. At that moment regret entirely consumed what was left of his heart as he thought of how much the choice to come back to his wife had cost him. He had left more than just the love of his life behind; a large piece of himself was with her there too. He knew better than anyone that choices had to be made and, once made, could not be undone. He wished with all his being that he had decided differently. Henry yearned to go back to her, back to his beautiful Arabella.

****

Interposed between the joyous sounds from the celebration party, a baby's cry distantly resounded from the upstairs nursery. Brought back to the harsh reality of the present, Henry looked up from "Greensleeves," the poem he had written out of his pain and love for Arabella. At that moment, regret entirely consumed what was left of his heart as he thought of how much the choice to come back to his adulterous wife had cost him. He thought back to Mitch's phone call and wished with all his being that he had tried to see Ara to explain what had been going on in New York. He could have at least *tried* to see her.

A clinking of glasses and cheers sounded from the dining hall. He looked around his office with a sudden loathing. He needed to get out of this mansion, a place filled with Anne and her betrayal. He jumped up and started filling his briefcase with anything vitally important that he might need. Once his briefcase was stuffed to breaking point, he creaked open the office door to see if any party-goers were in the main hallway. Not seeing anyone, Henry snuck outside and quietly shut the door behind him. He turned and locked the office before stealthily moving up the stairs to the master bedroom.

He listened carefully for any sounds of movement before entering the suite. He was not in the mood to encounter Anne again, at least not until the divorce papers were re-drawn up. Grabbing his suitcase and several large duffle bags from his closet, Henry began packing hastily.

While he packed, Henry began to plan what was left for his life. He would soon be without Anne, a sweet and welcome freedom. But he was still without the love of his life. A life without Arabella was a life he did not know if he could survive.

Looking down, he saw that his favorite Wrangler jeans from Wyoming were in his hands. Suddenly, he needed to rid himself of the ridiculous suit. He stripped it off quickly and pulled on the jeans, reveling in the familiar comfort. Something crinkled in his front right pocket, and he reached inside and pulled out a wrinkled piece of paper with faint writing sprawled across it:

"And fare thee well, my only Luve
And fare thee well, a while!
And I will come again, my Luve,
Tho' it were ten thousand mile."

It was Arabella's note! It had gotten smeared and wrinkled, but the note had survived the washer. Love for Ara surged to the surface, and he realized that he would come again to see his love. It was not too late to fight for her, even if he should have fought sooner. Filled with hope and shaking with adrenaline and excitement at the thought of even seeing Ara again, Henry finished packing, making sure to include his cowboy gear.

He pulled the bags onto his shoulder and wheeled the suitcase behind him as he left the suite and crept down the stairs. Again, seeing no one in the main hall, Henry quickly walked to the front door and opened it.

"Oh, isn't he darling?" Henry heard one of the guests say from the dining hall.

Asher!" Henry thought, pausing momentarily. "What kind of father leaves without saying goodbye to his own son?" His mother was also inside at the party. But Henry knew if he stepped inside the room, all Hell would break loose, especially now that he had changed into his cowboy clothes! He decided to call his mother and have her bring Asher to him while he waited on the divorce papers to be drawn up, as those would take a bit anyway.

With a last look around the mansion he had grown up in, Henry knew with certainty that he would not return. He walked outside and closed the door behind him with finality.

As he loaded the luggage into his car, Henry reveled in the fact that he was going back, back to his beautiful Arabella.

53
NEW YORK, NEW YORK
April 4, 1993

Logic is a funny thing. Henry had always seen himself as a logical man, never letting emotion cloud his judgment. It was what made his work so successful, but what had happened in his personal life? Everything was a tangled web of mess, if that were possible. Nothing was in its proper place. But that didn't mean the web needed to be de-tangled or simply just taken down.

Henry had called Anne with no reply. He left her a very convincing message that she needed to meet him at his hotel this morning.

"We will be civil, or things WILL get ugly," he recalled saying. He and Anne weren't talking but things needed to be said. They had left things unfinished, and all Henry wanted to be was done. He had checked himself into a hotel after that night, after he found out. But today was the day to put anger aside and make things clear.

He heard a rap on the door and went to answer it.

Anne, dressed to the nines, walked in, looking cool and collected. She didn't wait for permission to take a seat on the sofa.

"Anne." Henry didn't feel like pleasantries were really welcome, but he had to start the conversation somehow.

"No need for awkward conversation starters, just say what you needed to say to me." Anne wouldn't look him in the eye.

"So, you and Thomas?"

"That's what you want to talk about? If that's the case I'm leaving. I don't need to be humiliated any further." Anne started to get up and leave.

"I think I have a right to know what went on. I'm not going to lash out on you. I just want to know. What happened?"

Anne hesitated. "I don't know what you want to know. I suppose it was just your run-of- the-mill affair…"

"Was? You ended it? When?" Henry was intensely curious, and he wasn't quite sure why.

"Well, no, I mean, it's been a month or so, but nothing was ever ended. I just had a lot going on with the baby." Anne spoke casually, as if every word wasn't crushing him.

The baby. Henry's heart sank. Was Asher even his son? The room was spinning, and Henry felt like throwing up. He steadied himself and sat down on the chair across from Anne.

"Anne…" Henry could barely form the words he needed to say. "Is he mine?" Henry stood up from his chair and walked over to the window. He stared down at the world below, so peaceful and unaware of his misery.

He turned his attention back toward Anne. "Tell me. I have a right to know." He said with a steady, monotone voice.

She finally quit her fidgeting and looked Henry in the eyes. Hers were filled with fear. Her lower lip trembled as she tried to open her mouth and speak, but nothing came out. She blinked and returned to her usual demeanor.

"Like you care, Henry, like you have ever cared!" She screamed at him. "You would be grateful if he wasn't yours wouldn't you? You are so sick, you know that? SICK!" Anne kept yelling.

Henry could tell he would not get his answer, yet, not like this. "When did it start? The affair, I mean." He changed the subject. He had other questions. He would just have to leave one the most daunting for later. Looking for some semblance of calm, Henry reverted his gaze back to the window.

Anne looked at him discourteously, like she was pushing the knife further into his back. "Before we were even married." She said dryly.

The same question resurfaced in his mind, and he couldn't push it back. "Anne. Is Asher my son?" Henry's hands were shaking.

"I don't know." She started fidgeting with the rings on her fingers and refused to look Henry in the eye.

"I can't believe you." Henry's head fell into his hands, and he just sat there silent. He could tell Anne was nervous and wouldn't be able to keep from speaking much longer.

"Really? I mean what is the difference between you and me anyway? You are no better, so don't act all betrayed and hurt." She was justifying her actions, like the two were even comparable.

"You want to know the difference, Anne. The difference is I felt remorse, I stopped."

"Oh please! You think just because you weren't sitting next to her this whole time that means you stopped? For the first time in our marriage, Henry, just be honest! You haven't stopped loving her this entire time."

"I have never lied to you about loving her." Henry said firmly.

"You lied to me! When you said you loved me, when you said you would love me forever. You have never loved me the way you love her. Ever! And all I ever tried to do was be the stupid person you wanted me to be, but that was never enough. I loved you, and you never once opened up to me." The tears streamed down her face, but her voice never quavered.

Henry couldn't help but laugh, "You didn't love me; you never loved me. You were screwing Thomas the entire time! My word, you are so blind!" Henry could feel anger welling up in him once again, and he pushed it away. Anger wouldn't solve anything, and anger was exactly what she was looking for. It would keep them from talking about the truth.

Anne opened her mouth to speak, but nothing came out.

"How could you even think you love me? Because if we loved each other why would we put each other through this? Frankly you probably love Thomas more than you love me, but point of fact, you don't know what love is. If you did, you wouldn't be married to me when you are in love with another man."

"Again, you have done the EXACT same thing. We are no different."

Anne's words cut him. Henry suddenly thought about all that he had put Ara through with all of this and cringed with guilt. Nothing about this was ideal; he was just trying to do what was best for everyone, even Anne. But was his choice what was best for everyone or just for him? They weren't right for each other, he knew that, but then he wondered if he was being selfish. All he really wanted to be was happy, and Ara brought him that happiness. But was he making Ara happy? At this moment in time, he highly doubted that. It had been months since he had seen her, she never replied to his message about his father dying. Maybe that should have been his first inclination, maybe he just needed to let go of her, if that meant her being better off. But with Anne, things would never be right with her and this conversation they were having right now, had to be done, for the sanity of both of everyone.

Anne interrupted his thoughts. She was always interrupting him, even when they weren't speaking. "You can't leave us Henry. How can I support this child on my own? I will not accept that I lost in this. I can't. I won't" Anne was shaking her head and staring at the floor.

"I don't even know if he's my child! Is your mind so warped that you can't see how disgusting this whole thing is? We can't come back from this!" Henry was raising his voice, but it was warranted. "It's over, Anne. This isn't some contest you can win. And since money seems to be all that you're worried about, you can stop worrying as you signed a prenup. Besides, I'm sure Thomas will be right there by your side, like he always has been. Just sign the papers and let me be free." Henry handed her the divorce papers he had had redrawn up just the day before.

She snatched them from his grasp, furiously scratched her name on the line marked with a "sign here" sticker, threw the pen on the ground, and turned to leave the room.

With one final glance over her shoulder, she cemented the final engravings in their marriage's gravestone, "And...no, he is NOT yours, Henry." She smiled wickedly, "Take care, love." She blew him a sick and twisted kiss and was gone.

54
JACKSON HOLE, WYOMING
April 4, 1993

"But to see her was to love her, love but her, and love forever."
-Robert Burns

"Ladies and gentlemen, we are beginning our descent into Jackson Hole. The local time is 2 p.m., and it is a brisk thirty-three degrees outside. If this is your final stop, we wish you well, and, if you have another destination, we hope you have safe travels. On behalf of the crew and I, it was a pleasure serving you this afternoon, and thank you for flying United."

Henry's eyes were dry from lack of sleep, but his veins were pumping with adrenaline at the thought of landing in Wyoming. He remembered his first long and depressing journey here and was thankful he flew this time, even if he had had to fly commercially. Trace had called him to let him know that the jet was in the shop for routine maintenance. Henry hadn't wanted to wait another second.

The plane trembled as it met the landing strip. Henry could not see the lights of the airport as it was snowing quite heavily. It was almost dark outside even though it was the late afternoon. The seatbelt sign lost its illumination, and people began pulling down their bags from the overhead compartments and filing their way off the airplane.

Henry stood up and gathered his own things before waiting behind a line of people. Everything around him moved so slowly, but his mind was running a mile a minute. He checked his watch and calculated the length of the drive ahead of him.

The person behind him bumped into his back.

"Oh, sorry, mate. Lost my footing." A short, balding man with a British accent smiled up at him apologetically.

330

"No problem." Henry turned back to face to the exit.

"What do you make of this weather? A bit blundery, huh?"

Henry sighed quietly and turned around again. "Yes." he said curtly, anxious to get off this plane. A mother was five rows ahead, holding everyone behind her up.

"Can you imagine being caught out in this storm? A dreadful thought." The man shivered at the idea.

Henry stayed quiet, the line started moving again, and the conversation ended.

"Have a good evening, sir." The flight attendant cordially bid every passenger adieu and finally, Henry was out, finally in Wyoming again.

He made his way straight for the rental cars, noticing there was no line. No one wanted to drive in this storm. He made haste and filled out the proper paperwork and information to get a Land Rover. He took the key from the lady and headed out the door. A bitter cold wind chilled his face. He was used to the cold from his morning runs. He lifted his collar around his neck and found his car. After throwing his bag in the backseat, Henry was on his way. Blizzard or no blizzard, he would see Arabella tonight.

****

Snow clung so thick to the windshield that Henry had to stop every few minutes to manually wipe it off the glass. It had already snowed up to eight inches in some areas, and the snow was still coming down in thick sheets of white. As he slowly made his way up into the mountains, Henry felt a rock of nerves form in his belly. He hoped it was only apprehension at seeing Ara again, but his gut told him it was something else.

He flicked the headlights from low to high, trying to decide which one gave him the clearest view of the snow-covered road. Deciding neither choice made much difference, Henry leaned forward and concentrated. He occasionally looked for landmarks when he stopped to clear the windshield and was surprised at how slowly he was travelling. In normal conditions, Henry guessed he still had about fifteen minutes to Arabella's ranch.

He stopped to brush more snow from the windshield, throwing the snow off the vehicle as if it was poison. Frustrated at how long it was taking to get to Ara, Henry flung himself back into the car and was prepared to resume his journey when he saw something a little ways ahead. It was something dark, just off the road, next to a large tree.

Henry put the Land Rover into drive and moved closer to the large object. He saw that a dark blue pickup truck had driven off the road and crashed into the tree. Judging by the amount of snow covering the truck and lack of tire tracks from the road to the tree, Henry estimated that the vehicle had been there for several hours already. The vehicle was dark, with no signs of life.

Deciding to keep moving, he drove on slowly. Suddenly, he saw something move from inside the cab of the truck. He slammed on the brakes, and his rover started losing traction. He came to a sliding stop just missing a tree on the opposite side of the road. Henry felt like he needed to get to that truck as fast as possible, something was wrong, very wrong.

He forced open his door and began trudging through feet of snow. The accumulations were climbing. His run felt like more of a walk, and the blue truck looked like an infinity away. He trudged on, breathing in and breathing out. He could barely feel his fingers as they met the cold metal of the truck's driver-side door.

He wrenched the door open, and the cab illuminated with light.

Henry was frozen, not from the cold, but from what he saw.

Arabella was sprawled across the front seat moaning in pain. The thick black winter coat obscured much of her body from view, but he thought her right arm was bent at a strange angle. The matching hat hid some of her blond hair while the rest spilled around her neck and shoulders.

She lifted her head, and her eyes flashed with recognition and then utter shock. "H-h-henry?!" Her voice was shaking, but Henry couldn't tell if she in shock or dreadfully cold.

"Ara! What...I...are you okay?" Henry examined a deep gash on her forehead closely, thinking that her head must have hit the steering wheel when she crashed. A small stream of blood was flowing down her cheek.

"I... I crashed and...Henry. I think I must be hallucinating." Ara said in a daze.

This was not the reunion Henry expected not at all. He froze as he tried to think of what to do. Ara was hurt, injured. His beloved Arabella … he couldn't breathe.

"How can you be here?" She lightly giggled, as seeing Henry could not be possible.

Henry snapped out of his paralysis and grabbed her hand and found that it was ice cold. "Ara, you are freezing." No longer hesitant, Henry ran around to the other side of the truck. He opened the door and lifted her head into her hands.

"You're going to be all right. I'm here now. I'm just going to carry you over to my Rover. Can you hear me, Ara? Say something to let me know you hear me." He took off his coat and tried to wrap it around her.

"Henry." She was smiling, but her blue eyes were opening and closing very slowly, like she was sleepy.

"Ara, I think you might have a concussion. You have to stay awake, do you hear me? Just keep talking to me." Henry got his arm underneath her back and was pulling her out the door. When her legs reached him, he swung her into his grasp. He almost lost his footing on the snow but caught himself.

"Whoa, whoa! I got you. Just relax, keep talking, Ara." He patted her cheek repetitively to keep her awake as he started heading toward his rover.

"Henry, I ... missed your hand." She tried to lift her hand to his but was too weak.

"Oh, Ara, you have no idea how much I missed you." He was breathing heavily as he tried to trudge through the thick snow carrying Ara. He could barely see in front of him, but the lights on his rover showed him the way. "Ara?" He asked while moving around a large drift, still moving toward the lights.

"Yes, Henry?" She whispered, not opening her eyes.

"Open your eyes, Ara."

They fluttered open.

"I love you, Ara. With my whole heart, for the rest of my life. Did you know that?"

"Love." She answered with her eyes shut again.

"Ara!" He yelled her name, and she jumped, waking up a bit. He had reached the Rover. He pulled open the back door and lifted Ara inside. The passenger door was too close to the tree to open. He settled her in the back seat and pulled his coat around her a little tighter.

Jumping inside, Henry pulled the vehicle into drive and guided it into the center of the road. Fortunately, he could still see his tire tracks and that enabled him to drive a little faster than before. All he had to do now was keep driving and keep Ara awake. Henry didn't know which one would be harder.

"Ara? How you doing back there?" He turned the heat up on high and turned the backseat fans on as well. Not hearing an answer, he reached back and shook her.

"I ... think I'm ... dreaming." She answered back sleepily.

He needed to get her attention and decided on something might startle her. "Ara? I am divorcing Anne; she signed the papers today." He looked back and saw that her eyes were on him, even if they were a little unfocused. "Also, my son ... is not my son. He is actually the son of my former best friend, who was having an affair with Anne even before we married."

"No son?" She asked, seeming a little more awake.

Encouraged by her growing alertness, he kept talking. "Yes, a divorced man with no children. How's that for a mess?"

"Divorce." Ara mumbled. "Baby."

Just ahead, he thought he could make out lights of the town.

"You." Ara whispered as she fell unconscious.

"Ara! Ara, stay with me!"

****

"Henry?" The man in blue surgery scrubs asked. "You brought Arabella in, right?"

"Yes, that's me." Henry said in a shaky voice as he got out of his waiting room chair to speak to the doctor. He had been waiting, terrified, for the last few hours as the medical team had taken Ara into surgery the second they had arrived at the hospital. "How is she? Arabella?"

The doctor rubbed his hand on his neck. "Arabella is still in surgery. She has some internal bleeding she sustained through the accident. We are working on it and will keep you updated."

"Uh, okay." Henry had a million questions, but the doctor obviously needed to get back to work, so he decided to let him go. "Thank you, Doctor."

The doctor nodded, turned, and walked quickly back to surgery.

Henry sank back into his chair. Ara had internal bleeding and was still in surgery. He should have gotten to her sooner.

"Henry?" A nurse had arrived at his side without him noticing.

"Yes?"

"I'm helping on Arabella's case, and I'm trying to get in contact with her family.

"Uh … I'm not totally sure." Henry was shrugging his shoulders like an idiot. He was trying to remember what Ara had told him about her parents. They lived out of state, of that he was sure. His mind was jumbled with terror and exhaustion.

The nurse seemed impatient with his less than helpful answers. She sighed before interrupting his attempt at an explanation. "Look, does she have family we can contact? She didn't come in with identification. And the situation is quite serious."

The pieces finally connected in his minds. "She, um, her parents live in Arizona, but she has friends who are just as much family as anyone. They live here. I have their number. I can call."

"Good."

"Nurse, can I see her yet?"

"She's still in surgery, as the doctor just told you, but we will let you know when she is out." The nurse smiled mechanically and briskly walked away.

Sighing, Henry headed to a nearby payphone, dreading the call he needed to make. He punched in the numbers and waited.

After quite a few rings, Henry heard a few curse words and then, "Mm, Hello?" Mitch's voice croaked out.

"Mitch, it's Henry."

"*Henry*?" Mitch asked incredulously with sleep still thick in his voice. "Why on Earth are ya callin' me? It's the middle of the night!" Sounding more awake, he finally yelled. "And I do remember I told ya never to speak to me again!" Mitch continued shouting.

"Mitch, Mitch!" Henry broke in quickly before Mitch could hang up on him. "We can fight this out later, but I have something very important to tell you. Ara is in trouble."

Mitch stopped yelling into the phone. "This better be good, Tudor."

"I went to see her." Mitch began yelling. "Just wait, Mitch! I found her just outside her ranch. She was in a car accident. I drove her to the hospital … and," Henry's voice broke as he realized how twisted this nightmare had become " … She is … in surgery now."

"What? Arabella?" Mitch stammered out.

"Uh, well … They said the situation with Ara is … serious. Can you guys come down here as soon as possible?"

He could hear Mitch pulling on his boots and coat. "We will be right there. Nicole!" The line went dead.

Henry hung up and rested his head in his hands. He felt a little better knowing Mitch and Nicole would soon be here, but he was on the edge of losing it. He sat in his chair fiddling with a loose thread on the cushion until the string had been entirely pulled out. He threw it away from him and started tapping his fingers on the armrest. He remembered this feeling, of being helpless, of excruciating love that may never be returned again. When his father was dying, Henry only did one thing that actually made him calm. Pray. Even though he didn't have much practice, he knew that praying after his father had passed had seemed to help. He had turned to God before in a desperate time, so it seemed like the thing to do once again. It was, no doubt, what Ara would want him to do.

He hung his head and rested his elbows on his knees. He began to pray silently and the tears seemed to naturally follow. He didn't know how long he was praying when he heard a bustle of activity. Henry unfolded his hands and sat up, wiping his face quickly. Looking up, he saw Mitch and Nicole, dusted with snow and looking harried and stressed as they rushed in.

"Henry, where is she?" Mitch asked impatiently.

He stood up with his hands in an *I don't know* gesture. "I haven't heard anything new. They said when she was done with surgery they would let me know." Henry smiled at them both. He had missed them so much; he couldn't help it. "Long time no see."

"Not long enough," Mitch snapped, pushing his hands into his front pockets to, it seemed to Henry, keep from punching him.

Nicole frowned. "I am going to see if I can get someone to talk to us." She turned to Mitch. "Just don't get too worked up while I'm gone." She walked away, looking back over her shoulder to make sure Mitch didn't pounce on Henry the moment she left.

Henry tried to smooth Mitch's anger a bit. "Look, this situation is literally just a pile of crap." Suddenly, he felt his own anger flare up. "You don't have to like me or whatever, but I am grieving too. Maybe you don't think I have a right to grieve or to love her, but I do. You have NO idea what happened in New York because, if you did, I doubt you would be sitting here trying to make me feel worse than I already do!" Henry lost it. He never intended to yell at Mitch.

Mitch looked just as surprised by his outburst, but he said nothing.

"My father died. Did you know that? He died right in front of me. My ex-wife tricked me into thinking I had a son, that, in fact, wasn't even mine, and what's worse is that I left the woman I loved thinking I had a responsibility to my son. My best friend and business partner has been sleeping with my wife, well ex-wife, since before we were even married. I have lost ... everything, most importantly, Arabella. And all I want right now, from you, is to put all your hatred for me aside and just sit here with me in peace. And just to clear up, when Ara saw me in New York, it was a rare moment that I was sharing with my mother. Not Anne or anyone else. I was just so happy to see my MOTHER smiling again, so I smiled with her, for her, but inside I was yearning for Ara because she is all I EVER yearn for."

Henry had just let everything flood out of him, everything that he wanted to say to Ara but couldn't because she was in some room, surrounded by doctors and bloody sheets and things, possibly dying. He had to say these things to someone because he didn't know if he would get the chance to say them to Ara before losing her for good. And he was scared, trembling and losing-his-mind scared.

Suddenly exhausted, he sank down into his waiting room chair and put his head in his hands.

He heard Mitch sit down beside him. "Well, sounds like a rough few months ya had, partner." He took off his hat and held it in his hands.

They sat in silence, deep in their own grief, waiting for news. Henry had a distant thought that he should ask Mitch about something important … a baby! They had announced that a baby Taylor was on the way before Henry had left Wyoming. "Mitch, where is the baby?" Henry asked looking around as if a baby might suddenly appear out of nowhere.

Mitch looked up at him, seeming surprised that Henry remembered. "Oh, Owen is at home with Nicole's mother. She moved in with us to help with the baby for a few months."

"Congratulations." Henry told him, trying to sound happy, but his mind was mostly consumed with terror and worry for Ara.

They fell back into silence.

A few minutes later, minutes that felt like hours to Henry, Nicole walked back in the room, followed by a tired-looking doctor. "Ara is in recovery now." The doctor said. "But her condition is very fragile. You may see her for a few minutes. But keep your words calm and quiet; you may say absolutely nothing that would cause her stress."

Henry jumped out of his chair, hearing only, "Ara is in recovery."

Nicole grabbed Mitch's hand, and he stood up as well.

"Henry, maybe you should just wait here. I mean, I think it just might not be good for her right now." Mitch looked genuinely concerned, and Henry understood.

"Yeah, I understand. Just go. Please just tell her … just let me know how she's doing." Henry's voice quavered and felt like he was about to cry. What if he never got to tell her?

Nicole put a hand on his cheek and wiped away the tears he hadn't yet cried.

"We will," Mitch said.

They turned, hand in hand, and disappeared around a corner, and Henry was alone.

Henry stared at the dusty clock that hung on the grey wall in front of him. One minute, two minutes, five minutes, the time kept ticking way.

After ten minutes, Henry saw Mitch round the corner. He stood up and met him halfway. "What's wrong?" Henry spoke frantically.

"Nothing, Henry, she's fine. She's … she's asking for you." Mitch laughed to himself. "She thought she was dreaming up the whole thing that you came to rescue her. She won't believe it until she sees you." There Mitch was with that big old smile of his.

Hope sprung up inside Henry, like when one would dig a hole right along the water of a riverfront, and every time the person removed one cup of sand, it just filled with water. Hope was dangerous, though. It made rejection earth-shatteringly devastating. But he still hoped.

"Just don't go off on her like you did me, you know, just be cool, partner."

Henry clasped his shoulders, like they were friends again. "Okay. Where is she?"

"Just around the corner, Room 122."

"Thanks." Henry was nervous but ready. He walked down the hallway and saw the light that illuminated her room. He took a deep breath to clear his head.

He stood in her doorway as Nicole was leaving the room. She touched his shoulder and left them alone.

"My Arabella." Henry smiled at her as he stood in the doorway.

Ara took a deep breath before turning her gaze toward him. "My Henry." Her hair was pulled back from her pale face, and dark shadows shown under her eyes, revealing the ordeal she had been through. The white hospital gown made her look quite thin. Her tiny feet were peeking out from under her blanket, and they looked almost blue in the hospital lights. Even with the large bandage wrapped around her forehead, she was breathtakingly beautiful.

"I'm so glad to hear you say that." Henry stepped forward to her bedside, tucking her feet under the blanket as he went. He grabbed her hand, not thinking whether or not it was the right thing to do. He just knew. Their fingers intertwined and tingles shot up his arm and through his body. This was right.

"Yeah, well, there's nothing like a life and death situation to bring some perspective to life." She smiled weakly. She looked pale and weak, which worried Henry.

"So it's official … I'm not a dream." He had pulled a chair up to the bed and was holding her hand to his face. "Tangible, real. I'm here."

"You've always been a dream, Henry, just so dreamy." She laughed to herself. She was loopy. The medicine was obviously making her groggy.

"You sound like you have had a little too much to drink, pretty lady." They both laughed together and fell into silence. Henry had so much to say, but felt like he could say nothing at all. "They told me not to stress you out because you're pretty fragile right now." Henry felt the need to bring up why he wasn't talking about the elephant in the room.

"I have a lot to say to you, I think," Arabella's eyes were opening and closing very slowly now. He could tell she was trying very hard to stay awake to talk to him.

"Same here." They fell silent again. "So, what can we say?" Henry treaded lightly.

Arabella held eye contact with Henry, her blue eyes dancing. She was not scared as she told him, "I fell in love with you, Henry."

"And I, you." Henry squeezed her hand and tears splashed onto her finger tips. "I do still. Ara," He held her hand between both of his now and kissed each fingertip. "I love you, My only luve$_{11}$.'" He quoted a piece of their poem and smiled at her.

"I love you too, Henry. Always have, always will." As those words rolled off her tongue, tears dripped down her cheeks, and her bright blue eyes were an ocean, wild and fierce.

And Henry was lost in their depths. They gazed fiercely at each other like they had never been apart before Arabella closed her eyes. "I will never leave you again," he promised in a whisper.

A faint smile remained on her face, but her eyes never opened, like she had just fallen fast asleep. The trail of tears still stuck to her face, and Henry reached out and held her face in his hands, kissing her goodnight.

Like the sirens of a thousand cities ringing at the same time, Henry was jolted out of the moment. Machines started beeping and an alarm sounded, an alarm that sounded horribly familiar to Henry. "Ara?"

Nurses and doctors suddenly flooded the room with blue scrubs. Everything around him was flooded. "Code blue, code blue!" Blue like her swelling ocean eyes.

Someone was pulled him up out of his chair and escorting him out of the room.

"Sir, you need to leave now!"

"No, I can never leave her. I promised her!" They kept pushing, and he kept fighting to keep her in sight. Her blonde hair against a white pillow was all he could see now. She was swarmed by people she didn't even know. "Just don't let her die!" He needed to be by her side, but everyone was pushing him away.

Then his ears were filled with a horrifying, single note as the heart monitor depicted a single line running across the screen. The floor was falling away from him; the ceiling was surely caving in. "Arabella!" He cried out desperately.

The door shut on him, and he was alone in the hallway.

"Arabella." He whispered with his hand flat on the door. Tears cascaded from his eyes like a flood of pain, and all around him was the storm.

"Arabella."

Citations (Marked by subscript numbers in the text).

1. John Donne - "A Valediction Forbidding Mourning"
2. Emily Dickinson - Poem 1472
3. "Don't You Forget About Me" by Simple Minds
4. "I'll tell you how the sun rose, a ribbon at a time" by Emily Dickinson
5. The Kinks - Strangers (1970)
6. "The Passionate Shepherd to His Love" by Christopher Marlowe
7. "Ode to the West Wind by Percy Bysshe Shelley
8. "My River Runs to Thee" by Emily Dickinson
9. "I Have Been One Acquainted with the Night" Robert Frost
10. "Annabel Lee" by Edgar Allan Poe
11. "A Red, Red Rose" by Robert Burns
12. "i carry your heart with me (i carry it in my heart)" by E.E.Cummings
13. *** *It has been said that Henry VIII was the author of "Greensleeves." However, the author remains anonymous and the poem shown in the text is a copy of that author's work.*

ABOUT THE AUTHORS

TALIA JOHNSON *is an English teacher in Bismarck, ND. When she is not working with her wonderful students and colleagues, Talia enjoys spending time outdoors in her beloved state of North Dakota. She loves taking her beautiful Boxer, Maximus, on long walks and runs, walking with family and friends, and spending many hours on her family's farm. She is also passionate about reading, especially young adult novels she can share with her students, and looks forward to writing additional novels with her extraordinary friend, Amber.*

AMBER DURAN *is a stay-at-home mother with a passion for the written word. Though she currently resides in Springfield, MO, she will always be a North Dakotan at heart, having spent most of her life growing up in Mandan. She's a Christian, hiker, reader, writer, painter, singer, and artist. When she's not raising her son with the best husband in the world, Andy, Amber enjoys the outdoors and has a touch of wander lust, hoping to one day travel the world with her family.*